WRATH OF THE CURSED WITCH

ALSO BY ROCIO CARRANZA

NOVELS
Blood of the Blackthorn
Flame in the Silver Storm
Wrath of the Cursed Witch

NOVELLAS
Beneath the Sacred Well

COLLECTIONS
My Dreams Come True

SHORT STORIES
Lana Lang
Miss Reliable

WRATH of the CURSED WITCH

THE ETERNAL CURSE BOOK THREE

ROCIO CARRANZA

QUEEN OF WANDS BOOKS
since 2024 | Austin, Texas
contact@queenofwandsbooks.com

Wrath of the Cursed Witch is a work of fiction. Names, characters, places, and incidents either are the product of the author's imagination or are used fictiously. Any resemblance to actual persons, living or dead, events or locales is entirely coincidental.

Copyright © 2026 by Rocio Carranza
All rights reserved. Published by Queen of Wands Books.

No part of this publication may be reproduced, distributed, or transmitted in any form or by any means, including photocopying, recording, or other electronic or mechanical methods, without the prior written permission of the publisher, except in the case of brief quotations embodied in critical reviews and certain other noncommercial uses permitted by copyright law.

Library of Congress Control Number: 2026902129
eBook ISBN 979-8-9933391-4-6
Paperback ISBN 979-8-9933391-5-3
Hardcover ISBN 979-8-9933391-6-0
www.rociocarranza.com

Cover Art by Irina Koryakina
Cover Design & Map by Rocio Carranza
Editing by Heather Hudec, Simply Spellbound Edits
Interior Formatting by Mariska Maas, Rubre Art
Interior Illustrations by Irina Koryakina, Natalia Tyczyńska, Maria Erić, Karolina Wucke, Sam Gaitan, Wiktoria (@maniagania), Guilia Martini, and Zuzanna (@sno0zie)

First edition March 2026
Published in the United States
9 8 7 6 5 4 3 2 1

*For those who don't fit in the box they've been given.
Break it and make something new and wonderful instead.*

CONTENT WARNINGS

Wrath of the Cursed Witch is a dark fantasy novel and book three of The Eternal Curse series. This story contains content that might be troubling to some readers, including, but not limited to, depictions of and references to abuse, attempted sexual assault, blood, death, genocide, gore, manipulation, PTSD, strong use of language, and violence

Unclaimed Wastes
Gods Protection
Horned Cove
Teros
Dragon Sea
The Clutches
Alcanza Peaks
Mytar
Rubianes Keep
nsmir Realm
Larrea
Bay of Chaos
Azurea Sea

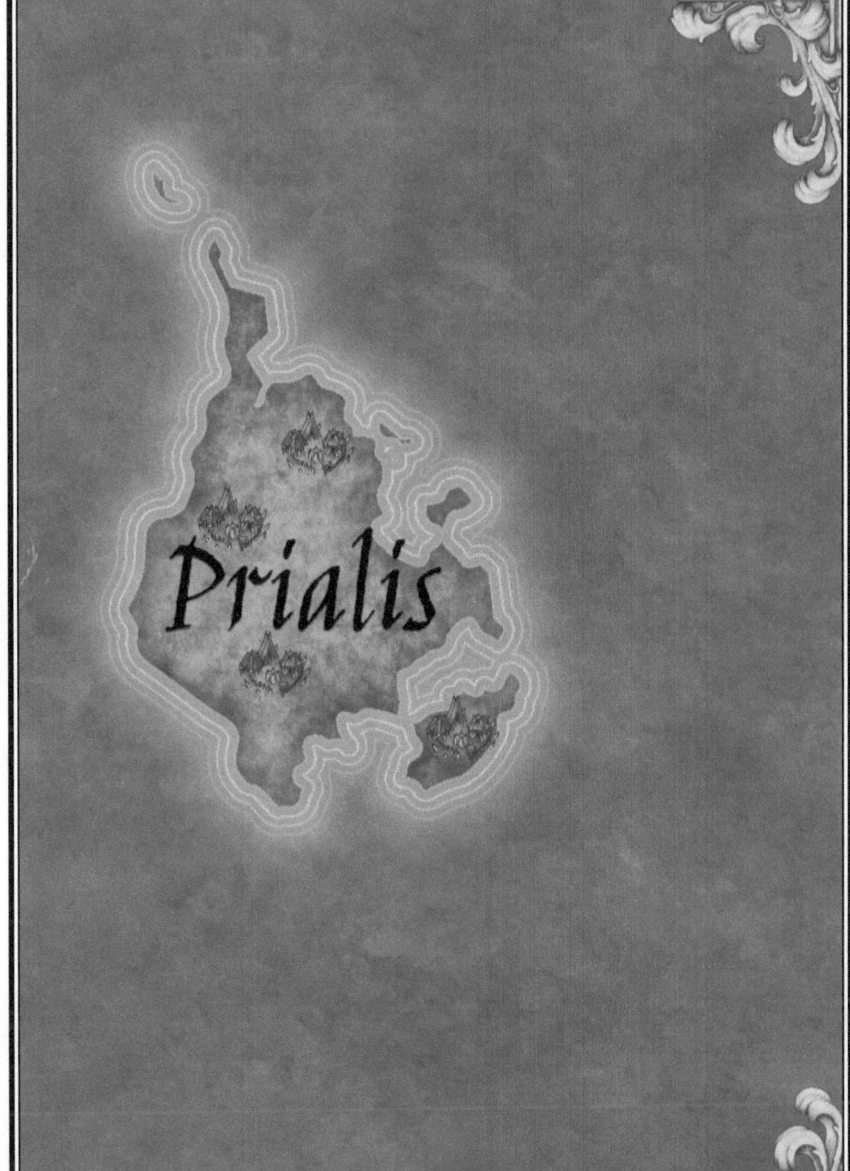

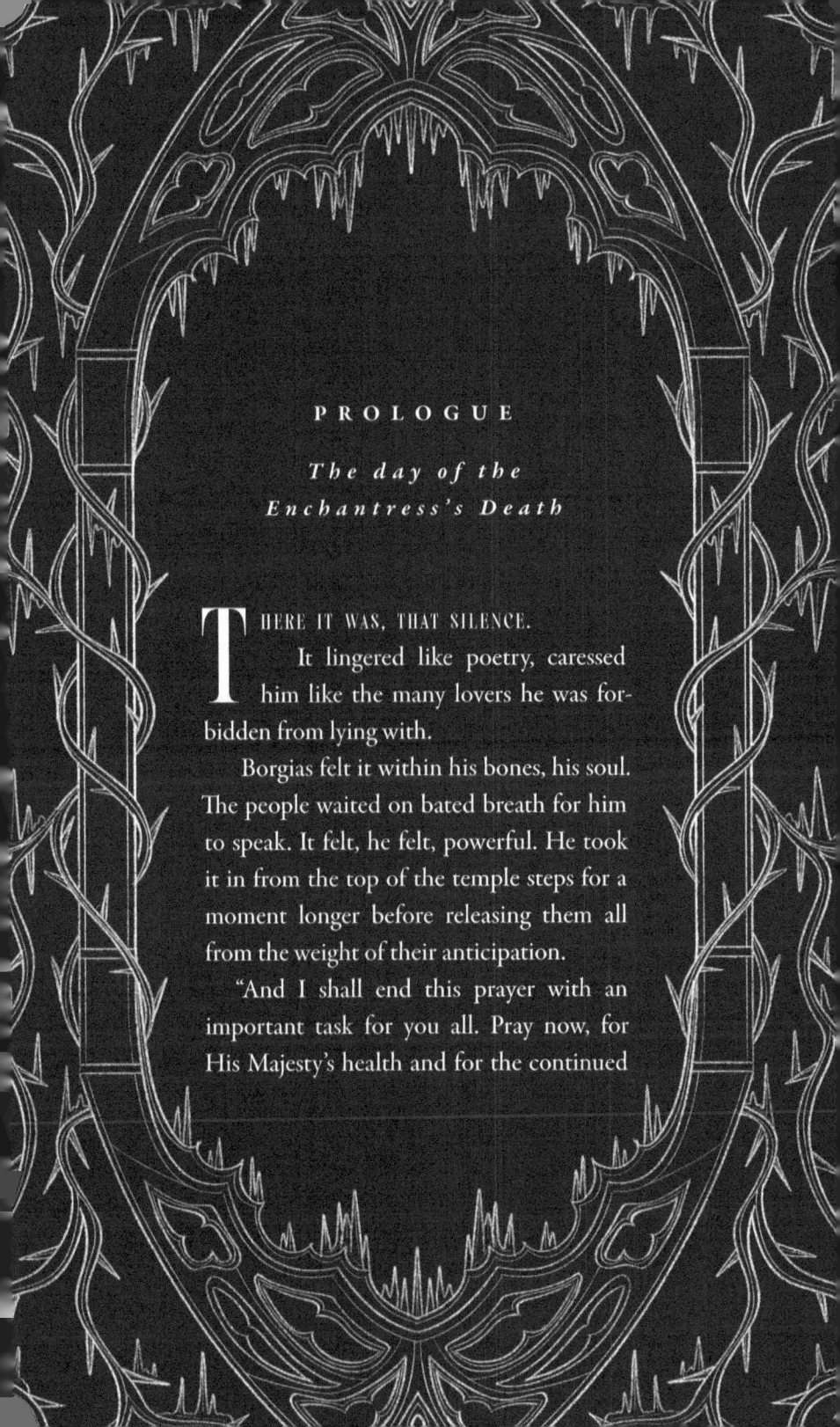

PROLOGUE

The day of the Enchantress's Death

THERE IT WAS, THAT SILENCE.
It lingered like poetry, caressed him like the many lovers he was forbidden from lying with.

Borgias felt it within his bones, his soul. The people waited on bated breath for him to speak. It felt, he felt, powerful. He took it in from the top of the temple steps for a moment longer before releasing them all from the weight of their anticipation.

"And I shall end this prayer with an important task for you all. Pray now, for His Majesty's health and for the continued strength of our kingdom. By the will of the gods!"

"The will of the gods!" they repeated.

Borgias grinned, raising his hands in farewell as the crowd began to disperse.

He made his way back into the Temple of the Five which was rather empty, hollow, save for a few apprentices working about and the royal elder waiting for him inside. Too soon he missed the admiring faces of the city folk. Here, he was naught but another body dressed in spiritual robes.

"You did well, Borgias," Elder Osvald praised him.

The locking of the doors and windows sounded behind Borgias. The midday sun was trapped outside, leaving the inside of the temple shrouded in darkness penetrated only by faint candlelight.

Elder Osvald gave him a faint, knowing smile. "One would think of you as the elder instead of me."

Elder Osvald looked every bit of his seventy-three years. Wrinkled, loose skin hung like his robes, patches of hair clung for life on the sides of his balding head, his brown eyes, pale and weary. All of it proof that time had not favored the kind-hearted.

He took Borgias into a brief hug, gesturing him to the other side of the temple where the sculptures of the gods rested. Young apprentices in their taupe robes cleaned the statues, placing fresh flowers as an offering at each of their altars, a hope that their king may soon be restored to good health.

"Perhaps, one day," Borgias replied, his eyes unable to meet the lingering stares of the sculptures, "but my duty is to the gods."

Elder Osvald nodded agreeably, gesturing to the apprentices for privacy. The young men bowed and hurried away, one accidentally dropping a yellow rose on the marble floor. As their footsteps faded down the hall, the temple grew eerie.

Borgias was unsettled with the silence as he bent to pick the stray flower up. In his haste, he accidentally pricked his finger on the stem.

Borgias pulled back sharply. A bead of blood pooled in the center of his thumb.

"Do be careful, Borgias." Osvald traded his handkerchief for the rose, wiping it with his sleeve and placing it gently on the altar.

Borgias cursed under his breath, wrapping the handkerchief around his finger. The bright red blood stained the white cloth, spreading quickly.

Borgias swallowed, trying to ignore it as he turned to Osvald. "Did you bring me here to pray, Elder?"

"No, not exactly," Osvald said. "I simply wish to talk."

He led Borgias along the statues, pointing them out as they walked. "The Creator, The Sage, The Lover, The Warrior, what do they all have in common?"

Borgias looked upon the four sculptures, all robed and carved intricately in gray. "They are gods?"

Osvald nodded. "That they are, but what else?"

Borgias tried to see the tethered thread between them but couldn't think of one. They were gods, they ruled over all, they were four of the five living gods. He tried to hide his irritation beneath a mask of curiosity.

Old men and their riddles.

He gave a feeble, final guess. "They are not Death?"

Osvald's lips thinned. He gestured to the statues. "They have faces, Borgias. They are not covered beneath their robes. They are here to guide us, give us mortals faith, justice, truth, and strength."

Borgias nodded along with the old man, but he bit the inside of his cheek to temper his annoyance.

What is the meaning of this nonsense?

Osvald continued, walking to the last sculpture. He rested a hand on its altar. "Whereas Death is hidden, final. No mortal can escape it, nor can they predict their own demise. Death is cloaked in darkness where we are born and shall return to one day when it is ready to collect our souls."

Borgias stared at the foot of Death's statue. It was nothing more than a large figure dressed in floor-length robes, the tip of its nose peeking from beneath the hood, a long-fingered hand reaching out from within as if holding the robes closed. It was the only statue of the five gods that did not bear a face, it was true.

Ever since Borgias was a boy, the lesson had been imparted on him. Death was everywhere, coming for everyone.

Borgias cleared his throat, blinking away from it. "Why am I here, Elder?"

Osvald did not turn from the statue as he spoke, "I heard the most curious confession today."

"Oh?"

"Yes, it was from a young boy who worked in the stables."

"A stable boy?"

"Yes, a child."

Borgias let out a short laugh. "What could a stable boy say that bothers you, Elder? Did he steal the kitchen sweets?"

Osvald's returning smile did not reach his eyes. "These child servants. Children. They often see things not meant for their eyes, hear things that they do not understand."

Borgias fell silent.

Osvald brushed a piece of dirt from the robe of Death's statue as he continued. "We mere mortals are creatures of habit who tend to grow bored of the habits we create. It is in this boredom that we forge new ones, breaking the cycle only for a moment of pleasure."

"I see."

"That pleasure, that brief release, is the most dangerous time for any man. It makes us mad with desperation and hope, clinging to the promise of something new. And sometimes the promise of something... forbidden."

Borgias' jaw tensed. "What could this child have said that is making you speak so—?"

"Our king has been poisoned . . . by a witch."

Borgias stilled. "Who was the boy?"

Osvald turned slowly to Borgias, his face grim. "You did not ask the right question, Borgias."

Borgias took a step forward. "You are not answering mine."

Osvald's eyes darkened knowingly. "You forget yourself, Borgias. Tell me it is not true."

"Who is the boy?" Borgias grabbed the elder by his collar, forcing him off his feet.

"He is a child!" Osvald choked. "We are men of the five, we are bound by—"

"Damn you, tell me now!" Borgias shook the elder, losing his grip on sanity as he demanded again and again from the old man who the boy was. This filthy child would be the end of him, would uncover his darkest secret, his treason, would sentence him to death.

Death.

He was desperate for an answer. A name, a simple name.

But when he finally stopped shaking the elder, he took in Osvald's pale face, his eyes staring at nothing, his body limp in Borgias' hands.

He let him go, petrified. Osvald's corpse hit the floor with a sickening thud. Borgias's hands shook so violently the handkerchief wrapped around his thumb loosened and fell atop the dead man, the spot of blood on the white cloth marking its new flesh.

Who was the spy?

What did the boy see?

He bent down to Osvald, tapping his face. "Elder? Elder, wake up. Wake up!"

A name! I need a name!

Borgias heard the footsteps behind him too late, an apprentice held a candle, his eyes widening as he beheld the scene before him. "Borgias, what happened!"

Borgias lifted Osvald's body onto his knee quickly, "Elder Osvald, he—he fainted as he was speaking! Get a healer, quick!"

The apprentice trembled, but nodded, running back down the hall calling for someone to help. When he was far enough away, Borgias pushed the man off him, sickened and terrified.

I will be killed.

If the boy speaks, I will be killed.

The prince will do it himself.

As he breathed raggedly, his gaze trailed to the elder's face.

Osvald's mouth was slightly agape, his dead eyes wide with fear stared behind Borgias.

Borgias slowly followed his stare, turning and coming face-to-face with Death.

PART 1

THE SEEDS OF WAR

*The kingdom of Givensmir was
shrouded in flame and smoke,
bodies of witchcraft burnt to ash,
covering the once lush land in gray depression,
the new king unwilling to give another the
chance at the power he had lost.
War broke out like a plague throughout the continent,
tears and bloodshed covered the footworn paths of the weary,
and soon the world forgot of peace,
as life tasted bitterly of misery.
And throughout the mortal lands,
talk of magic and sorcery soon became
the truth among folklore,
spoken upon the lips of those who marveled at what could be,
but feared what it now symbolized.
Death followed magic like a shadow that
clung to a body beneath the sun,
and the witches waited under the shade of the Blackthorn.
While the mortals rejoiced, singing
short-lived songs of victory.*

— RECOVERED DIARY ENTRY OF
PRINCESS ADRIANA OF GIVENSMIR

EVE

CHAPTER 1

Sixteen Years Later

DEATH. Eve could see it before her as the dragon roared into the snowy night, sending shards of ice toward her and Dakon. But it was no match to their flame; so welcome it was in the silver storm, she barely noticed how frigid the air had been. Dakon's grip on her tightened as they beheld the creature emerging from its icy cave.

"It was the honor of my life being your familiar, Eve," Dakon breathed.

Eve's lip quivered, holding back tears as the dragon loomed over them, so easy it would be for its sharp teeth or massive claws to crush them. Her heart thundered in her chest and ears so fiercely, even the flames that engulfed her and Dakon in a fiery embrace did little to quell her rising panic over what was to come.

"There is no one I'd rather see the end with," Eve managed between shaky breaths.

The dragon took a step toward them, quaking the ground beneath them.

"Ready?"

"Yes."

The dragon roared again, snapping its jaws at them. Dakon shoved Eve aside just in time, thrusting a fiery fist at the creature's snout. It screeched in pain, taking monstrous steps backward.

Eve got to her feet, throwing fire at its body before it could recover. Dakon mirrored her, picking up stones and sticks from the snowy path, setting them ablaze and throwing them at the dragon.

It continued screeching into the night, backing into the cave and shielding itself with its wings.

"It's weakened by fire," Dakon shouted. "Keep going!"

Their flame was the only light shining in the darkness of the icy woods, and Eve could barely make out the dragon as it disappeared into the dark cave.

Then it was gone.

"We should chase after it, make sure it doesn't follow us," Dakon managed between ragged breaths, he lifted another large stone, setting it on fire.

"Hurry, then!" Eve gulped in the cold air. It stung her throat and the brisk wind dried her mouth.

There isn't much time.

"We don't know how deep the cave goes. We can't lose it."

She set her fists to fire once more, racing toward the cave alongside Dakon when she heard a panicked shriek.

"Stop! Stop, please!"

She turned, but only Dakon stood behind her.

"Did you hear—"

"Please have mercy!"

Eve turned to the voice, raising her hand like a torch to light the mouth of the cave.

A naked man with burn marks on his jaw and ribs lay on the snowy ground just inside. His hair was a tinted silver hue smoke emanating from the strands as the wind blew out the embers, his skin was a deep umber brown beneath the frosted white scales that were shedding onto the ground before him.

"Who are you?" Dakon asked, his eyes wide. "Where is the dragon?"

The man cleared his throat, his arms raised defensively before him, "I—I am the dragon."

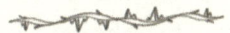

EVE AND DAKON SAT INSIDE THE CAVE, WARMING THEMSELVES AROUND the fire. Instinctively she reached to feel her necklace, a sun affixed to a golden chain she had yet to remove since that night she was arrested by Lord Wesley. But her neck felt bare. It was the last tie she had to her father who had gifted it to her as a child. Perhaps it was the last tie to her mortality.

She thought of Izan, hoping against hope that the Strix had given him a swift death. She tried and failed to suppress the memories of their capture, how he fought to no avail against them. Her heart ached for him and even for Theo.

I fell in love, and they fell to their deaths...

She shook her head.

Pazel lay just behind them, neither her nor Dakon willing to leave him outside. Eve snuck a glance at him, and for a moment believed he was simply sleeping until she caught sight of the dried blood on his chest.

The events of the night prior returned. The chanting, the spell that held them down, the blood, the fire, the grimoire, the knife in Pazel's body. She trembled, too fearful to close her eyes and see it so vividly.

The man who claimed to be the dragon entered from within the depths of the cave. He was wearing a cloak of fur hides, patched together in loose stitching. He carried a few more in his hands.

Before Eve could ask, the man answered her unspoken question. "I found these left behind by those who've ventured this far."

"You mean, those you have killed?" Dakon quipped.

The man shrugged. "A dragon has to eat." He handed the cloaks to Eve and Dakon, and she wrapped herself quickly with it.

Weak and tired, the fire within them slowly gave way and the cold returned once more, brisk and frigid. The tips of her fingers became numb, and soon her teeth chattered even though she was nearly touching the fire in front of her. She needed a distraction.

"What is your name?" she asked as the man sat across from them, warming his hands.

"Depends."

"Depends?"

"I have gone by many. Dragon, Witch, Dragon Witch—"

"But what do you want us to call you?"

He smirked. "Call me Victor."

"Victor," Eve tested it.

"It's been a long while since I've heard my name from another's lips. Say it again."

Eve scoffed, scooting closer to Dakon.

Victor laughed. "Come now, I'm only fooling. I've been bored and alone in this wretched place for a lifetime."

"How long exactly have you been here?" Dakon asked. "And how long have you been a—uh . . ."

"A dragon?" Victor raised a brow. "It must be at least a few centuries now."

"A few centuries!" Eve remarked.

"And probably centuries more if not for you two and your fire."

"I don't understand."

"You are looking at a cursed witch, my dear." He made a gesture as if to bow while he sat. "Unless I come by fire or warmth, which is rare here, I am cursed to be in my dragon form. Take it from me, you two, never piss off a goddess." He whistled, rolling his eyes.

Eve stared, the man before did not appear much older than her. "When was the last time you were mortal?"

"Never in this life," he replied, "but I believe what you meant to ask is when is the last time I've been a man."

Eve nodded.

"I cannot recall, truthfully. It is rare for anyone to venture in the Unclaimed Wastes and even rarer for them to have time to build a fire before I find them."

"Why not wait for them to do so?" Dakon asked.

"A dragon has to eat," he repeated.

"Why shouldn't we kill you now first?" Eve snapped.

"Because I like this better," he raised his hands in front of his face, inspecting them. "You'd be surprised what you'd forget when trapped in scales and ice."

"That's not very convincing," Dakon mumbled.

"Would you rather brave the snow outside?" He pointed toward the mouth of the cave. "Be my guest, though you can leave your friend behind, I'll be hungry when this fire goes out."

Dakon stood, flames building at his fingertips. "Don't you dare touch him."

Victor raised his hands. "I am doing you and him a favor. If he is left to the elements, even in a shallow grave, there are other creatures that will feast on him. And they take their time with their meals . . ."

"Are there other dragons out here?" Eve stood next to Dakon, lowering his fists.

"No, but there are other things that will haunt you til the ends of your days." He warmed his hands by the fire. "We are among ancient magic here in the wastes. Ones that would wear your friend's body like a second skin."

Eve shuddered.

Dakon turned to her, his eyes full of fresh grief. "What do we do with Pazel?"

She shook her head, placing a hand comfortingly on his cheek. "We cannot drag him along with us forever, but we will give him an honorable burial."

Victor scoffed. "I told you they will come for his body—"

"We will burn him," Eve interrupted, keeping Dakon's gaze. "The creatures will not feast on ashes."

Dakon clenched his jaw, nodding.

"Then it's settled," Victor clapped, standing. "A funeral, gods I haven't been to one in ages." He made to walk toward Pazel, but Dakon stopped him, pushing him back.

"Stay away from him."

Victor stilled for a moment, before his face crumpled into a chuckle. "Ah, of course, where are my manners? You must make the preparations, yes?" He took a step back. "Now what gods are we praying to here? What is your stance on death? Or *Death*?"

Eve narrowed her eyes on him. "Don't believe yourself safe, Dragon, I can still burn you alongside him."

"Wouldn't dream of it, my dear. Though you can't be one to judge when you're murdering friends." He gestured to Pazel.

"We didn't kill him." Dakon took a step toward him.

"You're right. None of my business." Victor backed up a few paces further into the cave, his hands raised in mock defense.

"We didn't!" Eve called after him.

"Of course not." Victor turned, calling over his shoulder, "And I didn't eat the mortals whose cloaks you're wearing."

MARC

CHAPTER 2

The throne room was bathed in blood, smeared across the floors so vividly Marc nearly forgot they were made of a white-gray stone before. He could feel his own, boiling beneath his flesh, even after he ordered his guards to execute whatever witch remained inside, save for Reyher and Talesa.

Though, no amount of death seemed to temper the rage within him.

"The ritual was incomplete, Your Majesty. But I have my witches . . . my other witches combing the streets looking for her. We will bring the fire witch and her familiar back to try again. It will work this time, I swear it."

Marc sat on his throne, looking down at the pitiful witch bowing before him. Reyher had sworn the ritual would work before and now here Marc was, sitting without magic, a grimoire, or Eve.

Eve.

Even the name in his mind brought a sour taste to his mouth, a venom he wanted to lash out and release. He would find Eve, and when he did, he would pin her to the ground with daggers if he had to to keep her in his sights.

This was a mess, a fucking mess.

"I've grown quite tired of your broken promises," Marc replied.

"We did not expect the witch to have the grimoire. She was supposed to be non-magic."

"Well, it looks like she has it, doesn't she? Did you not listen when I told you she burned my father's tower?"

Reyher flinched. "I—I apologize to Your Majesty. But as I said before, we *will* find her. And we will succeed next time."

Marc was tired of his groveling. He tilted his head to his guards who began moving toward the oblivious Reyher. Another locked the throne room doors.

Let it consume you...

Marc stilled.

He heard the voice echoing throughout the throne room and shifted his eyes.

Marc saw no one speaking.

He shook his head, certainly the chaos of the evening was getting to him. He focused again on the witch.

"Remind me again, what kind of witch are you?"

Reyher raised a brow. "I don't understand—"

Marc gave him a coy smile. "What kind of *tricks* can you do, hmm? Eve can manipulate fire, what makes you so *special*?"

Reyher's eyes began to glisten with tears ready to be shed. The groveling would increase tenfold very soon. The guards were only a few steps away from him now.

"I can move things or keep them where they are, Your Majesty."

"And your co-conspirator?" He gestured to Talesa, the only other Strix kneeling beside him. She was an older woman with dark curls and pointed features.

She swallowed and faced the ground, trembling.

Let it consume you...

Marc heard the voice again. It was as if someone was whispering in his ear now and the overwhelming sensation of ease came over him. The voice, how it coaxed him. Thoughts of power, the Blackthorn, glory, Eve clouded his mind.

Eve.

Let it consume you...

Marc could faintly hear Reyher speak. "Talesa can shapeshift, too, Your Majesty. I have told you this all before, we hide nothing from you."

Marc blinked, concentrating on Reyher's words. "I—I was simply confirming," he managed after a moment. He nearly forgot what he was doing in the throne room until the sight of blood reminded him once more. Suddenly, he felt quite parched...

He stood and Reyher flinched, squeezing his eyes tight as if readying himself for Marc to make contact. Yet, to the witch's surprise, the guards snapped shackles on him.

Let it consume you...

Reyher tried to fight, but it appeared his magic was gone. He was nothing more than an old man now, and his feeble attempts to escape against four of the king's guards were fruitless. One of them hit Reyher in the back, forcing him down on his knees once more as Marc approached him.

He could have sworn that he could hear Reyher's heart beating from where he walked, feel the fear emanating within him, feeding his now insatiable hunger.

Marc bent down and grinned, flicking his finger against Reyher's shackle. "Iron makes you mortal, isn't that right?"

Reyher didn't respond, refusing to look into his eyes as he panted against the hard stone steps, his face bloodied and bruised from the impact.

Let it consume you...

That voice. It made Marc feel powerful, invincible, *immortal*. He grabbed a fistful of Reyher's hair, forcing him to meet his gaze.

Reyher's eyes bulged, his mouth trembling as he spoke. "I-it can't be."

Let us consume him...

Marc felt a delicious thrill run through him, the throne room darkening as if shadows fell like blankets over the space, his thirst painful, his hunger desperate. He couldn't stop himself, and he didn't want to.

This voice, this power, promised him everything and more.

More, more, more.

Talesa screamed, trying to escape, but the guards caught her, shackling her as she tried to shapeshift into a bird. She fell on the bloodied floor, shifting back into her mortal form as the shackles and guards held her down.

Consume him...

Marc gripped him tighter, bringing the old man closer as Reyher's face twisted in horror. He was stunned into silence, unable to scream or beg for help as Marc unleashed the thing from within him.

MARC SAT IN HIS BATHING CHAMBER, RESTING HIS BACK BETWEEN Jayne's thighs as she ran her fingers through his hair. He did not pay attention to her as she bathed him, her hands making their way down his chest in gentle motions, nor did he comment on anything she said. He could only think about the voice, wishing it would return, to give him what it promised. Instead, much to his frustration, Jayne prattled on about the court and the destruction of the dungeons.

It irked him to hear her voice, irked him to listen to her speak at all. He thought about how it would feel to watch her be consumed by the thing instead. He willed it to return, wanting to feel that power once more, wanting the fear in Reyher's eyes reflected in Jayne's.

". . . I suppose I shall have to request a new funeral dress. Such a shame Adriana perished in the dungeons. Just this morning, Gabrielle demanded to know where the princess was, but I told her that you had sent her on an errand to Mytar." Jayne giggled. "I can imagine the look on her face when she discovers the truth. I swear I don't know who was more insufferable, Adriana or her."

Marc couldn't hear anything but Jayne's high pitch anymore.

What in five hells did I ever see in her before?

He twisted to face her. "Who?"

"Your sister, Your Majesty?" She smiled.

"No," Marc grabbed Jayne's wrist. Her smile quickly fell. "The other one."

Jayne froze. "Gabrielle?"

"Interesting." He tightened his grip on her wrist, and she let out a small squeak.

Jayne's wet hair spilled over her bare shoulders. Her freckled face and murky green eyes reflected his wicked face back. He noticed his eyes appeared darker than his normal hazel hue . . .

"What do you call a woman married to the king?" He smiled slowly.

Jayne's eyes watered, her lips quivering.

"I said—" He squeezed tighter.

"A queen, Your Majesty," she cried out, trying to pull herself from his grip.

Marc nodded, fixing his gaze to hers. "And what do you call a wench who sleeps with the king?"

"A—A royal mistress," she said quickly, tears rolling down her cheeks.

Marc brought his face close to hers, drawing in the same breath as Jayne, who for the first time actually had the common sense to look terrified. "And you have not been appointed as either. Be sure to remember that when you even think of speaking to me without permission."

A shamed flush rose on her cheeks. "I—I . . . of course, Your Majesty. I only wish to serve you."

Marc saw, disappointed, that his eyes were hazel once more in the reflection of hers. He let go of Jayne's wrist. "That's better."

Jayne's cheeks began to redden, her eyes still watering, but all Marc could feel was annoyance. "If you are going to cry, leave and I will call another to finish what you've started."

Jayne quickly sucked in a breath and wiped her eyes. "No, no need, Your Majesty." She picked up a small wet cloth and positioned herself for Marc to lay his head on her bare lap again as she continued her task. He didn't bother looking at her, closing his eyes to try and hear out for the voice as she ran the cloth along his body. After a few moments, she stilled.

"What is it?" Marc said, not bothering to open his eyes. "Why have you stopped?"

Jayne cleared her throat. "There is a large scratch along the back of your neck, Your Majesty. Th-there's quite a bit of blood. Would you like me to get a healer?"

Let it consume you . . .

Marc smiled, his eyes still closed as he relaxed. "No need, it's not my blood."

ADRIANA

CHAPTER 3

THE RED RAYS OF DAWN PERCHED ALONG the Temple of the Five, the gold details of the structure shining across the city as if the day held promise instead of torment. Adriana peeked at it as Callum pulled her hand gently, but firmly, from the shadowed alley they had been instructed to hide in.

Emilio was speaking to someone in an adjoining tavern, and he must have given them the signal to come inside, but she could barely think, barely speak anymore. Her eyes fixed on the glinting gold and the statues of the gods in the distance, wondering if they were even real.

A thought that made the goosebumps

on her flesh rise, but one that she couldn't force herself to ignore. Not anymore.

She could feel the tension in the air, or perhaps it was her nerves. People were waking, walking outside their battered homes with their heads hung low, their eyes downcast, their bodies drifting through the streets to tend to their business like spirits.

She wondered if she looked the same.

Adriana, Callum, and Emilio had traveled through the night, painstakingly slow through the dense, dark forest that surrounded the castle. The sounds of the hounds growing closer and farther and closer again felt like a knife to her sanity all the while. They were forced to hide behind trees, brush, in holes meant for large beasts, praying that they wouldn't return while they waited for the hunting party to move far enough away so they could run again.

Her heart pounded as her imagination fervently crafted the most macabre consequences she and her friends would face should Marc get his hands on them before they could escape the capital. Her hand shook in Callum's, tears pricking in her eyes—would he kill them quickly or slowly?

How slowly?

She naively believed that making it to Catalina's Port would give her a sense of relief, but as they entered the port city, guards combed through the paths on horseback and foot. Alleys were the only source of concealment, and now as the sunlight was gracing itself time was running out.

"Adriana, we must go now before anyone notices us." Callum gave her hand a gentle squeeze and without another word, pulled her toward the tavern. They dashed inside and Emilio shut and locked the door, peeking out from the window before closing the shutters.

"No one saw you?"

"No one, I waited until it was clear." Callum nodded, releasing Adriana's hand.

"Good." Emilio let out a shaky breath as he took Callum into an embrace, softly placing his lips on his. "Come with me."

He led them across the empty tavern into a back area with a private room. There was a large table and chairs, the curtains were drawn, and the candles were being lit by a young woman. She turned to them as they entered, and Adriana met the bluest eyes she had ever seen.

Emilio closed the door behind them and gestured them all to sit.

"Thank you again for taking us in. I know how much this puts you at risk, and we do not take it lightly," Emilio said to the woman.

She nodded, pushing her blonde hair behind her and wiping her fingers on her apron. She was clearly someone who worked at the tavern, with hands that had seen labor and eyes that reflected late nights and troubled patrons.

"I owe you my life, Emilio," she said.

She and Emilio exchanged a knowing gaze before he turned to Adriana and Callum. "Forgive me, this is Clara. She is a barmaid here at the tavern and has been quite helpful to Teros and the growing rebellion."

"How is that possible?" Adriana asked. The woman before her was nearly her age, young and innocent enough.

"Drunken words are spoken secrets here, *Princess*," Clara responded. "A man with too many tends to tell the pretty barmaid quite a bit."

Adriana bit her lip, silenced.

"What is our next move?" Callum asked. "Can you help us get to Teros?"

Clara folded her arms, assessing them. After a long moment she asked, "Are you aware of what is going on in the city?"

Neither of the trio spoke, and Clara continued. "There have been daily witch burnings in the square, curfews, disappearances, and bannings on shipments from other ports. One cannot simply go out to sea anymore without the required permission from the city official."

Emilio's eyes widened. "What are you saying?"

"I mean that escaping is not going to be simple. Even the pirates have been avoiding Catalina's Port as the royal navy combs the waters as far as the eye can see. You are going to have to stowaway on a vessel."

"A vessel of the king's fleet, you mean."

"Yes."

Adriana's heart sank. While she knew Marc's last voyage to the Blackthorn left their fleet nearly decimated, in the time since he had grown it to nearly twice the size at the detriment of the laborers. If pirates were avoiding this port, the sheer force of Givensmir's navy must be remarkable.

"Now, how in the five hells are we going to do that?" Callum shook his head.

"Well, it is easy for you two." Clara gestured to the two men, then pointed at Adriana. "For you, not so much."

Adriana paled. "I don't want to stay here. I—I can't be alone," she said, her voice shaking as she nearly spat the last words. "There is no one left here to help me."

"Agreed," Callum replied, taking Adriana's hand in his. "We need to go together, not separate."

"Unless you can fool a ship of men into believing you are one of them," Clara looked Adriana up and down, raising a brow. "Not likely—then you have only two options."

"Which are?"

"Go aboard as a mistress to the ship's captain or stay here and see if you can stowaway on a merchant's cart. Though, most are headed south to Zafira with blockades for inspection. I imagine a merchant would charge a high price to risk taking you on . . . and it looks like you are short of coins at the moment."

Adriana swallowed.

"She will not sell herself—" Callum began, standing.

"Look around, sir. We are all giving up something for safety, and even that is not enough. The truth stands. Your princess has one of the most recognizable faces in Givensmir. You either make her unrecognizable or pay a high price to make sure others pretend she is."

Emilio placed a hand on Callum's arm coaxing him back to his seat, "I want us *all* to be safe, and we will be. But we have to think clearly." He turned to Adriana. "What do you wish to do? We do not have much time before the guard triples and begin breaking down doors looking for us."

Adriana's lips quivered, and she bit them as she considered her bleak options. For all three of them to brave the Winding Roads together would be a sure death sentence. Yet, to separate . . . she couldn't force herself to think about what would happen now that she was without the protection of the kingdom. The memories of the crowd chasing her through the city streets sent a chill down her spine.

And there is no Dakon to save me now . . .

She looked up at Clara. "Do we know which captain is looking for a mistress?"

"Adriana!" Callum stood, incredulous.

"I am trying to live, Callum! I don't want to be alone with a strange man headed to Zafira. The roads are already dangerous as is, and Emilio is right, we are running out of time." She pointed at Clara. "Can you tell me who it is, and how soon they are planning to leave for Teros?"

Clara's mouth raised into a sly smile. "A dead man."

Adriana must have heard her incorrectly. "A—a what?"

"You heard me, Princess. A dead man."

"I don't understand."

Clara leaned closer to Adriana. "As part of His Majesty's growing forces, Lord Matias, the commander of ships, has recruited men from across Givensmir to fill vacant posts. One is a Ser Fraunces from Larrea set to take the post of captain for a vessel headed to Teros in two days' time. However, he has neglected his duties—and has yet to check in with the port official. He has instead frequented the brothels and this very tavern nearly every night since his arrival. His sailors know nothing of him but his name."

"You think one of us can impersonate him?" Emilio asked, arms crossed as he leaned back against his chair, thoughtfully.

Callum shook his head. "I think the real question is can we not tie him up and take his post before he can stop us? Does he need to die?"

Adriana knew the answer to this and suspected Callum did too. She stood from her chair and paced in front of the curtained window, trying to think through the weariness of her mind. Even in all the chaos of the last few days, if she closed her eyes for even a moment, she would succumb to sleep. She urged herself to keep them open, to focus on something other than the difficult decision she would have to make.

Callum, Emilio, and Clara continued speaking on the matter, but Adriana couldn't force herself to engage, her spirit heavier than ever. Instead, she peeked from behind the curtains and saw the temple like a beacon in the distance through the window. And like before, the sight did not bring her comfort, only dread building inside of her as it grappled its way through her insides.

Today an innocent woman would die, another would be imprisoned, and another would be ripped from her life because her brother and all the men feral for control decided so, using their gods as reasons to force their will upon them all. And even so, the Temple of the Five stood proud, as if it blessed them all with Death's kiss. It was easier for Adriana to pretend the gods didn't exist, than to believe they stood idly by as their people were killed for the vanity and glory of mortal men.

She grew angrier the longer she stared at it. Her breathing heavy, her heart pounding, her skin hot. Part of her wished that staring at it alone would make it crumble to little pieces on the ground, every statue and gold detail torn apart and carried off in the wind.

She pulled herself away from the curtain, turning to the three who were now in a heated discussion about Adriana's safety. She scoffed, unable to hide her irritation and pounded her fist on the table, getting their attention.

They stared at her as if she had appeared from thin air, as if they were looking at someone completely unexpected—a woman on the verge of madness and not the pious, precious princess.

She didn't give herself a moment to think before the words came from her lips. "I don't want anyone to make decisions on my behalf, not anymore. Not ever."

"Then what do you want, Princess?" Clara asked, narrowing her eyes.

Adriana met her gaze. "I want to leave and come back with a force so powerful my brother will be on his knees begging *me*, and only me, for mercy." Her voice shook with rage as she spoke, and no one dared to interrupt her. "I want to be free from his shackles, from his nightmare of a reign he has inflicted upon *my* people. Of every woman—" She choked back an angry sob, for the woman killed for running from the guard, for Gabrielle surely enduring the wrath of her brother, for everyone who had fallen because of him, and for Dakon who left her helpless and alone . . .

Clara took a ginger step to Adriana and slowly pulled a small knife from her apron. She held it out to her. "This is the price of your freedom, Princess."

Adriana took it in her hands, the cool steel like ice on her palm. She could see her reflection in it, but it didn't quite look like her anymore.

AMARIN

CHAPTER 4

"*Oh, Amarin? Oh, Amarin, I've been looking for you...*"

Amarin's eyes shot open to his dark captain's quarters. He could faintly see the fog from outside his porthole, the bit of moonlight trying to peek from behind it. His heart raced as he sat up quickly, retrieving the knife he kept under his pillow.

It had been days since his men landed at the Crooked Port, days since he last saw Eve and the rest of her group. They had exhausted their search of the village, the surrounding jungles, and even resorted to searching the waters.

But hearing Cassandra's voice now, he

knew. Somewhere in the depths of the soul he lacked, he knew...

His eyes searched around; his cabin was quiet, too quiet. And he felt her before he saw her, that familiar chill in his bones, the sensation of being watched and always two steps behind.

"Amarin."

He blinked and beheld the sea witch lying next to him. Amarin jumped, startled from the bed. Cassandra laughed wickedly, getting to her feet and walking around him before he had a chance to put a sizable distance between them. He shivered as she ran her fingers along his beard, his shoulders, down his chest. He pushed her hand away as she tried to press further down. Amarin tried to compose himself, to pretend as if he had some semblance of bravado in her presence.

"What do you want, Cassandra?" He gripped the knife tighter in his hand.

She brushed her long, dark strand of hair behind her shoulder. "You, always, my handsome pirate." Cassandra reached out to touch him again, and he took a step back.

"Where is Eve? Where is Dakon, Pazel, Izan?"

Cassandra scoffed. "How should I know."

Amarin's nostrils flared. "No, more lies. You tried to kill us."

"I did no such thing." She lay back on the bed, giving him a wink.

"The sea is yours. The sirens belong to you," Amarin pressed. "I know you were behind this."

Cassandra grinned. "My dear, you know what happens when these sirens grow hungry. Your ship happened upon their territory. What am I to do about it?"

"Bullshit, you sent them after us."

"Now, why would I do that?" She bit her lip, beckoning him with a finger.

"No." He shook his head, taking another step back. "Tell me where they are."

She sighed dramatically. "Always business with you, Captain."

"It keeps these visits short," he spat.

Cassandra lifted her lips, revealing an enchanting smile. "Then I won't waste your time." She pushed herself up, brushing past him to his desk. Maps and papers were littered about it. She shoved it all aside, letting it clatter to the floor as she procured a leather pouch from thin air. With a simple flick of her fingers, the candles of the quarters lit, revealing the mess pooled around the ends of her blue silk dress.

Amarin didn't have a chance to chastise her before she spoke. "So it seems your crew is four short this evening." She smirked as she placed the pouch on the desk, not bothering to meet his eyes.

Amarin's heart stopped. "So, you do know."

Please, be alive.

"I suppose that makes life easier for you, Captain," Cassandra said, grinning. "Four less to worry about, and now you don't have to face the witch kingdom . . . you can thank me now."

"Th-Thank you?!" Amarin pulled the knife out toward her. "Tell me this is a cruel joke, Cassandra!"

She raised a brow, amused. "Is that not what you wanted?" She walked toward him, her silver eyes shining mischievously. Amarin felt sick as he kept the blade raised, but she didn't flinch, didn't stop moving toward him.

"Tsk, tsk, Captain. I'm rather disappointed in you."

Amarin had half a mind to try and stab her, death be damned, and as his grip tightened around the blade, he felt he may actually go through with it. "Where are they?!"

Cassandra's eyes lit up, the silver hues catching the candlelight, a flicker of something dark and demented within them. Amarin's flesh crawled, but still he did not lower his blade. Cassandra placed her hand on his knife. "Do it, Captain. Perhaps it will make you feel better."

She held his gaze as the tension thickened, Amarin could feel himself choking on it. His jaw tightened, his arms shaking.

"I said, 'do it.'"

He imagined what it would be like to stab her in the heart, to pierce her skin and take all the years of heartbreak and rage out on her. He was not above murder, and hers would certainly be most appeasing. Captain Amarin had taken lives, more than he could ever hope to remember. The faces of his foes and those at the bidding of Cassandra he couldn't recall anymore. For decades, his life had been bound to hers, his soul hers to command.

Cassandra pushed his blade hand toward her chest, the tip of the knife settling there. "I know what you want, Amarin. I know how much you ache to see what lies beneath."

Amarin's eyes watered. His heart thundered furiously, beating loudly in his ears, the echo of a man who wanted death be it hers or his. But her words, *four short*, he couldn't risk not knowing what happened to them, to *her*.

Guilt consumed his anger, smothering it with shame.

Lucia's daughter.

I have failed her again...

Before he could think to shove the blade further, he let it go. The knife clattered to the floor with a loud thump, the weight of his burdens heavier than ever. He let out a frustrated grunt as he breathed raggedly, warring with himself to remain calm.

"Where are they?" he demanded.

Cassandra grinned. "You mean, where is *she*?"

"Damn you, where?!" Amarin could barely control himself, he was losing time. He shoved his face in Cassandra's, a rare startled expression came over her before she hid it beneath her usual malice.

He needed Eve to be alive, *please gods let her be alive.*

"She *was* on a ship to the kingdom who sought them." Cassandra smirked.

"The Blackthorn?"

"No, my dear." She blew him a kiss, and he fell backwards as if hands had shoved him away from her. "To Givensmir."

Givensmir?

He could feel the heat on his skin, the rage. No, that was too simple a word for what came over Amarin. He was nearly blinded with it, his vision clouded with tempestuous anger.

"To the fucking mad king?! He will have her killed!"

"Calm yourself, Amarin." Cassandra sighed. "She escaped."

Amarin could strangle her; he breathed deeply to keep himself from acting on it and uttered the only thing he could manage. "Why?"

"For power."

"P-power?! You have it all." He gestured to the sea that lingered outside of the foggy window. "Why do you need any more?"

She scoffed, pushing him back. "Simple mortal."

Amarin fell to his knees, trying his best to bury his fury, knowing with each second that passed it was becoming more uncontrollable. It was futile. "Take it, take my body, my heart, my air. Anything else you fucking want, just bring her back to me."

Cassandra didn't bother looking at him, untying the pouch on the desk as she spoke. "My, my. I feel like we had this discussion over thirty years ago, haven't we?"

"Anything, I beg you."

"If I didn't know any better, I'd suspect you were in love with the witch." She finished untying the knot, glancing briefly at Amarin before focusing her attention on the pouch once more. "Though, I think we both know seeing the last tie to your dead lover be taken away is what truly upsets you. I can nearly hear your heart crying out for them both."

"Cassandra, anything."

"My handsome captain, there's nothing more I need from you. Not when I have your soul."

Cassandra lifted the pouch, opening it and plucking a single object from within. A large black coin with a silver *A* inscribed on it faced him.

Amarin stilled, his eyes beholding something he had not seen since that night over the sea. The night Cassandra visited him as he was dying on a small boat drifting over open water. The night he cursed and damned the gods with his last breaths. The night he knew he had no hope to save Lucia...

He wished he had been brave enough to die that night.

"Oh?" Cassandra picked it up, holding it for Amarin to see. "Do you recognize this?"

Amarin's lips trembled.

Anger. He could only feel anger.

"If I remember correctly, you begged to live, to have revenge. I gave it all to you and more."

Amarin couldn't speak, hot tears rolled down his face. He wanted nothing greater than to see her body cast into the sea, to die and never return to torment him or anyone else again.

She continued, "I gave you life, and you used it to kill the guard that took your precious Lucia the moment he sailed from shore. I have made you into the greatest pirate in all of Serit. Countless treasures and epic stories are yours. Now here you are after all I've done... so ungrateful and crying over a witch who didn't even know you existed until she stepped foot on your ship."

Amarin let out ragged breaths from where he knelt, watching as she gave the coin a gentle kiss.

"Or perhaps it upsets you because you were hoping for another chance at your sweet Lucia. The witch that got away—"

"Damn you." Amarin spat. In one foul swoop, he grabbed the knife from the floor and hurtled himself toward Cassandra. She didn't have a chance to move as he shoved the blade in her stomach, driving it deep within her wicked flesh.

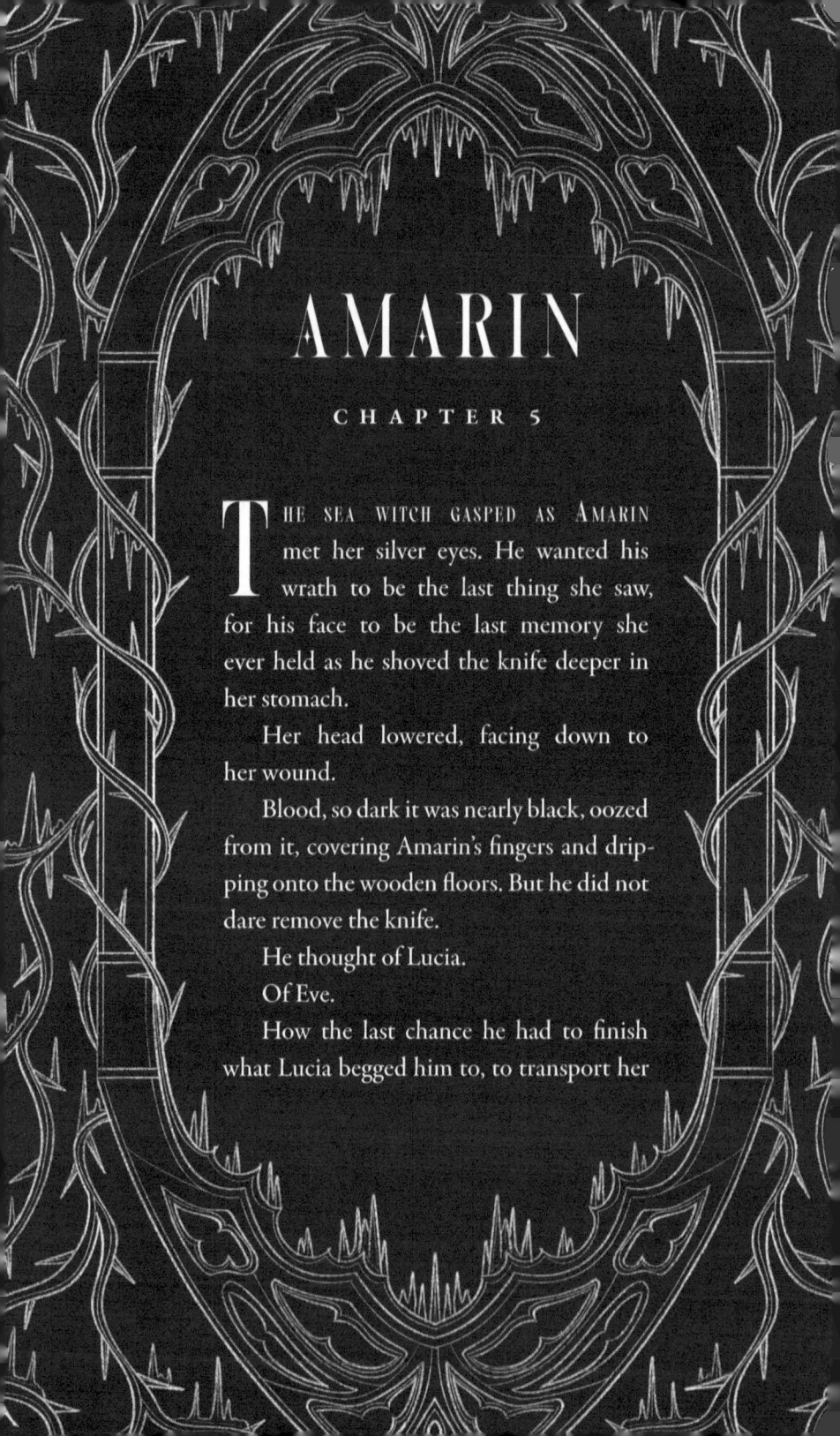

AMARIN

CHAPTER 5

THE SEA WITCH GASPED AS AMARIN met her silver eyes. He wanted his wrath to be the last thing she saw, for his face to be the last memory she ever held as he shoved the knife deeper in her stomach.

Her head lowered, facing down to her wound.

Blood, so dark it was nearly black, oozed from it, covering Amarin's fingers and dripping onto the wooden floors. But he did not dare remove the knife.

He thought of Lucia.

Of Eve.

How the last chance he had to finish what Lucia begged him to, to transport her daughters to the Blackthorn, was gone because of Cassandra. No matter what he did, Lucia would forever slip through his fingers, and Cassandra would never let him forget it.

Over three decades of torture, of grief, all leading to this knife in the sea witch's belly.

Cassandra raised her head slowly to Amarin, her eyes turning from their silver hues to a dark brown. Amarin could scarcely believe it. His hand shook as he held the blade in a white-knuckled grip, too terrified to release it.

Could it be?

Her eyes held a fear within them as she spoke, her voice trembling. "A-Amarin?"

No, it's not. No.

Her long hair was no longer black, but brown, the curls falling loosely over her shoulders. Her dress was not blue, but a soft cream color. She smelled of chamomile like that from his home.

"Amarin?"

A tear sprung from her eyes, falling gracefully down her cheek. Her lips, the very ones he remembered kissing oh so long ago, quivered.

"Lucia?" He pulled the knife out, and her body collapsed on him. He held her in his arms, the blood was too great. He threw the knife aside and removed his tunic, pressing it against her wound, trying to stop the blood.

"No, Lucia. Please, I'm sorry." He cried into her, trying to keep his shaking hands calm, trying to think of anything he could use to stop the bleeding.

"Amarin," she choked.

"No! Lucia!" He held her tight. "Get the healer!" he screamed out loud, praying the night crew would hear his cries.

But instead of movement outside his door, he heard laughter, cackling, coming from Lucia. He blinked through his tears and instead Cassandra lay in his arms, unharmed. He shoved her aside, crawling back away from her.

How, why?

It was Lucia. It had been Lucia!

"You're a monster." He shuddered, seeing her rise to her feet.

She picked up the black coin, his soul, from the ground and grinned. "I must admit, I'm impressed. Though it took you long enough."

"No, no. It's impossible."

"You are quite lucky I am fond of you, Amarin. But try that again and I will not be so merciful." Cassandra raised a brow. "Now, are we going to behave or do I have to punish you?"

Amarin trembled with shock on the floor.

Lucia. She was in my arms. She was...

"You asked where your precious witch was and I told you, though those incompetent fools let her escape and can't seem to find her."

"Who?"

"Why the Strix, of course. They resurrect a fallen goddess, and I would have reaped the rewards of helping her return."

Amarin's eyes widened. "You, you never wanted me to take Eve to the Blackthorn?"

It was not a question, but as Amarin thought over their journey, it all began to make sense. The sirens, the storm, being forced to dock at the Crooked Port when his maps had initially shown they were supposed to have been far west of it.

"Their offer was less appealing to me. I simply needed you to buy the Strix time, and you did so beautifully. Well, you and the other one."

"Other one?" Amarin asked.

"Oh yes, though it seems he would do more harm than good, switching sides like a flipped coin. One night with your witch and he was willing to *die* for her." She made a show of placing his soul in the pouch once more.

"Who are you speaking of?"

"Think real hard for me, Amarin. I cannot give you all the answers." Cassandra pushed her hair behind her shoulder. "But if you see him again, be a dear and kill him for me." She kicked the bloodied knife with her heel, and it landed next to him.

A traitor with Eve. On his ship.

It dawned on him and Amarin stood slowly. "Kill him?"

"Yes, my dear, do what you do best." She took a step to Amarin, her silver eyes taking him in. He swallowed, nervously, but this time didn't dare reach for the knife.

"If I kill him"—He swallowed, willing his courage to carry his next words—"I—I want them back alive."

Cassandra laughed, turning away from him. "That alone is worth more than a thousand dead nymphs."

"Then name your price."

Cassandra stilled for a moment, before turning her bright eyes on Amarin. "I have told you already, there is nothing you can give me—"

"You hold no power over land." He stood, taking a step toward her. He quickly added, "But I can do your bidding there. Anything you want from land, Cassandra, name your price. I swear to find and bring it to you." He forced the revulsion down his throat as he caressed her face in his hands. "Tell me, and I will make it yours. Just please, bring them all back safe and alive."

Cassandra kept her iron gaze on his, as she slowly wrapped her arms around his neck. Amarin cleared his throat, trying to maintain any bit of confidence he had.

"Well"—she smiled slowly, wickedly—"there is something I would like."

"Name it, anything."

"I have had a change of heart since the Strix failed with Eve. I want something more." She grinned. "I want the grimoire, the one your precious witch is rumored to have."

"A grimoire, I never saw—"

"Of course she never showed you." Cassandra laughed. "She barely trusted you."

"How would I get it?"

"Find the witch and you'll find her book. Then we can both have what we want. Perhaps, I may even leave you be for another thirty years."

Amarin furrowed his brow. "What will you do with this grimoire?"

Cassandra's eyes brightened. "Anything I wish."

He nodded. Every second he spoke to her was time wasted, but he had to ask for one more thing...

"I will find Eve and bring you the grimoire, but if I am risking my life for this book I—I want something more."

Cassandra sighed. "Go on."

"I want my soul back."

Cassandra raised a brow. "Your soul?"

"Yes, my soul and Eve for your wretched grimoire and whatever nightmare you may procure from it. I say it is an even trade."

She narrowed her eyes, staring at him for a long moment before speaking. "Deal. Cross my little black heart."

He let out a shaky breath, unable to hide the shock from his face.

What kind of grimoire is worth her releasing me?

"But, Amarin"—She turned, grabbing the pouch of souls—"if you fail to bring me the grimoire, then consider your witch dead. If she so much as touches the sea, I will make her mine." She patted the pouch, tying it to her dress. "And I've been meaning to add another to my collection."

Cassandra made her way to the door.

Amarin faced her. "But wait, where is she now?"

As the words passed his lips, the candles went out and the fog in the window disappeared.

Cassandra was gone.

He collapsed to his knees, all the events of the evening catching up to him.

Amarin didn't know where to go. There was no solid word of their whereabouts, no witnesses.

Save for one...

He got to his feet.

I need to find him to find her.

And then kill him.

NAVIR

CHAPTER 6

Navir watched as Clarisa slept. "Do you think we have pushed her too far?"

The crystal dangling from its silver chain about her neck glinted slightly in the moonlight that peered into her chambers. He could hear it—*tink, tink, tink*—so profoundly from where he leaned against her window, the tapping of the midnight rain against the glass was hardly noticeable.

Navir's eyes never left Clarisa, lingering far too long. He barely noticed Aris speaking next to him.

"—I believe we can push her farther," Aris said, following Navir's gaze with a raised brow. He was no fool. He wouldn't question

Navir's intentions, despite how obvious it was turning out to be.

Navir straightened. "And her familiars?"

Clarisa sighed, barely discernible as she slept, as if the worries of her world had escaped in the shadows of a dark night. She was the semblance of peace and bliss. Her chest rose and fell in calm waves much like the gentle ones that lapped against the castle now. He had never seen her like this except when Ana was in her presence.

Ana . . .

Bitterness coated his tongue at the thought of her.

She can't hide for long.

"In due time we will find them, Your Highness," Aris whispered. "Right now, the magic is doing its work. I imagine it will only be another evening of silence before she awakens. By then, we must be prepared."

Navir nodded slowly. It seemed the tapping of the oracles against their crystal cage grew louder with every second that passed. It chilled him how much stronger they were getting, how much stronger Clarisa was getting with them . . . they had lingered like ghosts at her bedside before her familiars forced them back into the crystal days ago.

From the corner of his eye he could have sworn that the oracles' dark hooded figures lingered there still, waiting to consume him when his guard was down. He shifted his eyes slowly for good measure, releasing his clenched jaw when he confirmed they weren't there. The mere thought of them, their ancient magic and vile souls, made his flesh crawl and his breathing thin. What would happen should they escape? Would the oracles kill her in her sleep . . . or him. He wondered many other things as they watched Clarisa.

He cleared his throat, trying to compose himself.
It was the third night since Ana and Theo's escape, the first since her familiars slipped through his fingers—the last bits of leverage he had against Clarisa and her fire witch sister slipping through his fingers. It made him uneasy, but he wouldn't admit that to a soul, not even to Aris, with his motives he had yet to uncover.

Tink. Tink. Tink.

Navir ripped his gaze from Clarisa and the smoke within the crystal that turned darker with each breath he took. He looked down at Aris. "How do we keep *them* from escaping without her familiars?"

Aris did not return his gaze, he too seemed to notice the crystal's peculiar change. "By keeping them fed."

"Do we—"

"Yes, there is enough to last us . . . for a while."

Navir cleared his throat. "Good. Excellent." He gave a final look to Clarisa, who still slept soundly before them. Impatience, a festering energy, made him want to shake her awake, but instead he relented, taking long strides across her room.

The oracles watched him, both from within the crystal and the shadows his mind had conjured up at the corners of her chambers as he moved. He half-believed they would appear from thin air and take him before he could think to scream; it took everything within him not to run.

Aris followed close behind, and when they were over the threshold of Clarisa's doorway, he spoke. "Shall I make the necessary preparations?"

Navir nodded, turning once more to face Clarisa's bed.

She whimpered slightly in her sleep as shadows grew on the wall behind her. He didn't get the chance to see what they were going to do as Aris closed the door and turned the key, locking it.

"That is not for our eyes, Prince," he said, placing the key in his pocket. "There is no turning back now."

THEO

CHAPTER 7

THEO SHIVERED AS THE WINTRY MOUNTAIN winds made their way through the cart he lay in. It felt like ice on his skin, keeping him fervently awake when all he wished to do was sleep the pain away. The cart flap opened and closed with the breeze, revealing the white snow and the narrow paths. Would he more likely die from the cold or from the cart falling off one of the steep mountain passes?

He could see little else through the wet fog as thunder rumbled somewhere in the distance. He did not know where they were; Givensmir's maps of the Blackthorn were not detailed, save for the capital and major coven villages. Landmarks were few and far between, measured in estimates and calculated guesses based on spies that the Golden Council kept—spies that belonged to Lord Wesley, rather.

They had been traveling for three nights, hiding out in the daylight within dense forests as they ate the food in the cart. Their horse, a beautiful dark mare by the name of Midnight, slept soundlessly as the three of them—Ana, he, and her mother Rinya—woke in shifts anticipating Prince Navir's guards at any moment. Yet, as the days rolled by and the nights sank further into plummeting cold rain, their fear lessened.

He pulled the thin blanket over him, huddling in the corner of the cart furthest away from the open flap. It did little to help, but it made him feel as if he were trying to live as opposed to succumbing to misery.

In these long stretches of painful silence and bitter cold, Theo closed his eyes and reminisced. The warm memories distracted him from the doom that lingered. He recalled the hot shores of Givensmir, the sun on his face, the warm water lapping back and forth on the sand. He could nearly taste smoking ham from the castle kitchens, feel the welcoming embrace of candlelight, of the fireplace in his chambers, the warmth of Eve's skin beneath his fingertips.

He thought of summer.

That summer.

The heat in the not-so-secret garden, the pond that swayed with the gentle breeze, the chirp of the insects, the hoot of the owl, and always Eve.

Behind his eyes, he could see hers like sparrows in the summer skies and the warmth of hearths in the winter. He could see her precious smile, hear her laugh as they ran through the gardens passing the years of their youth hidden within its embrace.

Does love look golden-brown?

He was certain it did, and it pained him more than the blistering

cold to know that he was the sole reason for losing it. He, so stubbornly the ever-obedient son of madness, the prince of propriety, left her to die.

Theo could avoid the truth no longer. He chose duty over Eve, over every day spent in their childhood, every moment in the gardens, every glance and beating of his heart when she was near him.

The stolen kiss in the moonlight, her body and trust given to him beneath the shaded gardens, every inch of her . . .

Now she was gone, forced to save herself because he chose not to.

He could still hear her begging him, the fear in her voice breaking his heart.

"Please, help me escape . . . let us run away and be free together."

"You foolish idiot," he growled at himself, his shaky breath making a small fog before him.

Eve deserved better. He meant it when he told her that that night in her chambers.

But he wished he would have said he would do everything to make himself worthy of her. To let her know through every word, every deed, that she was the fire in his life and without her he was nothing but cold and alone.

The wind whistled again, and the cart shook. They were dangerously close to the edge, and if it weren't for Ana, Rinya, and Midnight, he would have accepted his fate should he be damned to fall down.

Eryce is gone.

Pedro is gone.

Eve . . .

Theo closed his eyes once more and prayed shakily, to nothing and no one but himself, hoping, wishing, begging that Eve was somewhere far from Givensmir, safe. That her escape was not short-lived. That his brother would never find her, wherever she was.

As the cart rocked back and forth through the winding, frigid mountains Theo vowed that should he survive this torment, he would spend the rest of his life searching for her, through every city, every village, every kingdom in and out of Serit. He would find her and beg for her mercy.

Because his winter desperately needed her summer.

EVE

CHAPTER 8

"**Y**ou were the greatest apprentice I could ever wish to have," Eve whispered to Pazel as he lay atop a bed of stones and branches outside the cave. She crossed his arms over his chest, grimacing at his fatal wounds there.

He didn't deserve to die like this.
He didn't deserve to die at all.

Dakon placed a fur cloak over him to hide the brutality of it all. With his wounds covered, Pazel looked peaceful, serene. Eve placed a gentle kiss on his temple.

Dakon whispered something to him, but the morning wind was blowing fiercely, carrying most of his voice away with it. "... I will tell stories of your great adventures until the end of my days."

Victor lingered close by, surely waiting to reap the benefits of a large flame before him. Eve chose to ignore his presence, focusing on Dakon who straightened and placed his hands over Pazel.

Eve did the same, trying to keep the tears that stung her eyes at bay.

Together they set his body ablaze, the fire roaring powerfully in the wind. Victor rushed to it, staying close enough to feel the heat but far enough to avoid burning his skin.

The flames roared and covered Pazel, hiding him in a blanket of red and orange, smoke thickening the air around them. Eve reached out to Dakon, and he took her in his arms as she sobbed into his chest. Their greatest friend, the heart that kept them whole, everything she never knew she lacked until he was gone, became ashes the wind swiftly carried away.

"We will kill them," Dakon said, holding her tighter. "We will kill every single one."

As she began to shiver in the cold, the fire within her dying out and giving way to exhaustion, she wanted nothing more than to take Marc into her hands and burn the names of every person he took from her into his skin.

Eryce.

Callum.

Theo.

Izan.

Pazel.

And all the countless women and witches who perished under his rule.

He would pay for every death.

And she would be there to bear witness.

"We must go to Teros," Eve said, finally. "It is the closest kingdom to the Unclaimed Wastes, and since I was betrothed to Callum, they should favor me."

"Are you certain they have not sided with Marc?" Dakon asked.

"Would you side with the king that killed your heir?"

"Fair point."

Eve turned to Victor, who rested on the cave floor, admiring his hands next to the fire. "How far is Teros from here?"

Victor didn't look at her as he responded. "Nearly six days on foot."

"Six days?" *We would freeze to death.* "Are there any friendly villagers, clans, covens along the way?"

"None that have survived this far north." He sighed, picking at a small scab.

"When is the last time you've gone to Teros?" Dakon pressed.

"Never."

"Then how would you know?"

"Because I've tried, both as a man and as a dragon."

"Tried?"

"Yes, but I'm damned to remain in the wastes, remember? A woman scorned is an eternal curse." He whistled, shaking his head.

"You mean Isila?" Eve asked.

Victor nodded. "The very bitch. Do you know her?"

Eve huffed. "You mean witch."

"Did I not say that?" He sighed noncommittally.

"No, and I know more than I wish to."

Victor peered at her. "Now I'm intrigued."

"I gave my soul to her grimoire, and now we are tethered. There is not much more to tell."

Victor sat up, raising a brow. "Where is this grimoire?"

"I'm not certain," Eve admitted. "One moment we are being sacrificed in the throne room, and the next it appeared and took us here." She shook thinking of how powerless she felt; they would all have met death with Pazel if not for the book. As much as she abhorred the grimoire, it had saved them when she needed it most.

If only it came sooner, then Pazel might have—

"Is that how you happened upon my cave?" Victor asked.

"This wasn't a planned adventure," Dakon replied, gruffly. "As you can see we aren't dressed for the winter."

Victor whistled. "Forgive me for asking a simple question. You two are my first source of amusement in over a hundred years."

Dakon muttered something under his breath.

Eve rubbed her aching head. "I gave my soul to the grimoire for our safe passage, but I don't know why it brought us here. Nor where it went."

Victor shrugged. "The better question is what it expects of you now that it has you."

Eve swallowed. In all the chaos the grimoire had been far from her mind, but now that she sat in the cave, she couldn't help but only think about it now.

I gave it my soul. But I do not feel different. Will I feel different soon?

"Have you tried summoning it?" Victor waved a dismissive hand, then focused on his fingers, distracted again. "Hmm, I nearly forgot I had knuckles."

Eve rolled her eyes, turning to Dakon. "Do we want to summon it? What would we even do with it?"

"It has you, Eve. Which means it has me too. Whatever may come, we must confront it sooner rather than later."

"But what about Givensmir?"

"Trust me, we will go back, but we cannot save anyone if we are being possessed and haunted by something we do not understand. Perhaps there is a way we could use it to our advantage."

Victor whistled again.

Eve raised her head to him, but he was still admiring his hands.

Gods, the vanity.

"Is there something you'd like to add to the discussion, Dragon?" Dakon snapped.

Victor sighed. "You forget I am a witch too."

"I'm not certain that taking wisdom from a cursed witch is in our best interest."

Victor stood, stretching. "We have more in common than you think, Familiar."

Dakon got to his feet, approaching him. "Give me one reason—"

Victor smirked. "I say you beckon the grimoire, destroy it, and our souls are free. You two can skip to the warring kingdom and kill off the mad king, and I will go back to living as a free witch far from this frigid hell."

"But how do we destroy it?" Eve asked.

Can it even be destroyed?

"Ah," he chuckled. "I've thought long and hard about this, centuries even."

"And?"

Victor held their gazes as Eve waited on bated breath for his answer.

Would it be simple?

Impossible?

Deadly?

He finally shrugged. "I'm not certain, truthfully. I was hoping one of you would have the answer."

"I can't take this, Eve. I'm killing him." Dakon stepped forward.

"No, Dakon. Wait." Eve shoved him back down. "He can still help us."

"I am quite handy." Victor grinned wickedly.

Dakon clenched his jaw, ignoring him and turning to Eve. "It is my duty to protect you. I don't want this *imbecile* leading us astray or harming you."

"He wants the same thing we do."

"And what is that anymore?" Dakon asked. "Because last I remember, we were escaping a throne room full of Strix who killed Pazel and nearly took us with him. The only thing I seek is revenge and to save whoever we have left." He clenched his jaw, clearing his throat. "If the grimoire can help us then I don't want to destroy it. Not yet."

Eve considered this.

But no good can come from something cursed, can it?

"The grimoire is the only reason the Strix killed Pazel in the first place. They want our magic." She held his hands, urging him to meet her eyes. "It is dangerous, Dakon, and I couldn't forgive myself if something happened to you too."

He lowered his head, closing his eyes and knitting his brow in frustration. "What then?"

Eve sighed. "Their ritual failed. Whatever they tried to do with us didn't work."

Dakon nodded. "He didn't die in their circle, but . . ."

"But they will try again." It wasn't a question so much as a certainty. And her voice trailed off as the truth of her words dawned on her.

Dakon rested his forehead against hers, eyes still closed. "Finding it hard to reason going back?"

"A bit," she admitted.

"It's okay to be scared, Eve. But I'm here. I'm always here."

Clapping echoed in the cave, and Eve and Dakon turned to the source.

Victor approached them, feigning a swoon. "That is sweet. Truly, my heart is singing your praises."

Eve straightened, narrowing her eyes at him.

"I rather wish you weren't here," Dakon grumbled.

"And miss such bliss between lovers?"

Eve released her grip on Dakon. "We aren't lovers."

She could feel his gaze as he cleared his throat next to her, agreeing. "We are all we have left, if we don't get back to Givensmir. There are people there who need us."

Eve stepped toward Victor before he could respond, trying to sway the conversation. "You said you've tried venturing south as a dragon. How long did it take you to reach the edge of the wastes then?"

"Two, perhaps three days." Victor raised a brow.

Dakon smirked. "I say we take the dragon."

"No!" Victor stepped back. "I have only just started enjoying myself."

Eve held firm. "We have to get back and stop the king."

"A king? You are worrying yourself over a mortal king?"

"He's killing women, witches. He's attacking the Blackthorn."

Adriana, was she even safe anymore?

Victor waved his hand dismissively. "These kings are all mad. There is war, then peace, then war again. Wait until this one dies, or at least another century, and your odds with the next ruler are better."

"We don't have a century to wait," Eve snapped.

Victor lay back down, chuckling. "Ah, of course. How could I forget?"

Eve huffed, standing and pushing past him, heading further inside the cave, anywhere that gave her space from this wretched man.

DAKON

CHAPTER 9

Dakon followed Eve into the depths of the cave. The floor was slick with icy rock. She managed to walk across effortlessly, whereas he had to take precarious steps to keep his footing. He could nearly see the smoke emanating from her skin; the rage within her would soon become uncontrollable.

"Eve!" he called out. "Wait!"

She stilled but did not turn to face him.

Damn Victor. Damn ice. Damn the wastes.

"Eve," he repeated, gently touching her arm. She did not recoil, but he could hear her breathing, see the smoke slowly giving way to a gray mist as she calmed herself.

"Ignore the man, he's delusional from all

this isolation." Dakon gestured about the cave.

It was grander than he expected, a large and formidable castle made of crystal. Icicles hung about the ceilings as if waiting to impale them, the surfaces blanketed in a sheet of blues and whites, glistening with the bits of light that made it through the top. Together it appeared like jewels set upon the surfaces of the walls. He had never seen anything like it before, how grand and elegant it felt, though he supposed a dragon needing to live there would require such space. As he turned about the cave, taking in how massive it was, it reminded him of something from a dream or one of Cerene's tales.

How could something so beautiful harbor such a monstrosity?

He glanced ahead of them. The cave separated into various corridors leading endlessly to nowhere but darkness. He wasn't sure he wanted them to venture any further.

"Delusional or not, it is his fault he is here." She glanced behind them, and he followed her gaze. Victor was in the distance, tending to the fire.

"He wishes to be a man as long as possible; he won't leave from where he sits." Dakon gestured to the first opening on the left. "I think this would be a good time to talk about . . . everything."

They made their way into the opening. Inside was a small chamber-like room with an open ceiling. Snow drifted inside, and the wind howled above them. On one side was a pile of cloaks, furs, weapons, and other such objects. Dakon shuddered, knowing full well where they came from.

Eve ignored it, pulling out one of the blankets and placing it on the floor. She sat atop it, positioning herself along the edge of the cave wall. Dakon sat alongside her.

She closed her eyes and he could see beneath the veneer of frustration how tired she truly was. Her hair was in a mess of tangles, the lids of her eyes darker than usual, her face red from the wind burns. He placed a friendly hand on hers. "I know it has been quite the arduous journey."

Eve raised her lips in a grim smile. "I want to sleep."

"Sorry, I can leave you be—"

"No, I want to sleep and dream again." She knit her brows. "Not of nightmares or monsters or blackthorn branches coming to consume me. I want to sleep." She tightened her grip on Dakon's hand.

He held his silence, waiting as she took a shaky breath.

"I fell in love with summer once. I want to dream of summer. Sometimes, I close my eyes and I forget . . . I forget how he looks. I can only see his body falling off the ship."

Dakon raised a brow. "Izan?"

"Theo." She loosened her grip and blinked her eyes open. "I wish to dream of someone I'll never see again, someone whose face I had once committed to memory that is now more of a distant longing muddled in fog and anguish."

Dakon nodded silently. He knew too well what she meant. He hated that he could only remember Adriana's sweet face from the siren that wore it not so long ago. He wished he could hold her in his arms, caressing her face until he was certain he'd never forget it.

"It haunts you, doesn't it."

"Worse. It lingers."

"That is worse."

Eve let out a short laugh. "You have a way with words, Dakon."

"A rare compliment. I'll take it."

Eve turned to face him. "What are we doing, Dakon? What do we want to do?"

Dakon sighed. "With escaping or with each other?"

"Both."

He swallowed. "We are quite the tragedy, don't you think?"

"Yes, a story for the ages. A witch and her familiar get lost in the snow and die by the ice dragon that is waiting to feast upon them."

"I would laugh if it were a tale and not our truth."

Eve straightened, taking Dakon's hands in hers. She was cold to the touch as he looked within her brown eyes. He admired her most when they were brown. She always looked more like herself with them.

"I love you, Dakon. Truly."

His heart stopped.

Oh...

"But I am not in love with you." She let the last words trail off as she apprehensively met his gaze, a nervous energy festered down to her hands, and he was sure it wasn't the cold making her shiver.

He didn't break her gaze. Instead he willed his magic to the surface. "And I am not in love with you, Eve." He raised a warm hand to her cheek, and she rested it there, visibly relaxing. Her bright brown eyes gazed upon his green ones, a slow appreciative smile stretched across her lips. She was a vision even in this horrid place.

"Though, I wish I did," he admitted.

She placed her hand on his once more. "It would certainly make things easier."

He laughed. "But what is the fun in that?"

She grinned. "None, I suppose."

The wind howled louder now, getting their attention. They both looked up into the darkening gray sky.

Dakon cleared his throat. "Since we are being honest, I wanted you to know something. The reason I wish to get back to Givensmir as soon as we can."

"Hmm?"

"I—I am in love with Adriana."

Eve stilled, blinking a few times. "Adriana?"

"Yes, the princess."

Eve crumpled into laughter. "Princess Adriana? Sister of the mad king, youngest of the royal family?"

Dakon felt a flush on his face. "Yes, the very one." He crossed his arms uncomfortably, and Eve's laughter slowly quieted. A long silence stretched between them.

"Oh."

Dakon rubbed his eyes. "We are not strangers. We fell in love in the spring."

Eve's eyes widened. "Does anyone know?"

"I don't believe so. We used to exchange letters—"

"Oh, oh, oh no." Eve stood. "It *was* you!"

Dakon stood quickly. "What are you talking about?"

"Adriana, she lost a letter in her chambers. We nearly tore it all apart searching for it. She told me it was a noble and you were the courier. I—I truly had no idea."

He shook his head. "I was both the pen and dove."

Eve began pacing. "That day we discovered a handmaiden found it. We caught her as she returned to the chambers."

He furrowed his brow. "It was Cerene, the woman who raised me."

Eve paled.

"What are you not telling me?"

Eve bit her lip, turning from him.

"Eve." Dakon took a step toward her. "Eve, I'm your familiar, we need to be honest, no matter how difficult."

She slowly turned to face him. "I accidentally set the letter in her apron ablaze—"

"I know."

"It was in front of Adriana."

No.

"Adriana was forced to give a confession about the incident to the king. She thought it was Cerene, not me—"

"Stop, please," Dakon said, raising a hand to silence her. "No more."

Eve stood shaking in front of him. "I'm so sorry."

"I—I can't... I cannot, will not, let myself drown in misery again." He looked up to face Eve. "It is not your fault, nor Adriana's that she was set to flame. It was the king's and all those who would see magic burn."

She lowered her gaze, but Dakon raised her chin with his hand. "No. We are done mourning, Eve. We are done running and being weak. The time for anger, for revenge, is now."

"I would say wrath is a better choice."

Eve and Dakon turned to the voice. Victor leaned against the opening of their chamber.

"Why can't you leave us be?" Dakon groaned.

Victor grinned, ignoring him and facing Eve. "Wrath, my dear. It's the only thing that brings a smile to my face. If I am not smiling, then you should be worried."

"Wrath is what gets innocent people killed." Eve huffed.

"No, wrath is what gets people in the way killed."

"Has the fire gone out? Is that why you're here?" Dakon crossed his arms.

"No, it roars. Just like your discussions." Victor gestured about. "These caves echo." Victor made his way inside. "I see you have found my collection."

He walked toward the objects cluttered along the wall, picking up random trinkets.

"We haven't taken anything if that is what concerns you," Eve snapped.

"Not at all, in fact, I would feel better if my flames were safe." He tossed a few daggers, a sword, and other weapons aside. "And despite what you think, I would like to keep you alive . . . for pure and selfish reasons."

Of course, the fire.

Dakon leaned down, picking up a set of twin daggers. They had black hilts and silver blades in need of a decent sharpening. He supposed he could find a stone somewhere that would do the job nicely. He twirled them in his hands. They felt balanced, familiar. Something about having these made him feel more prepared for what was to come. He placed them in his belt.

Eve moved next to Victor, rummaging and picking up a satchel and a small knife, placing it inside.

"I think it's time, don't you?" She looked at Dakon.

Their eyes locked knowingly.

Victor looked between them. "Are we going to summon someone?"

"Something." Eve sighed. "And it's better to do it now."

ADRIANA

CHAPTER 10

The day came and went, settling into an evening shrouded in fog and little twilight as Adriana peeked from behind the curtain in Clara's room outside. She couldn't see much of anything save for the light of candles in the windows of neighboring homes and establishments that lined the streets. The weary people of the morning had disappeared into the night making way for the more nefarious that lingered outside of the brothels and taverns with dirty faces and smug grins as they traded coins in the alleys. She didn't want to know what deals of the dark they were making.

Adriana closed the curtain, moving back toward the small makeshift bed in the corner. The three of them spent most of the day sleeping to prepare for the evening. Well, for the moment Clara would usher Adriana into a private room that Ser Fraunces tended to buy for the hour.

She shuddered.

Callum and Emilio had already been moved to it, hiding beneath the bed inside for the moment Adriana would bring Fraunces in. Their only compromise to the plan.

Her hands shook as she eyed the small blade resting on the chair next to her. It glinted slightly in the candlelight, a single one nearly burned to the wick, and she wondered how it would feel to pierce someone, to end their lives, to be the executioner.

She recalled her reflection in the blade earlier that morning—an angry woman, hair in tangles, and face bruised by the chaos of the collapsing dungeon and her brother's hand. It didn't make her feel powerful, not like she had expected. In truth, it scared her to see her bitter eyes staring back, marked with something she had only seen in Marc's. She swallowed and took a step away from the blade, fearful her unwavering stare would lead it to cut her. A ridiculous notion, but . . .

Do not think about it.

Do not think about it.

Do not think about it.

No matter how much she tried to tell herself this, her mind conjured up visions of a stranger, a man bloodied beneath her, or atop her . . .

There was a knocking at the door, and Adriana nearly fell over herself as it opened.

"Adriana?" Clara entered quickly, the noise of the busy tavern carrying up the stairs toward them. Men shouting, a lute playing, glasses clinking, women singing—but even so Adriana's heart pounded above it all, thrumming in her ears so loud she was sure it would deafen her. Even as Clara closed the door, the pounding continued.

"Y-yes," she replied, straightening herself. Adriana had donned one of Clara's simple peasant dresses, a faded blue that appeared gray in the darkness, but she found herself patting it down nonetheless. A habit of needing to look presentable, though she supposed those days were long behind her. Adriana's gown from the palace had been burned in the stove earlier that day, along with everything that tied her to royalty. But now she felt naked before Clara, unsettled and vulnerable.

"Ser Fraunces has arrived and is drinking downstairs. I informed him I would ready the private room." Clara stepped toward Adriana, placing a gentle hand on hers. Adriana met her tired, blue eyes. "You only need to lock the door when he enters, your friends will do the rest."

Adriana nodded, her hands shaking as Clara retrieved the blade from the chair and handed it to her.

"Use this to protect yourself and keep it when you leave. The world outside the castle walls is far more dangerous than you may dare to believe."

Adriana swallowed, pocketing the knife. "I know—"

Voices shouted beyond the window, and Adriana flinched as she quickly looked toward the dark curtains. It was no doubt a skirmish in the alley or perhaps something worse, but she tried to blink the latter thought away.

Clara snuck a peek behind the curtains. "It is only drunk men. Nothing to fear." She placed her hand on Adriana's arm in gentle, soothing strokes meant to calm her, but Adriana could only think how the curtains were her only shield separating her from the outside world.

The memory of running from a riotous mob surfaced once more and her lips trembled. "I was chased by a crowd in the city once."

She wasn't sure why she said it, only that the words left her lips before she could stop herself.

You may not have many words left if this fails...

Adriana pushed the thought away, wishing to speak the memories from her mind before having to give herself to a strange, and perhaps deadly, man.

Clara raised a brow. "Yes, I heard."

Adriana sat on the bed. "I suppose I would have died, been stoned, or whatever it was the people wanted from me. I'm not certain this blade would do anything against those who hate me."

Though the knife was safe in her pocket, she felt as if it were burning a hole through the fabric, as if speaking of it gave it life. She swallowed.

"You are beloved, Princess." Clara knelt before her, taking her hands in her own. "Those who tried to harm you . . . well, they were different. I promise."

Adriana met Clara's eyes, genuine sincerity reflected back to her. She nodded, it was all she could think to do.

"We were relieved to hear you escaped, truly."

"I cannot take all the credit, Dakon—"

"Dakon?"

"Yes, he saved me that day." Adriana turned from her, the thought of him sending an ache in her chest. She could nearly see his green eyes and the promise of spring and sunlight if she closed her own, the haunting memory of the man she loved and may never see again, a man who took her heart as he escaped the castle with another. She choked back a sob. "I never had the chance to thank him. To tell him how I loved him."

Clara stilled. "Was he a servant in the castle?"

Adriana met her eyes once more. "Yes."

"I don't suppose Dakon is a common name for castle servants." She seemed to say it more to herself than Adriana.

Adriana narrowed her eyes. "No, he is the only one I've met."

Clara's eyes widened slightly, and after a moment slowly took a seat next to her. "Oh." Her eyes then shifted to the floor, her face paling.

"What is it?" The pounding of Adriana's heart stopped, and now she wished she could hear anything but the silence that stretched between her and Clara. She tightened her grip on Clara's hand. "Do you know him?"

"I met him once."

"And?"

"It was so long ago, Princess. I thought I'd never see him again."

Adriana's heart fluttered. "Did you see him leave with Eve? The witch?"

Is there a chance to see him again?

Clara shook her head. "I saw him with another castle servant. Rumor had it they were set to join a pirate's crew."

Adriana nodded remembering him and Pazel running away. "Is that all?"

Clara took a deep breath, meeting Adriana's worried gaze. She shook her head. "I overhead castle guards the other night in the tavern. They spoke about a witch and servants who had run away." Clara cleared her throat, closing her eyes briefly before continuing. "He was captured, Princess. Taken to the king along with the witch."

"What?!" Adriana stood, unable to keep her limbs from shaking.

No, no, no, no.

Clara now appeared to be as young as she looked. The facade of maturity melted before Adriana as she struggled to speak the final words. "He, he—"

Adriana wanted to know what they were.

Adriana begged herself not to let her finish.

Adriana couldn't bring herself to listen but couldn't find the will to leave.

"Is he . . ."

Clara stood, taking Adriana's face in her hands. "I'm so sorry."

ADRIANA

CHAPTER 11

Was there anything stronger than grief?
  Was it sorrow?
Was it agony?
Misery?
Adriana mulled over this as she met Ser Fraunces at the base of the stairs, hidden just down the hall from the main tavern floor. No one seemed to care, or they were drowning far too deep into their mugs to notice the drunken man being led by another lady of the night toward the private rooms upstairs.

She could smell the stench of liquor and sweat as he approached, his gait was crossed and his speech slurred as he took her in his sights. His pale eyes were a murky blend of grays and blues that seemed to try and focus on her but stared just beyond as if trying to determine where the nearest room at the top of the stairs would be. As if he hadn't enjoyed the splendors of this tavern dozens of times before according to Clara.

Adriana noted how much older he was than she expected, nearly twice her age. A large tunic barely covering his belly was stained with ale. She bit her lip, trying to calm herself and remember Clara's instructions. She looked behind him. No one else was there watching them; the crowd of the tavern seemed far gone, as if they were a lifetime away. For once that evening, she could barely hear the patrons or the noise of the night.

Fraunces grinned slowly, and she tried to ignore the menacing countenance lurking beneath his crooked smile.

The room on the left. The room on the left.

Adriana did her best to return it, grabbing his hand and ignoring his fingers trailing down her waist as he followed her up the stairs.

She had not taken more than a few steps when he pulled her back.

"What are you doing?" Adriana protested.

Fraunces didn't seem to care that they were halfway up the stairs as he pushed her up against the wall.

Adriana's eyes widened, she couldn't mask the horror and panic clawing its way through her.

"The room," she squealed. "We need to go to the room."

The tavern was too loud, too rowdy, her voice certainly lost in the thick of it. Panic welled in the pits of her stomach as she tried to breathe.

Fraunces pushed his face into the crook of her neck, and it took everything within her to keep her senses, to think about how to escape his fierce grip.

"You're new, aren't you?" he hiccuped into her ear.

"Yes, now please, the room." She tried to push him off, but he forced her back to the wall.

"We don't need a room," he slurred.

Adriana began to scream but Fraunces put a hand on her mouth. "Uh uh. You scream, and I cry witch." He cackled lazily in her ear, his hot breath reeking of stale liquor.

Tears fell from Adriana's cheeks as she tried to kick him off, but his body was pressed into her forcing her still.

"I hear that's the magic word," he continued, loosening his grip on Adriana as he focused on kissing her neck. "The word that makes you women jump at our command."

Adriana nearly retched at his voice, his stench, his proximity. She tried to push once more, but he pushed her hands down as he continued. "Don't make me say it." He hiccuped. "Behave and I will keep your secret, my little witch."

Witch.

Witch.

Witch.

The word echoed in Adriana's mind, her body hot with the anger, the fury, the rage.

Women like you will always burn before men like me.

Wrath.

Red and bloody.

Adriana could not see past it. The burning fire within her clawed its way out like a monster from the pits of the five hells.

She pulled the knife from her pocket, and without a second thought shoved it into the side of Fraunces's neck. His blood covering her arms and face was less putrid than his hands on her skin. She didn't stop, couldn't stop, shoving the knife again and again into his flesh, losing herself in the act of complete fury.

All the time watching women's bodies pile up in dungeons and fires of the pyres burning ash into the air from their corpses, clouding the kingdom in gray skies and misery seizing hold of her sanity was too much to ignore. Too much to bear.

Witch!
Witch!
Witch!

She screamed loud and hard, her throat going raw as she continued stabbing his body. "You're the witch! You're the witch! You're the witch!"

The door at the top of the stairs opened, panicked gasps and footsteps running down to her, but all she could see was the red that filled her soul.

"You will burn before me!" she screamed as hands roughly pulled her from Fraunces's dead body and the knife was forced from her hand. "You will all burn before us!"

Witch!
Witch!
Witch!

"Get her out of here," Emilio shouted at Clara, as he wrenched her toward the top of the stairs, "Quick!"

Adriana fought against them, but Clara shoved her up the steps, locking her in the room.

"What happened?" she demanded, her blue eyes piercing Adriana.

"He attacked me. He wouldn't let me go," she stammered, her hands shaking so violently she nearly believed they would fall from her sides.

Clara pulled the blanket from her bed, throwing it over Adriana's shoulders. "Sit, now."

Adriana did as she demanded, shivering as if she were in a brutal snow storm. The memory of Fraunces, his rotting breath, his drunken touch, his words, *witch, witch, witch*. They echoed in her mind, taunting her with the terrifying truth.

"I—I killed someone." She breathed, choking back a sob.

Clara sat next to her, holding her close. "And it may not be the last time, Princess."

Adriana's eyes trailed from the dark, black curtains before her, down to the floor where blood drops led to where she sat. She trembled as she beheld her bloodied hands, the small cuts from how hard she stabbed him, Fraunces, *him*.

"I—I—" Words were at the tip of her tongue, but they did not free themselves from her shaking voice. She swallowed, trying again. "He-he's truly dead?"

"He is," Clara said, taking out a small cloth from her apron and wiping Adriana's hands.

"Did anyone see?" She turned to Clara, the daunting realization settling on her, how she screamed, how she shouted.

"You will burn before me!"

Never in her life had she lost control like this, never had she imagined, truly imagined, how it would be to see the life leave someone's eyes, to be the reason for it leaving. She clutched Clara's hands in a tight grip. "Are they coming for us?"

Clara's eyes widened but she shook her head. "Princess, no one stops for a dead man in Catalina's Port."

Adriana nodded. "What does this mean now?"

"It means you must finish what you started. You must go on the ship, masquerade as Callum's mistress, and find protection with Teros."

Silence lingered between them as Adriana tried and failed to keep Fraunces from her mind, how she looked in his eyes. She wondered if perhaps she was more like Marc than she ever dared to think.

"Am I damned?" she said, looking at her stained hands, the blood that refused to leave, like ink on parchment. It certainly would spell the words of her deed for the rest of her life, she was sure of it.

Clara shook her head. "You have only paid the price of freedom."

NAVIR

CHAPTER 12

TORCHES LIT THE CONFINES OF THE castle windows, and Navir craved the warmth as raindrops fell upon his wings. He glided through the wet skies, rain weighing him down until he was forced to fly into his open balcony doors. He shook his black feathers, watching as they disappeared into the air replaced by his bare, wet arms.

He had flown for nearly an hour, searching for any trace of Ana and Theo, any sign of them hiding in the dark forests surrounding the capital. He passed by homes, open windows, and even carriages desperately searching for even a trickle of conversation about a witch on the run or a mortal trapped in the Blackthorn.

There was nothing.

His chambers were silent and dark, and he seethed as he paced back and forth inside. His anger rose with each step he took.

"Where are they?!" He shoved a lone chair, and it broke as it made contact with the stone floor. The wooden pieces clattered across his path. He didn't care, he only wanted to wrap his hands around Ana's throat—no, he wanted to make Clarisa do it. End her life and cut off the last tie Clarisa had to her mortality.

Perhaps, I could wake her now...

The thought was quickly eclipsed by the memory of the oracles tapping against the crystal, subduing him. Besides, she would wake soon, and according to Aris she would be more powerful than ever, the oracles taking over and gaining strength with each witch they forced her to consume. They had just enough of them to last through the next steps of their plan, but he shuddered thinking of what would happen if he took too long to execute it.

His mother. She would notice very soon that her favorite assassin was acting differently. It was inevitable. The Clarisa they all knew was dead, wasn't she? Replaced by the monster he molded from deception and promise of power. A power that his mother held in her clenched fists...

He breathed deeply, the air filling his chest as he tried to calm himself for what he needed to do, what he should have done long ago.

"Good evening, Son," Queen Saryn said as she peered into her cup.

"Mother," he replied curtly.

He could faintly hear screaming, so quiet he had to strain his ears, but it was silenced as his mother drank, leaning against her open balcony door. Drops of rain made their way inside, pooling at her feet and dampening the ends of her nightgown. The thunder was quiet, though the lightning flashed occasionally behind her in the sky, revealing her tangled hair and tired eyes. She was nothing like the vision of royalty she held in front of the kingdom.

He barely recognized her himself.

"Who is the unlucky witch?" he asked, taking a seat at her desk. "Does this one float or fly?"

His mother's blue eyes met his, narrowing. "No. But you are not here at this hour to speak about unlucky witches."

It was a threat. He knew it as he held her gaze.

"You are right, Mother. As always." His fingers traced circles aimlessly on the wood, tinkering with objects atop it as she sighed, staring into her now empty cup.

"I hear you have Clarisa locked in her chambers."

"You are quite nosy, Mother." Navir cocked a smile.

"You are not nearly as cunning as you believe yourself to be."

"And you are not nearly as powerful as you would have us all believe." He gestured to the cup.

She placed it down slowly on a side table. "What are you here for?"

Navir straightened. "The mortals are preparing for a second brutal attack on our shores, and while you sit here drinking your woes away, I think it's time to confront the truth. We do not have the strength to prevent their invasion. Not as it stands now."

Saryn's lips thinned. "And you believe you can stop them?"

"I know I can."

Saryn scoffed. "You have always been a dreamer, Navir, but you lack commitment."

"Just as you lack the magic you steal from other witches. It must bore you to solely rely on your spells."

She turned, ignoring him. "Leave if you only wish to insult your mother. I am in no mood to temper your naivety."

Navir moved toward her. Rain pattered against his skin as he stood on the threshold of the cold balcony and the warmth of her chambers.

"Naivety? I believe you mean disappointment. You, who put these ideas and dreams in my head as a child, now wish for me to cast them aside because I turned out more like you than my father."

"Your father was a waste."

"Which one? The one you married for power or the one who was keeping your sheets warm when heads were turned—"

He felt the slap on his cheek before he could utter another word, hard and nearly blinding. Every bit of anger and frustration his mother felt put into a single blow. And every bit of mercy within him splintered with it.

His mother stood tense before him. "You know not what you speak of."

Navir clenched his bruising jaw, swallowing down the rage that made his limbs shake. "You wanted me to be the child Clarisa is, a half-witch with all the power at my fingertips. Someone to be admired and praised. But when I ended up the bastard of Malin, you hated me for it."

Angry, hot tears rolled down his cheeks as he took a step to close the distance. His mother took a step back, her eyes widening. "You hated me, and it wasn't even my fault. It was you, all you!" His voice shook, and rain fell upon his head, running down his blistering cheek. He wanted it to drown them both, to drown her.

"I gave you a crown."

"It was always mine to have!"

She stood silenced, her blue eyes a mixture of hurt and anger.

"You have done nothing but allow these mortals to force their will upon us. For the first time in decades, they nearly reached our shores, and you did nothing but sit in your chambers waiting for them."

"I am not a fighter, Navir. We had our own forces out there."

"Ah, yes, our high priestess and her witches prayed to Isila, but did she come? Did she save us with her mercy?"

"Do not speak of our goddess—"

"I speak of you! If not for Clarisa, we would have perished. She is the reason we are standing here breaking each other."

"You place far too much trust in that half-breed."

"And you did little to use her when you had the chance, save for killing your foes when they upset you. She was nothing but a pawn in your game of pride."

"You have no idea what it is to rule knowing your greatest confidants could be plotting your death. Do you know how many spies we have employed in the mortal lands that broke their oaths to us, to me?"

"And that is why you killed Malin, isn't it?" Navir challenged. "Was sleeping with a mortal woman enough to damn him?"

His mother stood rigid, breathing hard. "He betrayed me."

"You betrayed yourself." Navir refused to acknowledge the pathetic, drunk witch before him. "He was the last one loyal to you until his dying breath."

"You know not what you speak."

"I know this. You are scared, Mother. You have started a war you couldn't stop, and now you find yourself drinking the blood of witches hoping one will give you enough strength to feel powerful again."

"Don't—"

"Or what? You'll have me killed too?" He spat the words with such vitriol, she looked at him as if he struck her too.

She shook her head slowly. "I have coddled you for far too long, my son." She closed the distance between them, her maternal stare wet with unshed tears. "Here is the brutal truth: We witches are nothing but mortals with tricks up our sleeves. And when you strip away the magic, the mystery, we die like they do. Bleed bright red and coat the grounds of parched lands begging for sustenance. And when these mortals cross our shores, and they will, the Dallise Sea will be painted in our misery."

Navir clenched his jaw. "That is the difference between you and me, *Mother*. Where you see bloodshed, I see power. Where you see our downfall, I see promise."

His mother's brows furrowed as she beheld him. "You have placed your trust in the wrong hands. She will kill you the moment you cease to benefit her."

"Not if I kill her first."

Saryn's eyes widened. "This ends now, Navir."

"You're right, Mother, it does."

Before she could respond, Navir grabbed her by the arms. "Here is the brutal truth, *Mother*. Malin never betrayed you. He was given a potion that forced him to. *My potion*."

His mother's eyes widened, her mouth opened in shock. But before she could utter a single word, Navir shoved her off the balcony.

She hadn't a chance to scream, to shriek, as she fell down into the rocky shore below. The long fall ended with a sickening thud as her body made contact with the jagged rocks that rested along the side of the castle.

He flew down, watching as she was dragged into the high tide, her eyes still wide in disbelief. And he waited there until she was out of sight, pulled into the dark depths of the sea.

CLARISA

CHAPTER 13

It's ours.
All ours . . .

Clarisa could hear the voices, but she couldn't see past the darkness.
Couldn't feel anything but the cold air.
Couldn't feel anything at all.

EVE

CHAPTER 14

"Have either of you summoned something before?" Victor asked doubtfully.

Eve laid the blanket out, taking a candle from Victor's belongings. "Usually the book finds me, but I have a feeling—"

"Great, *feelings*."

She ignored him. "I have a feeling we can bring it here."

Dakon pulled the blanket to the center of the chamber, and Eve sat atop it, placing the candle before her. Dakon lit it easily.

Victor's eyes were on them, judging their every move.

Dakon sat before her, taking her hands in his.

They sat in silence as she concentrated on the grimoire, thinking about how she wanted it before her, needing it to explain what happened and what to do next.

The night wind breezed along her face, blistering cold; it howled desperately beyond the cave. No matter how she concentrated, the cold kept seeping through her thoughts.

"You're doing it quite wrong, you know," Victor said.

She let out a frustrated breath, raising her chin to face him. "Well, are you going to offer any help or simply stare and judge."

Victor ignored her, retrieving a knife from his belongings. Eve flinched and Dakon began to rise, but Victor gestured to them both to sit. "I want you alive, remember?"

Dakon slowly sat down, his eyes narrowed on Victor.

Victor sat with them. "One cannot summon something without giving something." He gestured for Eve's palm, and she handed it to him slowly. Before she could ask a single question, he sliced her palm in a single swoop.

"Ow!"

Victor gestured her palm over the candle, wetting it with the blood. "You are the summoning witch. It is your duty to give something in return." He turned to Dakon, handing him the knife. "Carve the name of the grimoire in the candle."

Dakon looked annoyed but did as he was told. Eve's blood spilled over the edge of the wick and filling the carved spaces of the candle.

Blood of the Blackthorn.

"Let me heal you, Eve."

"No," Victor interrupted him. "She needs to give to take. If she cheats the spell, there could be nasty consequences."

"It's all right, Dakon. I will heal by morning, I'm sure."

She straightened. "Now what."

Victor smiled, pointing at Dakon. "You light the candle."

Dakon did and Eve was surprised how brightly it burned despite the blood that trickled down the wick. "Now, both of you close your eyes."

Eve closed hers, seeing nothing but darkness behind them. Victor shuffled about them. Dakon's hand was in hers. They were not entirely cold, but neither were they warm. The wind howled but sounded further and further away.

She tried to concentrate on the grimoire, the weathered pages, the owl beneath three stars, how heavy it felt in her hands that day she tossed it over her balcony and into the water. She recalled how it forced her to touch its pages as it enveloped her chambers in a horrific blizzard. Or even how warm it was beneath her shaking, numb fingers.

Time felt like it stretched an eternity, and she was growing impatient.

Certainly, this witch had been a dragon for far too long to remember anything about witchcraft. She doubted he had even practiced out in these wastes.

When was the last time he even summoned anything?

Perhaps, a century or more before he was stuck in scales and claws and ice.

"This isn't working," she said, opening her eyes.

Her heart stopped.

Eve was no longer in the cave, and no longer was she holding Dakon's hands.

She was in a dark chamber with a single, large mirror facing her. She stood.

"Dakon? Victor?" Her voice was thin, barely reaching out from her lips.

No one responded.

She took a step toward the mirror; it was the only light in the darkness. She could see herself, confused, alone, and afraid as she faced it. Eve swallowed, raising a trepidatious hand to the glass.

Slowly, she placed a finger on it. To her surprise it went through the glass like water.

She whipped her hand back inspecting it, there seemed to be nothing wrong with her, no scars nor scratches on her fingers.

What magic is this?

She heard a tapping sound. Eve looked back at her reflection and saw herself, tapping on the glass.

"Come inside," it said.

Eve felt a chill as her eyes widened. Her reflection followed suit, appearing stunned before offering Eve a gracious smile.

Is this a trick?

"It is not a trick," her reflection said, answering her unspoken thoughts. "Come inside."

Eve's skin crawled, and she took a step back.

Her reflection smiled warmly. She walked out of view and came back a moment later. "Is this not what you are looking for?" She raised her hands and in them was the grimoire.

"The Blood of the Blackthorn."

"Come inside, and I will give it to you."

Eve took a step. "This is how I get the grimoire?"

"Yes." Her reflection smiled. "I've been holding it waiting for you."

Eve raised her hand, her fingertips barely brushing the mirror, when a hand snatched her back. "Don't touch it," Victor said, pulling her away, "or we may never see you again."

Eve's heart thundered in her chest as her reflection screamed at Victor. A loud, shrill shriek that shook the ground they stood on. Her reflection was not in the mirror anymore, but shifted into one of Victor, screaming as he held the book in his hands.

"Eve!" Dakon pulled her into his arms. "We've been looking for you."

Victor turned to them. "We are in the veil. And here, I would advise you to stay very far from mirrors. They will snatch you in and your reflection will be free to roam in your place."

"The veil?"

Victor smiled. "Yes, we are not in our world anymore, but we've hedged to one of spirits and gods."

"I—I thought we were simply summoning…"

"My dear, you cannot summon a goddess's grimoire without coming to get it yourself." He walked past them into the darkness. "Now follow me. We don't have much time."

THEY WALKED TOGETHER INTO THE DARKNESS THAT SLOWLY SHIFTED into a dense forest. A moon lit their path as they continued walking between the large, twisted trees. They looked familiar.

"Are these blackthorns?"

"Keen eye," Victor responded, taking out a knife and cutting through the thorny branches.

"Do you know where we are going?" Dakon asked.

"Not at all," Victor responded. "But I have a *feeling*."

"Are you trying to trap us in here?"

"If I was trying to trap you, I would have gladly let the reflection take you."

Eve grabbed on to Dakon's arm, the feeling of dread creeping up her spine. "I don't feel very safe here."

"And you shouldn't," Victor murmured. "That means we are getting closer."

They came upon a clearing, all around blackthorns tangled the edges of the forest. In the center was a large fire. Victor led them to it.

"Is that what you are looking for?" He pointed to the inside of the flame, where a book burned.

Goosebumps popped up on Eve's flesh. She could only stare at it.

Dakon reached for it. "Let us get it and be gone."

"No," Victor said, pushing his arm away. "It has to be her. She is the witch summoning it."

Eve looked to both of them. "Should I do anything?"

"We won't know until you reach for it, my dear."

Eve swallowed and slowly reached for the book.

S̲ʜᴇ ᴏᴘᴇɴᴇᴅ ʜᴇʀ ᴇʏᴇs.

Dakon and Victor were staring at her.

"You may be new at this but nothing from a goddess comes without a price," Victor cautioned. "I would be wary of using it unless you truly need to."

Eve slowly lowered her gaze. In her hands was the Blood of the Blackthorn.

And it felt heavier than ever.

DAKON

CHAPTER 15

"Even think about killing us and I promise I will personally make you suffer when we change you back." Dakon pointed at Victor as they walked outside in the cold.

"You have my word." Victor placed his hands over his heart.

"Your word is shit until you can prove it."

"Ah, you wound me, Familiar." He raised a hand dramatically over his temple, peeking with one eye for Dakon's response.

Dakon refused to take the bait. "I mean it. Hurt her or me and you will be begging for the death you have avoided all these years."

Victor smiled. "Do you promise?"

Dakon scoffed, turning to Eve huddled in one of the fur cloaks beside him.

"Remember," she said to Victor, "take us to Gods' Protection, the river between the wastes and Teros. If you don't kill us, we will find a way to help you out of here too."

"Are you sure you wouldn't want to figure this out here?" Victor murmured as he continued walking past them outside. "I rather like the warmth."

Dakon shook his head, and Victor grinned wickedly as he turned forward.

The wintry air was crisp this morning, an insufferable blanket of snow covered the ground in white save for Victor as he trudged through it, making a path leading toward the edge of the forest. Beyond him were gray trees covered in ice, their branches burdened with all the winter it carried, hanging low in a perpetual state of submission. The snow fell like rain but sounded like despair. If not for the gray skies, Dakon wouldn't tell where the days and nights ended and began.

He recalled how Victor spoke of the ancient magic that lingered on this land; he wondered why Victor had been allowed to live so long if they were as dangerous as he believed.

He could be lying as well.

"Won't you join me?" Victor called out to them, pushing against the waist high snow. "Or better yet, we could always go back inside!"

"No," Eve replied, "We need to go somewhere less . . . less—"

"Lonely? Cold? Miserable?" Victor turned around, walking backwards.

"Less deadly," Dakon snapped. "We can't stay in this cave forever."

Victor laughed aloud, finally reaching the edge where the trees did not cover the snow that fell upon him, leaving wet, crystal-like trails down his face. "Why not? I need the company."

Eve rolled her eyes, shouting, "How long will this take?"

He shrugged. "I have to freeze to death first." Victor shivered as he removed his cloak, calling out to no one in particular. "Any moment would be nice!"

Dakon watched as the witch trembled in the snow, waiting in anticipation for him to change into the enormous ice dragon from before. Eve held onto Dakon for warmth, even inside the mouth of the cave where they stood the cold seeped into his bones making him feel less magical and more mortal than ever.

He longed for warmth without fire, for silver birches, for blue skies and verdant meadows. He longed for Adriana, in her favorite rose-colored gown sitting next to him as they spoke about nothing of consequence. He reached for his pocket, but stopped himself, remembering how he dropped her letter into the sea thinking he would never see her again.

Damn fool.

He thought of the treachery that became of Givensmir's castle, the burnings, the Strix, Marc wreaking havoc on the people—Dakon was nearly sick with desperation to lay eyes on her again.

Thinking of Adriana made him ache for her like never before, knowing they were only a few stone walls and corridors apart. He wished that he could have managed a way to escape and find her, no matter how impossible it was.

Please, let her be safe. Let her be alive.

"Why is it taking so long?" Eve wondered aloud.

Dakon barely heard her through his thoughts, muttering in response. "I don't know, maybe it takes time?"

Victor whistled weakly as the snow piled around him. His arms wrapped around his bare body, his face turning red as the wind whipped at it. Dakon was not particularly fond of the dragon witch, but neither did he want him to suffer long. He shifted uncomfortably next to Eve, hoping Victor's transformation would happen very soon.

The silence stretched until Eve finally broke it.

"Dakon?"

"Yes, Eve?"

"Do you believe the ritual could have worked?"

Dakon raised a brow. "We've discussed this. It couldn't have. It wasn't finished properly."

"But what does that mean?" Eve let go of him, straightening. He met her brown eyes, wishing he could remove the hint of uncertainty growing within them. "What happens when a spell is incomplete?"

Dakon hadn't thought of that. So much had happened in such a short time, he admittedly couldn't think about much else save for the next problem before them. He wished he had Cerene's book, the one he lost somewhere between being captured by the Strix and ending up in shackles before Marc.

She would have known what it meant.

"I don't know, perhaps that it didn't take. That it goes away? Why?"

"Do you think the Strix taking our blood, calling forth our magic, giving my soul to the Blood of the Blackthorn . . . everything, could have manifested something else? Even if it wasn't what they wanted? Change things we didn't expect?"

She shuddered as she finished, but no longer from the cold. The uncertainty within her was giving way to trepidation, and the unwelcome pricking of dread clawed into Dakon's chest too. Witch blood was powerful alone, what could the Strix have done with it in the absence of a mortal sacrifice?

What could they have summoned instead?

He bit the inside of his cheek, thinking about that night in the throne room. The Strix chanted in a language he did not understand, and the grimoire appeared shortly after. Their blood was given to Marc, and . . .

Their blood was given to Marc.
And then the book was summoned.

He raised his eyes to Eve, finding the courage to voice the question he knew was on both their minds. "There's a reason we were able to get the grimoire easily, isn't there?"

Eve's eyes widened, but she nodded all the same. "I don't believe it's hers anymore. It's complicated, but . . . I don't feel her soul within it. No longer does it beckons me as it used to."

"But if her soul has left the book then—"

"Then she is out there using a host," Eve finished for him.

Dakon's heart raced.

"Marc." It had to be. The mad king was ready to receive their magic, his body open for the taking.

If Eve's eyes reflected trepidation before, now they were spiraling into panic. She turned from him, pacing back and forth, running her fingers through the tangles of her hair nervously. Dakon could only watch as she pondered the very dire truth settling upon them both.

Isila did not save us from the throne room . . . she used us to free herself.

And the Strix gave her the chance to come back to life.

Eve released a shaky breath, speaking aloud as she continued pacing. "I know it should be impossible. She's been trapped for centuries. How could she—"

Victor shouted aloud, cursing into the wind that whipped at his shivering face. "Damn you, Isila!"

"Isila . . ." she repeated under her breath. "Isila . . ."

"Yes." Dakon replied, trying to ignore Victor's curses. "Isila is the reason we are here. It would explain why we were cast away to the wastes out of every other place in Serit. She wanted to be rid of us like she did with Victor, to prevent us from stopping her. She sent us here hoping he would kill us."

Eve stilled. "This is a curse, not her mercy."

Dakon took a step toward her, grabbing her arm gently to face him. "Eve, think of every folktale you've ever heard as a child. What do you remember of grimoires?"

"They are books of magic." Eve searched his eyes, the answer slowly coming to her. "Books that contain the soul of its owner." Her eyes widened. "It needs a soul to survive."

Dakon nodded, and he silently thanked Cerene for all the tales she told. "And if Isila's soul is truly gone from it, if she has taken a host—"

"That means the grimoire is mine now," Eve said, her voice, a shaky, barely contained whisper. "It was her plan all along to use my soul to replace hers, wasn't it? It is why the book appeared to me once my magic returned." She grabbed Dakon's shoulders, her eyes fervently searching his. "She used the chaos in the throne room to free herself knowing I would take the bait to try and save Pazel."

Dakon couldn't speak, shock taking over him.

Eve's mouth opened and closed, and they stood together for a long moment before she managed to speak again. Her voice trembled. "I-it's mine now."

He straightened from her grip, looking to and fro as if the path to the castle would somehow appear before him, but Eve wrapped her hands around his arm, pulling him back. Her fingers trembled as she struggled to force the words from her lips. "Dakon. If we are cursed, if Isila banished us here, then that would mean . . ." She closed her eyes for a long moment, swallowing her fear before meeting his gaze once more. "It would mean that we may not be able to leave the wastes, either."

No.

Fear seized him now, holding onto his body in its icy embrace, a grip that clawed its way through him, tearing apart every hope he held on to since arriving in this godsforsaken place.

Adriana, I need to get back to Adriana.

Dakon turned back to Victor, trying to suppress his agony, when he heard a thunderous roar. Before them, Victor finally shifted into the ice dragon. In the bleak day, the dragon was immense and terrifying.

It towered to nearly the tops of the evergreen, snow-capped trees, its sharp teeth enormous and powerful, its white and silver scales glinting.

This was truly a monstrous beast.

Beast.

Dakon squeezed his eyes shut, missing his companion's dark fur and bright vermilion eyes.

Oh, Beast, you would be able to show us the way.

He opened them, facing Eve. "We need to go south and see for ourselves. There has to be a way back home."

Eve managed a nod, as her wide eyes beheld Victor before them. The dragon huffed, and Dakon felt the icy breeze on his skin, the cold was becoming nearly unbearable now. He watched as Victor lay down, stretching his long tail toward them like a staircase.

Dakon sighed, pulling the hood of Eve's cloak over her head as she shivered next to him.

Now or never.

"It's time, Eve. Let's see what we're facing."

Together they climbed atop the dragon's back, the chill of his scales made Dakon wish he'd grabbed another fur blanket. Eve wrapped her arms around Dakon, and he held onto one of Victor's scales.

Then they set forth into the gray sky.

THE THREE OF THEM HAD FOUND A SECLUDED CAVERN FOR THE NIGHT, the cold still insufferable as they huddled around a fire. Dakon laid out an old map he recovered from Victor's cave and stared at the lands of the wastes sketched out in faded ink. By Dakon's estimate, they were still a day's flight away from Gods' Protection, a day until they would find out the extent of their banishment.

He hoped.

"So, am I a free man?" Victor groaned in his witch form from beneath the blanket of furs. The fire cracked next to him, and he squinted as a few stray sparks landed near his face.

Dakon was certain he preferred Victor as a dragon, when he could do nothing but fly and listen. Now, he talked and interrupted them as if his voice would be plucked from his body at a moment's notice while Dakon and Eve explained their suspicions.

Dakon picked up a stray stone, placing it in the crook of his arm along with the others. He didn't bother meeting Victor's excited eyes as he responded.

"We aren't certain," Dakon muttered. "Though if you wish to step outside again, be *my* guest." He rubbed his face with his left hand, it was cold to the touch, and he shook the chill away as he stepped over Victor. He lined the wet stones in a circle around Eve, it was the best he could do without a rope or thread. In all of Victor's treasures, they had brought what they could, and the only candle it seemed he had was the one burned to the wick when they retrieved the grimoire. Dakon settled for a branch he broke into tiny pieces until one finally stood straight before Eve.

This will have to do.

"Damn," Victor groaned. "So close."

"If you are going to be with us, you might as well help," Dakon said, waving his fingers gently above the branch, setting it on fire.

"No, I would dare not interfere."

"You mean you don't want to."

"Well, not in so many words." Victor turned over, resting his chin on the palm of his hand as he watched them.

"It didn't stop you last time." Dakon lifted his gaze to Eve who sat cross-legged with her eyes closed, concentrating. Before her the grimoire was opened to a blank page, all the pages were blank it seemed.

"This is your duty, Familiar." Victor sighed.

"And where is yours?" Dakon asked as he continued placing the final stones down.

"Dead. Isila didn't see the need for a dragon to have one out here."

"So, you made a stupid decision, and it cost the life of your friend?"

"We were far from friends."

"Enemies?"

"Lovers."

Dakon let out a short laugh, the irony not lost on him. "A goddess and your familiar, I am quite surprised you had time to do much else."

"I didn't. It's how I was caught. The souls piled up and so did the lies I told them both."

"A liar and a cheat; we are so lucky to have you," Dakon murmured. He retrieved one of his daggers, cutting the palm of his hand and reaching out so his blood drops mixed with the fire.

"But an *honest* liar and cheat." Victor lifted his chin, having the audacity to look prideful.

Dakon shook his head, ignoring him. He turned to Eve once more, the last stone placed on the cold ground, closing the circle. She released a breath, her eyes closed, her soft, brown hair hanging loose down her back. She had grown so much into her craft since they first began, and Dakon could scarcely remember the haughty, spoiled noblewoman he first met so long ago.

Eve trembled slightly as she reached out to the flame. It began to burn at her fingertips, the embers reaching up her arms and slowly consuming her until she was more fire than witch. The grimoire opened, the pages flipping before her until it landed on one stained with orange-brown ink.

"Remarkable," Victor breathed.

Dakon couldn't speak, watching as branches grew from the ink, reaching toward Eve until it finally consumed every bit of the woman before them.

"She is where she is meant to be now."

ADRIANA

CHAPTER 16

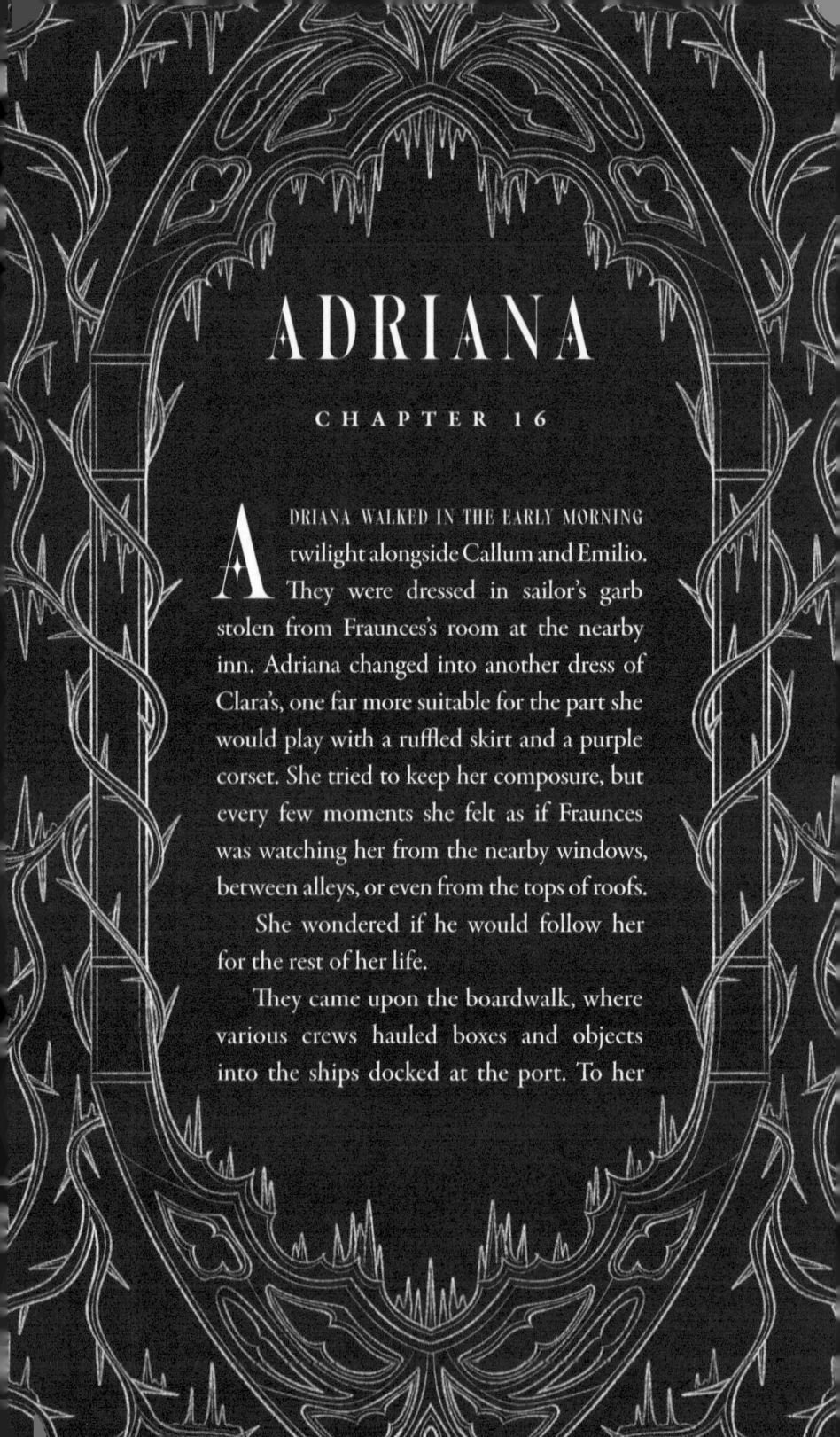

ADRIANA WALKED IN THE EARLY MORNING twilight alongside Callum and Emilio. They were dressed in sailor's garb stolen from Fraunces's room at the nearby inn. Adriana changed into another dress of Clara's, one far more suitable for the part she would play with a ruffled skirt and a purple corset. She tried to keep her composure, but every few moments she felt as if Fraunces was watching her from the nearby windows, between alleys, or even from the tops of roofs.

She wondered if he would follow her for the rest of her life.

They came upon the boardwalk, where various crews hauled boxes and objects into the ships docked at the port. To her surprise, no one seemed to pay her any mind.

"I thought mistresses were not common on ships," she whispered to Callum.

"They are," he whispered back, gesturing her to the far end of the harbor where other women in tight fitting dresses stood.

"Oh."

"Do we remember our names?" Emilio asked, stopping them before they reached the start of the port.

"Ser Fraunces," Callum said.

"Thalia," Adriana said.

"And I am a lowly sailor that no one will care for. But if it matters to either of you my new name will be Oliver."

"Oliver?" Callum asked.

"Yes, does that bother you?" Emilio crossed his arms.

"Oliver... it doesn't suit you."

"I happen to like the name."

Callum rolled his eyes. "If it pleases you."

"Well, why shouldn't it?"

Callum paled, and Adriana bit her lip, knowing the answer but unwilling to get in the middle of their quarrel.

"Never mind, it's not important, *Oliver*."

"No, I'd like to know," Emilio demanded, louder than intended.

Adriana sighed. Their squabbling was getting the attention of a few passersby. She pulled them both aside, irritated. "Oliver was a noble Callum favored when he was younger. They may have shared a kiss, I am not certain. Now can we please get on with this? We still have to make it out of the port."

Emilio turned to Callum. "Fuck Oliver. My name is Noah."

Callum stifled a laugh. "Noah it is."

They walked to one of the ships, Callum introducing himself to the first mate, a stanch man with long, dark braids, as he climbed aboard with Emilio.

"It's about time you made your presence, Captain. My name is Hidalgo." He shook Callum's hand. "There are too many new faces here that need someone to follow."

"Right." Callum nodded. "My apologies."

As Adriana began to climb the steps behind them, the first mate stopped her. "There is still a lot to be done. It's no place for a woman, m'lady. You can speak to the other mistresses, and we will fetch you when it is time to board."

"I am quite capable, I assure you," she pressed.

"The last lady who said that lost a finger when she ventured out of the captain's cabin before we were fit to sail. No, you can stay and wait. I am certain your captain will not leave you."

"I will take the risk," Adriana said, making her way past him and hurrying to reach Callum. Emilio was quickly tasked with helping lift cargo on board, and Callum led Adriana to the captain's quarters.

"I have to look the part until we sail. Stay here, and I will return as soon as I can." He gave her a gentle kiss on her head, and she gave him a fierce hug in return.

"Thank you, Callum."

He held her back. "We are almost out of here. Just a little bit longer."

Callum released her, and soon he was gone. The captain's quarters were large, with massive windows behind a wooden desk, but it was otherwise empty and looked rather new. There wasn't much save for what Adriana assumed to be the necessities of any captain: maps, ink, a few quills, parchment, and other such objects. She peeked at the maps, they were marked with routes and stops, the drawings quite similar to those she studied in the castle.

She sat behind the desk, making herself comfortable, trying to distract herself from the silence of the cabin, the rising of the dawn in the distance, and the faraway voices of the crew on the other side of the door. Adriana pulled the first map in front of her, there were

X markings over *O*s across the northwestern borders of Givensmir, familiar ports she recognized as those belonging to Teros leading all the way down to the capital where the last *X* mark was made. It appeared fresh, as if recently made.

She furrowed her brow, seeing the line through Catalina's Port making its way toward the south where the other ports had only *O* markings. Her breathing hitched as she recognized the pattern.

This ship is headed south.

She gasped, standing so quickly the chair fell down behind her with a loud thud. She ran to the door, needing to find Callum, or Emilio, either of them so they could right this somehow.

She opened the door and the sunlight outside nearly blinded her, so used to the dark she did not realize how powerful it was even in the early morning. She blinked through it, turning left and right, seeing men and women aboard working.

"Wait!" she called out to no one in particular. "Where is my captain?"

Hidalgo dashed up to her. "What are you doing here, miss?"

She ignored him. "Where is Fraunces? This ship is set to sail for the south?!"

He seemed surprised but ignored her question. "You were supposed to go on the other ship. One of my men was supposed to take you to that one over there." He pointed at a ship drifting in the opposite direction going further and further into the distance.

"I don't understand!" Adriana was trembling again, her heart certainly in her throat as she struggled to find breath.

"Your captain and a sailor were moved to another ship set for Teros, we ordered a sailor to take you to them."

"Then take me there, now, please!"

"We will do no such thing." The man with a deep voice approached them.

Adriana turned, meeting dark eyes with a hint of silver . . . or so she thought. The man had thick, black hair and a stubble on his sharp jaw, a tattoo of vines ran up the length of his neck.

"And who are you?" she demanded.

The man crossed his arms, revealing dimples and a sly smile.

"Miss," Hidalgo answered for him, "this is Izan, captain of this ship."

CALLUM

CHAPTER 17

"I WILL HAVE YOUR GODSDAMN HEAD for this!" Callum roared, taking out Fraunces's sword and pointing it at the poor sailor.

"I-I'm sorry, Captain. She came on to me!" he cried out flinching. The woman next to him, blonde with pale skin and a red dress cowered behind the sailor.

"You kissed me first!"

Callum cursed. He'd found them entangled in an embrace in his captain's quarters, and much to his horror, the mistress was not Adriana. Even worse, that sailor was the one who was supposed to retrieve her from the other ship.

"You were tasked to bring the Miss

Thalia on board!" He gestured to the vessel that was nearly out of sight now, so far away he wasn't certain the sailor could even see what he was pointing at.

"My mistake, Captain Fraunces, but this lady will do, won't she?" He pushed the woman forward and she took a step back, her eyes wide with fright.

Callum pushed past the woman, pointing the sword at the sailor's chest. "Tell me one reason I shouldn't throw you overboard!"

"Captain Fraunces," Emilio said, placing his hand on Callum's and forcing his sword down, "might I have a word."

"Not until I kill him," he snapped.

"I think it's bad luck to have bloodshed on our first day, *Captain*," Emilio pressed. "Can I please have a word?"

Callum narrowed his eyes at the sailor who was shaking in front of the sword's blade. "This isn't over, yet. Get out of my sight, both of you!"

The sailor and the woman ran below deck, not bothering to look back. When they were out of sight, Callum raised his eyes, no longer able to see the other ship in the distance.

Fuck.

Emilio pulled him into the captain's quarters as the rest of the crew pretended to work, their eyes peeking up at them curiously.

Callum was panicking, he could feel it on his face and in his voice even through the anger. He seethed as Emilio closed the door behind him. "We need to turn this ship around, *now*."

Emilio rubbed his temples. "Now, Callum—"

"Bring me the first mate, someone who could change course. If we turn now, we may be able to catch them."

Emilio grabbed Callum by the shoulders, staring him into silence. "I want Adriana safe as much as you do, but we need to look at this plainly or all three of us may not have heads by the end of this."

A lump formed in Callum's throat. Guilt was worse than the panic. It was consuming.

"Adriana is headed on a merchant ship to Zafira, you saw it yourself. It is new and built for swiftness in the water. Now look here." He gestured around the cabin. "This ship is much older, *slower*."

Callum followed his hands; the wood was chipped in spots, the window glass yellowed and faintly chipped in the corners.

Emilio continued, "Even if we wanted to try and catch them we couldn't. You remember what Clara said. These waters are full of the king's ships, do you not think they would report a wayward ship headed off course? Do you not think they would try to chase it down and discover who was on board?"

Callum swallowed, his heart beating fast. He couldn't think of a suitable argument, it was true, even as they left the harbor, they had passed by at least half a dozen ships with soldiers, and there were checkpoints to even leave the vicinity.

They were lucky that no one recognized them this far as the escapees from the castle dungeons, but how long would their luck last if they were forced into more encounters with the royal ships?

Callum hung his head, leaning against the desk to keep upright. "We can't leave her. We made an oath to be together."

"And we will. I swear to you we will find her again." Emilio bent down to meet Callum's crestfallen stare, his golden-brown eyes serious as he spoke, never wavering. "But we cannot do it alone, not with our potential enemies aboard, not in any way that could draw attention to who we are before we are amongst our allies."

"What if they find out who she really is?"

Emilio pulled Callum into a tight embrace. "She is more clever than you think. Our girl will make it. I know she will." He gently lifted Callum's face between his hands, locking eyes with him once more. "I swear to you, my love, we will find her."

Callum could do nothing but nod, hoping against hope that Adriana would forgive them, that their mistake would not be fatal. He had to believe she would survive, had to believe she was no longer the young lady he grew to know as delicate and precious, but the woman who did what she had to to survive.

"Onwards then to Teros," Callum managed.

"Yes, Captain." Emilio embraced him once more and turned on his heel, leaving Callum alone to his thoughts, his regrets, his mistakes.

We will find you again, Adriana.

I swear it.

AMARIN

CHAPTER 18

Amarin raced off the Wretched Sentinel and toward the Crooked Port. Eve's last known whereabouts were the jungles that surrounded the port and the village within. And while his crew had exhausted every effort, Amarin needed to try one more time.

Just one more time.

He needed to find anything in the jungle that would lead them to her . . . or him.

The jungle.

He cursed under his breath as he ran up the sandy shore with nothing but his sword, a torch, and the clothes on his back next to a few of his crew. It was the middle of the night; a crescent moon and the stars like small candles in the sky, shone on the land and sea, but did little to light the jungle as he approached.

His heart sank. This jungle was a massive, dense cluster of palm trees, brush, and tangled vines.

Niani raised a torch. "We should split up, Captain."

Amarin nodded, clenching his jaw as he watched Niani and the others move further down the line and enter the jungle, disappearing as they stepped foot in the darkness.

He retrieved his sword, slicing at the brush before him and taking a step inside.

It was nearly pitch black, and Amarin turned around once to confirm the beach still remained in his sights. It was, but that did little to settle his nerves.

He turned back to the darkness, his sword held before him as if readying himself for a sure attack from a beast or one of the Strix. In the distance, he could hear Niani giving orders and the rest of their party pushing through. It made him feel less alone.

Amarin focused ahead, wondering how Eve, with all her fire, could have been taken so easily. He wondered if Dakon and Pazel were still alive.

"Damn these fools," he muttered, "running off like children and getting killed."

His thoughts trailed to Izan; the simple healer had turned out to be something far more menacing than he expected.

You're an old fool, Amarin.
You're an old fool without a soul and wits.
Trusting anyone as if you don't have bounties on your head.

He slashed at some vines angrily, moving further inside the jungle until he could no longer see the light of the moon or the beach behind him. He raised his torch higher, hoping it wouldn't die out before he could escape.

As he continued through, he began to wonder what it was he was searching for. A body, clothes, a trinket? Certainly, Izan or the Strix wouldn't be hiding out in the jungle, or had they been waiting for him this entire time?

He mulled over these thoughts pushing further into the brush until he realized something. He had been wandering a long while, and he should have reached at least the edge of the village by now...

"You damn fool," he huffed at himself. He raised the torch, trying to see where it would be best to adjust course. The vines, the trees, the jungle. It all looked the same.

An unsettling feeling crawled along his skin, and he turned too quickly, tripping over a tree root as he tried to run.

Amarin groaned, thankful that the torch did not go out. As he pushed himself up from the dirt floor, he felt something smooth beneath his fingers. He felt around the small object and picked it up as he brought the torch to get a better look. It was a green pocketbook.

Amarin stabbed the bottom of the torch into the earth, using both his hands to open the book. Inside were drawings of bones, of herbs, of spells...

His heart raced as he flipped through the pages, this had to be something important, something that belonged to one of the witches. But as he neared the last page, he was disappointed by a lack of name or a clue to anything further.

"Damn, I just need to find them."

He rubbed his eyes, a throbbing in his head pained him to think. He strained to listen for Niani or any of the other crew nearby, but all he could hear were the chirping of insects and an occasional hoot of an owl, all else was silence.

"I'm fucking lost with a diary of bones." Amarin scoffed at the little book, thrusting it down onto the dirt. "And it's not like you can help me find it, can you?"

He stood, thinking about how to return when he heard the sound of parchment flipping. He followed it, looking in stunned silence as the pages of the book flipped back and forth.

Amarin clutched the sword tighter in his hand, the hairs on the back of his neck rose. He turned, trying to see the path he came, but it all looked the same—as if he had never cut through.

Certainly, he was going mad, perhaps there was a wind blowing the pages awry. But even as the thought came to him, Amarin knew it wasn't true, the heat of the night was worsened by the lack of a breeze.

This book is moving on its own.

His eyes trailed back to it. The little book was opened to a page with seven words. Amarin bent down, reading them slowly aloud, "I am lost and need you."

He furrowed his brow, picking up the book and leaning it toward the torch to read it better.

I am lost and need you?

Amarin swallowed, flipping the page and the next and the next, though now they all bore the same words.

I am lost and need you.

"I am lost and need you," he said once more, confused. As the words parted from his lips, Amarin could feel something watching him, eyes burned into his skull. He turned and saw nothing but trees and vines.

Sweat pricked at Amarin's temples, his eyes wide with the realization that he could hear nothing but the low growl of something very close by. Even if Niani and the crew could hear him scream, they would not be able to save him in time.

He was hopelessly lost in a strange jungle, following broken leads on a fool's errand. He should have sailed for Givensmir instead of searching haunted jungles.

The growls grew closer.

He stood, the torch in the ground casting a long shadow behind Amarin.

He tightened his grip on the hilt of his sword imagining a feral jungle beast stalking his prey—stalking him.

"I'm sorry, Lucia," he breathed, shame and fear taking over.

He would not find Eve. He would not bring her to safety.

He had failed her.

Orange-red eyes peered at him from the shadows, and Amarin could scarcely breathe. It took all his strength to keep himself from dropping his sword.

A large beast, dark as the night around them emerged from the brush, on all fours it nearly reached Amarin's chest. Its teeth were bared, the ends of its fur like mist in the air.

Amarin had never seen anything like it, this creature of the night. He grasped his sword with two hands now, knowing that his mortal weapon would do little against what was approaching him.

He was ready to strike, to fight.

But deep inside, with the heart he had left, Amarin knew it was futile.

This beast was certainly Death.

EVE

CHAPTER 19

Eve opened her eyes and recognized the tan-colored stones before her. She raised her hand, feeling the walls of the castle once more bathed under the midday sun. The scent of pork wafted through the air and she turned toward it, following it to the kitchens. It was rather crowded and the bodies of people moving to and fro pushed past her as if she weren't even there. She knew she wasn't.

This is the servants' quarters.

"Cerene!" a voice called from the other end of the corridor.

Eve whipped her head in time to see her mother race into the servants' quarters, rushing down the corridor. Eve quickly followed her to a weathered, wooden door that appeared as if it would break in two by simply staring at it.

Her mother knocked quickly before letting herself in. Eve made her way inside behind her.

The room was tight. There was barely enough space for a little wardrobe and a makeshift bed of planks beneath straw and blankets next to a side table. The walls were bare stone, with small holes at the bottom Eve knew mice would travel through.

She huddled in the corner as she watched her mother and Cerene, a tightness in her chest.

There must be something I need to see...

Cerene sat on her bed, unmoving as her mother closed the door tight behind her, placing a small chair in front that would do little to thwart any attempts to break in.

"Cerene," she repeated, kneeling before the old woman, grasping her hands tightly in hers. "What do I do? I haven't heard a word from Amarin!"

Cerene squeezed her mother's hands back and released them. She patted the bed, gesturing to her to sit next to her as she grabbed a small cup from her bedside table.

"Here, drink this, my dear."

"But—"

"Drink."

Her mother drank, and Eve watched as her nerves calmed as she finished the cup. "Thank you, what is it?"

"Lavender water." Cerene smiled sadly.

Her mother laughed unexpectedly. "Lavender water?"

Eve couldn't help but grin, she had forgotten the sound of her mother like this. It warmed something cold inside her as she watched her continue into a fit of giggles like the child she wished she could be once more, carefree in the castle among other children she would perhaps never see again. Many of whom would be lost in time or death. *Theo. Callum. Eryce. Adriana?*

Eve hugged herself trying to focus on the women before her instead.

Her mother laughed until the tears that came from her eyes turned into choking sobs that made her body tremble.

Cerene wrapped her in a fierce hug. "He will come, Lucia. I have seen it. You have seen it."

Who is he?

"You have seen what I have seen, Cerene." She cried into Cerene's shoulder. "I will not make it past the night, but my daughters. He said—"

Cerene lifted a brow. "He? Did you meet with Borgias?"

Lucia pulled back, her tear-stained face meeting Cerene's solemn gaze. "I did."

Cerene's lips thinned. "Whether the king dies tonight or not, you are in grave danger. Borgias is not to be trusted."

"I'm desperate, Cerene. And I—I have leverage."

"Lucia, leverage needs more than your word alone. He could turn on you.

"I have no choice! Lord Marcelo has all the entrances guarded. Our daughters are stuck in their rooms. It was either trust him or Lord Wesley, they are the only ones who know these tunnels—"

There was a knock at the door, and her mother stilled. Eve backed into the wall as if it would take her in and hide her from whatever was on the other side. She wasn't ready for them to come for her mother, if this was how it happened. She still didn't know what she was supposed to gain from this.

Cerene held a finger to her lips and pointed for her mother to hide behind the small wardrobe.

Her mother rushed there, crouching behind it as Cerene moved the chair and opened the door. Two small boys rushed inside. "Cerene! They're coming for us!" one of them cried.

Eve watched as her mother peeked from behind the wardrobe,

the crying boy, no older than five, held onto Cerene's legs in a fierce, terrified grip. The other boy Eve recognized as Dakon, who was but seven and shaking in Cerene's embrace.

Dakon.

That must mean the other boy is . . .

"Pazel"—Cerene closed the door quickly—"what are you speaking of?"

Eve's breath caught and she held her hand to her mouth to keep from gasping.

"They are looking for the stable boys," Dakon stammered. "They are killing us, Cerene!"

"I don't want to die, please, Cerene!" Pazel cried harder.

Cerene shushed them as shouts carried through the halls. "What happened?"

"The guards came to the stables, th-they killed our friends."

"How did you escape, my children?" She brushed their heads with her fingers as the shouts grew louder, and the boys cried harder in her lap.

Eve tried to steady her breathing, but she found herself shaking instead.

They were killing children?

Eve walked past them to her mother who was concentrating on them from behind the wardrobe. She recognized that look from when she was a child, watching her mother channel her magic.

What did she see?

Eve reached out slowly and touched her face. Her mother stilled but did not look at her.

Eve closed her eyes, taking in her thoughts. She could see Dakon and Pazel through her mother's eyes. They were frightened children, their minds racing, revealing the events that had unfolded moments before.

The guards missed them because they were playing with sticks as swords in the garden maze, forgetting their duties until they saw the rush of golden armor.

The other boys were executed in the stables as Dakon and Pazel were about to make their way inside.

She could see clearly how Pazel nearly gave them away until Dakon placed a hand over his mouth and dragged him away. She could hear the terrified cries echoing in the distance as Pazel and Dakon ran straight to Cerene.

The only mother they knew. The only protection they had.

Eve withdrew her hand, breathing deeply.

I never knew . . .

Her mother stood, facing them. "They are cup bearers," she said firmly. "You are cup bearers."

The banging of doors down the hall grew louder, the cries of the servants and roars of the guards ordering them around carried like omens of death in the air. Eve backed into the corner again.

They won't be harmed. I know it. They can't be.

The boys continued crying, and her mother ran toward them, grasping their chins in her hand and forcing them to look upon her face. "You are cup bearers! You work for me and Lord Marcelo. You have accompanied me here to retrieve lavender water from my handmaid."

The guards were close and her mother repeated this again and again as Cerene handed the boys a plate of cups and a kettle.

The guards' shouts were outside the door, and her mother patted down her skirt trying to temper her shaking.

The door burst open and three guards entered.

Eve, knowing she was nothing but a spirit in this past, still flinched as if they meant to strike her.

"We are looking for any stable boys, on matters of the crown!" one announced, pointing at Pazel and Dakon.

Her mother stood in front of them. "There are no stable boys here, ser. These are my cup bearers, and I do not appreciate you yelling at me in the presence of my handmaid. We shall be going now."

The guard stepped in her path. "I said it is a matter of the crown, of the utmost importance."

"Then you best not waste his time." Her mother narrowed her eyes.

The guard narrowed his in return, gruffly moving aside. "You, boys! Who do you serve?"

Dakon shook, but answered, "Lord Marcelo and the Lady Lucia, ser."

The guard clenched his jaw, turning to Pazel. "And you, boy, what are you holding in your hands?"

Pazel was on the verge of tears, shaking.

"You are scaring my cup bearers!" Her mother held onto Pazel.

"Take the young one." The guard gestured.

"No!" Cerene cried. "He is just a boy!"

No!

Eve could do nothing, watching in horror as the guards made their way to the little boy. Their hands about to rip Pazel from her mother when he finally found his voice. "Lavender water! Lavender water as it calms the lady!"

The guards stopped, and the one who gave the order grunted after a tense moment. "Very well. Next time speak with your chest, boy."

He gave a nasty glare to her mother and the rest of the room before leaving with the other guards.

Cerene closed the door again, shaking as she held her mother and the boys together. "Why are they doing this?"

Dakon and Pazel clung to her and Cerene, whimpering too fiercely to pay any mind to their words. Her mother was silent for a long moment, before bending down and taking Pazel's hands in hers. He could barely speak for all the sobs choking him, covering his reddening face in splotches.

"These boys saw something they weren't supposed to. Something they need to forget."

Eve's mother loosened her grip on Pazel. Suddenly her eyes widened. "No," she gasped.

"What is it, what do you see?"

Her mother stood slowly, her lips trembling as she raised her gaze to Cerene. "I made a grave mistake."

"Dakon," Eve breathed. Her eyes met his as he knelt outside of her stone circle. A brisk chill carried through the cave, and she swallowed down the bite of the wind.

He blew out the candle and removed the stones from around her before entering. "Yes, Eve? What did you see?"

"That is what I wanted to ask you."

DAKON

CHAPTER 20

"I truly hit the luck of the gods, haven't I?" Victor laughed. "The lore that builds on ancestors and stable boys."

"Quiet!" Dakon snapped.

He sat next to the fire, trying to think, trying to remember.

In truth, he only thought about how much chaos and turmoil his life had been that only the rare moments of normalcy stood out to him. He wrestled with himself, trying to salvage the memory Eve spoke of. The one her mother had seen once.

She cradled the grimoire in her hands, clutching it as if it intended to leave at any moment, vanishing in thin air.

The Blood of the Blackthorn.

It was the third time he ever laid his eyes on it, and it was nearly unrecognizable without all the blood stained on its pages from the throne room, or in Eve's possession. He stared at it, unable to keep his eyes from it. The binding was old and weathered, the parchment yellowing and frayed at the edges. The grimoire appeared heavy as Eve adjusted it to her lap.

He shuddered. It felt wrong to be in its presence.

"What exactly did she see?" Dakon asked again.

"I'm not certain, I should have touched her hand again to see."

"Touch her hand?" Victor asked.

"Yes, it is how Eve can see memories," Dakon answered, shifting his weight to face her.

"Intriguing," Victor mused. "You carry quite the depth and mystery."

Eve ignored him, sighing as she beheld Dakon. Her brown eyes were weary. "Does it matter?" she asked, melancholy. "Would it change the past that so many mortals, an entire kingdom, was willing to accept? My mother will forever be the enchantress that succumbed to madness."

"But it will matter to you." Dakon held out his hand.

Eve raised her eyes. "Are you certain? I may fall into memories you may not wish to share."

Dakon hesitated. He thought over his most precious and private memories.

Adriana.

Silver Birches.

Spring.

"It is all right," he breathed. "I trust you."

Eve gave him a ghost of a smile and placed her hand in his.

"I told you not to play in here. Cerene will have our hides," Dakon whispered urgently as he chased Pazel. The boys, far distracted from their duties, had found a cellar under thick entanglements in the garden and decided to venture within.

There were few torches lit as Pazel ran excitedly toward the darkness, sure they would find a magical door of sorts, no matter how ridiculous the notion was to Dakon at the ripe age of seven.

Dakon had to admit, despite the carcasses of rats and other vermin scattered about the narrow tunnels, he was quite excited to find something new. He was even more intrigued as the walls began to bear slivers of light from the outside. He imagined it was the light of somewhere far beyond the castle walls—a forest of fairies, an island of dragons, anywhere adventure could spark.

"Come now, Dakon," Pazel pleaded, "just a few minutes more, and I'll go back. I swear it."

"Fine. But only a few more."

They raced together up a few steps until they managed to reach a lone door. Pazel pushed and pulled on the brass ring, but it didn't budge.

"It's locked," Dakon said, disappointed. "We have to go back."

Pazel groaned. "I don't want to work."

"Me neither." Dakon sighed.

The boys turned to leave.

"I hate the elder's horse. He leaves the worst mess—"

"Have you done it?" The voice trailed from one of the open slits in the wall.

Dakon and Pazel stilled.

"Certainly, My Queen."

Dakon held a finger to his lips, silencing Pazel as they moved toward it. Dakon peeked through it, seeing the queen's solar with her gold-and-black tapestries hanging about. Her desk sat in front of her large windows.

Princess Alondra leaned against the desk. "I am not a queen, yet."

"But soon you will be." Borgias took a step from out of view and reached toward her. His hand caressed her face.

Dakon felt sick. He wasn't sure this was something they were supposed to be looking at, but he couldn't explain why.

"Is he supposed to touch her like that?" Pazel whispered, and Dakon nudged him, once again placing a finger to his lips.

Princess Alondra grinned. "I have been waiting for far too long. I married him thinking I would be queen in my youth, and here I am all these years later..."

Borgias kissed her neck. "Ask and you shall receive, *My Queen*."

Alondra embraced him. "And the prince?"

"He will be restrained, I assure you."

"He needs a muzzle on both his heads. Lusting over that filthy witch."

"All taken care of." Borgias brushed his hands along the strands of her hair.

"This is his idea."

"His idea," Borgias repeated, placing his lips on hers.

Their lips pressed against each other, and Pazel moved back, disgusted. Dakon wished he could look away but couldn't force himself to.

Alondra pushed Borgias back gently. "And he drank it all?"

"Every last drop. He even complimented the tea." Borgias grinned, reaching into his robes and procuring a tiny, empty vial. "A gift fit for a king."

There was a knock on their door and the two parted immediately, Alondra pretending to fiddle with her desk and Borgias stepping aside as if looking out the window.

A guard spoke. "Your highness, Prince Eryck."

At the mention of his name, Dakon removed his face from the slit.

Even all the while as they ran down those steps outside, Dakon could only feel fear at the thought of the mean prince finding out what they saw.

"Pazel told the elder," Dakon breathed, the memory coming back to him. "We were charged with cleaning his horse's stable, and when he arrived to ride, Pazel confided to him privately about what we saw."

Eve was silent, bringing her grimoire back into a cradle.

"But what does this have to do with where you are now?" Victor asked.

"My mother was killed as a traitor to the realm," Eve said slowly. "Everything that has happened to us is because she was wrongly accused."

"Quite the stretch, isn't it?" Victor mused.

Eve huffed. "My sister and I were separated because of it. She was taken to the Blackthorn where she still resides, while I was left and raised among my enemies as a mortal. I was unprepared for the grimoire, and now my soul is trapped by it. I'd say it's more than a fair statement."

"It was much simpler when witches ruled these lands," Victor replied. "Far less witch hunts and far more deception."

Dakon scoffed. "Take one step in that castle and there'd be enough deception to last you lifetimes more."

"I understand how my mother was wrongfully accused, I just never imagined how complex the plan was, how many people were involved," Eve murmured. "All of this for power? Is it really that morbidly simple?"

"Oh, to be blessed with power or cursed by those who do," Victor murmured.

"Or both," Dakon said quietly. He raised his gaze to Eve. "Why does the grimoire only focus on your mother?"

"Because all I've ever wanted was the truth."

"And now that you have it, do you suppose it'll give you something else?"

"I fear the full truth is still far beyond my touch." She looked down at the book in her hands. "But I suppose it can help with our plight now."

Dakon moved his gaze between Eve and the grimoire. "How do we use it?"

"Like any grimoire." Victor smirked, his hands raised as if itching to take it.

Eve turned from him, gently touching the cover, running her fingers from the three stars at the top and down the symbol of the owl in the center. "It told me of my past, of my mother's past. It has always been linked to my magic. I suppose it uses it to some extent."

"Can I?" Victor reached out for it.

Eve pulled it to her chest. "Why?"

"I am not going to steal it. I want to *see* it."

"This is Eve's grimoire." Dakon pushed him back down. "Unless you know how to use it, I suggest you wait for us to discover what more it has to tell us."

"You forget, Familiar. I have been a witch longer than your bloodline has existed."

"I wouldn't know, I'm an orphan," Dakon snapped.

"That's evident."

Dakon stood, ready to strike, but Eve pulled him back down.

"What is your sage advice?" Eve narrowed her eyes at Victor. "Only then may I consider it."

Victor took a step toward her. "You can destroy it or you can use it. *We* can use it."

Dakon clenched his jaw.

Victor continued, "My dear, this is no ordinary grimoire. This is one forged from the soul of a goddess who has now willingly sacrificed it to you."

"So she could trap me in it instead of her."

"Yes, yes, however, we can fix that, save your kingdom, and still use it far beyond our years."

This felt wrong.

"How?" Dakon asked.

"Because magic is not immortal. And neither is a fallen goddess."

Dread. It was clawing its way up his spine again.

Dakon tried to ignore it as Victor spoke. "The five gods still rule over our world, but Isila is not one of them anymore. She is of ancient magic, but not immortal magic. If we can destroy her host, her soul, we can still have her grimoire of centuries worth of spells and witchcraft. All of it at our very fingertips."

Victor stretched his hands out to touch the binding, but Eve stood quickly moving away.

"I do not wish to rule over anything. I want to go home. I want everything to be as it was."

"Forgive me, dear Eve, but nothing will ever be as it was. Witches and mortals have been fighting for centuries, and they will fight for centuries more. Kings and queens will go mad with power and die for the next of their spawn to take over. It is a cycle of life, power, and death. *We*, us three, we can live apart from that."

"No." Dakon stepped between them. "Whatever it is you have planned, we want no part of it."

"Then free me, and I will trade my soul for the grimoire."

Silence followed.

Would he truly want to give up his soul?

Does he even have one?

Eve looked between the grimoire and Victor. "I won't."

"You can't." Victor lifted his lips into a grim smile.

"No, I—"

"What do you know of the book you're carrying? What do you even know of me?"

"We know that you were cast to the wastes, that Isila created the book to save her soul before she was cast away by the other gods. The original three witches hid it and were killed by the gods for it," Dakon said, frustrated.

"Not exactly."

Dakon scoffed. "Then what?"

Victor gave him a sly grin. "Isila created the grimoire before she was ever cast by the gods. It was her pride, her vanity, that made her. She only shared it with the original witches. Every spell, every vicious piece of witchcraft stolen from other witches, placed inside." He shook his head, pointing at the book. "That is more than a grimoire. The Blood of the Blackthorn lives to its namesake. It is a tomb of magic stolen from magic folk bound in service to it. A graveyard of lost witches and creatures who trusted us to save them."

"Us?" Eve whispered.

From the corner of his eye, Dakon saw Eve nearly drop the book. He reached out and lifted it back into her arms, steadying her.

"How do you know this? How can we trust what you are telling us?" Dakon snapped.

"Because you are looking at one of the original witches."

It can't be.

"No, that's not possible," Eve said. "All of them died."

"Did they? I must have missed that funeral." Victor scoffed.

"Wait, am I your heir? Are we related?" Eve asked nervously.

Victor smiled. "Not in the slightest. As I was banished, the other two witches chose a young girl, an apprentice they trusted, to take their magic. She is your ancestor, not I."

For some reason Dakon couldn't quite name he was glad that this man was still considered a stranger of sorts. No blood ties, nothing to keep him from killing him should it come to it.

Eve seemed to feel the same, as Dakon saw her let out a deep breath.

"So, as I was saying"—Victor smirked—"I know this grimoire well. And I know that even if you don't wish for it, you are tethered to it. Each moment that passes, the ties grow stronger and soon you will not even remember what your life was without that power, that curse, in your hands."

Dakon glanced at Eve, watching as she clutched the book tighter.

Victor continued, "Thus, when I offered to trade my soul for yours, I knew your answer would be—"

"No..." Eve breathed.

"Precisely." Victor nodded, pleased with himself. He brushed off the dirt from his shoulders. "Well, I suppose we better hurry before that 'no' turns into threats and promises of death, shall we?"

Dakon looked to Eve as she placed the grimoire in her satchel. "Eve, you can give it to me, if you wish. You are not alone, remember? It has me too."

"I know," Eve affirmed. "Though, I wish to end this all before I'm not sure anymore."

ADRIANA

CHAPTER 21

Adriana lay on the floor of the captain's quarters, refusing to sleep in Izan's bed and refusing to tell him anything more than her false name.

He left her alone in the cabin as he tended to his business on the main deck, and she had half a mind to lock his cabin door when she was alone. The only thing stopping her was how little she knew of this man and his temper.

Was Izan the kind of person to break down doors and strike women?

She shivered at the thought and turned the other way, hiding beneath the blanket as if it was a shield to protect her.

Adriana was not a skilled swordsman,

not a knife wielder, nor a fighter of any kind. On a ship alone over the Dallise Sea, filled with sailors strapped with weapons of steel and sharpened wood. She prayed she would survive unharmed. Perhaps if she stayed in this cabin the entire journey, they would soon forget about her.

A pitiful wish.

She groaned, listening to the water lap against the sides of the ship and the occasional voices of the night crew as they moved to and fro about the ship.

Adriana wondered how long it took before Callum and Emilio realized she was gone. She wondered if they tried to chase her ship down, if they killed men to look for her, made a mess of their plan in drawing unwanted attention to themselves.

Selfishly, she wished they had, because lying here in the dark on the wooden floors, she was scared of what would happen to her, of what Izan would expect from her when he inevitably made his way inside.

"Why did you not listen and wait outside with the other mistresses?" she whispered to herself, feeling foolish for not taking the first mate's advice. Now she was here, lying on the floor of this damn cabin, sharing a room with a stranger.

As the shadows of the evening turned pitch black under a moonless, starless sky, Adriana cursed her foolishness, Callum and Emilio, the ship, the night crew, her damn corset that was so tight she could scarcely breathe properly.

"When I see them again," she huffed, moving to lay on her back, taking slow, deliberate breaths.

If she saw them again.

She stilled. That was the sad truth. She was headed for Zafira, with nobles kind to her as the princess of Givensmir, the place she lived for years as a small child once, the place where her former betrothed, Jos, had gone to negotiate their protection from Marc.

But he was killed before he ever made it there. Thoughts fought for purchase on her sanity, or rather, her lack thereof as fear took over once more.

What if they were behind Jos being caught?
What if their alliance with me has changed?
What if they are spying for Marc, hoping I show up at their doorstep?

These questions plagued her as she tried and failed to sleep. There were no more tears, but her eyes stung as dread overcame her. She imagined wild scenarios of being imprisoned in their sandy dungeons, carried through the streets like the witches in the capital, lashed until her skin was raw, or sold off like a broodmare to a stranger.

How could I prove to them I am who I claim to be?
Would Izan help me if he knew?

That was the worst part of it all, the daunting truth that she was dressed like a mistress aboard a ship sleeping in the cabin of the captain. It had been years since she visited the Zafira capital, years since she lived in their castle and walked their halls. She could only imagine how much time had aged her, changed her, in their eyes.

Who would believe her if she claimed to be the lost princess of Givensmir?

A light knock sounded at the door.

Adriana sat up, pulling the blankets around her as the door opened.

Izan entered with a candle in his hand, closing the door softly behind him. He turned to face her, his eyes widened as he gazed upon her face. "Forgive me, miss, I thought you'd be sleeping."

Adriana raised her chin. "I—I am surprised you even ask my forgiveness after your insolence earlier."

"I hope you understand." Izan walked about his cabin, using the wick of his candle to light a few others. The cabin felt less ominous in the presence of the dim light. "I cannot change course, even if I wished."

"We had barely left," she snapped.

"Yes, and the checkpoints would have noticed if we turned a merchant ship of the crown off course."

Adriana couldn't think of a suitable response.

Izan continued, placing his candle slowly on the desk. "And seeing as though you do not talk like a mistress nor act like it, I will assume you are looking to not be found."

"Perhaps I am new to this," she challenged.

"Then why are you not naked in my bed?"

Adriana gasped.

"See." He gestured to her pale face. He pulled the chair from behind his desk and dragged it toward her. It made a low scraping sound against the wood that unnerved her, and she squeezed her eyes shut until the sound ceased.

Izan sat before her, looking down at what she assumed was a woman at the edge of fear and desperation. She swallowed.

"Who are you, really?"

"Thalia."

"Lie."

She narrowed her eyes. "Why does my name matter?"

"Because I think I know who you are."

Adriana scoffed to mask her rising panic. "Why should I tell you anything when you have not been forthcoming yourself?"

There is no reason to believe he knows who you are.

Calm yourself.

"What do you wish to know?"

"I don't know, anything? Why did you change ships?"

"Because I received orders from the Lord Matias's clerk to send this ship to Zafira. The other captain was moved to the one for Teros."

That was too simple.

"Why is this ship going to Zafira?"

"I'm not certain, Princess."

"How could you not—" Her blood ran cold, and her eyes met Izan's grave ones. They stared, cat and mouse, for a long, tense moment before Adriana did the only thing she could think of.

She threw the blanket at him and ran for the door, not thinking about what she would do or where she would go as they drifted in the middle of the sea.

Izan fell backwards on the chair, cursing aloud.

Adriana ripped the door open, hearing Izan get to his feet and give chase. She pummeled through a few of the night crew workers on deck, racing as fast as she could to the other end of the ship. If not for the few torches lit on the main deck, she wouldn't have been able to see in front of her, the darkness encompassing all but where the fire touched.

"Come back!" Izan yelled between breaths not far behind her. She knew he was gaining on her, knew that he would catch her very quickly if she did not think of a way out.

She ran into the wooden end of the bow, Izan only a few feet away. Adriana grabbed hold of the bowsprit, climbing onto it and pulling herself to the edge.

"Stop! Come back!"

Adriana kept pulling herself forward, terrified of what Izan would do knowing what he knew. She couldn't go back to the dungeons, couldn't go back to the castle where her brother would be waiting to unleash his wrath upon her.

"No!"

"You'll fall in!"

She could see from the faint light of the torches how the night crew crowded around Izan as he removed his sword belt, handing it to one of the other crew mates. Hidalgo raced toward them in only his trousers, clearly sleeping before all the commotion she caused.

Izan grasped the bowsprit, climbing behind her.

"Don't come any closer!" Adriana screamed, pushing herself into a sitting position, holding on to the sides of the shaky bowsprit.

She made the grave mistake of looking down, the sea beneath her concealed by the darkness, she wondered how far she would fall before she became one with the sea.

"Fine, I will stay where I am." Izan didn't move, his wide eyes staring at her. Adriana was surprised to see the panic within them. "But you must know that if you fall from the front of the ship, you will die. It will be painful."

"I can swim," Adriana quipped.

"It's not the water that will kill you. It's the ship itself. Listen."

Adriana tried to ignore the fervent beating of her heart in her chest as she listened. The waves were powerful as they pounded against the ship, clashing together in a terrifying show of strength.

"Would I die quickly?"

Izan stilled for a moment. "Slowly, in my experience."

Damn him. Damn them all.

Her lips trembled, the fresh tears falling from her eyes. She couldn't stop crying. All she did was cry, and now she let herself be racked with desperate sobs.

"Leave!" she choked out. "I want them gone."

Izan turned back to the crew. "You heard her, be gone."

The crew was still, confused.

"Now!"

Hidalgo pushed them away. "Move it, the captain says." He shoved them away, and they disappeared in the darkness the torch couldn't reach. Izan, much to her detriment, stayed.

"You too."

He didn't move. "Please, I won't hurt you, *Thalia*." He stretched out his hand, close enough to Adriana that she could reach out and touch him if she chose to.

She recoiled from him. Adriana couldn't trust him; she couldn't trust anyone. Izan could be lying through his teeth, saying anything to get a hold of her. She could see it clear in her panicked heart, this stranger trading her to the capital for a large sum, leaving her at the mercy of her brother. She would be hanged, beheaded, burned, sold to the man her brother promised her to . . .

She listened to the water once more slamming against the ship.

Death or death, her options seemed plain now.

This is the price of your freedom.

"Let me help you back onto the ship. I swear no harm will come to you."

Adriana ignored him, looking down once more into the dark.

It will be painful...

She wondered if Dakon would be there to meet her when it was all over, if he was waiting for her, seeing her right at this very moment. She let out another sob for the man she loved and never saw again in this life.

"If you give me a chance to explain—"

Adriana kept her eyes downcast, sniffling through her tears. "Have you seen what my brother does to women who displease him?"

Izan didn't respond.

"I have," she swallowed. The darkness, for some reason as she pondered death with Dakon and the thought of life without him, seemed less ominous than before. "He would consider a swift death to be too kind a punishment for me."

"You are his sister."

Adriana shook her head gravely. "I am a woman."

Izan sat up. "Yes, you are, but let that be your strength. Do not give him victory over you."

Adriana raised her arms, feeling the gentle breeze cool against her wet cheeks. She closed her eyes, saying more to herself than Izan, "I want eternal spring and green eyes and silver birches."

Izan raised a brow, confused. "Y-you can have all of that, but please come back."

"I would rather die than be a prisoner of his."

"I know you have no reason to trust me, but I swear to you now, on this very night that you will be safe from him so long as you are with me."

But Dakon.

"I have someone waiting for me, wherever Death takes our souls. I know he is there waiting."

"I have someone who might be waiting for me too. I hope not, but they may be. But please, tell me this"—he raised his hand again—"would this person want you to fall?"

Adriana met Izan's dark eyes. Her heart sank and even the cool air that waved her hair about didn't quell the heat of her shame.

"No, he wouldn't," she whispered finally.

"Take my hand."

Adriana scooted forward carefully, raising her hand to place in Izan's.

"Do you promise not to send me back?"

His silver gaze never wavered. "I promise."

Their fingers brushed just as the ship hit a harsh wave, lurching forward and shaking the bowsprit. Adriana's grip slipped from Izan's, and she spiraled down into the depths below.

ADRIANA

CHAPTER 22

The descent was slower than she anticipated. Adriana could see Izan screaming out for her, his hand outstretched, their fingertips splayed open reaching to close the space between them. But it was too late, she was descending quickly and the bowsprit grew smaller in her vision.

Izan leapt after her.

It will be painful.

She closed her eyes, waiting for the force of the ship to pummel into her, breaking her bones and body like her spirit in the capital. Adriana couldn't breathe, couldn't scream out, her voice gone with any hope she had to live another day.

Arms gripped her tight, she wondered if they were Dakon's. If maybe she had gone into the arms of Death. But the crashing of her skin against the frigid water, forced her eyes open. She was in Izan's embrace as he swam them swiftly beneath the surface of the sea barely missing the bottom edge of the ship where surely she would have met a grisly fate.

All around her was silence and darkness, piercing her soul with terror as the tales of creatures of the Dallise Sea took over her fraught mind. She cried out under the water, a grave mistake as she sucked in the cold sea, trying to choke out a breath that did not release.

She was too deep, too far gone to reach the surface, wherever it was now. She was fading, her vision only taking in the pitch-black sea, her body giving in to the lack of air.

Before she completely lost herself, she saw a pair of silver eyes shining in the water.

SHE GASPED AWAKE, COUGHING VIOLENTLY AS SHE TOOK IN HER surroundings. She was in the captain's quarters, lying in his bed, wearing his ivory blouse and trousers. A soft morning light peered from the large window behind the captain's desk, the sea rocking peacefully beyond it. She shuddered, holding herself tight.

I nearly died.

Did I die?

She felt herself, her warm skin, her shaking limbs, the goosebumps on her flesh. She winced as she felt a large, dark bruise on her forearm. No doubt from the fall into the sea. But she didn't feel dead.

Adriana stepped off the bed, shivering at the cool wood beneath her feet as she walked to one of the windows behind the desk. They were rather large, spanning across the length of the cabin. She could see the water just below, gentle, peaceful.

She shuddered, lifting her eyes upward toward the sky. It was a soft blue, the clouds painted in the sky with masterful strokes, the daylight bringing catharsis to the horrors of the night prior.

Adriana sat on the floor before it, bringing her knees to her chest and hugging herself. Life had taken such precarious and disastrous turns so quickly, and now it seemed that it wouldn't even let her die to escape it. She would be forced to face the tragedies that had yet to unfold, and she trembled as she considered what waited for her after this ship docked.

She placed a tender hand on the glass, wondering if Dakon had had the same thoughts as he sailed away from her.

Was he scared when death finally called or did he embrace it with the courage she lacked?

She heard the door open behind her but didn't bother looking to see who entered. She supposed it didn't matter anymore.

"I brought you something to eat." It was Izan's voice.

She kept silent, bringing her hand back from the glass to hold herself again. She could hear as he placed the plate down on his desk and his footsteps as he made his way next to her.

He rested an arm against the window, following her gaze to the water. He cleared his throat after a few silent moments. "I used to love it once. The sea. I spent my life in it until I was taken away as a young boy."

Adriana peered at him from beneath her lashes. "You were raised on a ship?"

Izan shook his head slowly, bending down to sit next to her on the floor. "No, in the water."

She turned to him, knitting her brow. "I'm not certain what you mean."

"I mean that I have secrets too. Ones that would get me killed or sold for a pretty coin."

She bit her lip.

"I was taken by a . . . a group, captured from the sea as a child and raised as one of their own when they discovered my gifts."

"And what are those gifts?" Adriana whispered.

He lowered his gaze to Adriana's bruised arm, then back to her eyes. "Do you trust me?"

"I'm not certain," she admitted.

"Smart, very smart," he said gently. Izan raised a hand, gesturing for her arm. "Then allow me to at least show you."

Adriana slowly raised her arm, and he took it gently, placing his hands over the bruise. "I heal. Mortals, witches, creatures of land and sea . . ."

She watched with utter fascination as the bruise slowly moved from her arm to his hands to his own forearm. He groaned slightly. "It seems this hurts far more than it looked."

Adriana pulled her arm back inspecting it. "How?" She was completely healed, not even a scratch left behind.

"Because I am not mortal." He pulled his sleeves down, covering the bruise.

"Are you a witch?"

He smiled. "No. Were you hoping I was?"

"It would have made this less complex."

"The world outside your castle walls is far more complex than witches and mortals."

This feels like a dream or a nightmare.

"Do you . . . eat mortals?"

Izan laughed, tears springing into his eyes and she was sure the crew outside could hear even through the closed door. Adriana felt a pricking at her skin, she leaned back. "I-is that funny?"

"No, no. I apologize. I simply have never been asked before." He wiped his eyes with the back of his hands and at Adriana's trepidatious silence, corrected himself. "I do not consume mortals. I am nothing but a sea nymph."

"A sea nymph?"

He nodded. "I heal, sing, and occasionally lead lost ships ashore if I am feeling generous. We are not particularly violent."

Thank the gods.

"I'm sorry," she said. "This is all new to me." She tried to steer the conversation elsewhere, gesturing to his new wound. "And I wouldn't have let you if I knew you would be harmed too."

A ghost of a smile crossed his lips, but he turned back to looking out the window. "It will heal quickly. But it is I who am sorry I scared you the other night."

Adriana recalled how easily he confronted her. She shook her nerves.

What else does he know?

"Thank you. And I will keep your secret," she said carefully.

"And I yours. But I think if we are to remain civil on this short journey, we might have to build some form of trust between us."

She nodded. "Agreed."

He faced her, sitting back against the window. "What is a princess doing aboard a merchant ship of the crown?"

She let out a shaky breath, casting her eyes down. "My brother, the king. He killed my betrothed and imprisoned me along with my allies. When the dungeons were falling apart, we escaped, the three of us."

To her surprise, Izan straightened, leaning toward her. "You were there when it happened? When the throne room went to chaos?"

She raised a brow. "The dungeon is far beneath the throne room. Was the destruction born from there?"

Izan nodded, his eyes widening. "Yes, I saw it."

She narrowed her eyes. "Saw what exactly?"

Izan quickly reached inside the pocket of his trousers, pulling out a golden necklace, a sun pendant on the end of the chain, and a small diamond rested in the center.

Eve's necklace.

She gasped. "Where did you get that?"

"It belongs to a witch—a half-witch. She and her familiars were captured and taken to your brother. I followed them to Givensmir." He lowered his head.

"And what happened?"

"I found them in the throne room, but I was too late . . ." Izan whispered.

Adriana's heartbeat faster than she could think. "Because they were killed?"

"No"—he shook his head, meeting her eyes, a fear within them—"because they disappeared."

"What do you mean?" Pounding, her heart was pounding so loudly in her ears she was scared she would not be able to hear Izan's words.

"Your brother is working with the Strix, a powerful witch coven that was exiled from Blackthorn long ago. He wanted them to summon a grimoire, to take magic from—"

"Eve." Adriana finished for him. "Eve *is* a witch . . ." She knew it to be true, but hearing herself say those words aloud held different meaning now.

Are there good witches?

Is Eve a good witch?

"You know her?" Izan looked on the verge of pain and bliss.

"She was my greatest friend," Adriana breathed, reaching for the necklace.

Izan handed it to her slowly.

Feeling it beneath her fingers, she felt as if she could see Eve again in the far corners of her memory. Memories of when they were nothing but spoiled ladies of the court, gossiping about dresses and people, and not fighting for their lives in a world controlled by evil kings.

Does that mean Dakon is alive?

Adriana's heart sprang and she nearly spoke the words into existence until Izan continued.

"I'm trying to find her. She is out there somewhere and I want to—need to—tell her how sorry I am."

"Sorry?" Adriana raised a brow.

Izan hung his head, his eyes glazed with tears he would not let fall. "I was the reason she was caught. The Strix and a sea witch, they ordered me to distract her and I—"

Anger flashed across Adriana's face. "You're the reason they were taken?!" She stood, wishing she had a sword, a dagger, a piece of glass, five hells, even the pointed end of a quill would do.

Izan stood along with her, placing his hands between them to placate her. She wanted to rip them from his arms.

"At first, yes. But then I stopped. I refused, and they took matters into their own hands. I couldn't fight them all."

Adriana grabbed a flask from the desk, turning and raising it toward him. "Explain, or I swear by every one of the five gods I will bludgeon you with this!"

Izan answered quickly. "They sent sirens, they nearly killed everyone aboard, and Eve, she saved us but set the ship on fire. We were forced to dock at the Crooked Port, I didn't know they were there waiting for her. I was told by Cassandra they would be waiting for her in Givensmir, that she would force Amarin's ship to veer off course."

"Who is Cassandra?!"

Izan rubbed his face, groaning. "She is the sea witch, the powers that be here on the Dallise Sea."

"And she lied to you."

"Yes."

"Just like you did to Eve."

Izan turned. "I did. I lied. It doesn't matter that I changed my mind. I still lied to her."

Adriana forced him to face her, grabbing his bruised arm forcefully and turning him back around. "Then why are you looking for her? Are you trying to take her back to them?"

"No, and in truth, I don't believe she would want to see me. But I want her safe, I want to know she's safe."

"You're selfish." Adriana tossed the flask aside. "You're a selfish bastard."

"I love her."

"Can you even love?"

Izan flinched. "Even if she doesn't reciprocate, I need to know that the gravest mistake of my life did not cause her to lose hers."

Adriana shook her head. "Your choices have hurt me too." Tears sprang eternal, and she could nearly hear them meeting the floor beneath her. She wanted to rip Izan apart with her bare hands. She took a step toward him. "The man I loved was with Eve. He was taken there, too, because of you!"

Izan tried to step away, but the window behind stopped him. He swallowed. "I'm so sorry. But I promise I will find them."

"They never should have been lost!"

She was so close, she could see the silver glint in his dark eyes clearly now. "I would throw you in the sea if I didn't know you'd survive."

Izan said nothing, guilt and shame reaching across his face.

Good.

"I want to kill you," she whispered, that same feeling from the night she took Ser Fraunces's life returning. It scared her.

"I want you to."

She stilled, his answer not quite what she expected.

He continued, "I can't change my past, my mistakes. But neither can I sleep, nor eat without her. I'm in misery."

Adriana stepped back, watching him unfold into despair.

They stayed that way for a long while, until the sun sank and the sky painted itself a pink and purple hue beyond the horizon. It would be beautiful if everything else was not plaguing her.

Adriana reflected on her losses. The people. The kingdom. Eve and Dakon.

What would a future of peace look like when this was over?

She knelt down, placing a hand on Izan's shoulder.

"I need to go to Zafira to get an army and save my people," she began gently, standing. "But swear yourself to me, protect me, and I will do everything in my power, use every resource I have, to find them both."

Izan held her gaze, his of pain and hers of steely resolve. He tightened his jaw, and she was almost certain he would reject her offer when finally bowed his head before her. "Yes, Princess, I swear my loyalty to you."

Adriana shook her head. "I am not a princess. Not anymore."

Nor would I ever be again...

"My apologies, I—"

She straightened. "I am a queen."

PART 2

THE PRICE OF POWER

"It has become apparent, in my final hours, that no amount of magic can prevent fate's interlude. I would give up my soul for mortality, rather than spend these wretched moments knowing what is to come and being unable to undo it."

— RECOVERED DIARY ENTRY OF GIVENSMIR'S FIRST ROYAL ENCHANTRESS

THEO

CHAPTER 23

"**D**OES IT ALWAYS RAIN HERE?" Theo asked, adjusting his thin hood atop his head. It did little to keep the raindrops away from his skin.

"I can scarcely remember a time it didn't," Ana mumbled, pulling out a few fruits from the cart and handing them to her mother.

"Have you ever thought of leaving?"

"I never had a reason to."

"None of us have reason to," her mother quipped. "Why go where they would sooner murder us?"

Theo swallowed. "I'm sorry."

"Did you ever kill a witch?"

"No, never—"

"But I'm sure you've watched one be

burned, haven't you?"

Theo remained silent.

"Mother, please," Ana chided, placing a gentle hand on Rinya's shoulder.

Rinya took a long look at Theo and shook her head. "We should arrive at one of the smuggler's ports before morning." She passed a small apple to Theo as she spoke. "I expect that the queen's council would have sent a dove to all the covens and ports about their missing hostage."

She raised a brow to Ana.

Theo shifted uncomfortably. "Thank you for saving my life. I swear I will never bother you or your family again as soon as I gain passage back to Givensmir."

"Don't thank me," Rinya replied, "thank my daughter. She has a far gentler heart than I." She stood. "I will feed Midnight and take the first shift. Both of you should sleep."

She walked toward the cart where the horse lay, not far beneath the frigid, gloomy sky and the trees that barely covered them.

Theo ate his apple, watching the sparks of the small fire crack. He had a mind to shove his hands in the flame to rid himself of his fingertips' numbness.

Ana sat across from him, staring intently into the fire.

"One would think you get enjoyment from how the flames dance," Theo said carefully, feeling unnerved in the silence.

Ana shrugged, blinking away from it. "Scrying is not a strength of mine, but I try."

"Scrying?"

"Yes, it is how Isila speaks of our future to us."

"Your goddess?"

Ana nodded. "She has never been forthcoming with me, though, unfortunately." She scoffed. "If she was, I suppose I wouldn't be here."

"That makes the two of us. Though, I simply end up in places because of foolish decisions."

Ana let out a small laugh. "Perhaps it is the only thing I will concede to a mortal."

Theo tried to laugh, but he only managed a ghost of a smile. Silence carried once more, smothered only by the whispering breeze making its way through the trees and embracing them.

He peered up occasionally as he ate. Ana focused on the fire as if no one else existed, and he wondered what she wanted to know so desperately about her future.

He wondered if this Isila would tell him his.

As the fire died down, Theo settled beneath the thin blanket on the ground. Somehow it was warmer there than in the back of the cart. Ana lay a few feet across from him, facing his direction. He couldn't help himself as she began to close her eyes, knowing that this may be the last time he could speak so frankly to her before they arrived at the port tomorrow.

He cleared his throat. "Why did you save me?"

Ana opened her eyes.

Theo repeated himself. "Why did you save me?"

Ana blinked a few times, as if seeing him for the first time. "Because it was the right thing to do," she said simply.

"Was it not the right thing when Pedro was dying?"

Ana looked away.

"Please," Theo said, his voice hoarse, "I just want to understand. I have no one left to trust."

Ana nodded solemnly. "I did not think they would kill Pedro, nor did I realize he was in such horrid shape until I saw his wounds."

"Then why did you not save him?"

"I hold no power there in that castle. And I cannot heal those who are marked for death, not without killing myself."

"But he was living—"

"He was, until Navir cursed him to take on your fatal wounds."

Theo nearly forgot to breathe, remembering how quickly he healed and how quickly Pedro crippled before his eyes. "How is that possible?"

Ana stared at him gravely. "Magic is not immortal, Theo. But neither is it weak. It can be dangerous, bloody, vile. And there is always a price to pay for bloodshed."

"Will it kill him then? Will it kill your prince?"

She shrugged. "That is not for me to decide."

He shook his head, confused. "Why did you not leave me?"

Ana stilled for a long moment, and Theo nearly asked again before she finally spoke.

"The woman I love, she has not been herself for . . . quite some time. If she killed you, the final tie she had to her mortality, it would prove she was truly gone forever."

Her mortality?

Ana continued. "I didn't want to risk knowing the truth. I couldn't let her destroy herself, not completely. With you out of her sights, somehow I believed that there would still be hope for her."

"Clarisa? Is that whom you speak of?"

Ana nodded, a sliver of pain etched on her face.

"Does she know you wore her face?"

Ana flinched but nodded slowly. "She found out after Pedro's death. I couldn't bring myself to tell her, and when I tried . . . she cast me out. I have not seen her since the night I freed you."

"She had no idea?"

"None."

"I suppose there is hope for her after all."

The wind whistled through the woods, and Theo found himself remembering how cold it was. He curled into himself as he asked the last question that plagued him. "What does Navir have over you? Why do his bidding at all?"

Ana flashed her eyes to him, raising her brow. Theo was certain she wouldn't answer and nearly gave his apologies until she spoke. "Nothing . . . then everything."

Before Theo could question her further, Ana turned from him. The chill of the afternoon settled on him again, freezing his bones and numbing fingers. He brought the blanket over his head, covering himself in complete darkness from the rainy day.

Nothing, then everything.

As he drifted into a fitful sleep, he wondered which made her fear Navir the most. And which finally made her leave.

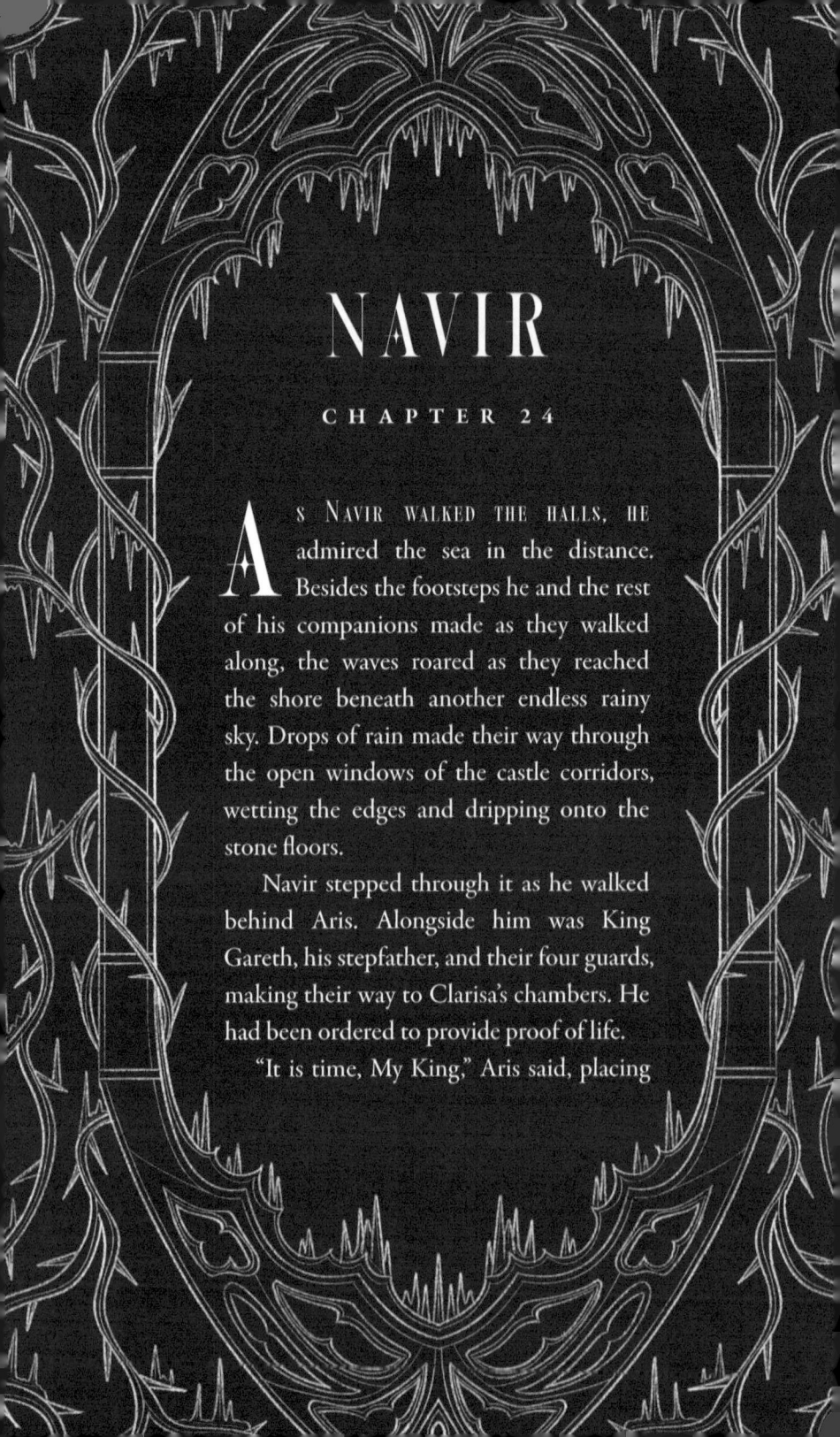

NAVIR

CHAPTER 24

As Navir walked the halls, he admired the sea in the distance. Besides the footsteps he and the rest of his companions made as they walked along, the waves roared as they reached the shore beneath another endless rainy sky. Drops of rain made their way through the open windows of the castle corridors, wetting the edges and dripping onto the stone floors.

Navir stepped through it as he walked behind Aris. Alongside him was King Gareth, his stepfather, and their four guards, making their way to Clarisa's chambers. He had been ordered to provide proof of life.

"It is time, My King," Aris said, placing

his hands in his pockets as he stood in front of Clarisa's door. The guards stood anxiously; it emanated off their flesh and into the air—sweat, regret, and festering nerves.

Aris pulled the key from his pocket, lifting it to the lock. "Now keep in mind, Your Majesty, she may not be the same witch you remember. This *sickness* has a way of . . . changing the afflicted."

King Gareth barely managed a nod, seemingly unbothered and bored of this affair.

Navir nodded impatiently. "Go ahead, open it."

Aris's stare lingered on him, then King Gareth, a moment longer before he relented, pushing the key in the lock and turning it with a resounding click. The guards tensed beside him, raising their swords as the door slowly opened, revealing the inside of the chambers.

Clarisa stood just in front of her bed, staring at nothing but the wall in front of her.

Aris cleared his throat. "Good evening, Clarisa. Are you doing well?"

She didn't answer but turned to stare down at him with fierce blue eyes.

Navir knew those eyes.

"Clarisa." Navir took a step forward, reaching out his hand despite Aris's protests. She turned to him, her face revealing nothing as he kept her stare, trying to ignore how dark her chambers were and the eyes that lingered from the shadows in the corner. "Are you well?"

"Perhaps, she needs another day," Aris managed.

Clarisa's blue hues were captivating, and Navir couldn't help but lose himself within them. He knew somewhere deep inside them was the woman he yearned for, but the witch in front of him was something far more promising.

He shook his head, silencing Aris. "No. She is perfect." He turned toward the shadows. "They are all perfect."

His arm still outstretched, he was pleasantly surprised when Clarisa placed her hand in his.

"We are quite hungry, My Prince," she—no, they—said.

Navir smiled. "Then we shall fix that for you."

He gave her hand a gentle squeeze before releasing her, turning to the guards and his stepfather. "I believe Clarisa would enjoy your company, Your Majesty, while I fetch something for her to eat."

King Gareth didn't seem to care much, making his way slowly inside as if each step was heavy on his soul rather than his body.

Navir ignored him and turned to the guard. "Be sure she doesn't leave this room."

He walked out as the guards came inside with curious, tense glances, staying close to the king who was only a few feet from Clarisa.

"We shall return shortly," Navir called out as he left the room, Aris following behind him.

"Why not send the guards to fetch a prisoner?" Aris asked as he closed the door.

"Because we will need them later."

Screams echoed from within the room, startling Aris so much that he dropped the key. Fists pounded against the door and someone within nearly opened it, when the pounding stopped suddenly, replaced with more piercing cries.

"I would lock that door if I were you," Navir said, walking away from Aris as he shoved the key and turned it. "We wouldn't want you to slip inside now, would we?"

Aris fell as a final thud hit the door, turning to see Navir as he reached the end of the hall. "Yes, Your Majesty."

CLARISA

CHAPTER 25

We will rule the kingdoms.
The power...
The power.

It echoed through the castle walls, but she couldn't find the source.
Why could she only see the dark?
Why couldn't she escape?

Find the grimoire.
Bring it to us.

DAKON

CHAPTER 26

Even in his wildest dreams, Dakon never imagined he would see the day when he would ride on the back of a dragon. He stretched his fingers up, touching the clouds, or perhaps it was the fog that lingered all the way into the sky. Even so high up, he couldn't catch the glimpse of a sun—the entire Unclaimed Wastes seemed lit by nothing at all.

He and Eve bundled together in fur cloaks and blankets, holding on to each other and the scales of Victor as he glided easily across the land. It was frigid, yes, but soon he found that his magic kept him warm even in the frost that clung to the ends of his hair and the fierce wind that whipped at his face.

In the hours they spent traveling south on the dragon, he couldn't see much around them save for the tops of trees and occasional mountain peaks Victor expertly weaved through. It made the experience far less exciting than he hoped. The gray skies were dull and there seemed to not be much life in the wastes.

Near the end of the second day, Dakon heard Gods Protection before he could see it. Victor lowered himself to the ground, and Dakon helped Eve climb down the back of the dragon tail. Moments later, when they warmed Victor and handed him the spare clothes they carried in their satchel for him, Victor was back to making his silent thoughts into loud remarks.

"A wretched place, isn't it?"

Dakon ignored him, taking in his surroundings. They were positioned on one side of two cliffs that faced each other, separated by a considerable distance where the river flowed far below. On the other side, the trees were far less snowy and more inhabitable than the side of the wastes they stood on.

Dakon made his way slowly to the edge of the cliff, aware that the ground, while covered in snow, may prove weak. The river was deafening, the sound traveling up the face of the cliff, carrying the noise of it crashing against the rock below. The water sped through the cliffs as if racing to reach the end first.

Where did this river lead exactly?

He peered over the edge. The rock was slick with ice and frost leading all the way down. At the bottom, a few rocks jutted out of the water, ready to impale them should any of them slip trying to climb down. It was more than a long way to the bottom; falling would mean certain death.

"I told you we can't go past it." Victor sighed, crossing his arms.

"You can't, but we can," Dakon quipped.

Hopefully...

"We have to find another way to Teros," Eve replied, peeking over the edge. "Certainly, this is not the only way there."

"Or at least a way to climb down," Dakon agreed, taking a final look.

They both turned to Victor who shrugged noncommittally.

"Are you helping us or not?" Dakon spat.

"I could ask the same of you. I've been with you all for days and have yet to see any progress on getting me out of here."

"Have you tried flying over?" Eve asked, exasperated.

Victor grunted. "Yes, and it doesn't work. Unless you want me to try now with both of you on my back, then I suppose we can all plunge to our deaths, though only one of us will come out unfortunately unscathed."

Dakon scoffed pushing past him and walking a safe distance from the cliff's edge, following it. If the dragon wouldn't help, then neither would he.

They spent the rest of the afternoon walking along the edge of the cliff until it gradually descended closer to the river. There was hardly any life where they walked, as opposed to the other side where he caught a glimpse of a stag running past the trees.

He faced the edge of the forest on their side—ominous, deprived of the beauty of nature. Even birds seemed a foreign concept to the wastes, no chirping in the trees, no animals even scavenged for food or water near the river as the three of them approached it.

He stared across, the river itself was rather wide, and with the current as strong as it was it would be near impossible to swim through it. A lone bridge hung in despair, barely held together, connecting the two sides with a fragile thread.

He cursed under his breath, moving to the water's edge to test the current.

Dakon lowered his hand into the river. It was fiercely cold and numbed his fingers. The touch alone sent goosebumps along his flesh, and he retrieved it quickly, shoving it into his pocket for warmth.

Could we make it across the bridge?

Would we live if we fell through?

"Should we try the bridge or find a new one?" Eve asked trepidatiously, tightening the strap of her satchel across her chest.

"This is the only bridge, my dear." Victor smirked.

"And you've tried to cross it, I'm sure." She rolled her eyes.

"Many times."

Eve nodded, turning to face Dakon who walked to the bridge. "We don't seem to have another choice, do we?"

"I suppose the greater question is what do we do if we don't go?"

"Fair enough." She approached him, and Dakon tested the planks, stepping on the first one and pushing down with his weight.

It seems to hold, but will it hold us both?

Eve stepped on the plank and while it groaned it did not give.

He swallowed nervously, shivers crawling on his skin. They still had an eternity's worth to go as the river raged close below. Some planks were missing, others broken, and the rope that connected both sides to keep the bridge intact was splintered and frayed in parts.

"Are you coming with us," Dakon asked, turning back to Victor.

The witch leaned up against a frail tree. "No, no. I would rather bear witness this time."

Dakon shook his head, irritated, and faced forward.

Good riddance then.

Eve placed her hand in his and held tight. With his other, he grabbed the rope on the side, balancing himself. Eve did the same, shifting her weight to keep upright with his help.

He took one last look at the rest of the bridge before them.

We may just be able to make it through if we don't break the bridge. Just don't step on the broken planks.

Don't pull too hard on the rope.
And we may stand a chance.

"Are you ready, Eve?" he said, his breath a fog of mist before him.

"Yes," Eve managed.

Dakon took the first step forward and the bridge rocked slightly. Eve tightened her grip, her nails digging into his flesh.

"We will make it, Eve," he said reassuringly, and she loosened her grip.

"I trust you."

They took another step, then another, and the bridge rocked with them, but to Dakon's surprise it did not break.

He glanced back to see Victor reaching into a nearby tree and pulling out a few winter berries. Victor noticed his gaze and grinned wickedly, waving toward him.

"You're doing quite well!" he called out.

Dakon ignored him, turning forward once more and focusing on the rickety planks in front of him. They creaked and groaned under their weight, but they stepped gently atop each one as if willing the air to take hold of them and carry them across.

He dared to peek up, they were halfway across the bridge now.

It's almost over. We're almost there.

As he looked back down at his feet, he noticed the wood planks were nothing like they were before. They were polished and new as if recently built, and not the tarnished, rotted wood that had borne centuries of neglect.

"D-Dakon, do you see it?"

"I do, but Eve..."

I don't trust it.

"Don't say it, Dakon. Just focus on making it across."

He turned around, but Victor was no longer there, and neither were the snowy wastes. It was only darkness, the bridge, and the water that rushed beneath them. Nothing more.

What magic is this?

"Eve" —Dakon's voice nearly gave way to fear—"I don't know what this is, but I think we have to run now."

"What?" Her eyes shot up.

A shriek pierced the air, and Dakon grabbed Eve with all the force he had and raced down the bridge. It creaked and rocked violently back and forth as they ran, but it did not break. He heard footsteps behind them, the shrieking getting closer.

Dakon kept his desperate eyes forward, too terrified to see what horrors chased them. The evergreen trees lay ahead, the animals making their way through the brush, pairs of curious eyes waiting in the foliage. The sun beat down from above them, guiding them across and to the verdant green grass ahead of them. The warmth on his heavy fur cloak made him sweat. Before them was not winter, but a spring sprung in a matter of seconds, inviting and wholesome. And despite the shrieking, the footsteps, and the breath of something close on the back of his neck, everything he missed while stranded in this wasteland was just within reach.

"We're going to make it now, we're going to make it, Eve!" Dakon cried out, his heart leaping in chest, the hope driving past the madness fear promised.

Adriana.

I will see her again.

I will see her.

The evergreen trees, dense and dark, wilted into silver birches. They parted for him into the meadow he and Adriana had lain in so long ago. He could see the ends of a lavender dress flowing through the trees as if she were running, wanting him to chase her. His breath thinned, his heart raced, his limbs screamed for rest, but he did not stop running.

I will never leave you again.

I will never abandon you again.

I will never stop loving you.

DAKON

CHAPTER 27

SOMETHING SHARP SCRATCHED INTO THE back of his neck; he screamed out in pain. The bridge, the end, it was so close. He gripped Eve's hand as they passed the threshold, leaping onto the snow.

Snow?

Dakon trembled, looking down. His hands were wet with snow.

Eve cried out an agonizing wail next to him, and Dakon's soul sunk into despair. He trembled as lone tears made their way down his face.

"No!" he screamed into the blistering cold air. "No! No! No!" He pounded his fists into the snow, and they reddened with the icy chill.

"I told you it wouldn't work."

Dakon lifted his head to look at Victor, still leaning against the tree and eating the winter berries gathered in his palm. Victor shook his head in mock pity. "I would know. I've tried."

Snow melted beneath Dakon's fingers as he watched Victor eat the damn berries. His face was smug as he gestured with his chin to the bridge before them.

Now it was back in a sad state of disrepair.

"Though I am curious what you saw?" Victor smirked. "The first time it was my familiar beckoning me from afar, handsomer than ever he was." He took a step closer, pocketing the berries as he continued, "Soon thereafter I would see Isila murdered in the most macabre ways—a dagger in the throat, tortured in some castle dungeon, or even by fire."

Fire.

It was all Dakon could think of as Victor stood by smugly passing off wisdom neither of them asked for. A fucking dragon that did nothing but murder passersby and stay stuck for centuries in caves and misery. He wanted to put fire to the land, torch it and see what truly lurked beneath, but more than anything he wanted to be rid of the damn ice dragon once and for all.

Dakon rushed Victor, punching him in the jaw with his fiery fist. Victor fell back into the snow, and Dakon scrambled atop him, raising another fist setting it ablaze. "Tell us how to get out of here!"

"Dakon, no!" Eve shouted, trying to shove him away, but Dakon couldn't help himself anymore.

Victor, with a fresh burn bleeding across his face, roared with laughter. "If I knew how to leave, don't you think I would have?"

"Stop playing games," Dakon said. "I will kill you. I swear I will."

"You won't," Victor chuckled. "Because without me, you have nothing but a witch who doesn't love you and a book that belongs only to her that neither of you knows how to use."

"Dakon, please, stop this!"
I need to kill the dragon.
He's the reason we are here.
He wants to keep us here."

"Our lives are better without you in it," Dakon snapped. "All you have done for centuries is waste away here—"

Victor shoved him off, pointing a finger into Dakon's face. "I spent fucking centuries here trying to escape, boy. And I have more wisdom, more magic than either of you will ever have. If I can't break this fucking curse, no one can!"

Dakon shook. He itched to tear this dragon apart; he wanted nothing more than to rip out his tongue and silence him forever. He needed to end this madness all because they decided to give this dragon a chance.

Dakon unsheathed his daggers, setting them ablaze. "We should have killed you."

"But you didn't." Victor narrowed his eyes.

"I won't make that same mistake again."

"A shame, though I suppose I can do with just one of you alive." Victor took a step forward, his eyes turning a crystal white hue.

"Stop it!" Eve yelled, but she seemed so far away now.

"Unless you are joining in"—Victor grinned—"I suggest you start preparing a funeral bed for your familiar."

"No one is killing anyone," shouted Eve.

Dakon heard enough. "This entire time he has been leading us astray. Five hells, he may kill us while we sleep if he's hungry enough."

"Don't tempt me with a good time," Victor snapped. At the tips of his fingers, ice crystals formed.

Kill the Dragon Witch.
Kill him and use the grimoire to break this curse.
Find a way home and save Adriana.

Dakon thrust a dagger at Victor. It flew swiftly through the air, certain to meet its intended mark. Victor quickly waved a hand, freezing the dagger, and it fell just before him shattering on the ground in a million tiny crystals.

"No!" Eve cried. "Stop this madness, Dakon!"

Victor threw the ice crystals from his hands, sharper than the blades of Dakon's daggers, sure to pierce through his throat with ease. Dakon barely dove out of the way, the crystals slicing through the bottom of his cloak, ripping the ends to shreds. Dakon raced behind a tree.

He held his other dagger in a white-knuckled grip, calling out from behind the tree, "In all the centuries you've had to practice, is that really the best you got?"

He no sooner spoke the words from his lips than the tree began to feel cool even through his torn cloak, Dakon turned, seeing it form into ice.

Gods!

He ran out of the way before Victor broke the icy tree in two.

"I'm just playing with my meal." Victor laughed.

Dakon jumped behind a tangle of brush. "Tell me, oh wise idiot, doesn't fire beat ice?" He thrusted fire at Victor who ran behind a thin tree. The fire caught hold of the snowy branch and died out there.

Victor looked at the snuffed out fire, and turned to Dakon smiling, "I think I have the upper hand here, don't you think?" He thrust his hands and from it more ice crystals flew in Dakon's direction.

Dakon rushed out, barely dodging the shards of ice piercing in his direction, one nicking the top of his ear.

Shit!

Eve was screaming at them, begging them to stop. But Dakon didn't pay attention, he didn't care to stop. He only wanted blood or death and damn him he was going to get back to Adriana. He would not leave until every obstacle in his path was destroyed.

Even if it meant coming back with scars beyond repair.

Dakon shot more fire at Victor trying to impede the onslaught of ice headed for him. He looked around for somewhere else to hide, but in their immediate vicinity, the trees were all cracked or split open from their fight.

"Seems like you have nowhere left to hide." Victor smiled, his hands growing their ice crystals once more.

"I was simply tiring you out," Dakon replied, his fire crawling up his arms. He retrieved his final dagger, setting it ablaze once more and readying; he had to make sure he didn't miss this time.

Victor lifted his hands, surely ready to send another shard of ice crystals at him when a large scream pierced the air.

"I said stop!"

Fire surrounded him and Victor, sending them onto their backs in the snow. He tried to stand but found he couldn't move.

She froze us.

Dakon tried to break through her hold, but she was too strong. He could barely shift his eyes to see her approaching. Eve was set ablaze, her eyes that familiar red angrily staring down at both of them.

"I said—"

A loud crash rang through the forest. Dakon shifted his eyes in the direction of it. The bridge had finally collapsed, but at the edge of the bank before it stood a woman he had never seen before. A woman who looked very much like . . . Eve.

Eve?

She stood glaring at them with deep blue eyes, tan skin, and her hair, a dark brown cropped just above her shoulders, waved in the wind.

Dakon and Victor couldn't move and there was nowhere to run as the fire engulfed them in a circle of Eve's magic and fury.

"Clarisa?" Eve breathed, but the fire still raged.

Clarisa didn't respond, she merely lifted her hand and twisted her wrist. A large door appeared between Dakon and Victor as if leading into the snowy ground like a tunnel. Dakon tried with all his might to crawl away from it, but he couldn't budge.

Release us, Eve!

It was a black, wooden, circular door with inscriptions he couldn't quite name in silver. Eve took a step forward, flicking her hand absentmindedly to Dakon and Victor.

What is this?

"Oh fuck!" Victor shouted. Dakon heard his shriek, cutting through the air as he managed to move once more. He turned; Clarisa waved her hand and the door swung open, revealing nothing but darkness. He and Victor jumped back, but Clarisa snapped her fingers and thorny branches, grasped their ankles pulling them inside.

"No! Stop it! They're with me!" Eve shouted, running to Clarisa.

Dakon and Victor grasped at the snowy ground, finding anything to give them purchase against the strength of the branches' grip. Victor thrust ice at it trying to break free, and Dakon did the same with his fire, but nothing seemed to penetrate the thorns that dug into their flesh, pulling them quickly inside until they were both grasping the edge of the doorframe.

"I know," he heard Clarisa say before the door snapped shut on their fingers, releasing their grip.

And together they fell endlessly down into darkness.

EVE

CHAPTER 28

Eve watched horrified as the door disappeared into the ground.

"Clarisa!" she screamed, clawing her fingers erratically through the snow and finding nothing buried beneath. "Bring them back. They weren't hurting anyone but themselves!"

Clarisa said nothing, appearing to not even hear her as she glared forward. Eve ran to her, barely able to believe she was truly here in the flesh, frightened about where Dakon and Victor were sent, and trying to understand what happened. The moment her fingers met her sister's shoulder, a cold shock sent her hand back.

Eve looked up, the sister she remembered

seeing in the great hall next to a dead princess looked the same as the woman before her. But instead of the remorse shown clearly on her face as she disappeared into the mist, this Clarisa seemed vacant, unmoved.

"Clarisa?"

Clarisa turned her eyes slowly on her, she opened her mouth to speak, but the voices that came from her sounded nothing like Eve imagined.

"We are Clarisa."

Eve took a step back. "Wh-what?"

"We are Clarisa."

Her eyes, they weren't brown, but a piercing blue, shining in the evening. The snow picked up, and the wind whipped at her face. Her lips quivered.

"Clarisa, what happened to you?"

Clarisa narrowed her eyes. "Where is the grimoire?"

Eve's eyes widened, trying in vain to keep her eyes on this Clarisa and not look right where it lay in her satchel next to the fire. "I—I asked first."

Fire.

Fire.

Come to me.

Clarisa took a step toward her, and Eve stepped back again.

"Where is the grimoire?" the voices asked again.

"I don't know what you're talking about." The fire raged behind Eve. It crackled and roared, fighting against the blistering cold that threatened to extinguish it. The wind blew furiously at the embers, forcing it to catch onto trees and brush despite the snow. Smoke filled the area, fogging her vision.

And still Clarisa was unmoved. "She lies."

Eve felt the magic rising from her fingertips, it burned within her as she convinced herself to strike. To strike and run.

This isn't Clarisa.

This is something wearing her skin.
This is not her.

"She is perfect," the voices said as Clarisa raised her palm facing up. "Keep her alive."

Water whirled in the center of her hand, growing larger and twirling in circles. Eve felt herself choking on something forcing its way up her throat.

Now! Move!

Eve spat on the ground, seeing fresh blood, and shoved Clarisa's hand away, turning to run into the fire.

She nearly tripped over herself as she raced behind a large tree, gasping for air and lifting her trembling fingers to her lips. She coughed out more blood.

How? Why?

"You cannot hide fire witch. We see you."

Eve peeked from behind the tree; Clarisa walked through the fire with ease, barely a mark on her skin as the flames danced around her.

Eve's eyes widened and her limbs trembled as Clarisa raised her hands, the water within them crawling like creatures toward the fire smothering it to mere smoke in the snow.

No.

"Clarisa, whatever it is, we can solve this," Eve said, raising her hands before her.

Fire.

Bring me fire.

"Take her alive."

Fire.

Eve's hands became engulfed in flames, and she shoved the fire at Clarisa, giving herself just enough time to run into the brush. The thorns cut her face and neck, snagging on her fur cloak. She tore it off her, running as the voices called out for her.

"Little fire witch, show us where you've hidden the grimoire."

The damn book.

She had to go back for it. She couldn't leave it to be found.

Eve pushed against the thorny, snowed-in brush, covering herself in the frigid branches. She could hear Clarisa approach, the voices growing louder.

"Fire witch. Fire witch. Find the fire witch."

She held her breath, peeking through the branches. Clarisa moved like a spirit through the frozen forest, her blue eyes a light in the pitch-black darkness guiding her forward. Eve bit her lip to keep from trembling, to keep from drawing attention to herself.

"We know you're near, fire witch."

Clarisa stilled in front of Eve's hiding spot in the brush. Eve didn't dare look up, didn't dare draw breath for fear her sister, or whatever had become of her, would find her.

"We can smell your fear. It consumes you, child."

Clarisa continued forward and silence followed, stretching in agony as Eve considered her limited options. To run or to stay and hide.

She nearly broke into a sprint, when the oddest sound came across her ears.

Tink. Tink. Tink.

She stilled.

Tink. Tink. Tink.

It sounded close, too close. She peeked through the branches again, Clarisa was gone. She let out a shaky, quiet breath.

Tink. Tink . . .

Then it stopped, and Eve's heart stopped with it.

"We found you, fire witch."

Eve whipped her head around and came face-to-face with Clarisa's piercing blue eyes. Eve hadn't a chance to move when Clarisa's cold hands gripped her throat.

"C-Clarisa," Eve choked, "don't!"

Clarisa squeezed. "Our fire witch."

Tink. Tink. Tink.

Eve grasped Clarisa's hands and saw . . . everything.

Amarin's ship.

The Blackthorn.

Her lover.

The prince.

The oracles.

The oracles. The sound is coming from the oracles.

But what does it mean?

The sound quickened, and Eve gazed upon the glowing crystal about Clarisa's neck. A thick, gray smoke swirled within knocking against the glass.

"You are our fire witch." Clarisa tightened her grip, and blood pooled on Eve's tongue.

Eve begged for every bit of magic to come through before she gave into the darkness creeping at the edges of her vision. Her fire sparked weakly, but she put everything she could into it as she shoved a hand into Clarisa's face, pushing her away.

"I love you, please," Eve choked.

Clarisa growled as the fire burned her flesh. "Fire witch!"

The tinking was louder now, deafening Eve with its relentless tapping against the crystal, and Eve twisted from Clarisa's grip.

They grappled for control, fire against water, sister against sister, blood against blood.

"Stop it, Clarisa!"

Clarisa, bruised and bloodied, pinned Eve beneath her, raising her hand above her. Eve choked on the blood in her throat.

Tink.

Tink.

Tink.

Eve screamed and coughed, ripping the crystal from Clarisa's neck. She squeezed it tight in her hands, willing her fire to destroy it. Clarisa's blue eyes turned white as she fought to remove the crystal from Eve's ironclad grip. The crystal cracked in her hand, piercing her skin as Clarisa shrieked into the night.

"She's killing us!" the voices within Clarisa screeched. "The fire!"

Break!

Break!

Clarisa shoved a hand onto Eve's throat; blood coated her tongue, rising in her throat.

"Fire witch!"

The crystal snapped in half in her palm, the sharp jagged edges nicking her skin. Clarisa screamed, holding her hands to her temple. Large clouds of smoke rose from the crystal. Clarisa reached out to touch them, but Eve kicked her off, running away with the crystal.

Clarisa gave chase, the whites of her eyes glowing in the forest. Eve waved her hands to freeze the time around her, but Clarisa would only hold for a moment, before rushing after her once more.

Eve ran back toward the river, setting her path ablaze, every bit of branch, brush in her way, anything to slow her sister's pursuit. The shadows of the crystal spoke. "Let us in, fire witch." Eve set the crystal ablaze and threw it into the forest.

The trees took to flame despite the snow, but still Clarisa raced after her.

Eve spat out blood, her body feeling faint, her magic slowly fading.

"Get back!" Clarisa screeched behind her.

Eve ran until she saw the satchel nearly buried beneath the fresh snow, grabbing it with her free hand.

She snuck a glance behind her. Clarisa burst angrily through the edge of the forest.

"Give it back!"

Eve ran harder, following the river as Clarisa gave chase.

Her body ached, the blood pooled in her mouth, the satchel felt like it weighed a thousand stones. And to her horror, the river stopped.

No.

The water fell over the edge of another cliff. A waterfall into nothingness.

She turned. Clarisa was closing in.

Eve did the only thing she could, and jumped in the icy river, succumbing to her chosen fate.

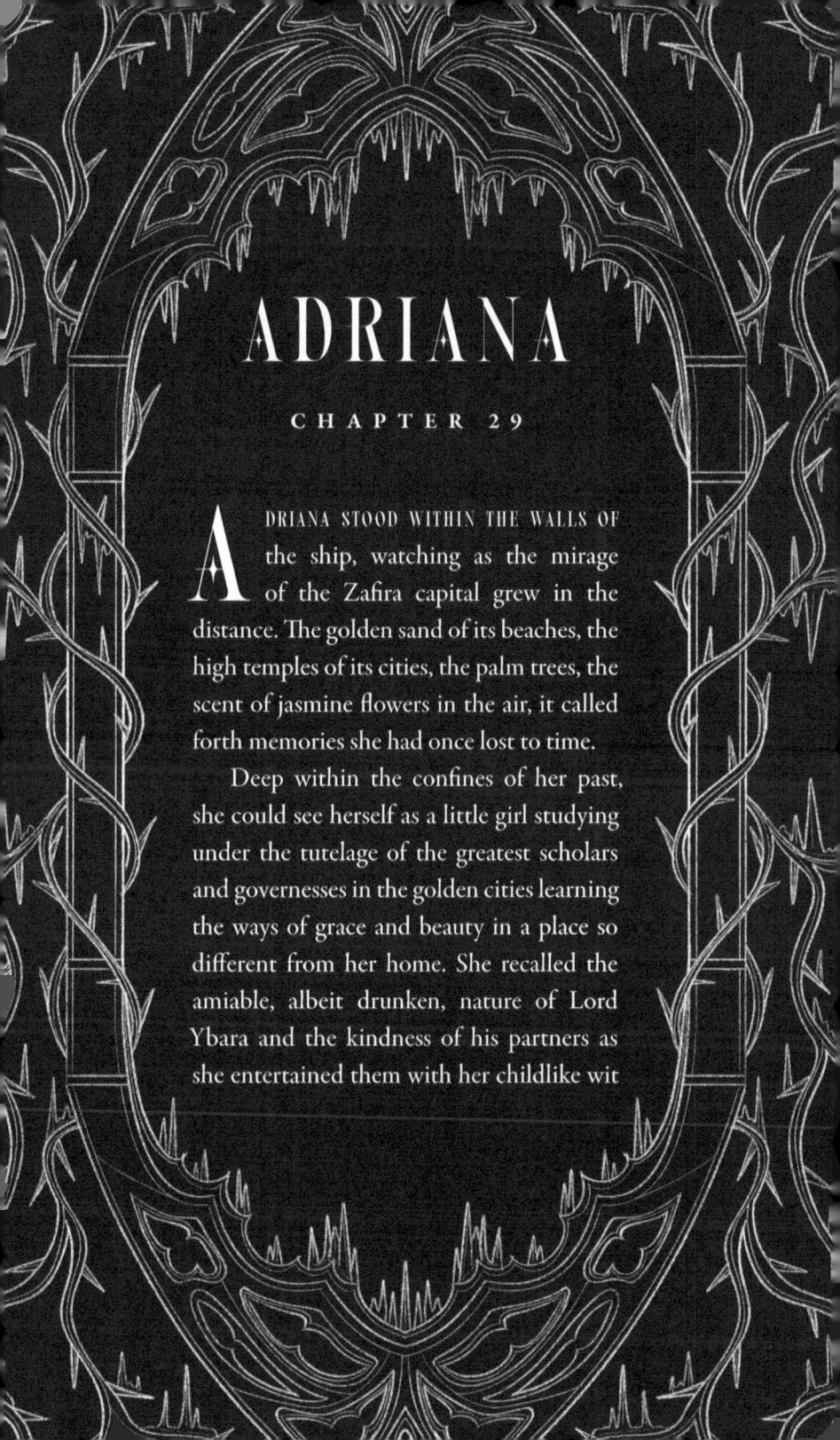

ADRIANA

CHAPTER 29

A DRIANA STOOD WITHIN THE WALLS OF the ship, watching as the mirage of the Zafira capital grew in the distance. The golden sand of its beaches, the high temples of its cities, the palm trees, the scent of jasmine flowers in the air, it called forth memories she had once lost to time.

Deep within the confines of her past, she could see herself as a little girl studying under the tutelage of the greatest scholars and governesses in the golden cities learning the ways of grace and beauty in a place so different from her home. She recalled the amiable, albeit drunken, nature of Lord Ybara and the kindness of his partners as she entertained them with her childlike wit and humor over dinners on the large balcony overlooking the water. Leaving at the tender age of eleven at the summons of her mother to attend court had been so intensely heartbreaking she clung to the lord's legs begging him to let her stay. She couldn't imagine they had forgotten her.

But would they remember me as I am now?

"Have you ever seen anything like it?"

Adriana didn't bother to turn, smiling politely as Hidalgo leaned against the railing alongside her.

"I lived here once a long time ago."

"Is that so?"

"Yes, in another life." She closed her eyes, relishing the warmth of the sun on her face. "It's quite enchanting, don't you think?"

Hidalgo shrugged. "The coast is beautiful, but don't let it fool you. If one ventures too deep into the barren lands I've heard of things that would take you beneath the parched dirt."

Adriana grinned. "My, aren't we superstitious?"

He nodded. "I wouldn't call myself a true sailor if I wasn't."

"I thought you sailors only feared what dwelled beneath the water."

Hidalgo lifted his lips. "The sea scares us because it's the unknown, but out there"—he gestured to the land—"holds things you can never truly escape."

Adriana considered this, thinking of Izan saving her from the darkness of the sea. He was a nymph and saved her life, whereas the men who took her to the dungeons of the castle, and her own brother, would have sooner seen her die than spend a moment considering her voice.

"Men then?"

Hidalgo gave her a grim smile. "Aren't you clever, Miss."

She didn't answer, and soon they stood in amiable silence as they watched the land and sea before them. The crew moved to and fro behind her, readying the ship to dock. She wanted to feel hopeful, excited even, to be far away from home, but the nerves of doubt creeped in.

What should I do if they don't remember me?

"I'm quite surprised you mentioned nothing of the jewels." Hidalgo broke her thoughts.

"Hmm?"

"The jewels," Hidalgo repeated. "Did you see any when you lived here?"

"There are far more precious things than jewels, Hidalgo."

"Is there?" He grinned.

"Of course, it can't buy you everything."

"But it does make life simpler." He pointed to the tower of the Zafira lord in the distance, "Imagine, all those royals sitting in their high towers filled with gold. What problems could they possibly have if at the snap of their fingers all their wishes could come true?"

If only it were that simple.

Her father's reign had marked the beginning of the end of peace for the kingdom, but she would be lying if she didn't admit that at court she was living quite comfortably. She need only ask, and nearly every wish she had would have been fulfilled.

But that was then.

Adriana lowered her gaze to the water, watching as the waves lapped gently against the ship.

Calm. Everything had been calm because her father was placated by the mess he caused to so many innocent lives—the battles he started, the families torn apart by his incessant need for more lands and power, when he had it all, why would he worry over the court or his own children?

Adriana rubbed her eyes.

She was a silly, little fool kept occupied by shiny things like jewels as the people fought for their lives and lands . . . and she only became humbled when she got a small taste of hardship after Marc's ascension.

Adriana realized she was biting her lip and released it.

"Yes, I—I suppose that that is true."

She could feel his eyes on her, but he didn't question her further. He simply nodded.

"This old man has kept you long enough." He stepped aside. "We'll be docking soon. Wherever you go from here, please take care of yourself, Miss."

"I will, thank you."

Adriana kept her eyes on Zafira as if it would slip through her fingers if she didn't pay it enough attention. She could hear Hidalgo walking away, his voice carrying over sounds of the seagulls in the distance and the waves against the ship as he shouted orders to the crew.

She took a deep breath, the salty sea air on the tip of her tongue. The golden city, the capital of Zafira, was far more impressive than she remembered. The buildings were made of near-white stone, some with decorated statues in gold and bronze that glinted too bright in the day. The palm trees danced beneath a cloudless sky, and the sun that had warmed her comfortably earlier was beginning to burn her cheeks.

She blinked a few times, squinting to make out the rest of it in the sun, but relented. She pushed away from the railing and walked back to the captain's quarters. Inside, Izan fumbled over maps and other loose papers about the desk. He didn't bother looking up as she entered, closing the door quietly behind her.

"There will be another captain taking over the ship. It seems my duties will be complete once we dock."

"Will they try to force you onto another ship?"

"Perhaps." Izan smirked, placing an X on the map. "But you and I will be long gone by then."

Adriana sat across from him. "Will I have to run?"

"No, the city is quite crowded near the port. We only need to slip within, and I can lead you to Lord Ybara."

"Do you know him?"

"I was raised mostly in Zafira." He marked another map, flipping it face down with the other as he spoke. "His name is uttered at least once a day there in jest or curse."

Adriana nodded. "With the Strix?"

"The very one."

"Is that why you wanted to come back? To rejoin with the witches?"

Izan dabbed his quill in the vial of ink. "No, most of the witches had moved up north to Givensmir."

Adriana swallowed. "To kill us?"

Izan grinned. "What stories did your governess tell you that you should think every non-mortal wishes to eat you?"

Adriana didn't have a suitable response and bit her lip.

Izan shook his head. "The Strix moved north to aid your brother in taking over the throne. Quite persuasive he was. Not certain what he promised them, but it must have been worth it to leave the golden cities."

"So, if there is no one here for you, why do you return?"

Izan stopped. "Do you really wish to know?"

"Why else would I ask?"

Izan placed down his quill, clasping his hands together before him. "Because there is a seer here, I believe can help me find Eve."

"A seer?"

"Don't tell me after everything we've discussed you are having difficulties believing in the work of seers now?" Izan raised brow, teasingly.

"Not at all." She tried to appear confident.

Save for the lore of their bloodthirsty tendencies.

"Are you planning to leave me once you drop me off at their castle?"

Izan smiled. "No, unfortunately for you, you are stuck with me. I made you an oath, remember?" He stood, placing a dagger in the hilt of his belt. "We both want the same things, My Queen. We wish for revenge against your bastard of a brother." He glanced at Adriana. "No offense."

"None taken."

"And we wish to find Eve and your lover. Both of them are bound to be together wherever they are."

Adriana did her best to hold back a smile but failed, straightening herself in a show of confidence.

"If we make it through this, you will be rewarded. I promise you."

"A mighty promise for a queen without an army," Izan teased.

"I have faced worse odds, and besides, I am a woman of my word."

"I believe you," Izan said, picking up his flask and taking a sip. He handed it to Adriana. "Do you want a drink?"

She took it, tilting her head back as she drank.

"Hold on, I don't want to have to carry you off the ship."

Adriana laughed, wiping her mouth with the back of her hand. She lifted the flask to him, and he groaned at the lightness of it as he placed it in a satchel.

There was a knock on the door, and Hidalgo peeked inside. "Captain, we are about to dock."

"Excellent," Izan replied, "prepare the crew and get the ship ready for the next captain."

Hidalgo nodded, closing the door behind him. Izan took a step toward it and stopped suddenly, turning to face Adriana.

"I meant to ask, which one of Eve's companions was your lover?"

Adriana raised her chin. "Dakon."

Izan nearly choked on air. "Dakon? The man with the green eyes?"

"Yes, that's him!" She stood. "Did you get acquainted with him?"

Izan shook his head, and a surprised cough escaped his lips.

"What is it?" Adriana asked, nervously.

Izan composed himself, flicking his eyes between her and the floor. "Nothing, My Queen. I am simply . . . surprised is all."

Before she could ask anything further, he made his way quickly outside of the cabin.

Adriana could hear him muttering under his breath, frustrated. "I swear, twice? Twice?! He must be more magic than man!"

"Now, before I get my head chopped from my shoulders, will these lords and ladies recognize you?"

Adriana shrugged as they waited in the great hall of Lord Ybara, ruler of Zafira. She patted down her trousers, regretting that she had not changed into the mistress dress she had on board for something even remotely appropriate. Her face was wrapped in a scarf, hiding her true identity from the masses in case they were stopped fleeing from the port.

To their extraordinary luck, no one had paid them any notice.

The guards faced them on all sides as they waited in the otherwise silent and empty great hall. It seemed familiar to her, the blue tapestries bearing the sigil of golden snakes hung along the pillars that lined the hall. The windows carved intricately through the white stone showed the tops of the palm trees and the rest of the city that reached out toward the edge of the sand and sea. She welcomed the sound of birds cawing somewhere nearby.

"So, I hear we have a visitor!" a voice boomed in the hall.

Adriana swallowed seeing Lord Ybara for the first time in years, followed by two women and a man.

He was larger than he had been when she was a child, the parts of his face not obscured by a thick, black beard was tinted a red hue like the wine he used to drink. He wore a tunic threaded with ivory and sea-blue beads. He no longer had hair atop his head like he once did, balding from age or stress, or perhaps both.

He walked slowly up to his white chair and sat. His companions stood on either side of him.

"Yes, Lord Ybara. I have come a long way," Adriana said.

"And you are?"

A prick of fear rose in the pit of her stomach.

Could he be trusted or had he long abandoned her as an ally?

She slowly removed her scarf, freeing her hair about her shoulders.

"I am Adriana from Givensmir, my lord."

Lord Ybara stood. "It's impossible."

"Do you not recognize me, my lord?"

He moved down the steps quicker than she thought possible. Izan tightened his grip on his dagger, but Adriana shook her head slowly.

"You are alive, thank the gods!" Lord Ybara said, astonished.

"Barely," she replied as he took her in an embrace.

"We were told you were dead. The doves were quick to announce your death when the witch attacked the castle." He placed a gentle hand on her cheek. "How did you ever escape?"

Adriana placed her hand over his. "We can discuss that later. But for now, I have far more pressing matters to discuss with you."

"Yes, yes," he replied. "Of course, freshen up and join me for dinner."

He clapped his hands together and a servant rushed toward them with a glass of wine. Lord Ybara took the drink and gestured the servant toward them.

"Follow me, please," he said, walking briskly out of the great hall.

Adriana and Izan followed, taking in the majestic corridors and large open windows overlooking the city and sea. When they were far enough away from the great hall, Izan leaned toward her and whispered, "I think I could get used to this."

Adriana remained facing forward, watching as the servant seemed to slow a step.

She whispered back. "Ensure I live, and your rewards will be boundless."

ADRIANA

CHAPTER 30

Adriana slept fitfully through the afternoon, haunted by dreams and memories of Dakon, the dungeons, and what rested on the Ser James spike as he rode into the castle grounds. She rose from the bed, expecting to see nothing but fire and stone walls that caved within itself, but instead was greeted by a beautiful night painted by stars through her balcony.

Laid out on the edge of her bed was a delicate gown of turquoise and silver beads. The handmaids must have placed it there while she napped. It should have made her feel comforted to be within luxury once more, but the only thing she could think of was that someone had entered her chamber when she was alone and vulnerable. In the dim candlelight, she turned about the chamber, wondering if it, too, had eyes she could not see.

She dressed next to the wardrobe in the corner, hoping she was wrong. As she fixed her sleeve, a knock echoed through the chamber. Startled, she froze.

The door opened to a handmaid. "Good evening, Princess. It is time for dinner."

ADRIANA WALKED ALONGSIDE IZAN AS THEY FOLLOWED THE HANDMAID to the balcony. The dinner was set there with delicacies and wines, fresh fruit and hot meat from the castle kitchens. Lord Ybara sat on one side with his two wives and husband. Servants and guards stood at the entrance of the balcony, ensuring none could enter.

Or leave.

Lord Ybara stood as they approached. "There she is, the beauty of the kingdom."

Adriana smiled politely. "Thank you, Lord Ybara. You are very generous."

"Come now, sit and let us speak. You look famished."

"Yes, please."

A servant passed Adriana a plate of fruit and she began to pick at the berries, placing one in her mouth as Lord Ybara spoke. "Forgive me. Allow me to introduce my wives and husband. Lilia, Tali, and Varik."

"I remember you were but a small girl the last time you walked these halls." Lilia smiled. "Quite the precocious child."

Adriana grinned. "I remember you gave me sweets when my governess wasn't looking."

"Don't tell her now. She will still pull my ear."

Adriana giggled. "You have my word."

She gave pleasantries to the others and turned to Izan who sat beside her. "This is my adviser, Izan. He is my sworn protector and the reason I was able to make it here to your shores."

Servants approached, filling their cups.

"Your sworn protector, hmm," Lord Ybara said as he took a long sip.

"Yes, my lord. I will guard her with my life."

Lord Ybara nodded. "Even against, let's say, seven guards?"

Adriana stilled, turning her head to the guards standing close beside them.

Izan tensed. "If I must, I will."

The silence lingered uncomfortably before Lord Ybara broke it, laughing. "Good. Only a test, you see." He tapped on his cup and a servant approached with two pitchers. He reached out for a cup but Lord Ybara swatted at his hand, grabbing the pitcher from his tray and shooing him away.

Adriana tried to swallow her nerves, an uncomfortable shakiness in her hands as she clasped them together on her lap.

"I must say again how honored I am that you sought refuge and protection in my home. I never thought we'd see you again," Lord Ybara continued.

"Nor did I," Adriana admitted. "My brother has certainly made a mess of things."

She could sense the tension as the servants brought more plates of food, placing them down carefully.

"Yes, about that"—Lord Ybara sighed—"how did you escape your brother when your betrothed couldn't?"

"It is quite a long story—"

"We have the time, though I must first offer my condolences. Lord Jos did not deserve to die as he did."

Adriana felt a flush rise on her cheeks. His head on the spike, lifeless and horrid, entered fresh in her mind as she rubbed her eyes. "He tried to save me, save us. I'm not certain how far he made it before my brother's men found him."

Lord Ybara cleared his throat. "No need to go over the macabre details, my dear. You are welcome to stay as long as you wish."

"No, I wish to speak of it." Adriana felt the heat of her skin as she spoke. "He killed my betrothed and then shoved me in a dungeon to keep me from escaping."

Lord Ybara lowered his cup. "He did what?"

"Can I have some more to drink?" Izan gestured not so quietly to the cup bearers.

Adriana ignored him as she replied to Lord Ybara. "Yes, I was in the dungeons and escaped with the help of other nobles imprisoned there."

"That is madness. He has truly lost his senses."

Adriana raised her chin. "Before I speak further, I must know, to whom do your allegiances lie?"

Lord Ybara raised a brow to his wives who kept their faces stoic. "That depends, Princess," he replied, carefully. He placed down his cup. "Are you here for protection or for rebellion?"

"I am here for my crown."

Izan stilled next to her, and though he bore no weapon, she could see him eyeing the knife on the table.

Lord Ybara narrowed his eyes. "And what makes you a greater ruler than your brother? What makes you think the people will accept you over him?"

"Because I am nothing like him."

"Didn't your people nearly kill you in the streets? It doesn't give me much confidence that you have the love of your people."

"Those were witches disguised as city folk under the orders of my brother to have me killed."

"If he wanted you killed, why would he send you to the dungeons?"

Adriana straightened. "Things changed. He chose instead to pawn me for more coin, marry me off to another who would fund his cause across the Dallise."

"Like father, like son, I suppose." He shook his head.

Adriana stood. "I want to rule over people, not ashes, and certainly not over chaos."

"My dear, every throne is a stepping stone to chaos."

"Says only the men who made it that way."

Lord Ybara's lips thinned, saying nothing for a long moment.

"What you are speaking of is treason. Why shouldn't I have you sent back to your brother? I'm certain he would reward me greatly for it."

Izan leapt between them, holding out one of the knives from the table. The guards rushed quickly holding out their spears. They were quickly outnumbered, but Adriana did not break Lord Ybara's stare, nor did she sit back down.

"Because you want to be on the winning side, Lord Ybara." She took a step around Izan. "Tell me, the wine you drink is from Rubianes is it not? How much has the cost risen since his rule began? How many nobles are buying jewels from your mines when they are far too preoccupied keeping their necks? You mention seven guards when I distinctly remember nearly a dozen at least when I'd dine here as a child. It begs to question: How many of your innocent people have been burned by his committees because of false accusations of witchcraft? How many of your guards?"

Lord Ybara clenched his jaw, saying nothing. She stepped closer and the guards nearly touched her with their spears before Lord Ybara gestured them to lower their weapons.

"My brother will lose this rebellion, if not by the kingdoms who oppose him then by his tumultuous rule that will bring him to his knees. You have known me since I was a *precocious* little girl, now join me as the queen that brings you prosperity."

She lifted his wine cup and drank the rest of it.

NAVIR

CHAPTER 31

"**W**HAT DO YOU MEAN SHE IS injured?!" Navir snarled at Aris as he entered Clarisa's chambers. Aris stood next to Clarisa as she lay in her bed, shivering in her sleep. The rain tapped against the window outside, and in the early morning light Navir noticed how frail and weak Clarisa appeared. Her pale face, fresh with burns and blood and bruises, was gaunt. Her lips blue as if she had kissed the sea and took all its color, and water or sweat, he couldn't tell which, dripped from her temples and the ends of her hair.

But he felt nothing but contempt.

She was supposed to be ready.

She was supposed to kill Eve and take the grimoire.

"Your Majesty, her sister, the fire witch, is far more powerful than we expected," Aris explained as he felt Clarisa's forehead. He flinched, grabbing a wet cloth and placing it carefully on her temple.

"No, no. Clarisa is the chosen one, she has the magic of ages, she—"

"And so does her sister. Clarisa is not invincible."

"You are telling me a simple fire witch was able to nearly mortally wound Clarisa—she had oracles and the magic of those she's consumed! It's unbelievable."

"There are far more pressing matters." Aris stood. "The fire witch has stolen the crystal. The oracles are no longer with us."

Navir flicked his eyes between Aris and Clarisa's bare neck.

His blood went cold.

"Do you think she knows how to use it?"

"I think there are many things we don't know, but one thing is certain, if these oracles get a hold of the fire witch, we will have more than a mortal war to worry about."

Navir grabbed Aris by his collar, lifting him off the ground so they faced each other. His nostrils flared. "Clarisa is useless then? Is that what you are telling me?"

Aris shook his head. "The oracles consumed her, yes, but they also controlled her. What they have done to her, what they forced her to do, can't be undone."

"What are you saying? Spit it out." Navir released him and Aris's body slammed against the stone floor.

Aris groaned as he got to his feet. "In the time we have allowed the oracles to consume her, she has grown used to a certain . . . appetite. She will need to feed on magic. She will do anything for it until the lingering effects of the oracles wear off. She will be desperate and uncontrollable with power."

"But can she kill the fire witch? Can she defeat the mortal armies? If not, kill her and be done with it."

Aris stilled, but his eyes never wavered from Navir's. "You would so easily discard her?"

"If she cannot win this war for me, if she cannot bring me the grimoire, I have no use for her."

Aris's eyes widened. "Clarisa can still be of use to us."

"As what? I've wasted years preparing her for this, gaining her trust, and she repays me by coming back broken and defeated? No, the ties end now."

His skin prickled with desperate nerves, he slammed his fist against a side table. The sound echoed through the chamber, settling upon Aris who flinched back.

Navir was done wasting his time. He needed to take matters into his own hands.

He needed to strike before the mortal kingdom galvanized enough forces.

Aris cleared his throat. "Give me one more chance to make this work. She may surprise us."

Navir narrowed his eyes. "You have one, last chance, Aris. Heal her and send her back to get the grimoire. Fail and you will be begging for death, I promise."

"I understand."

Navir stepped to the window, shoving a vase off the windowsill. It shattered on the ground. "And the oracles? How do we get them back?"

Aris cleared his throat, stepping over the broken pieces. "We don't, Your Majesty."

"So we leave them?" Navir twisted back around. "Have you gone mad?!"

"The oracles are rare, very rare." Aris placed his hands before him, trying to coax Marc into calm. "Without the crystal they will do what they do best and find hosts."

"So, what then? We leave them to be lost or used against us?"

"They are more likely to die off in the wastes. Oracles do not survive long without bodies."

Navir clenched his jaw. He hated losing, but even worse, he hated wasted time. "And what about the fire witch?"

"She will be back, but I suspect it will be to fight for the mortals. But one witch cannot defeat an army."

"But she is stronger than Clarisa."

"But she has a weakness. Everything has a weakness." Aris placed a fresh cloth on Clarisa's temple.

Blood ties.

Navir considered this. It was a risk, but if it worked, they could have everything they wanted and more.

"Excellent." Navir finally said. "Let her sister be for now. And as for her"—he pointed at Clarisa—"hasten her healing. I plan to give the mortals quite the surprise."

"She needs a witch, Your Majesty."

Navir waved his hand dismissively. "Bring the prisoners."

"Your Majesty, there are not any more left . . ."

Navir narrowed his eyes. "Then find someone, or you'll be the first volunteer."

Aris stared at Theo grimly. "Yes, Your Majesty."

Navir made his way across the chamber and toward the door when a sudden thought entered his mind. "How long until she goes back to normal?"

"From the how the oracles left her? It could be days or moons. In truth, I am not certain."

Navir gritted his teeth. "I plan to lead our ships across the Dallise very soon. She needs to be ready. If she gives you any trouble, tell her I will kill Ana personally."

"You found her?"

"No."

Navir turned from the chamber, walking down the corridor

toward his tower. The place where he would once again fly from to search the lands below for any sign of that wretched, traitorous witch. And when he found her...

CLARISA

CHAPTER 32

"**A**M I DEAD?"
 Her voice felt hollow and far removed as she spoke into the dark. It echoed against the barren castle walls, traveling down the hall until it made its way back to her. She barely recognized the sound anymore, and if she were not certain she had said the words aloud, Clarisa would have believed them spoken by another.

She could not remember the last time she saw someone other than her reflection in the puddles or cracked glass she stumbled upon as she ventured through the corridors.

Dread, the very kind she had promised to ignore the first day she found herself here, pricked at her skin reminding her that she was in the clutches of very powerful magic... or a very powerful curse.

Memories of her trying to escape the castle only to find herself back in her chambers or screaming until her throat was raw, only to have the echoes nearly deafen her, kept her nearly silent now. Every bit of magic she ever held was useless here, as if she were nothing but a mortal.

Mortal.

She stepped over the broken cracks in the stone floor and shielded herself beneath her blue hood from the snowfall that made its way inside the open windows. It was cold and damp here, the crumbling roof leaked making *drip, drip, drip* sounds that haunted her more as moments passed. She continued pressing forward, trying to pay it no mind. Anything was better than staying still, anything was better than being driven mad thinking about solitude.

Clarisa was not sure how long she had been trapped in the Blackthorn castle, wandering aimlessly down abandoned halls, dungeons, chambers, and even torture rooms she had never laid eyes on before. It may have been hours, days, moons, years, it all seemed to come together in an endless dream she could not wake from.

Outside she could see nothing but gray fog obscuring the grounds of the castle, the skies, the forests, the sea. It was as if she and this castle were on a cloud of rain, dreary and forlorn, an island of broken nothingness.

With all her years of lessons in witchcraft, none had ever prepared her for something like this. There was talk of spirits, of hedging between veils, of goddesses and ancient magic, but never how to escape the dismal abyss she now found herself in. And as time stretched, she soon discovered that she remembered less and less of her life before the fog.

Her footsteps were the only sounds filling the void as she turned down the hall away from the west wing and walked forward into the darkness that loomed toward the northern tower.

Ana.

Brisa.

Tabor.
Navir.
Eve.

She repeated their names to herself, committing them to memory, though she knew the list was longer before. She wondered whose name she would forget soon but pushed the thought from her mind.

Have no fear.
Have no fear.

As if by habit, she reached for her collar, trying to feel for the crystal that was no longer there. The comfort it had once brought as it clung about her neck was gone now in its absence.

And here in this eerie, abandoned castle she couldn't remember why it felt so important before.

She couldn't remember why.

She couldn't remember...

DAKON

CHAPTER 33

He hit the ground, shoulder first, hearing a pop as his body met the earth. Dakon turned on his back, squeezing his eyes shut, the pain nearly blinding him.

"Fuck!" He groaned, trying to sit up but placing his weight on his hand was excruciating, he fell back down.

His shoulder, it was coming from his shoulder.

He was too scared to open his eyes and see. His mind ran amuck with sights of impalement or worse, severance.

Shakily he reached his uninjured arm across to it, his fingers recoiled feeling the bone out of place where it should have been.

Even his gentle touch felt like a dagger dug into his flesh.

"Ah, shit." Victor's voice sounded next to him. He coughed a few times, and Dakon could hear him getting to his feet and moving closer. "You need to shove it back in."

Dakon's eyes sprung open. "Sh-shove it? Are you mad?!"

Victor stood over him. "The fucking shoulder, Familiar."

Dakon shifted his eyes to his wound, the bone making a lump beneath his flesh. He felt sick, shaking. He cast his eyes elsewhere, trying to distract from the horrid pain, and it nearly worked. He realized they were no longer in the eternal blizzard lands of the wastes, they were somewhere where the trees still held a hint of green beneath a patchy cloaking of snow, brightened by a melancholy afternoon sun. The creatures of the forest scampered about as the birds sang around them in the distance.

Clarisa sent them out of the wastes...

"Where are we?" Dakon breathed.

"Wherever that witch sent us. Is she another one of your lovers?"

"No," Dakon huffed.

"Interesting, she looked like the spitting image of your witch."

Eve.

"That was her sister." Dakon moaned, trying again to sit.

Victor grinned. "Looks like you need my help."

"Fuck off." Dakon grunted, lying back down. He tried to think about what to do next, wherever Eve and Clarisa were, they were certainly more than a day's journey from them. He wondered if Clarisa thought she was protecting Eve; he even wondered if at any moment they would be dragged back to the wastes when Eve explained it all to her.

But the look in Clarisa's eyes, the rage, the anger—was it possible she was there to harm Eve too?

The thought barely entered his mind when Victor pushed a finger on the bone. Dakon shoved himself quickly from the agonizing pain flaring across his arm. He kicked at Victor, missing. "I said, fuck off!"

"Your choice"—Victor raised his hands defensively—"but unless you fix it, you're in for a world of pain."

Dakon tested his arm, trying to raise it again but the ache was too intense.

Damn him.

He lay a moment in silence on the wet ground, trying to summon the courage to do what needed to be done. He had to go find Eve; he needed to make sure she was safe and help her escape the wastes too. And he wouldn't be useful on an injured arm.

Dakon released a shaky, angry breath. Squeezing his eyes shut once more and bracing himself, he said, "All right, then. Do it."

"Gladly," Victor said, standing over him. He shoved aside the opening of the fur cloak and his fingers gently made their way around the wound. He removed them and Dakon heard the sound of ripping fabric.

He opened his eyes to Victor, handing him a bit from the bottom of his tunic. "Shove this in your mouth."

"Why the hells—"

"Do it, or you may attract unwanted attention." He gestured to the woods around them, woods that now looked oddly familiar.

Dakon snatched the fabric from Victor's hands, shoving it in his mouth and biting down hard.

Victor laughed. "You're quite handsome when you're not arguing with me."

Dakon narrowed his eyes.

"Curious why the witch sent us here?" He looked around. "I quite like it."

"Hurry and get on with it," Dakon said, his voice muffled through the fabric.

"Oh, yes," Victor replied, "let me adjust my position here."

Victor moved as if to step over Dakon but instead placed his boot on Dakon's shoulder.

Dakon's eyes widened.

"Remember, Familiar, this will hurt me more than it hurts you." Victor pushed his foot down on the wound. Dakon writhed in pain, but was pinned down, unable to move away. "Or perhaps it's the other way around." Victor shrugged, chuckling.

Dakon tried to squirm away, the pain too intense; spots of color swam in his vision. He was certain he would faint from this bitter agony alone.

Victor pushed his boot down hard, and Dakon flinched, squeezing his eyes shut and waiting for the blinding pain. But there was none, it was only pressure now. The pain nearly went away entirely.

He looked back up to Victor, who stepped off him and held out a hand instead.

Dakon spat out the fabric and shoved his hand aside. "We're going back."

Victor laughed. "Now why would I do that?"

"We have to make sure Eve is alive—"

"She is alive or else you wouldn't be."

True...

"Still, I cannot abandon her."

"You can't... but I can."

"Damn you, Dragon. You're taking me back."

"On such a nice day?" He gestured to the sky, painting itself into an early evening blend of purple hues and dark blues. He stepped back. "Besides, you and your witch were bitching and moaning about getting out. And now that we've done the unthinkable, you are telling me to go right back to that cursed witch?"

"Cursed witch?"

"Did you not see the crystal on her neck? She's possessed, damned, out of luck as one would say." He shrugged. "Those oracles are nasty beings. Rots your brain and body until you are nothing but a carcass."

"Then we have to save Eve," Dakon urged.

"Not a good enough reason I'm afraid," Victor said, walking

backward toward the dense brush of the woods. "And for the first time in centuries I have a taste of freedom. Wouldn't want to waste it going on adventures that could get me killed."

Dakon sat up, ready to once again fight the dragon witch, when a rustling of the brush next to Victor caught his attention. Victor was oblivious, still bragging about his new chance at life when Dakon saw the flash of steel.

"Victor, wait!"

He barely coughed out the words when a blade was held at Victor's throat, silencing him.

"Look what we've found here." A man with a dirty tunic and fierce dark eyes stepped out of the brush. "Seems like we have some lost folk."

The man pushed Victor forward, dagger still at his throat, forcing him to walk. Three other large men emerged from the brush, their tunics and boots in various states of disrepair, torn and disheveled. They laughed under their breaths as they walked toward Dakon.

"W-we're not lost," Dakon managed, rising slowly to his feet. He cursed himself for stammering.

Bandits. Or murderers. Maybe both.

He raised his hand defensively, the other reaching for the dagger in his belt.

"Don't sound too confident," the man replied, shoving the dagger deeper against Victor's throat.

"Push it harder and I'll think you're flirting with me," Victor grunted.

"Shut it," the man growled.

"Slice his throat, Julian." One of the men laughed.

Julian ignored him, flashing a smile to Dakon. "I like your fur cloak."

Dakon released his grip on the dagger, shoving off his cloak and tossing it before them. "Take it. We mean no harm."

"But we do," Julian said.

"Do it, Dakon, set them ablaze!" Victor shouted against the blade.

Dakon tried to feel the magic within him, but it was weak. He made a small inconsequential spark, hardly noticeable. Panic rose, he felt too weak.

"I-it's not working." Dakon met Victor's eyes, they were wide and nervous.

He doesn't feel his either. It's not cold enough.

Shit.

"Do you have something we'd like? These woods have been mighty cold." Julian gestured to his companions who quickly subdued Dakon, taking his dagger.

"Nothing here, but this." One of them raised the blade, disappointed.

The men looked to Julian.

"So, we've caught a bunch of liars," Julian growled.

"Honest liars," Victor choked out.

"I said shut it." Julian smacked the back of his head. He looked to his companions. "I say we take them for a swim, what say you men?"

The men cackled as they tied Dakon and Victor together, shoving them forward and leading them deeper into the woods.

CALLUM

CHAPTER 34

Callum and Emilio raced on stolen horses through the forest. The trees, massive and evergreen, filled Callum's vision as they whipped past their snowy branches and leapt over fallen brush. He longed to see the Teros castle towers in the distance, but they were still too far from it. It would take nearly the entire afternoon to even reach the edge of the kingdom's grounds.

The sun battled with the misty clouds in the sky, providing light but not much warmth as they moved swiftly. The cool wind whipped at Callum's exposed face, numbing him uncomfortably. He breathed in the frigid air and felt his dry throat burn as it settled there.

He could not remember the last thing he drank, nor the last meal he ate. He and Emilio were far too nervous on their last day at sea to do much but wait for the port to come into view. And when it did, they nearly raced off the ship as the sailors and the first mate unloaded cargo, running in the twilight of dawn into the village until they came upon the horses tied outside the harbor. Much to their detriment, they had not thought of stocking supplies or food, only of escaping, and now as they rode, he regretted not taking an extra moment to be better prepared.

He turned around as he rode forward, fearful that he would see a hundred men mounted on horses giving chase, but there was nothing but snow glinting against the sun that trickled through the branches. He wasn't certain how long they had been riding, only that they had to have given themselves a considerable distance by now.

No one will miss two horses . . .

Or a sailor.

Or a captain . . . a dead one.

"Let us take a quick break," Emilio called out. "My horse is growing weary."

Callum slowed his pace to a stop and looked about. "There are creeks and ponds not too far from here. If only I could properly orient myself, I would be able to tell you where."

"I believe I hear rushing water that way." He pointed to his left.

Callum shook his head. "Let us hope it isn't Gods' Protection. The water is no good there."

"But are there other sources nearby?"

Callum nodded. "There should be, if memory serves me correct."

"Good." Emilio grinned.

Callum could lose himself in his smile. Even in his distressed sailor garb, his hair that had grown twice its length since they first met, and the stubble that was now a beard, Emilio was beautiful.

"I know I am handsome, but you can look at me all you wish when we stop next," Emilio teased.

Callum blinked, smiling back as he pulled the reins of his horse to the sound of the water.

THEY DISMOUNTED FROM THEIR HORSES, LEADING THEM TO THE EDGE of a small lake. The sound of a waterfall nearby was music to Callum's ears as they sat near the edge, watching their horses drink. For the first time, he felt at peace as he rested his head on Emilio's shoulder. He couldn't remember the last time he had heard the rushing of Teros's many waterfalls.

He had just become a man when he was sent to the Givensmir court by his aunt, Lady Tyrina, in hopes that he would make a suitable match.

Eve.

Callum bit the inside of his cheek at the thought. He wondered what she would think now.

"What concerns you?" Emilio asked, watching the horses.

"Nothing."

Emilio chuckled. "If nothing bothers you then I would believe you invincible. Come now, tell me."

Callum straightened. "I feel as if I have failed my people, Teros. I was sent to the capital to make strong bonds in the court, to find a wife, and here I am a fugitive of the crown."

"Not to mention you have no wife." Emilio shoved him playfully.

"Ah, yes. She turned into a witch, and I helped her escape." He laughed at the absurdity that had become his life.

"You have to be just about the unluckiest man alive."

"A laughingstock."

"A failure."

"A fool."

They laughed until they nearly cried as they held each other.

And slowly they gave way to silence as they lay on the snowy ground, staring into each other's eyes.

Callum didn't know when he fell in love with Emilio, but he knew he never wished to part from him. Never wished to live a day where he did not look into brown eyes and feel his dark strands of hair between his fingers.

A nervous flutter filled his stomach at the thought of asking if Emilio felt the same.

How does he see me?

Emilio placed his hand gently on Callum's cheek. "You can talk to me, Callum. You are safe with me."

Callum nodded. "I want to stay here."

"Then we will."

"By this waterfall lake, listening to the water... to you."

"Then our journey is done, and I claim this lake as ours."

Callum grinned.

"Because as long as you are by my side"—Emilio rested his temple against Callum's, closing his eyes—"what is a place but somewhere I lay my head next to you?"

Callum lifted his hand to Emilio's. "If only it were warmer."

Emilio smiled. "Tell me if this helps."

He pressed his lips against Callum's. They were soft and far more delicate than they should have been in this blistering cold. But they were warm, and Callum eagerly kissed him back, taking him in. They wrapped their arms around each other, holding on as if this day marked the end.

And perhaps it was.

Because when they left, they would find themselves beneath a dark evening sky climbing the steps to the great hall of Teros or perhaps the council chambers, listening as Lady Tyrina discussed the horrid war before them. And though Callum did not voice it, both of the men knew they would be first in line to battle for the rebellion.

But here, next to the peaceful lake, they could pretend life was far simpler than it truly was. This place would be theirs until it wasn't.

The horses neighed suddenly, and Emilio whipped his head up to them. They were clearly agitated, neighing and huffing as they stepped back from the edge of the water. Callum sat up but couldn't see what they were afraid of down the sloped, rocky hill.

"Stay here," Emilio said, taking out a knife from his belt.

"No, I'm coming with you." Callum stood, doing the same.

Emilio didn't have a chance to respond as the horses began to run toward them. Callum leapt to grab their reins as Emilio raced to see what they were running from.

They were spooked, and if Callum hadn't caught one of their reins by luck, the other would have been lost to the woods. He quickly tied their reins together, pulling them back to the lake where Emilio stood unharmed, but wet.

"Emilio?" Callum called out. "Was it a snake?"

Emilio turned to him, his face pale as he breathed heavily.

"What is it?" Callum tied the horses to a tree and ran over to him.

Emilio knelt down, covering something that lay at his feet.

"W-we need to hurry to your aunt."

"Wh—" Callum stilled. He was certain he wasn't breathing anymore, his eyes beholding the wreck of the person before him.

It can't be.

"Callum? Callum! She needs our help."

Emilio shook him, and he caught his senses once more. He rushed to the woman lying still as if she were sleeping on the cold, snowy bank wearing nothing but a tattered burgundy dress that stuck to her like a second skin. Her head was bleeding, her neck and arms bruised.

"It is a miracle she missed the rocks," Emilio said, pushing on her wrist with two fingers, "but the woman is still alive, thank the gods."

"This isn't any woman," Callum breathed, his hands shaking. "This is my wife."

CALLUM

CHAPTER 35

"So, where is your betrothed?"

The commanding, matronly voice carried through the council room as Callum and Emilio sat waiting with the other representatives of the rebellion—lords and ladies of Teros, Mytar, and Zafira.

Lady Tyrina was a stanch, fierce woman taking the sole attention of the council room as she walked inside and made her way leisurely to the seat at the head of the table. Her long black hair was braided delicately with tiny green jewels. Her dress was black no doubt in mourning, and her brown eyes held nothing back as she inspected Callum for the second time that day.

The first was when the guards at the

gate took them to her, clearly recognizing Callum and separating the three of them to the care of the healers. She was just as formal and proper then as she was now, save for a brief hug thanking the gods with grace for his safe return.

But that was earlier in the evening. Now it was near midnight, and the council looked a varied collection of weary and surprised.

"Sh-she is in the guest chamber with the healer, Aunt," Callum replied evenly.

Lady Tyrina thinned her lips. "Good. And it is about time you showed yourself. Only a true Tyrosi could escape such a dismal fate in the capital."

Callum nodded.

She faced Emilio. "Thank you for your attention to this matter. Teros owes you and Pleasant Peak a debt that could never be truly repaid."

"It was an honor, Lady Tyrina."

"Yes, yes. But honor would be nothing if you were dead, so again thank you for bringing my nephew back to me." She looked at the rest of the members in the room.

"We have discussed this at length and now we will do this once more for my nephew. It is time for a new ruler in the capital. This mad king has done nothing but disgrace our kingdom and wreak havoc upon the innocent people of this land."

"Do we have enough forces to dethrone him?" Callum asked.

"We have enough to do damage. Larrea has remained staunchly supportive of King Marc as has Rubianes. But damage is all we need to remove him if we strategize correctly."

"Princess Adriana is alive. She supports our cause."

"Last we heard she was imprisoned and died when the dungeons collapsed." One of the council members spoke gruffly.

"No, she escaped. We helped her."

"Then where is she now?" Lady Tyrina waved a dismissive hand.

"Sh-she is on a ship headed for Zafira."

"You had the princess, our potential queen, and you let her slip through your fingers?" Another council member scoffed.

"It was complicated," Emilio replied. "We were separated at the harbor."

The council turned to Lady Tyrina, who narrowed her eyes. "Scribe." A young man shuffled to her with a parchment and quill. She didn't look at him as she spoke. "Write to the Lord Ybara, tell him to expect and search for the princess if he hasn't received her already. Send the dove at once."

The scribe bowed and rushed from the room.

Lady Tyrina pursed her lips. "I suppose we can send a dove to Lord Marcelo as well to see if we can sway him once he finds out his dear daughter is in our possession. We need only to marry the two of you to force his hand."

"Is that truly—"

"One of you"—she pointed at one of the councilmen—"send a letter to Lord Marcelo."

The council members stared at one another, unsure of who she meant.

"Do I need to repeat myself?"

Two men stood and one rushed for the door, leaving quickly.

"Do you think Lord Marcelo will change course?" Emilio asked. "His daughter was convicted of treason and killed the former king. Would he throw out his new alliance, risk his lands and possessions for her?"

Callum raised a brow, but Emilio pretended not to see.

"No," Lady Tyrina said, "but it is always good to salt the wounds of rigid men."

"What is the decision if Lord Marcelo refuses to join us?" a councilwoman asked.

"I suppose there is nothing else to do but kill her."

"No." Callum leapt to his feet. "I will not stand for it."

"She is a witch that went mad with witchcraft and killed our last king, though he was scarcely better than this one. Leaving her alive complicates things."

"She is the very reason I am alive." Callum pounded his fist on the table.

"At least hear her reason, Lord Callum," Emilio whispered, trying to pull Callum's arm gently to force him back into his seat.

Callum ignored him, pulling his arm back. "The king tried to kill her and me. She saved us!" He did not realize he was shouting until he finished his words, and the silence weighed heavy with tension.

Lady Tyrina sat straight, unmoving.

"This council is dismissed."

The people quickly stood, bowing to Lady Tyrina and moving out of the room. Callum stayed where he was, unable to break his gaze from his aunt. Emilio moved beside him.

"Callum, please."

Callum didn't look his way.

"You, too, are dismissed, Lord Emilio."

Emilio didn't move.

"She said, you, too, *Lord Emilio*," Callum breathed.

Emilio's gaze lingered for a moment longer and then he left, closing the door behind him.

"I will not let you hurt her," Callum said when they were finally alone.

"That is not your decision to make."

"We are betrothed. It is my decision."

"You were betrothed to a mortal girl from a powerful family. Tell me, does this witch still hold the lands and titles she once did?"

"Damn lands and titles; I gave her my word."

"And she left you to rot."

"I helped her escape. Does that not make me a traitor to the realm too?"

"You are my nephew. Your only crime was standing by a witch who used you."

Callum pounded his fist on the table. "Stop calling her a witch. She's a woman—a living, breathing, kind woman. And she never forced me to do anything. I loved her all on my own."

His aunt stood. From her side of the table, she looked every bit of the regal leader he used to wish he could be, tall and proud and staring at him as if he were a tantrumming boy.

"And what of your new lover?"

Callum blinked. "Wha—"

"You don't fool me, child. That man could barely keep his eyes and hands off of you."

"He saved my life."

"Quite a number of people are saving your life." She raised a brow.

"I thought that would make you happy."

"I am relieved, of course. You are alive, and I don't have to carry my torch to one of your other petulant cousins." She scoffed. "But that doesn't mean you have to give your life to everyone who saves it."

"I love Emilio." It was the first time he had spoken it aloud, and while he felt the conviction of his words, he was rather disappointed that it was said to her and not him. "And not just because he saved me."

"Of course you do." She waved a dismissive hand. "And what does he think of your deep affection for the wit—for Lady Eve?"

Callum lowered his eyes.

They never had a chance to speak too much about Eve.

"He knows of my past; he knows that I was promised to her. That she was supposed to be my wife."

Lady Tyrina moved to one of the large windows, looking at the cold, but lovely evening outside. He could see clearly under a full moon the tops of the snowy trees and the ponds that were scattered about twinkling under the stars. If the tension wasn't consuming him, he would appreciate it more.

"I do not judge you for your trysts in the capital, but I only wish you had been more mindful of the precarious position you put yourself."

"Trysts?"

She gave him a rueful ghost of a smile. "A prince, a lady, and a lord. You have certainly made connections in the kingdom."

Eryce.

"I—"

She raised a hand to stop him. "As I said, I do not judge you. But to hear these reports from my spies, it is concerning. It means you were not careful. It was most likely why the king brought you to his chambers that night to begin with. You were meant to die in that tower and not because you were betrothed to a witch."

Callum moved toward her. "I don't know what to say."

She sighed. "There is nothing to say, I suppose."

Callum stared out the window alongside her, "I want to do right by her. I do not want to be the man, the ruler, who breaks his promises."

"My dear, promises are for fools. If it is not signed in ink or blood, it is worth nothing."

He shook his head. "I thought Eve was gone. I thought she had escaped, and then to see her . . ." He swallowed, thinking of all the blood of her wounds, wondering if she would die in her sleep. The thought scared him, and he shivered trying to concentrate on hope instead. "She is back, for reasons we have yet to discover. I cannot lose her again, not after all I've been through."

"She is dangerous." His aunt took his face in her hands willing him to meet her serious eyes.

"Then so am I, and if you kill her"—his voice cracked—"you will have to kill me too."

MARC

CHAPTER 36

"We have seen record numbers at our sermons, Your Majesty. The gods have bestowed many blessings and good tidings upon your rule," Borgias said proudly, placing the cup of tea in front of Marc, bowing as he retreated to his chair.

Marc didn't meet his eyes, not bothering to pretend he even cared for something so trivial.

"A-and we have burned nearly seventeen witches this week," Borgias added, taking a seat.

Marc clenched his jaw. "I thought I told you all to start imprisoning the witches. Why are we still burning them?"

"Your Majesty, the dungeons are destroyed,

and there are only so many holding cells throughout the city. They are quite at capacity."

Marc looked about the Gold Council, all the men there were silent and tense as he considered his response. Yet all he could do was fidget with the cup of tea before him, the dark liquid swirling in circles as the tendrils of mist rose from within. He pushed it aside, tapping his foot against the wooden stand of the table relentlessly.

Let us consume them.

It was all he could think about, that insatiable, desperate hunger he wanted to fulfill. The voice beckoned him to madness that made the dark appear like sunlight when it took over. And after...

He didn't like to think about how he felt after.

No matter how many people he consumed, it was not enough, it was never enough for the thing festering inside him.

The voice that begged for power, for magic.

He bit the inside of his cheek. Nearly all the prisoners left over from the fall of the dungeons were mortal.

All those imprisonments and not a single witch.

Marc was losing his grip on whatever this cursed thing within him was—he caught a glimpse of his reflection in the window beside him.

His hair had fallen out in clumps, and what remained were patches of graying strands that made him look very much like his father. His temper swelled every nightfall forcing him out of sleep to unleash his wrath, the lack of rest taking a toll on his once admired body.

Even Jayne, who worshipped the ground he walked on, was horrified when he summoned her to his chambers the night before. He squeezed his eyes shut, recalling her wretched screams as the thing within him took hold of her. And not a single guard dared to open his door to investigate, but sure enough they sent servants to clean the mess when the dawn brought to light his deeds of the night.

Because worst of all, dreadful of all, was his ravenous hunger.

Let us consume them.

Marc tried to ignore it, shaking as he tried to concentrate. He needed witches and needed them very soon.

The thing did not prefer mortal flesh.

"W-what of the ships?" He raised his head to Lord Mateo. "When are we expected to attack the Blackthorn next?"

Lord Mateo cleared his throat. "As soon as it pleases you, Your Majesty."

"Though, I wonder if it is wise to raid a kingdom that may be expecting us," Lord Wesley said, carefully. "My spies say the witches are preparing something particularly concerning."

"Such as?" Marc picked up a quill, bending it in his fingers.

Witches.

"Well, as you know, the witch, Eve, has a sister alive in the Blackthorn. She is rumored to be the reason for the failure of our previous attack."

"Then have one of your spies kill her and be done with it."

"We've tried, but she is heavily guarded."

Marc bent the quill further. "Am I to believe every assassin in our kingdom is occupied? Send them all to kill her then or better yet subdue her and bring her to me."

Yes, bring the witch...

"But, Your Majesty—"

"Lord Wesley, if I am not above sending my own sister to die in the dungeons, what makes you think you're any safer?"

Lord Wesley swallowed. "Your Majesty, I—"

"Make your doves fly and bring me better news on the morrow."

"Yes, but—"

"Which reminds me, have we recovered my sister's body yet?"

Lord Wesley paled. "I was meaning to discuss this with you... in private."

"Why in private? No. Tell me now."

He nodded, searching around the table nervously. "Her body has yet to be recovered, Your Majesty. We believe she may have escaped."

Marc snapped the quill in half as he stood. "Escaped?"

Lord Wesley flinched. "Yes. I have received reports that she was spotted hiding in a tavern. When I sent the city guards, she had already left. We are exhausting every possible resource to find her, Your Majesty, I assure you."

Marc sat back down. "No, let her die out there. By the next moon she will either be dead or held for ransom."

"But, Your Majesty"—Lord Wesley tried to straighten as he spoke—"there is another matter regarding the princess."

Let us consume them.

Marc waved him to continue, holding his head in his hands. He could nearly feel the breath of the voice on his neck, sending shivers there when all he wished for was peace.

"As you know, there is talk of a rebellion growing in the kingdom. The forces are growing strong from Teros to Zafira and Mytar." Lord Wesley straightened. "They are calling to dethrone you and replace you with your sister."

Marc wished he could care, and a piece of his soul buried beneath the thing inside him was rife with fury, but all he could do was clench his head as the voice grew louder.

Lord Wesley continued, "And Rubianes has now joined their forces."

Marc raised his head. "Rubianes?"

"Yes, it appears that Lord Marcelo has received a threat from Teros who is holding his daughter hostage."

Eve.

The witch!

Marc stood, grabbing the end of the table, spitting. "Why in the five hells have I not been told of this?!"

Lord Wesley stood, raising his hands before him. "I only heard of it just before this council meeting, Your Majesty."

"You are telling me that fucking witch lives, my sister has escaped, my greatest ally has abandoned me, and yet you listened as this old man"—he pointed at Borgias—"droned on about sermon attendance?"

He didn't wait to hear his excuse. Marc lifted the table and thrust it on its side, shattering the tea cup, objects, and ink jars on the ground. Everyone stepped quickly away from him.

Marc breathed raggedly, his rage carrying his strength, as he picked up the remnants of the cup and thrust it at the wall. It shattered against the stone, dark tea marks dripped down onto the floor.

"Why are you all here if the kingdom is going to shit?" he shouted at the council. A few flinched and others were scared into mumbling pathetic excuses.

Elder Borgias stepped forward. "Your Majesty, don't stress yourself. I can bring you your calming teas personally—

"I don't want teas, I want witches."

Ser James cleared his throat nervously. "If it pleases Your Majesty, I will go immediately and strategize with my forces to further temper the rebel attacks. We have already reinforced the lands and roads leading to and from the capital. No one comes in that is not meant for the good of the crown."

Kill him.

Marc turned, grabbing his ears with his hands.

Ser James continued. "There is nothing to fear. There will be but a few skirmishes, Your Majesty."

Marc leaned against his chair, trying to think beyond the voice that grew louder. "Take any of the traitors' representatives at court and imprison them. For every day they do not denounce their role in this rebellion, take a limb and send it to their houses."

"Your Majesty," Lord Agustin, who for once looked moderately sober, said, "I denounce my brother's actions at once. I will write to him to do the same."

"You aren't your brother, though, are you?"

Lord Agustin hitched a shaky breath as Marc gestured to the guards to arrest him. They quickly shackled him and removed him from the room. Lord Agustin's voice echoed through the halls, begging for mercy and a chance to speak to Lord Marcelo.

Marc turned to the rest. "Next time I come here each of you better have good news or you will join him."

Consume them.

Marc grunted, shoving his chair aside. He turned to a cup bearer in the corner. "Give me something strong. Now."

The cup bearer ran to the side table filling a cup.

"We are in the middle of war, Your Majesty," Lord Wesley said slowly. "There will be more bad news before it gets better."

Consume them.

Consume them.

Consume them.

The cup bearer handed Marc the cup, and he snatched it, chugging the drink. It cooled his throat and bits of it fell down the sides of his chin and cheeks. He felt fogged and dazed, but still the voice did not stop. It never fucking stopped. He could barely contain his anger and anguish, wanting to tear apart the entire council if it meant a few moments alone in his thoughts. The cup bearer reached out to take it, but Marc threw the cup on the floor, denting the gold.

His limbs shook as he tried to contain the thing within him, threatening to reveal itself to all of them. He couldn't control it anymore. This wasn't what he wanted. This wasn't the power he was promised.

He raised his bloodshot eyes to the council who beheld him with dread.

"I want witches, damn you," Marc breathed. "Bring them to me, every single one."

The men immediately fled the council room, rushing as if Marc himself were chasing them with lances and daggers. Lord Wesley made to join them, but Marc grabbed him by the collar and pulled him back.

"Bring me Talesa."

"Your Majesty, she is the last of the Strix in the castle. The only one who could alleviate your . . . many ailments."

Witch. We need a witch.

Marc pulled Lord Wesley close as he spat the words, his liver-spotted hands shaking. "If you do not return with her, then I will mount your head in this very room."

Lord Wesley tried to gain his footing as Marc shoved him toward the door. "Right away, Your Majesty."

Lord Wesley ran from the room. Marc could hear him shouting from beyond the council room doors ordering the guards to find the last witch he was truly certain of. The one who would give him the reprieve of this painful hunger, the one that took his youth and strength each day.

Marc made his way to the window overlooking the city, holding his weight against the stone windowsill, feeling far feebler than his age would ever suggest. It should have been a typical wintry day in the kingdom full of snowfall that covered the rooftops and the forests beyond, but instead it held clouds of dark smoke that emanated from the city square.

He lifted his hand to the glass, feeling the chill of the morning against his fingertips. It was far too cold lately, in his chambers, this castle, his soul, and even his fingertips barely held the warmth they once did. As he watched the smoke dance into the sky painting it gray, he wondered when he would stop feeling at all.

EVE

CHAPTER 37

EVE DREW BREATH, WARM AND WELCOME. She blinked until her eyes adjusted with the light of morning, a small fire burned in the hearth beside her. Its embers crackled weakly as the wood burned slowly to ash beneath it. Above her was a tall, stone ceiling, the smoke of the hearth crawling up toward it touching the top in a dance of gray hues. The scent of fresh bread would have forced her out of bed if not for her weak limbs and aching head.

She squeezed her eyes shut as the pain woke along with her. Her head, her chest, her bones, every bit of her felt broken and bruised.

But not cold.

Eve slowly looked down. There were

blankets, smooth and silky atop her, and she nearly cried for joy at that alone. She was warm and safe in a soft bed for the first time in ages.

She forced her body to sit up, looking around. There were trinkets along a small, filled bookshelf, a desk, a side table and the bed she rested in. She looked upward to see a green-and-silver shield with a large, dark warhorse painted on its surface—it was affixed proudly above the fireplace mantle.

Teros.

I made it to Teros.

Eve hugged her body, feeling the bandages wrapped around her torso and hands. She was too scared to look beneath them, remembering what Dakon had once told her. Magic is not immortal.

She tried to recall how she arrived, but the only thing she could think of was jumping off the cliff and into the waterfall. She could clearly see the rocks below, waiting to impale her and leave her dying in slow misery. It was a miracle she missed them, a miracle that she even lived through it.

But what of Clarisa?

Goosebumps raised across her flesh, and she pulled the blankets high on her chest. Clarisa tried to kill her, her own flesh and blood. After all these years and Eve trying to find her, all she wanted was Eve dead.

But it wasn't her anymore, though.

Was it?

Eve swallowed. Not if Clarisa's memories were to be believed.

She reached for the chain about her neck, touching the crystal. It felt wrong in her hands. Wrong to be there at all. Eve listened for the *tinking* but it was silent. She wondered when it would return.

She slowly removed it from her neck and faced it to her. There was nothing particularly remarkable about it, only that it was a clear, nearly white crystal with gray smoke moving within.

The oracles.

She wanted to destroy it, wanted to be rid of it like she did the grimoire.

The grimoire.

She pushed herself quickly off the bed, grunting against her injuries. She was in far worse shape than she expected, and the ache in her head pounded relentlessly as the sunlight trickling through the window brightened.

Her feet met the warm, bear-skin rug beneath her as the ends of her thin, white nightgown skimmed her ankles. The dress she had worn in the wastes was nowhere she could see. Someone had undressed her, brought her here to some lord or lady's castle and took her satchel.

She was on the verge of panic, kneeling with her bandaged body to look beneath the bed in vain when a knock sounded at the door.

Eve rolled herself under the bed, startled. It dawned on her that while she may be in Teros, she could also be in the home of someone who wished to turn her in. She felt foolish.

Were they working for the king?

No, then they wouldn't have saved me.

Or would they?

She wished she knew the sentiments of Teros to the crown after Callum's death. Were they angry at Marc . . . or had he blamed it on her too?

The door slowly opened and she could scarcely breathe.

Friend?

Foe?

Death?

She closed her eyes like a child, too weak to summon magic with her wounds screaming for relief. She winced as she lay on the stone floor, trying to stifle her breathing when her visitor spoke.

"A waterfall? Now, Eve, if you missed me, you should have sent a dove like a normal lady."

Her heart stopped.

She opened her eyes, unable to stop the tears that pricked at the corners of them. "Callum," she breathed.

"Eve?" His voice came again; she could see his boots walking into the chamber.

"H-here." She pushed herself out from under the bed, her wounds crying out from the pain. She groaned, lying on the rug. Callum rushed to her, smiling as he bent down to her.

"Lovely as ever."

He lifted her onto the bed, grinning as he placed her blankets carefully atop her once more.

"How long have I been asleep?" she asked, bewildered.

"Too long. I came here to check on you . . . and bring you this." He removed her satchel from his shoulders, placing it on her lap.

She couldn't care less about the grimoire, tossing the satchel next to her. The true miracle was before her, and should she look away she feared he would disappear into thin air.

"Thank you," she managed.

He sat on the bed facing her, his warm hands taking hers. "Eve, you are a vision."

A small blush rose on her cheeks; she had nearly forgotten how charming he was. She took in his bright brown eyes, his hair that had grown considerably since they last saw one another, even his beard. She ran a hand through it.

Has it truly been so long?

She couldn't stop looking at or feeling Callum's face, certain he was a ghost. "I can't believe you're truly here. I can't believe you escaped the knights. You were surrounded, I-I—"

"Yes, there is quite a bit to not believe." Callum took her hand from his face and placed them back in his lap. "But I am so grateful you are alive." He gave them a gentle kiss.

"How did you ever find me?"

"Luck, truly." His gaze darkened. "Eve, what happened to you? You were nearly on the brink of death. If Emilio and I had not found you at the lake . . ." He couldn't bring himself to finish, his wet stare burning into hers.

She turned, shamefully. "I know how it must look."

"Then tell me, help me understand."

Callum stood next to her window, looking outside at nothing in particular. His hands were gripping the edge of the stone windowsill so tight Eve was worried he may break the stone. Time had hardened Callum. He no longer masked his frustration under a veneer of politeness. He shook his head, finally turning to look at her.

Even beneath the blankets and nightgown, she felt exposed and vulnerable. Not a single detail spared between them, every pain and grief laid bare for each other. Tears, now nearly dried, stained her cheeks as she ran her fingers through the fabrics on her lap, certain she would tear them at any moment.

He sat next to her again, tucking a strand of her hair behind her ear. "Well, I did once say that I wanted to hear your thoughts for the rest of my life."

Eve smiled weakly, saying nothing.

"I simply never thought I would get a lifetime's worth in a single morning."

Eve laughed through the tears. "There is nothing more I want than to be a bore again."

He rested his temple next to hers. "Unfortunately, Eve, you are anything but boring."

"Callum," she breathed, "I don't know what to do. I'm lost."

"You are never lost with me, Eve. You are home."

Home.

What was *home* anymore?

She raised her chin to face him, knitting her brow as she took in his hopeful gaze.

"I can still be your home." He kissed her knuckles gently. "Stay here in Teros with me, let me protect you."

His request held more than promise, it held commitment and truth.

Eve's heart dropped as she looked between his hands and his hopeful, though weary, gaze. She could see herself within them, brown eyes to brown eyes, one of sparrows in the summer sun and one of does in the autumn forests. So similar and yet . . .

She could feel the rise of magic within her, weak but present, and she kept her stare as she raised a gentle hand to his cheek and let herself see.

With Callum, she would find safety behind the war-ready, legendary Teros armies. She would free herself from the shackles of Isila and the oracles that took her sister. And time would heal the wounds of their losses.

She could see her and Callum walking among the evergreen trees, dancing under moonlit skies into their old age, and sitting on their bed talking of life and passions until the end of their days. And through it all, he never ceased to look at her as if she were the most precious thing in all of Serit.

But still, there would forever be the faintest hint of wistfulness, of longing, in his eyes.

Eve lowered her hand slowly from his cheek. She could see that look now in his gaze. And perhaps she loved him more for it, because he would keep every oath, every vow, every promise, no matter how it pained a part of him.

They held a bittersweet gaze for a long moment. Her cheeks warmed, her eyes damp. She could scarcely remember the last time she was in someone's arms, breathing the same air, holding such an intimate gaze. He leaned in slowly, carefully, and placed a gentle, welcome kiss on her lips. They were soft and warm. Callum was always warm.

She selfishly wanted to pull him in, knowing this would be the last time she would ever be with him this way. With the entirety of Serit collapsing to war and chaos, it was no secret that when it was all over, this moment would be the last they would spend together truly alone.

Theo.

He entered her mind, bittersweet as she wished she stared into hazel eyes. It brought her back to the fire that consumed her and Callum that day in the king's tower, their long-awaited kiss for others who had long gone to perish. Callum would not be Theo, and neither would she be Eryce.

And that is what would linger between them should she stay. She wished the aching of her heart could be tempered with bandages and ointments like her bruised body, but it still throbbed sad and unwelcome.

She slowly removed her hand from him, and he raised a brow, confused.

"I died somewhere between losing and finding you," she whispered. "The girl you were betrothed to back in the capital is gone forever . . ." She kissed his temple. "I only wish for you to *live*."

"But I want to live with you."

Eve shook her head, repeating. "It is time you lived, Callum."

His lip quivered, tears threatening to fall from the corners of his eyes. For the first time in her life she watched as Callum let go of the mask of propriety before her and choked out a blissful sob. "Thank you."

He placed his hands on the sides of Eve's face. "Thank you," he repeated.

She relented, pulling back slowly. Eve was lonely as they parted, her chest hollow and cold once more.

She wiped her eyes. "I suppose I shoul—"

The door sprung open and inside came a man Eve had never met before, tall with dark eyes and darker hair that fell just above his collar.

"I won't allow it. I won't Callum!"

Eve straightened. "Who is this?"

Callum stood, raising his hands. "Emilio, it's fine."

"No!" Emilio rushed to Callum. "I love you, damn you. Do not go through with this."

"Go through with what?" Eve demanded.

"The sham of a marriage with you. He loves you, but he loves me too!"

Eve couldn't help herself; she crumpled into a fit of giggles like a child.

Callum tried to push Emilio away, but he pointed at Eve. "This is no laughing matter!"

"Emilio, Emilio listen to me." Callum grinned, taking Emilio's face in between his hands.

Emilio tried to speak, but Callum brought him close and pressed his lips on his. Emilio ceased to fight, breathing shakily as Callum released him.

"We are not betrothed," Callum said. "And I love you too."

DAKON

CHAPTER 38

DAKON HATED THE COLD.
If he had enough strength to torch the entirety of the woods to make an everlasting fire, he would do so. He cursed his weak and aching body as the thieves nearly dragged him and Victor to the frozen lake. He could scarcely feel his face or hands when they finally threw them into the snow near the bank, tying their bodies together, backs facing the other.

In the brisk evening, the moon only peeked from behind the cloudy night sky, the stars hidden shyly away. It was fierce, the cold; the thin, crisp air made its way through his body. Dakon's bones ached. The snow, damp beneath his red cheeks, clung to the ends of his copper hair, clumping it together on his face and neck.

Not a soul besides them lingered near the lake, as if this place held only the promise of death and none wished to face it. Dakon squinted his eyes to make out anything besides the tree line and the glint of ice before them, but the light of the torches was weak in the blowing wind.

"Oh, what a pity, I suppose we must return to swim another time on account of ice." Victor feigned a frown. Together, he and Dakon lifted themselves to sit, his trousers and tunic nearly soaked through from the snow.

"Don't you mind that." Julian raised his chin, and the three men raced the edge, pounding their daggers and swords against the ice.

"Now, what fun is it to swim when you can't see any of us?"

"That's the point." Julian sneered, pulling out Dakon's blade and moving down to help the others.

The ice chipped away slowly, the clattering of steel on ice rang in Dakon's ears. It was thick, he was certain, and when they threw them in, it would be near impossible to break the ice from within. He tried to wrestle with his ties in the dark, but his fingers were numb and nearly immoveable.

"Turn into a dragon," Dakon hissed to Victor. "It's cold enough is it not?"

Victor turned his head. "Don't you think I would have if I could? Look around, this is not nearly as cold as the wastes."

"Horseshit. I'm more ice than man."

"You weren't much of a man before this either."

Dakon shoved his head back against Victor's, and he could hear his snicker. "Make me dead weight, and you'll die sooner. I hear drowning is a horrid way to go."

"I don't intend to die."

"I'm quite certain another dead man said that once."

"Oh, and you're ready to?"

"Not at all."

Dakon could nearly feel Victor's smile.

Will he kill me to live?

A raucous cheer pierced the air, and Dakon whipped his head to see the men had finally made a large hole in the ice. They stowed their weapons in their belts and began moving toward them excitedly.

Shit.

"If I must go at least it was in the presence of such endearing friendship," Victor said, coyly.

"Hurry, find a rock or something to fight with."

"No, I'm much too tired."

"Damn you, Dragon, I will not die with you."

The men approached then.

"Victor!" Dakon turned his head, trying to meet the witch's eyes. "This lake is frigid. You'll be able to—"

"Excuse me, gentlemen," Victor called out. "Can one of you kill me now and be done with it. I'd rather not deal with the consequences of my actions."

"What are you doing?" Dakon hissed.

"It is hell to turn into that monstrosity. Might as well end it now." He tried to whistle, but the wind carried it away.

"No." Dakon shoved him. "You'll do it and save me, and then we'll head back to Eve."

"Actually, cut my throat, even death would be entirely more entertaining than this. I beg you."

Dakon tried to feel the magic, but it was still too weak as he tried to burn his ties.

The men stepped in front of them, Julian smiling wickedly. "Ready to swim?"

"We can give you gold, silver," Dakon said quickly.

"Yes, a silver dagger in your throat," Victor grunted.

Dakon shoved him.

"I don't see any of this gold or silver," Julian said.

"We can bring you to the castle—"

Julian and the men cackled. "The castle? The very one they are killing witches left and right? No, if you don't have it here, then you're no good to me now." Julian grinned, his lips cracking from the harsh wind. "All right men, get whatever they have and send them off."

"You already have everything," Dakon said.

"Not quite." Julian and the men snickered.

"If you would have told me I would be stark naked in front of a lake with a familiar that wouldn't shut up, I would have called you mad."

Dakon shivered before the lake, seeing the cold mist of the water within reach up to his face. The men were placing their clothing in satchels as Julian laughed.

"Let them swim!"

The men grabbed him and Victor, shoving them to their knees in front of the broken ice of the lake. He could feel the cold kiss of its waters as his breath made small misty clouds before him.

"L-let us free or you'll regret it," Dakon stuttered.

"I told you to kill me earlier, damn," Victor muttered under his breath. "And you call yourselves true bandits."

Julian knelt next to them, grabbing them both by their hair. The stinging pull of his strands forced Dakon's head up as Julian's breath reeked next to his ear. "I've thought about it, truly I have gentlemen, but I made a promise to my men. And what kind of man would I be if I didn't keep my promises." He released them cackling as he walked away.

The men shoved their faces in the water, the blistering cold unlike anything Dakon had ever felt. It was pure and utter darkness within. He couldn't help but suck in a breath, the water like daggers in his throat.

He felt the pull of his hair and the laughter of the men as he gasped for the bitter cold air.

"Dunk them again!" Julian roared.

"You're going to regret this!" Victor gasped before they were submerged again.

Dakon's head was forced further down, his ears ringing from the blistering pain. There was nothing beneath the ice. Nothing that could save them. Only the sound of silence. Utter, demented silence.

He was pulled once more by the hair, and he gasped, desperate for air, choking on the water coming back up his throat.

"Goodbye, lost boys," he heard faintly in the distance before hands shoved him completely inside the lake.

If Dakon believed the wastes were cold, within the lake was far worse. The moment his body submerged into the depths, he could no longer feel it. He tried to swim up, but his hands were bound so tight behind his back they cut into his skin. He kicked his feet, to reach the light from where they entered, but the current beneath the ice was fierce, pulling him away until he saw nothing but darkness.

Silver birches.
Rose gown.
Lavender flowers.
Spring meadows.
Hazel eyes.
All of it was a vision in the dark.
It wasn't so cold beneath the ice now that he thought of it.
He could scarcely feel the pain anymore.
He could scarcely feel anything anymore.

But he could hear something.

He squinted his eyes, concentrating on the sound.

It roared, shaking the water, reminding him that he was cold once more.

Dakon felt something wrap around his waist, clenching him tight and pulling him to the surface. He barely opened his eyes in time to see the light growing closer until finally he was ripped out of the water and thrust into the snow.

His body was blistered and scarred as he trembled on the freezing ground. The wind howled as he wretched every bit of water he had left in his stomach, the bitter taste breaking through his senses. His vision was a blur as he barely made out his nearly white-blue hands in the snow before him and red sprinkled around. He rubbed his eyes and blinked.

Blood coated the snow before him, he turned quickly seeing the limbs and bodies of the bandits strewn about the edge of the lake. He clamored to his feet as Victor, in his dragon form, nudged him with his snout. Clenched between his teeth were bloodied clothes that Dakon grabbed quickly and threw over his body. Anything to cover himself and block the rising winds.

He nearly fainted as he threw on the boots, only snatching his dagger before Victor lowered his tail before him. With every bit of strength Dakon could muster, he climbed atop.

"Take me somewhere warm, please," Dakon breathed, before falling into a deep sleep.

IZAN

CHAPTER 39

Beneath his dark hood, Izan moved through the crowds like a shadow. People lingered in the dark around him, seeking nefarious pleasures only afforded in the midnight hour. No one bothered him as he rushed quickly through the alleys, his dagger seated firmly in his belt. He passed the familiar stone buildings further into the slums of Zafira's capital and away from the castle walls.

Izan turned at a bend in the narrow pathway, moving past the women who beckoned him into shadows of their own and the men who hissed at him for coins as he brushed past them. He stepped down the small flight of stairs toward a neglected set of homes shackled together with nothing but stone and straw and rotted wood. He ran to the one at the end, not bothering to knock as he entered.

Inside was a feeble woman with long, graying hair sitting on an old chair. A faint candle burned beside her. Her eyes were nearly white, blinded by magic or man, the rumors were never certain. A feral cat with matted, orange fur hissed at him as it ran into the woman's lap.

"You've upset my pet," the woman said.

Izan removed his hood, closing the door behind him. "My apologies, Ria."

"Sit, Izan." She gestured to a stool across from her. "I was expecting you earlier."

"I was a bit preoccupied"—he moved to kneel next to her—"but I am here now."

She felt his face beneath her callused fingers. "You have grown since we last met. The beard suits you. Though the silver in your eyes deceives you."

"I know."

"You come with many questions."

"And to see you, of course."

Ria gave him a ghost of a smile. "You do not fool me, child. You want something bad enough that you would risk showing your face in Zafira."

"Once you answer them, you'll never see me again, I swear it."

"Death comes for us all, Izan."

He stood. "Yes, well. I better get on with it before it finds me here."

"Do you have payment?"

Izan removed a vial from his pocket, handing it to the woman. She closed her eyes, feeling the glass in her hands. The dark liquid moved around inside. "Yours?"

"Only the best," Izan replied, taking a seat on the stool.

"Yes, this should fetch a good price." She pocketed it and ran her hands through the cat's fur. It glared at Izan before standing and walking out of the room.

"You get three," she murmured.

Izan nodded, knowing better than to argue with her. "Where is she?"

"She was in waste."

"Waste," he muttered. It had to be a riddle of sorts.

Sewers?

Slums?

Stalls for horses?

He considered asking for an explanation but thought the better of it. He only had two questions left.

"Where should I go to find her?"

"You won't. She has already found you."

Izan scoffed. "I forgot how unhelpful you can be."

"You aren't here for help. You are here for clarity."

"Isn't that the same?"

"It's never the same."

Izan scoffed. "I feel slightly cheated."

"I'm the one cheated, I have answered three of your questions and am willing to answer one more for less than we bargained for."

Izan shook his head. "How long will it be until I see her again?"

"Not in this life."

Izan stilled.

"Not in this life?"

"I have answered enough, Izan."

He took out his dagger. "Let me give you more."

"No, desperation spoils it, you know that."

The whites of her eyes lingered on him until he looked away uncomfortably. "But there is something else you have that interests me."

"What?" He straightened.

"A certain necklace, can I hold it?" She reached for his neck before he could protest, feeling Eve's sun pendant on a thin, golden chain. A diamond affixed to the center glinted in the candlelight.

"One of mortal heart and wicked nature..."

Izan gently placed his hand over hers. "This isn't for sale."

Her white eyes flicked to his. It unsettled him.

"Everything is, my child."

"Not this." He placed the necklace inside his tunic, standing.

She sat back, grinning, showing off her rotted, blackened teeth. "You do not yet know what you hold, do you?"

Izan clutched the necklace through his tunic. "Why don't you tell me."

Her white eyes stared off behind him. "Anything that carries a witch's blood is powerful, my dear. And that diamond has seen plenty of it."

Eve?

He stepped back as Ria kept her blinded gaze in his direction. "Do be careful out there, Izan. There are more eyes than you know looking for you."

Izan tensed, raising his hood once more. "The Strix have always had eyes."

"Mortal ones may prove your downfall." She cackled and coughed. "Oh, and be mindful of the fire."

In the candlelight, she appeared far more menacing than ever, the shadow of her on the wall growing taller, its limbs reaching out along the wall to grasp him.

Izan took a step back. Her cackling echoed through the room, growing louder. It was time to flee before she drew the attention of other things that lurked in the dark outside.

He raced out, rushing up the stairs to the main narrow path through the alley. He barely turned the corner when he heard the whooshing sound of a blade.

He fell onto his back, the blade barely missing his face as it stuck into the stone next to him.

Someone found me.

He clamored to his feet, taking out his own dagger and turning just in time to see a large, dark animal making its way toward him. Izan stepped back, blade drawn and pulled out the one from the stone. Its eyes were nearly red, its fur like mist enveloped in the shadows of the night.

A gytrash.

Harmless to mortals, but deadly to magic folk.

He turned on his heel, set to run away from the beast when he slammed into someone who shoved him back rough to the ground. His daggers fell, and he couldn't see where they landed in the dark. He looked up, coming face-to-face with a hooded man and the sword he carried angled at Izan's chest.

The gytrash behind him growled, low and menacing.

The pointed steel pushing against Izan's beating heart as he raised his hands, praying neither of them would tear him apart in the slums. He briefly wondered what Adriana would think when he didn't meet her in the morning.

He looked about. No one was in the alley, no one to call for help. Not that they would come. Most would lock their windows and doors, place their hands over their ears and pray that the danger would stay outside their walls.

It's what he would do when he was a boy.

It's what they all did here.

Because unlike the royals hidden behind their guarded palace walls, blood stained the sandy paths of the poor.

"What do you want?" Izan whispered shakily to the man. The man ignored him, raising the sword to his neck, Izan tried to crawl back but the snout of the gytrash stopped him. He stilled, trying not to swallow for fear the sharp blade would pierce his skin.

The man finally spoke. "To find her."

Izan's eyes widened as the man removed his hood, laying it about his shoulders. Out pooled red hair and a long beard barely visible in the midnight hour. He stood tall and brooding, obscuring the moonlight that tried to peek over the tops of the buildings.

"Amarin?" Izan managed. "How did you find me?"

Amarin grabbed him by the collar, his sword still taut against Izan's neck. "You betrayed them, you betrayed me."

"I—I did. And I'm sorry."

"Easy to apologize when you have a sword at your throat."

"Easy to ask for one when you have a sword and a throat to shove it in."

Amarin grunted, shoving Izan aside. "Give me one reason why me or my wolf shouldn't kill you."

"His name is Beast." Izan coughed. "This is Dakon's gytrash."

Amarin faced Beast, who focused on bearing his teeth to Izan.

"Gytrash, wolf. Doesn't seem to care for you, should make this easy enough."

He doesn't know how to use one...

"Gytrashes aren't guard dogs." Izan raised himself slowly against the wall of the alley. "They are meant to lead you when you're lost... or send you astray."

Amarin didn't lower his sword. "So, can it help me find Eve?"

"It's not a map; if it likes you well enough it'll take you where it thinks you need to go."

"Then why in the five hells did it take me straight to you?"

"I'm asking that myself." Amarin's sword was nicking his skin, and he pushed his chin up to give him a reprieve. "What use is my death to you?"

Amarin cocked his head. "Cassandra."

Shit.

Izan swallowed. "She wants everyone dead at one point or another."

Amarin seemed to consider this. "Why did you do it?"

"Because when she and the Strix gave me an order, I did it. Same as you."

"I would have never turned her in."

"I didn't turn her in. I changed my mind after the siren attack. I swear. I had no idea they were waiting to attack us in the Mistral Islands."

"Why not fucking tell me?"

"And say what? I thought they were gone. I couldn't even make it back to the ship after they took her. I had to stowaway on theirs just to follow them. I barely made it inside the castle after them."

"Is she dead?" Amarin's sword hand shook.

Izan lowered the tip of the blade. "No. I found them in Givensmir before they disappeared with a book. I don't know where."

"She has it." Amarin was conflicted, his gaze going quickly between his sword, the gytrash, the empty alley, and Izan's eyes.

Izan continued. "Now you know as much as I do. Eve is alive. I don't know about her companions, but with the gytrash we could find her together. It is bound to you for some reason."

"How do I know you aren't lying to me?"

"You wanted to find me to find her, is that right? And did the gytrash not lead you straight to me?"

Amarin took a step back, lowering his sword.

Izan let out a shaky breath. "Eve is all I want. Desperately. I have given my own blood to find her. I will spill more to make sure she is safe. I know my word is shit now, but I swear with any bit of trust I might have left with you, I am telling the truth."

Amarin narrowed his eyes. "For your sake, I hope so."

The words barely parted from his lips when screams echoed throughout the alley. Izan turned to Amarin, confused. Beast was gone.

Shit.

A crowd of people ran down the end of the alley toward them. Others woke from their homes, rushing out to see all the commotion.

"The castle, it's on fire!" someone cried out as they passed them.

Izan's heart sank.

Adriana.

"What the fuck is going on?" Amarin asked over the shouting.

Izan looked between him and the flames in the distance. He grabbed Amarin by the shoulders shouting back, "Head for your ships, take heed of the gytrash to lead you to her."

He began to run, but Amarin clenched his arm tight. "Where the hells are you going?"

"I have another oath I'm bound to." Izan gave him a desperate look, taking Eve's necklace from his pocket and handing it to Amarin. He didn't wait for Amarin to ask as he shouted. "Now, go! Find her!"

Amarin released him, and Izan didn't turn back, rushing against the crowd. And toward the fire.

ADRIANA

CHAPTER 40

SHOUTS IN THE NIGHT RIPPED ADRIANA from her sleep.

She opened her eyes to flame and the scent of blood in her chambers. The smoke, thick and heavy in the air, nearly choked her as she leapt off her bed and raced toward her balcony. She looked over, seeing hundreds of men in armor fighting against the Zafira guards not far below. Blood spilled onto the sand and walls of the castle, and Adriana watched in horror as Lord Ybara was brought before them.

"You can have whatever you wi—" he cried out.

But a knight in golden armor didn't

bother to let him finish as he swung his sword and took off Lord Ybara's head in one stroke.

Golden armor.

He's found me.

Adriana could barely move in horror. Lord Ybara, the man who promised her an army was dead. She could nearly breathe with how quickly she gasped at the gruesome sight. She stepped back hearing the screams of handmaids and servants filling the castle. The men in golden armor threw torches into whatever windows they could. One flew in her direction and she ducked just in time, but the torch caught the curtains, setting them quickly ablaze.

Adriana pushed herself away from the balcony, running into her chamber and thrusting open her door. The corridors were in chaos; people ran amuck with wounds or on fire. She swerved to miss a fallen, burning tapestry that banged against a guard cowering in an alcove. Outside, the open windows were filled with black smoke and the orange-red hues of fire. Golden armor glinted, and Adriana hurried away from it. The sounds of smashing of objects and cries of death behind her sent her running to the stairs for Izan's room.

She climbed the steps as fast as she could. People shoved her aside as they raced down. She was pushed against the banister, which groaned beneath her weight, until she fell to her hands and knees crawling up the final steps as they trampled upon her.

Adriana screamed Izan's name, but she couldn't even hear herself through the sounds of swords and panic. On the higher floor, there were few people running for the stairs, and she clambered to her feet, moving in time as they rushed down. She ran to the door near the end of the hall that she remembered Izan staying in and didn't bother pounding on the door as she pushed it open. Flames nearly consumed her, forcing her back.

They roared to life, and Adriana panicked knowing no one could survive such a beast of a fire.

"Izan!" she screamed, crying as she ran from the flames. Her only protector was gone, and she didn't know what else to do or where to run. Golden armor shined against the flames as one of the knights raced up the stairs.

Adriana ran for her life further down the hall, trying to make the next set of stairs down below. But as she reached the first step, she saw more of the men rushing up from the bottom. She looked back, the knight was running toward her, but if she ran down they would catch her there too. She looked to the banister, clutching it with shaky hands. Below was nothing but smoke and fire; she couldn't make out anything else in the dark.

I have to jump.

Even if it kills me.

Marc will kill me worse than anything at the bottom.

Adriana cried as she lifted herself onto the banister, nearly jumping when rough hands grabbed her back. She screamed, fighting against their hold.

"It's the princess!" one of the men yelled. "We've found her!"

Adriana spat and clawed and kicked to rip herself from his arms, but he wouldn't let go as more came.

"Help!" she screamed to no one, anyone.

"The king's been looking for you," the knight said, shoving her away from the banister.

"Let me go!"

"And miss a mighty high price for your head?" The knight cackled, pulling her toward the stairs.

"She said let her go!"

Adriana whipped her head to the voice in time to see Izan stab the knight in the neck. He released his grip on her, and Adriana pushed herself away, running to Izan.

"Izan!" she cried. "I thought you were dead!"

Izan gripped her in a fierce hug. "I'm sorry I'm late, My Queen."

He pulled her by the hand as they rushed down the other set of stairs. Adriana choked and coughed against the intensity of the smoke. She could barely make out movement in the thick of it, golden armor and servants clothes ran to and fro, the latter screaming and crying for mercy.

"This way, quick!" she heard Izan's voice through it all.

They reached the bottom landing and raced down another corridor. She could see the doors leading outside wide open as she and Izan pummeled through it, choking on the smoke and gasping for the clean air outside. He pulled her hand to run once more when another shout rang out.

"Stop! By order of the king!"

Adriana raised her head; they were surrounded by dozens of knights. Izan pulled Adriana behind him, raising only his dagger.

"Come now, you've lost. Let the princess go."

Adriana stilled.

She knew that voice.

Slowly, as if time had slowed to her shallow breaths, she turned to see him.

Timothy raised his long sword, grinning at her. "Did you miss me, Princess?"

No.

"Take a step, and I will slice you open," Izan said.

Timothy smirked. "The numbers are not in your favor, peasant. There are at least fifteen of me and only one of you."

Adriana couldn't stop trembling as the men closed in on them, all of them armed with swords. She could feel Izan shaking, too, but he didn't lower his dagger.

"Take a step and you die," he seethed.

"Fine," Timothy raised his hands.

Adriana blinked, confused, but then felt her hair pulled back. A knight ripped her from behind Izan, and he turned just in time for another knight to stab him in the back.

His eyes widened, his mouth went slack, and the silver hues in his eyes turned dark as he fell.

"M-my Queen."

"No!" she screamed. "Izan!"

More knights pummeled him to the ground as the one holding on to her shoved her roughly to Timothy, throwing her on her knees before him. She cried out, watching helplessly as the knights threw Izan's body into the roaring flames of the castle.

Timothy bent to her, placing a hand on her shoulder.

She smacked his hand away, crawling away from him. But he only laughed. "I'm a man of my word, Princess. Isn't that what you most admired about me?"

He gripped her arm, bringing her to her feet. "Now look at the mess you've made." He dropped his sword, and with his free hand gripped her face to look upon the carnage of the castle. Hot tears sprung down her cheeks, and she tasted blood, wishing she had the strength to rip Timothy apart. "This is something no ordinary kiss will save you from I'm afraid." He sighed, smiling.

Adriana spat at him, and he released her; she fell hard on the ground as the knights returned to grab her.

"Oh, you are going to regret that, *Princess*."

Timothy looked to the guards. "Take her into one of the open cages. Let her see what the people truly think of her on the ride back home." He shoved her toward them, and she was quickly shackled and taken in nothing but her nightgown.

As Adriana was thrown in the back of a caged cart, riding away from the fire that had become Zafira's capital, she could only cry hot, angry tears. They burned as they fell down her face and onto the straw riddled floor. There was nothing she wanted more than to see Timothy burn like that fire. She would do everything she could; in this life or next, she would see him burn.

PART 3

THE BATTLE OF MORTALS & MAGIC

*A storm approaches as the winds of the
west tear our sails asunder.
Outside my cabin door, I can hear the shouts
of sailors trying to temper its fury.
I opened it ajar a moment ago to peek at the chaos unfolding
and saw the monstrous lands beyond the horizon drifting
above the sea in the distance like clouds in the sky.
It is a tale I have heard once in a book I
cannot recall at this present moment.
Though the message is clear.
Magic will plague the lands of Givensmir once more.
The sea reaches my porthole, beckoning me to let it inside.
But I write with ink I have unfortunately smeared on this
parchment for a distraction of its relentless tapping and
from the half-witch who will awake at any moment.
I can hear the calls to ready the weapons outside.
Time will not favor the wicked as we begin our assault.
But in my final moments, I must make
my darkest declarations known.
What is a prophecy but a curse of distraction
to its most ardent followers?*

— RECOVERED ENTRY OF ARIS,
HIGH PRIEST OF THE BLACKTHORN

THEO

CHAPTER 41

"**D**ON'T LOOK BACK, WHATEVER YOU do. It will wear down the spell and both of you will be seen," Rinya whispered to Theo. "Keep your head straight and your body forward. When the sun rises at high noon, you will be safe to look as you please."

Midnight neighed from a nearby tree atop the rocky hill, and Rinya glanced back, shushing her. Rain fell as it did every night and day, this time carrying bits of hail that pelted at his cloak. He pulled the hood tight against his face, though it did little to resist the damp droplets that buried themselves in the fabric, making their way to his skin. He shivered beneath it, hoping the weather beyond the Blackthorn was fairer.

The three of them—he, Ana, and Rinya—stood at the edge of an isolated cove. The dark water reached the shores, trying to claw at their boots. Beyond was nothing but a horizon blended between gray skies and grayer waters. He wondered if anyone was watching them, or if the Blackthorn crown gave up their search for them completely.

He hoped for the latter.

Theo looked between her and the small boat resting on the sand. Its sails were fashioned with cheap fabrics, its wood gnarled in spots; the inside barely had enough room to fit he and Ana and some supplies to last them for a short journey.

If they were lucky, it would lead them to the Mistral Islands in a couple of days. Though, admittedly he was not much of a sailor and doubted Ana was as well. This journey would either kill them over the Dallise or save their lives if they landed in the right place with people who did not recognize him.

He looked to Rinya. "Thank you, again. I don't know how I could ever repay you."

"Keep my daughter safe. Don't let Prince Navir find her. That is all I ask."

"You have my word."

He turned to Ana. "I will give you both a moment." He made his way to the boat, ensuring the food sacks and waterskins were tied tight inside the boat. There were a few blankets folded at one end of the boat from their cart, a few ropes, daggers, and not much else. It was enough, barely, but enough.

Selfishly, he was glad that he would not have to brave the journey alone. Though he wished that Ana did not have to flee her home either. Certainly, her saving him marked her as a traitor. And if the rumors of the Blackthorn were to be believed, traitors suffered worse fates than mortals who crossed the crowns.

He heard Ana approaching and turned to help her inside. She

huddled on the far side of the boat, her eyes swollen and red, biting her lip. Theo cleared his throat uncomfortably as he positioned himself behind the boat.

"Are you ready?"

Ana sniffled. "No."

Theo gave her a sympathetic nod and pushed the boat into the water. Together they rowed until they reached the far end of the cove and finally the water took them further away from land. Theo adjusted the sails best he could remember and hoped. As he did when he was saved from the castle by Ana and how he did every night for Eve's safety before he fell asleep.

Ana cried quietly to herself and all the while, both of them faced away from the land, not daring to look back. Because what Rinya didn't mention was that the sun didn't show at high noon in a land that was destined to rain forever.

THEO HANDED ANA A BUNDLE OF PURPLE GRAPES, AND SHE TOOK them carefully in her palms. Their waterskins were thankfully full, and he untied one, taking a small sip before giving it to her. It had been nearly a full day, and they hadn't spoken much. The graying skies turned to silver-blue hues that battled in the winter season. He wished he knew where they were headed and hoped that if it was the shores along Givensmir that he would be able to find refuge with friendly allies—Teros, Zafira, maybe even the Mistral Islands, if Marc hadn't usurped their family there.

Ana handed the waterskin back, and Theo tied it with the others.

"What is your plan when we finally get off this wretched boat?" he asked, as he finished the knot.

Ana, who had been staring out to sea turned to him. "I'm not sure."

"Come now, we can't be far from land. You can talk to me."

She sighed. "I suppose find others like me or blend in with the mortals. Though, I do not wish to stay in Givensmir long, just enough to buy passage somewhere new. Or stowaway on a ship if I can help it."

"Outside of Serit?"

"At the very least. I hear there are lands that are far more tolerant of witches and other magic folk. A paradise of sorts."

Theo sat up. "Paradise sounds like a folktale."

"Perhaps, but better to find out than wonder, isn't it?"

Theo gave her a soft smile. "Well then I wish you the greatest luck in finding this paradise."

She nodded. "And you? You've gone from prince to prisoner and now a fugitive of both crowns."

Theo cleared his throat. "Sounds far more treacherous when you say it so."

"I'm sorry, that was forward of me."

"No, no. It's the truth." Theo shrugged. "But I only want to find Eve. If it means traveling to whatever world is out there beyond Givensmir, so be it."

Ana smirked. "And do what exactly? Apologize for abandoning her?"

"It would be a start, yes."

"I would say it's romantic, but knowing you mortals, you will lose interest once the season has passed."

"Not at all. She is worth a thousand seasons at least."

Ana leaned to stare into the water, her chin resting on her hand. "Ah, so it is numbered."

Theo ignored her. "What about Clarisa? You left her."

"I had no choice." Her voice faded as she spoke, not a hint of anger, but doleful.

"Do you think she will get better?"

Ana tapped the water with her finger. It rippled beneath her touch. "I wish I knew."

Theo lay back, watching as the blue-black clouds moved slowly overhead. The rain had ceased earlier that day, and though it was cold as the evening began to set in, it was not unbearable. He felt excited and nervous at the prospect of nearing the end of his escape. He wondered if Eve felt the same.

"Do you think they think of us?"

Ana touched the water again. "Of our betrayals? Certainly. Of the love we shared before it all? Perhaps when they are lonely."

"Lonely?" Theo couldn't help but laugh.

Ana raised her eyes to him, grinning. "I imagine you've thought of your dear Eve far more in captivity than you ever had when you were next to her. Loneliness is a heart in turmoil."

"You say it so poetically."

"What is life but a long poem of tragedy and happiness?" She sighed.

"Fair point."

The sound of a squawk caught his attention, and he sat up quickly. Ana removed her hand from the water and twisted her body to see it. A rather large seagull glided through the air, diving its beak into the water and coming out empty handed. It flapped its wings and turned away from them toward a few specks in the distance. Hidden behind the darkened evening fog was the faintest outline of land, a few ships, and a small boat.

Theo nearly jumped to his feet. "Do you see that?!"

Ana pulled herself up, her eyes wide as she beheld it. "We've made it somewhere."

Theo's heart leapt in his throat, this part of his journey was nearing its end, and he only hoped that wherever they were it was not among enemies.

Please, please let this end well.

NAVIR

CHAPTER 42

Navir sat in the captain's quarters, looking over the maps.

He wasn't certain how long they had been sailing through the Dallise, only that the sea witch had tried to slow them at every turn. One would think the Strix had promised her immortality with how hard she tried to bury his fleet.

After being forced south in a tumultuous storm, she finally relented, and he adjusted course to Givensmir once more.

Navir only hoped the element of surprise was still a viable option, as his spies reported the mortals planned to attack the Blackthorn before the next moon. He was left with no choice but to fight and be the first to draw blood.

Clarisa was recovering in the healer's quarters below deck and had yet to show any improvements. During this journey he swayed between wanting to throw her in the sea and holding out hope that the prophecy still had a chance to reveal itself through her.

But even better, if Eve was still working for the mortals, there was a good chance he could use Clarisa as leverage. With the oracles driving her to insanity by now, she would be begging for help or a witch to consume. He would have both at his disposal.

Aris sat across from him, silently taking notes in his book.

Navir stood, tossing his quill on the desk. Outside his window, he could see dozens upon dozens of his warships and transport vessels black as the night they sailed in. He needed to time his assault right, ensure they attacked before any of the mortals could rally enough forces against them.

Witches were not known for their fighting abilities, but perhaps with the right conditions they could sway the mortals from any future raids under his rule until he had enough to conquer them completely.

But that is another matter . . .

There was a knock at the cabin door and Navir looked to it, then to Aris.

Aris clamored out of his chair, walking to crack open the door.

"What is it?" Aris asked, impatiently.

The voice on the other side answered but Navir could barely hear him. Aris paled, turning to face Navir.

"What is it?" Navir demanded.

"They've found them," Aris breathed in disbelief.

Navir stilled. "Both of them?"

Aris nodded slowly. "Three of them, in a small boat. They've taken them aboard."

Navir grinned. "Well, bring them in."

Navir sat behind his desk, hearing the commotion on the other side of the door. Aris stood beside him nervously. Navir bristled at the sound of his fiddling hands.

There was another shout of protest, this time louder than the one before. Clearly their new prisoners were not going without a solid fight, banging and thrashing against the walls of the ship leading all the way to his cabin. It was music to Navir's ears.

The door swung open and it took nearly five witches to hold the two prisoners, even in their iron chains. They brought them to their knees, their hoods covering their faces.

Navir got to his feet, nearly running toward them. He took out a blade, ready to mangle their faces for daring to defy him.

"Remove their hoods." Navir gestured to his witches. His hand was twitching with excitement as they pulled off the leather sacks from their heads with a bit of resistance.

But once they were exposed, Navir was sorely disappointed.

There must be some mistake.

He stood, turning to Aris. "I thought you found three of them!"

Aris flinched, stepping back. "That's what I was told." He turned to the witches. "Did you not tell me we had found our escapees?"

"Apologies, we must have spoken incorrectly, but these are her familiars," one answered.

Aris let out a shaky breath, waiting for Navir's response.

"I know who they are, damn you." Navir knelt before the familiars looking upon the bloodied, battered faces of Tabor and Brisa. He stowed his knife, feeling too furious to do anything but laugh.

He lifted Brisa's chin to face him. It was clear these familiars had been out at sea for quite a while with their blisters and gaunt cheeks. He idly wondered how they even managed to escape and where the boat had come from.

He pinched Brisa's cheeks hard and tears sprung in her eyes. "Should I kill the witch who gave me hope?" he asked her, almost kindly. "I'll let you play executioner this time."

She trembled at his touch.

"Leave her alone!" Tabor spat.

Navir released her, looking to Tabor. He lifted a brow. "Or what?"

Tabor's nostrils flared, but the hint of uncertainty in his eyes was all Navir needed.

Navir smirked. "You're both quite lucky my ships found you. Not many would give two stranded witches a second glance. No, they would have left you to be picked on by hungry birds or whatever likes to dwell in the sea." He stood. "And if someone picked you up out here in the middle of the water where none could hear your screams, I could imagine all the heinous things they would do to you."

"Damn you."

"No, it is you who are damned. What kind of familiars leave their witch in their time of need? She has taken quite the beating since you left and all for what? You haven't even made it onto mortal land. You never had a fighting chance to escape now did you?"

"You are nothing without her magic, and she is everything without you," Tabor said. He lifted his chin taking a swift breath. "But the Clarisa we know is gone. You saw to that."

"I suppose you're right. These oracles are nasty beings. It has taken nearly my entire dungeon to keep her satisfied."

Brisa gasped. "No."

"Yes." Navir lifted his lips. "She's become quite the monster. But there does seem to be one problem."

Neither of the familiars answered as Navir picked up his knife, twirling it in his hands.

"One fight with her sister, and she has come back broken. One would say nearly mortal. It makes me wonder . . ." He slashed Tabor's cheek, so quickly he hadn't a chance to flinch. "Thank you for that."

Navir took the knife and shook the blood inside of an empty cup. "It makes me wonder if you are mortal too."

Tabor tried to stand.

"Oh, that won't be necessary," Navir said, handing the cup to Aris who began adding the ingredients inside. One of the witches pushed Tabor back down as Brisa moved against him, trying to hide from Navir's lingering stare.

Aris handed the finished cup back to him.

Navir lifted it before the familiars. "Now if I drink this will it be blood or magic?"

Neither of them answered. Tabor clenched his jaw, turning away. Brisa closed her eyes, still shaking in the witches' grips.

Navir drank until the cup was empty.

"Well, Your Majesty?" Aris asked trepidatiously.

Navir grinned. "I say we toss them overboard and see how their water magic works."

Tabor angrily tried to rush Navir; Brisa pushed and kicked against the witches, but to no avail. They were weak, famished, and lacked drinking water. Their fight was in vain, and Navir watched smugly as they were pulled from his cabin with curses under their breaths.

"Are you going to see?" Aris asked when the cabin was empty. He could still hear their screams through the door.

"No," Navir replied, looking out his window.

Aris swallowed. "Your Majesty?"

Navir didn't bother to face him, watching the evening settle as he pulled out his handkerchief and wiped the blood from his lips. "I already know the answer."

CLARISA

CHAPTER 43

"*Clarisa.*"

"*Clarisa.*"

She stilled.

"*Clarisa, come here my child.*"

Panic seized her heart, as she turned to and fro trying to find the source of the voice. She heard the crumbling of stone somewhere nearby, and a light filtered through the ceiling to her right. Clarisa backed away from it, running down the corridor.

"*Clarisa.*"

The voice, it sounded familiar, soft and gentle from a memory she could no longer recall but one that awakened some part of her soul that craved the presence of another.

Is someone else lost here too?

She continued running down the hall, the stone ceiling crumbing around her, the walls trembling, the floors littered with rock and dust. And all the while the voice beckoned her with its soothing lilt. It lured something in her, something she tried so desperately to understand, to remember.

Who is this?

Why is the castle falling apart?

She reached the end of a hall with a few doors before her. She looked between them, but they were all the same—dark wood with silver embellishments and a ringed knob. Clarisa didn't have a chance to peek within each one as the castle was falling to pieces around her. She shoved open the first one and raced inside just as a large rock pummeled to the ground where she had stood not even seconds prior, smashing into thousands of pieces.

She shut the door quickly behind her and the room stilled. Not even the faintest tremor beneath her feet. She squeezed her eyes shut as she rested her forehead against the wood. She breathed heavily, trying to calm the furious beating of her heart and control her trembling hands.

"You made it, you made it," she breathed.

Slowly, she opened her eyes and turned.

Before her was not a misty, gray existence, but a bright set of marble stairs leading around to the top of a tower.

"Clarisa."

It didn't sound menacing, but warm.

Ana.

Eve.

Navir.

She repeated their names as she tried to recall the others but couldn't.

Certainly her list was longer, wasn't it?

Her curiosity led her to take the first step. Here, the stone was not broken, the windows not cracked, the fog did not appear to reach this high in the castle. She peered out of the windows carved into the walls as she climbed the steps.

She watched as the gentle sea rocked against the shore, as the sun sank in the distance beyond the horizon. The birds flitted through the sky, their chirping like a song of hope and promise to her ears. She wanted to join them, to jump out and fly with them to the ends of the sea.

She nearly did so, climbing onto the windowsill and feeling the breeze on her face, as the birds whispered for her to take that final step, when she heard the voice again.

"Clarisa, I need you to come here."

The birds flew away, and Clarisa stopped, lowering her gaze. It was a long way down from this stairwell window in this strange tower.

Below there was only gray. It was always gray, wasn't it?

She carefully stepped down from the window and continued walking up the last steps.

When she reached the landing, there was a final door and she pushed it open. Inside was a forest, shrouded in twilight and filled with trees and brush.

She could scarcely believe her eyes as she stepped inside.

An owl flitted across her vision and she moved back, expecting to feel the door behind her, but felt nothing but air.

She whirled around.

And there stood her mother.

She felt like a frightened child, wanting to run into her mother's arms for comfort, but Clarisa couldn't do anything but stare. The moon's glow shone through the tops of the trees, bathing her mother's beautiful face in light. Clarisa nearly forgot how her mother looked, time had repressed the memory of her long, chestnut strands that cascaded down her back that she would sometimes brush as a child, and her sweet, kind eyes most reserved for her daughters.

Eyes that nearly mirrored Clarisa's.

She hitched a breath. Before her was a painting, an art, ethereal beauty unmarred by the hands of mortals all those years ago.

"Clarisa," her mother said gently, "I've been calling for you."

Clarisa still couldn't speak, the vision of her mother more surprising than finding herself in a strange tower that held strange forests.

Powerful magic, indeed.

Her mother lifted her hand. "Come, my dear."

Clarisa felt herself move, her feet taking each step so gracefully she was nearly floating. Her mother touched her face as if she couldn't believe Clarisa were here either.

Her touch felt warm and inviting, she felt real. Alive.

"How I've missed you, Clarisa." Her mother placed a gentle kiss on her temple.

"Are you really here?" Clarisa asked. "Please tell me I am not alone."

Her mother held her close. "You are never alone, even when I am not in front of you."

Clarisa considered this, as she heard the wind rustling through the trees. She raised her head, "Where are we?"

"Somewhere near the king's castle."

"In the Blackthorn?"

"Givensmir."

Clarisa turned. This forest did look faintly familiar, but she couldn't quite place it. Not yet.

"Why are we here?" She loosened her grip on her mother.

Her mother pointed toward the brush as two small figures emerged from it, one holding on to the other as they rushed past them. They didn't seem to notice Clarisa or her mother as they ran through them.

Is that . . .

Her mother held her hand. "Watch and see."

CLARISA

CHAPTER 44

Sixteen Years Ago

RUN TO THE COVE.
Get on the ship.
Find Captain Amarin.
Go to the Blackthorn.

Clarisa repeated Borgias's instructions to herself, committing them to memory as best she could as they hurried through the thick, dark forests of the Givensmir realm. She held her sister's hand as they broke through low-hanging branches, bushes, and spiderwebs barely seen in the faint moonlight that trickled through the tops of the trees. Her legs were screaming for relief, her lungs were on fire, and she tried to keep her tears at bay as Eve sobbed beside her.

She could hear the horses and calls of the knights in the distance. They had to move faster.

Clarisa looked down at her sister, a frail, frightening child that she had tricked out of her room and through the broken stone wall with promises of playing a game in the forest. Anything to lure her away from the castle as quietly as possible.

She felt ashamed as she pulled Eve roughly through another tangled set of bushes, but she began to pull away.

"Where is mother?" Eve cried out, as Clarisa practically dragged her now through the wilderness.

"Shh," Clarisa said, kneeling down to a trembling Eve, "we have to be quiet or they'll find us."

She panted deeply, trying to catch her breath as the shouts grew closer.

There isn't enough time for this.

She pushed her long, dark hair away from her cheeks as it tried to cling to the sweat there and grabbed Eve's petrified face between her hands. "Mother wants us to go on a boat ride, a ship, a big ship that will take us to a fantasy land. But if we don't leave now, we will miss it."

Eve's lip trembled. "But what about father? Or Theo?"

Clarisa felt the tears prick as she lied too easily. "They will be waiting for us there." She wiped her sister's eyes and brushed her knuckles shakily along her reddened cheeks. "But if the knights catch us, we may never see them again. Do you understand? We have to run until we feel we are flying."

Eve only nodded, her eyes full of panic as she gripped her hand.

Clarisa stood, hearing the barking of hounds; they were too close now.

Borgias's warning echoed in her ears.

I can only give you enough time to escape but whatever you do, you must not let them catch you.

She turned her dark eyes sharp and focused on the unmarked path ahead of them, she knew it led to the cove. And if they made it there, they only had to climb down and run for the boat that waited for them.

It had to be there.

She pulled Eve to follow her and to Clarisa's surprise her sister kept pace until they slowed, gasping for air against one of the trees. They were near the edge of the forest now. She could see the edge of the cove in the distance and the twilight turning to the faintest pink over the sea's horizon.

We're almost there.

Eve cried once more, taking in choking, sobbing breaths as she tried to calm herself. Clarisa tried to understand, tried to feel a morsel of sympathy for the child before her, but all that clouded her mind was the hounds that growled and the fearsome knights that rode ever closer toward them.

If they didn't escape, their mother would die.

Borgias had made it clear.

"I'm scared, Clarisa." Eve trembled, staring toward the dark woods. Clarisa followed her gaze, the trees, tall and spindly here were like shadows waiting to embrace them.

"I'm scared, too, Eve," Clarisa breathed, looking fiercely into Eve's eyes. "Mother would want us to be brave for her. Can you do that?"

"I want to go home."

"Me, too. But we are going to a new home, a better home. I promise," Clarisa replied.

"Why did we have to leave? Why isn't mother coming with us?"

"Mother is always with us, always."

"But I want her here, please. I don't want to play anymore."

Clarisa pulled Eve in a brief hug. "Look there." She pointed, beyond the edge of the forest nearby. There, the rocky cove waited for them, all they needed to do was climb down, and they would be safe, she repeated to herself. "We are so close, and once we get to the ship we will see everyone again, I promise."

Eve nodded, tears falling from her chin to the ground as Clarisa took her hand again. "But first, we need to run one more time."

The girls rushed, just as a hound broke through the trees.

"Over there!"

The moments before they ended up in the forest took over Clarisa's mind as she raced with Eve's hand in hers.

She wished they were able to give their mother a final goodbye before Borgias ushered them into the tunnels with nothing but the shoes on their feet. She recalled trying to quell her rising panic as she distracted Eve with promises of play as they were lost in the depths of the castle, hidden behind walls with no sense of direction. It was pure luck that she even found the cellar door that led them to the broken stone wall where they raced out of the castle gates.

She turned, seeing the peak of the castle towers far in the distance. This was her home, their home, in the court of Givensmir. And now it was nothing but a speck in the distance, hidden behind the tall trees that blocked their view. She felt the stinging on her face as branches swiped at her, trying to keep her within its thorny depths.

A hand barely clenched her sleeve, but she pulled away just in time.

Clarisa and Eve never ventured outside of the castle walls and never needed to. Their father was a close friend to King Paul. He was a lord of one of the richest lands and houses in the kingdom; they had everything they ever wanted there. Their mother was a royal enchantress. Clarisa herself was primed to take her post in a few years. They were noble, good daughters beloved by all who knew them. And yet, they were running for their lives, for the life of their mother for reasons unknown.

She couldn't imagine a single reason why they would be forced to escape like prisoners far away from their paradise on earth.

But she wouldn't forgive herself if her mother died for her hesitation.

They passed the threshold of the forest, and Eve slipped on the rock.

"Clarisa!" she screamed as she tried to pick herself up, but her leg was weak. "Don't leave me!"

The hounds broke through the brush, growling and barking as they went. Men raced on foot and horse, closing in the distance. She had a moment, a single solid moment to turn to the edge of the cove. Below was a small boat and just beyond the water was a ship waiting in the distance. But they needed to climb now. Now or never.

"Stop!" one of the knights yelled.

Clarisa whirled around, rushing to carry Eve with all the strength she could muster. Together, they made it to the edge of the cove, pulling themselves down.

"It hurts, Clarisa!" Eve cried out as she tried to bear weight on her foot against the rock face.

Clarisa looked down. It was a drop, but not too far. She could make it and catch Eve. She could make it if she tried. "I'm going to climb down, and then I want you to let go. Promise me you'll let go, and I will catch you."

"I can't hold on!"

"Try, please!"

She lowered herself as fast as she could, missing the final rock and falling on her back against the sand of the beach. She coughed, her vision blurring as the knights finally reached the edge.

"Eve!" Clarisa screamed at her sister. Eve was petrified, holding on to the rock face with a fierce grip.

"Jump, I will catch you!"

"I'm scared!"

"Stop, both of you, stay where you are!" She looked further up, the knights were removing their armor, reaching out to Eve.

"Eve," Clarisa screamed, her voice raw, "let go!"

She shook watching her sister tremble, terrified. She nearly thought she wouldn't do it, that they would both be caught and taken to a dead mother. But Eve released her hands, falling.

Clarisa opened her arms, readying herself to catch her.

But Eve never made it.

A hand gripped hers, yanking her up back to the edge.

It was her father.

Her father pulled a kicking and screaming Eve back over the edge.

"No!" Clarisa cried.

"We need to leave!" Someone rushed to Clarisa, pulling her toward the boat. "Hurry!"

Clarisa fainted as she watched her sister pulled away and the hands of someone strong carried her away to sea.

EVE

CHAPTER 45

It had been nearly a full moon since her discussion with Callum, and Eve felt an ache in her chest as she pulled her knees close. The grimoire lay beside her, but she no longer feared it, only what it meant to destroy it. Her soul was tied to it and unless she could find someone to replace her, she was doomed to forever remain bound to its weathered pages, even after death as Isila had.

Without Dakon, she felt unprepared to open and discover the truth of how to destroy it. But as time passed, and he didn't show, she began to wonder if Clarisa let him and Victor live after all.

Perhaps she already knew.

She was alone here in her thoughts as the days turned to night, barely on the cusp of a full recovery as the men outside readied themselves for war. Occasionally a servant would bring her food and drink, and a healer would change her bandages and test her strength. She only needed bedrest for another day more he told her this morning.

But she wasn't sure she was ready to leave this room.

When Callum visited and talked to her, bringing her books of fairytales that she read through quickly, he spoke of his love for Emilio and kept her apprised of the upcoming battles. The witches, it was rumored, were planning to attack the Givensmir fleet. And while that worried the rebellion initially, they found it would leave the flanks of the capital open for an assault. No word on what they would do to the remaining witches afterward.

She didn't want to know.

Eve only hoped that Clarisa was somewhere far away from it all.

Sometimes, when she slept, she would close her eyes and see Clarisa's piercing blue ones turning to white as she chased her through the forest. She could see the oracles leaving the crystal turning to shadows on the walls of this guest chamber and reaching out like vile spirits waiting to consume her. They had monstrous faces, long and misshapen as their long fingers pierced her skin, beckoning for her soul and the grimoire.

Those were her worst nightmares. And she would wake in a cold sweat, gasping for air and screaming until Callum came to check on her. He would lay with her until she fell asleep, stroking her hair until her eyes were too heavy to keep open any longer.

She never asked how he got to her so quickly, but as the days passed, she noticed a growing weariness in his eyes and once saw a chair by the door when she peeked out to look into the corridor.

After, she chose to scream into her pillow instead.

Yet, no matter what little distractions Teros provided her, Eve's worries, that shrieking voice in her head that made her doubt herself, sounded above it all.

She read through the fables and folklore of witches and grimoires. It all ended the same, the valiant mortal killing the witch and thus destroying the grimoires they possessed. The mortal would be knighted, crowned, rewarded for their heroism, and the witch would fade into obscurity, their evil nothing but a challenge to overcome.

All of these tales were written by people with great imaginations... or with a hint of experience. Certainly, in a land where witches roamed there were grimoires created and destroyed, taking and killing souls with it, the book that lay next to her was no exception.

She let her eyes wander to the book, peeking out from beneath her sheets. The owl beneath three stars that had followed her through land and sea and even spirit veils. She shuddered, never wishing to step foot back there again.

Eve wished she would have spent more time researching the scrolls and scripts of the royal library. In all the centuries of written works, the craft of destroying something like this book must have been studied by scholars of the crown or procured through the confession of witches. But no matter how she tried to reason with herself for more time, it soon began to dawn on Eve that she may not live through this.

Grimoires are bound to souls. Destroyed only when it's left without one.

But can you destroy the grimoire without destroying the witch?

"You can't," she breathed.

Eve lifted the grimoire onto her lap, looking at the door and listening quietly. There was nothing but the sound of horses and voices outside her window, but on the other side of the door there was nothing she could hear.

She pulled the covers over her for safe measure and opened the book.

It shouldn't have unnerved her, but to see her name in the book made her feel sick. She let out a guttural cough and placed her hand over her mouth until she was certain she was calm.

You need to see.

Waiting will do more harm.

She flipped the page. Instead of words, there were sketches. Ones of snowy trees, of shadows in the dark, of ships and hands that reached out to it from within the water.

These are all mine.

She kept flipping through the pages, seeing all her darkest memories laid bare before her. It was terrifying, but she couldn't stop herself. Revisiting these macabre depictions as if she were standing in the pages and watching it all unfold. She reached the last page, and it was of a woman, sitting on a bed, staring inside the book as blackthorn branches weaved across the whites of the page.

Me.

She removed her sheet and looked about her chamber. Nothing was out of the ordinary, no blackthorn branches, no darkness. It was light and airy, and the sunlight that filtered through the window promised only hope. She took a deep breath, settling her shaky nerves as she lifted the sheets over her head once more.

"Tell me," she whispered, to the book, "does Isila live?"

The pages began to flip back and forth until landing on a blank parchment with a single word written in the orange-brown ink.

Yes.

Her eyes widened, and her mind raced wondering what else to ask. She hoped no one entered the chamber and listened quietly to make sure. Nothing.

She leaned close to the book.

"Where?"

The ink settled and a new word formed just below it.

Castle.

"Marc," she whispered to herself, unsurprised. She wondered how long Isila planned to use Marc as a host before destroying him or going into another. Eve wished she knew enough about witchcraft to consider whether Isila needed another ritual to be completed to do this. Would the Strix do it? Would Marc risk his life to . . . no, he wouldn't.

But Isila would.

She leaned to the book again. "Can we kill her?"

Yes.

"How?"

Mortal.

Eve straightened. Of course, Isila was in a mortal body, without another she would simply die as anyone else. One of the rebellion men need only take the head from Marc's shoulders in battle and it would be done. Eve felt hope blossom over the crumbling expectation that it sounded far easier than it would be in truth. Marc was heavily guarded both by castle walls and rows of knights. Even a few loyalists, though aggrieved by his actions may still try to find favor with him and save his life.

She sighed, rubbing her forehead between her fingers. "Can I kill you?"

No.

"Impossible," Eve whispered, frustrated. "Everything can be killed." She considered the response and decided to ask again.

"Can someone else kill you?"

Yes.

"Temperamental are we not?" Eve huffed. "How?"

Fire.

She felt a lump in her throat. That couldn't be true. The grimoire caught fire in the castle libraries when she had taken it there. And yet, here it was without a scratch or burn mark. Her heart thundered in her ears as she peeked once more over the covers. It was relatively silent, and she used her chance to lift herself from the bed and to the side of the chamber where the fireplace rested unlit.

She thrust the book inside, its open pages splayed before her. Eve willed her magic to her hands, feeling the warmth spread across her skin and to her fingertips. Slowly, small flames began to dance there, and she placed her hands on the book. It took to fire, burning in the hearth.

She allowed herself a glimmer of hope until she saw that the pages did not curl, did not darken in the heat. She waved her hand, frustrated and the flame went out. The book was left nearly untouched.

"So, I cannot kill you. I understand fully now." She stood, groaning as she placed her head in her hands.

Eve needed Dakon, she had not realized how much she relied on him since they had been parted by her sister. Even if he didn't know what to do with the grimoire, at least they would be lost together instead of her fumbling around keeping secrets from the mortals who would set her to hang at a moment's notice.

In truth, she was surprised they hadn't already.

"No," Eve whispered, "one tragedy at a time."

There was a faint knocking, and Eve barely made it under her covers in time for it to open. A guard stood there, standing tall.

"Lady Eve, His Royal Highness."

Eve raised a brow but couldn't utter a word as the guard moved revealing him.

Theo.

EVE

CHAPTER 46

The grimoire had driven her to madness, or death, or certainly both as Eve looked upon Theo's face. He was older now, his light brown hair a shaggy, darkened blond. his chin held a darkened stubble, and his eyes crinkled slightly in the corners.

But within them were the same hazel eyes she looked upon all that time ago.

"Eve," he breathed. She could see the outline of his chest beneath his tunic, rising and falling with his shallow breaths. His eyes widened, and he didn't know what to do with his hands as he stood before her.

The door shut behind them and brought Eve to her senses. She blinked, waiting to wake up from this dream, but still Theo did not move from her vision. She carefully got out of the bed, not daring to take her eyes off him.

His lips gradually lifted into a hint of a smile. "You are a vision, Eve."

She didn't answer, taking cautious steps toward him.

He was dead.

I saw him die in Marc's memory.

She lifted her hand, and Theo raised his to embrace hers.

But instead of placing hers on his palm, she stood still before him. He looked very much like her Theo, but her Theo was dead. Just like she was.

Her Theo left her to rot in her chambers while his father tried to kill her.

Her Theo promised love and fled at the first sign of trouble.

She could feel the heat on her skin, the way she remembered him looking at her when she accidentally singed and blistered his skin when she first came into her power. But that was then.

"Eve, I—"

She slapped him before her magic could turn her hand to fire. She could feel herself breathing raggedly trying to temper herself before she set the entire chamber to flames.

Theo let out a grunt, squeezing his eyes shut as he rubbed the blow of her strike on his cheek. "Yes, yes, I deserve that."

Eve slapped him again, missing and hitting his shoulder. "No, you deserve far more than that!" She stepped back toward her bed, grabbing the sheets and tossing them at him. "You left me!"

Theo ducked, but not soon enough, as he became entangled in the cloth. "I know, I'm here to tell you—"

"I nearly died in that castle." She grabbed a pillow and threw it at him, sending him to the ground right as he released himself from the sheets.

"I'm sorry," he said, raising his hands above him as he stepped closer to her.

"Sorry?!" Eve scoffed, grabbing another pillow and shoving it at him, but he closed the distance.

"Yes, I'm sorry." Theo let the pillow hit him and fell to the ground. He knelt before Eve as she grabbed the last pillow, ready to shove it at him again. Her chest heaved as she looked down on him, seeing his glistening eyes and parted lips.

"Throw it at me if you must, send me away, and I will listen and never return. But please, let me speak for only a moment."

Eve lifted a brow, lowering the pillow to her chest. "A moment."

Theo nodded, staying on his knees as he spoke. "I have been afflicted with the pain of our parting since that day in your chambers. Not a day goes by that I don't think of you and how selfish I was in leaving you. I should have stayed by your side. I should have fought every knight and guard my father sent to your room. I should have done anything but sail away on a ship to certain death. And I'm sorry I wasn't braver, that I couldn't be the man then that you needed." He stood, carefully, his jaw tensing. "I have taken every punishment the gods could have bestowed upon me, and the look of hurt and betrayal in your eyes is still by far the thing that keeps me up at night. I have spent days wondering if you are alive, and I would be damned if I did not come and find you wherever in this bleak, war-torn, end of the world you fled to." He lifted a hand to her cheek, and she did not stop him as he wiped away her tears. "You are my summer, Eve. And I am nothing but a winter born of desolation when we are apart."

Tears welled in Eve's eyes and fell down her cheeks. She tried to turn to hide her pain, but Theo raised his other hand and gently faced her to him. "I love you, Eve." He bore his eyes into hers. "But if you wish to never see me again, I will honor it. But I mean every word, and I will love you to the ends of my days."

Eve took a step back, lifting her hands over her mouth as she let out gut-wrenching sobs. "And how do I know you've changed?" She cried, her tears blurring her vision. "How do I know that you won't walk out that door with all your promises of grandeur only to run away at the first sight of danger?"

He clenched his jaw. "I won't, I swear to you, Eve. I will stay and die if it means being here with you."

"I killed your father."

"I know."

"I'm going to kill your brother." She challenged.

"I will hand you my sword."

She scoffed. "Get out. Get out!"

The hurt in Theo's eyes was nearly too much to bear as he took a step back toward the door. Eve leaned against the bed, trying to keep herself upright. Her limbs shook, her head swam with confusion, and tears fell onto the sheets that were left behind.

The door opened, and she felt a sting of panic. She lifted her head, seeing Theo pull the ringed knob.

"Wait!" she called out, louder than intended.

Theo stopped, turning to face her.

Eve swallowed. "I—I suppose I will need your sword."

Theo let out a small laugh as he practically ran to her. She straightened, just in time for him to take her into his arms.

"Anything you want, it's yours."

THEO

CHAPTER 47

Eve's heart beating beneath Theo as his cheek rested on her chest. The slow, calm thudding made him smile as he felt her bare skin beneath his. She ran her fingers through his hair as they lay on the tangled sheets, their bodies together as one, breathing in tandem blissfully listening to the night birds singing somewhere outside the window.

"I wish I could stay here with you like this for the rest of my life."

Eve laughed. "When the winter blizzards come you would be begging to start a fire."

Theo grinned, hearing her heart skip a beat. "I'll order someone to come close the windows."

"You've truly thought of it all, haven't you?"

"No." He lifted his head until they were nose to nose, she giggled. "But where you're concerned, you're all I think of."

"Quite the charmer you are." She rolled her eyes.

He loved looking into her eyes, brown and soft even when she was irate or quarrelsome. He couldn't help but stare.

She tugged his hair gently. "Why are you staring at me?"

"Because I love you."

The words came naturally, as if he were breathing air. He wasn't even aware he said them aloud until her beautiful eyes widened.

He didn't wait for her response, pressing his lips against hers. Every kiss, every touch of her hand on him, warm and delicate, told him what he already knew.

"I love you, Theo," she whispered between kisses.

He lifted himself gently to his elbows, wanting to look upon her face once more, to commit it to memory before the night they wished they could stay in forever was lost to time. The golden flecks in her dark eyes, her rose-colored lips that parted slightly as she hitched a breath, the way her dimple revealed itself to him when she smiled. He brushed a strand of hair from her face, tucking it gently behind her ear. He wished he didn't have to go meet with the nobles.

"The gods truly defined perfection with you."

Eve tried to scoff but it came out as a laugh. "I was thinking the same of you."

She ran her fingers down his cheek and over his lips; he relished the feel of her touch, closing his eyes and losing himself. It heated his skin, and his breath hitched as he longed for more of her.

"Eve," he breathed.

"Theo." He could nearly feel her smile as she spoke his name. She slowly drew her fingers around his neck. He opened his eyes to her wanton stare.

"Stay with me," she whispered, "just a moment longer."

He nodded slowly. "Just a moment."

It was a lie. He would have given the rest of the night to her, honor be damned. Anything to stay in her embrace. He was torn between slowly letting her explore him and wanting to pull her onto his lap and kiss her as he had wanted to all these years and more. Nothing, not even snow, storms, nor swords would keep him from the feeling of Eve in his arms.

Her hands made their way down his chest, and a rush of excitement ran through him. She wrapped her legs around his waist and pulled him closer; he sank into her warmth. Eve squeezed her eyes shut, letting out a low moan, and Theo could barely contain himself.

He pulled out enough to lift her on his lap and let her lower herself onto him. "I don't want to share any bit of you, not even with the ground."

Eve let out a surprised laugh, and Theo couldn't help but laugh with her. "Who is the jealous one now?" She smiled, calming herself enough to rise and fall gently on him.

He hitched a breath, his eyes growing serious as he felt her, all of her. "Me, always me."

He stroked her delicate skin with his hands as she rode him, cupping her breasts and kneading her nipples in his hands. He bent to kiss them, softly, then sucking slowly as she moaned his name into the air.

It was a prayer, a warning, a promise.

He gave her breasts a final, gentle kiss as he drew her lips toward him, holding her body tight as she continued moving up and down his length. Tension built within him. She wrapped her hands around his neck, her tongue exploring his mouth. Theo was on the edge of release.

"Eve," he whispered, between ragged breaths.

It was enough to undo them both. She shivered in his arms as she placed her weight on him. He let himself go with her, feeling the warmth of her thighs pressing against him.

He could scarcely catch his breath, as he lifted his gaze to hers.

Her hair was long and wild, sticking to their damp bodies as she swallowed in air.

"Was that all right?" he asked nervously.

She grinned, scoffing. "That was just the beginning."

Then she asked him to kiss her, to kiss all of her again and again.

EVE

CHAPTER 48

"It is about time you woke," Lady Tyrina said thinly. Her lips were pursed as Eve entered her solar as summoned.

"I feel much better, thank you." She bowed her head politely.

"I see." She gestured to Eve to sit across from her.

Eve sat, trying to lay her hands gently on her lap, but found herself fiddling with her fingers, impatiently. She wanted to ask the grimoire questions, to find Dakon—if he was alive. He had to be alive out there looking for her.

"I see you come with bare hands."

Eve blinked, coming to. "Yes." She cleared her throat, "I wish you no offense."

"You don't offend me, but I know that my nephew made quite the case to save you. It would only seem right that you would do him the honor of your hand at the very least."

"I am not worthy—"

"I know."

Eve made to respond, but Lady Tyrina raised a hand silencing her. "But that is not why I have brought you here."

"Then why, if not to insult me?" Eve raised a brow.

"Because we are at war and need every able-bodied person ready to do their part."

"Of course, I am not much of a healer, but—"

"You are a witch who makes fire, are you not?"

Eve froze. "I don't wish to answer anything that can condemn me."

"It was not a question. We need all the help we can get, and I am willing to wager that with your... talents we could win a war to end all wars."

"Wars never end." Eve scoffed, not meeting Lady Tyrina's eyes. "Battles do."

"Perhaps, but I am in the final years of my life. I would like to see my nephew take my place in some semblance of peace before I go."

"And you think that sending me on a fool's chase to scorch the land will help? I am not immortal, Lady Tyrina, I am but a girl who can make fire and slow time."

Lady Tyrina raised her chin. "As I said, we will need every able body out there."

Eve met her steely gaze, her eyes were not soft and kind, and Eve wondered when was the last time she looked fondly at another. In her dark green dress and jewels, she appeared stoic and statuesque, speaking of war as if it were fought between flies and not men.

"Our armies will be leaving this afternoon, meeting the Mytar forces where they will take control of the trade routes and lay siege to cut off resources. Our friends in the south will battle on the sea against the Givensmir ships. And Rubianes will attack from the east."

Rubianes?

"My father is fighting for the rebellion?"

"Your father is dead, dear. As is your uncle." Lady Tyrina said it so simply that Eve was sure she heard her incorrectly. She tried to calm the sinking feeling in her stomach.

"Excuse me?"

"The king did not take too lightly to shifting alliances at court and sought to kill them swiftly. Seems it angered your father's men enough to rally forces for our cause."

Surely, she must be mistaken.

"My father can't be dead. He isn't. He would never betray the crown," Eve whispered, her voice failing her.

Dead?

"But he did, for you." Lady Tyrina picked up a scroll from her desk and handed it to Eve. "I let him know you were here alive. I admit I expected some resistance, but he sent this back before word reached me of his death."

Eve couldn't speak, couldn't understand. She closed her eyes, willing the tears that lingered behind to stay put. She took the scroll in her shaky hands, torn between wanting to look inside and tossing it away as if not reading his words would keep him alive.

She could see his gentle eyes and kind smile as he embraced her for the first time in five years when they spoke of Callum and the court. She remembered his broken body, his leg torn apart by wars fought for a crown that did nothing but rip his family away from him.

But most of all, she could see his forlorn face as the guards shut her door behind him. She could hear her begging him to save her as Lord Wesley whispered about their suspicions of her role in Princess Felicity's death.

It was pity and sorrow for a man who should have loved her and one that she never got the chance to see prove it. Because when it mattered most, he did nothing. And now he is dead with a change of heart she could not bear witness to.

Lady Tyrina reached out her hand, placing it atop Eve's. She gave it a gentle squeeze.

"These are bloody times, my dear. But more deaths will follow if we wait and mourn."

Eve raised her head, her vision blurred, but she blinked away the tears. "Thank you for telling me."

"I wish I came bearing good news, but alas this is what we are left with." She stood from her chair, moving to the door. "I will give you a moment alone in your grief, but when you walk out of this door it is as an asset to our cause not a burden to it."

Eve nodded.

Lady Tyrina gazed upon her for a moment longer, then left the room, closing the door behind her.

Eve wanted to sob, to wretch out cries and scream and toss the contents of Lady Tyrina's desk to the floor and smash windows, but as she sat in the chair, she couldn't force herself to move. She looked down at the scroll in her hands and unfurled it, reading the last known letter of her father.

Lady Tyrina,

Your letter finds me as does the lock of my daughter's hair. Give my daughter my love and deepest regrets for my hesitation and capitulation. It will not happen again. Keep her safe, and I will pledge my forces to Queen Adriana and fight alongside her armies. Correspondence has been sent thus forth. Discourse and riots reign in the capital as the people are weary and hungry. The Givensmir armies are weak and their ships manned by inexperienced crews. Now is the time.

Lord Marcelo of House Rubianes

Eve's chest heaved as she read the scroll twice over.

Her father truly did betray the king for her...

And Adriana is queen?

"She's alive." Eve felt a fluttering in her chest as she stood. She hoped that since the scroll was sent that Adriana was still somewhere safe. Rebellions as she remembered with the young King Fidel in Larrea, often ended with the head of at least one leader. She prayed it would not be Adriana's.

Eve moved to the window, looking out to see the Teros armies near as far as the eye could see, loading their weapons and carts, readying the horses and preparing to trek to the capital.

Behind one of the carts near the entrance to the gates were Callum and Emilio, speaking as they placed on their winter gloves and mounted their horses. Theo sauntered over to them, carrying a long sword and leading his horse to the entrance. His armor bore not a hint of gold but was gray and green as the Teros ones before.

He made it clear to her he wished for no crown and seeing him in this armor speaking with Callum and Emilio, she felt a hint of relief. Theo never expected a crown nor wanted it; she couldn't imagine he would have changed even after all he had been through.

Watching them leave the gates, heading into the paths through the forest atop their horses, she knew she needed to fight, to use whatever magic she could to topple Marc's reign. Because her family, the one that shared no blood between them, needed her.

She looked down at the scroll once more. It was more than she dared to imagine and the best apology she could ever hope for from her father.

Letting out a soft cry, she placed her fingertips over the dry ink as if she could feel her father's touch beneath her own. But there was no magic where there was no heart.

"Goodbye, father," she whispered, kissing the scroll and setting it on fire.

ADRIANA

CHAPTER 49

"I've heard the most curious of rumors." Marc's voice echoed through the halls of the throne room. The floor was cracked, the ceiling partially caved in, and Adriana looked down at the marble floor, refusing to meet his gaze. She could hear his footsteps as he walked down the steps from his throne.

"That there is a queen in my midst. Now, imagine my surprise when I found out that it was not our mother, but you."

Adriana said nothing, keeping her eyes fixed to counting the cracks on the floor.

There were thirty-seven thus far.

She could feel the eyes of the packed throne room on her, filled with the court of nobles, guards, and knights who did nothing as Timothy brought her roughly to her knees in chains.

"Our own mother died of shame," Marc continued, taking the final step.

Adriana released shallow breaths, trying not to give him the satisfaction of her tears.

"You killed our mother. And you have declared yourself a queen of the rebellion." Marc nudged her leg forcefully with the outside of his boot. "Dear sister, it pains me to say, but I believe the witchcraft has afflicted your senses beyond repair."

Witch.

Witch.

Witch.

Adriana looked up, ready to spit vitriol at her brother, when her eyes met a ghastly sight. She gasped, taking in the man before her.

Marc was balding; his long, light hair gone from his temples and around the crown atop his head. His skin was spotted and wrinkled, his eyes lopsided in a dark green hue. His teeth were nearly all missing, and those that remained were blackened and rotted. The only thing that seemed to remain of the brother she once knew was his cruel and bitter heart as he smirked.

She couldn't speak.

"What say you Elder Borgias?" Marc called out.

Adriana couldn't rip her eyes from the monstrosity her brother had become as Borgias's voice carried through the room.

"It is clear and simple witchcraft, Your Majesty. This is beyond the help of mortal hands. We must give her soul to the gods and pray for their mercies upon the dear *princess*."

"A burning, then." Marc grinned. He turned to the crowd of nobles. "One less witch by the will of the gods."

"By the will of the gods!" they repeated.

"Damn you!" Adriana shouted. "The only one who should beg for the gods' mercy is you!"

"I am a god!"

"You are sick with power," Adriana spat. She faced the crowd. "All of you are sick with power!"

The crowd began to throw items at her as Timothy dragged her to her feet.

"Burn the witch!" they shouted.

Adriana's blood boiled under her skin, her anger tempestuous and dangerous as she tried to writhe out of Timothy's grasp, but he held firm as he carried her away. Marc stood, a shriveled mess of skin and illness as he watched her with a grotesque, satisfied stare.

Drinks, food, and other objects were thrown at her as Timothy dragged her through the middle of the room and finally out of the door.

The nobles followed them outside as Timothy pulled her chains to the back of a cart. The wind was frigid on this snowy day, and the castle grounds were blanketed in white pierced by the muddy boots of nobles that stomped through it toward her.

She panicked, her heart thundering in her chest and ears, her hands trembling as she tried to pull away from the certain spectacle they would make of her death.

"Quit moving, witch," Timothy muttered, gripping her hands and hitching the chains to the cart.

"I'm not a witch," she shouted. "You know I am not a witch!"

"What are women but witches in disguise." Timothy smirked. "And to think you tricked me into kissing you."

Adriana's eyes widened. "That's not true!"

"It is if I say it is." He smacked the back of the horse, and it began to move, its rider gripping the reins and pulling it toward the open castle gates.

"Now, prepare yourself," Timothy said, unsheathing his sword. "The last witch was nearly ripped from her arms by the crowd. Best be nice if you want to burn peacefully."

Adriana eyed the scene before her. The castle gates opened to the cobblestone streets lined with guards and people that peeked around them. A light snowfall fell from the sky, sticking to her heating face and the tendrils of her hair that fell in front of her eyes. She wanted to hide within it as if it were the last shield she owned.

She remembered the crowd, recalled running for her life as they tore apart her guards. And no matter how much she knew it was galvanized by her brother and the Strix, it did little to quell the fear of knowing she would go back into the chaos once more.

She looked upon the faces of young and old, curiously staring at their tired eyes and slack shoulders. They appeared defeated, weary. She lifted her chin, ready for them to attack, to throw something, to carry forth with murdering her in the streets and finish what her brother started. The people, her people, wanted nothing more than an excuse to rage their frustrations out. And Marc made certain they were kept distracted as they protested and begged for morsels. This was Marc's victory, his way of winning.

Because what was better than burning a woman who fought unsuccessfully for a crown?

The cart pulled her forward, and Adriana took the first precarious steps, praying that her feet would not fail her, that she would make it to the end . . . or if she didn't that she would die quickly before she was burned alive.

SHE REMEMBERED THE FIRST WITCH SHE EVER SAW PARADED THROUGH the streets. So long ago, when she was a princess hiding in Eve's embrace at the sight of the witch pulled through the raucous, feral crowd. Now here she was, walking the same path as her, but this time it was nothing but silence.

The streets were still. Adriana would have been sure she had fainted if not for the sounds of her footsteps and the wheels of the cart groaning as they turned on the unforgiving, muddied ground.

She waited to feel the strike of a weapon or food wasted for the chance to throw it at her exposed body like the nobles in the castle had, but there were nothing but solemn faces.

Adriana raised her head, knowing the familiar route to the pyre where her death loomed around bends and buildings Her heart pounded in her chest and her breaths were shaky as she tried to walk as straight as she could in her chains. But the mud was slippery, and she gripped the back of the cart to keep her feet moving forward. It clung in murky brown stains to the ends of her nightgown, never changed since she was taken from Zafira. It flung onto her arms, her chest, her face. The cart never stopped and not a single guard helped her when she fell.

She snuck a glance at Timothy, whose jaw was tense.

He had not expected this.

She turned around seeing the rest of the guards looking curiously tense at the people around them.

"My Queen!" A shout echoed from nearby.

She turned to it; a guard pummeled a woman to the ground. Adriana didn't have a chance to speak before another shouted, "Queen Adriana, our true ruler!"

The voices overlapped as the crowd began to shout her name, fighting against the guards that tried to silence them.

"Release our queen!"

"Queen Adriana!"

"Save the queen!"

One man tried to shove Timothy aside, but he struck him with his sword. "Hurry! Take her to the pyre!" he shouted, thrusting Adriana into the back of the cart. The man riding the horse was pulled off by someone in the crowd, and Timothy stabbed him, before jumping into the saddle and giving the horse a swift kick. It began to race, running over those in the crowd that tried to stop them as Adriana screamed for the people being butchered in the streets. She nearly fell from the cart as Timothy swerved to and fro around the buildings and narrow city streets until finally reaching the center of the city square where more guards stood.

Timothy leapt off the horse, handing the reins to another.

"Hurry! The crowd is coming. We must burn her before the rest arrive. Hold off their approach there!"

He quickly undid her chains, shoving her off the cart. She fell hard onto the ground, and Timothy grabbed her by the arm and carried her to the stake. Adriana kicked and shoved, unwilling to go down without a fight.

It took three guards to subdue her, and Timothy hit the side of her head with the hilt of his sword. She stumbled, colors spreading across her vision. It gave them enough time to bind her hands in rope to the stake as the crowd roared close by.

"Th-they are coming," Adriana managed, coughing up blood.

"They won't make it," Timothy snarled, gesturing to the guards to light the wood. "Now!"

"But Elder Borgias isn't here to cleanse the space," one said.

"Damn the elder, light it or you'll die along with her."

She could hear the whoosh of the fire behind her as Timothy gave her one last look. "I told you," he spat. "I told you, you would burn before me."

Adriana coughed, the smoke filling her chest as he walked away. She could feel the heat gaining behind her as the crowd, larger now shoved against the feeble defense of the guard. She looked to the sky, praying to die quickly, to not suffer, holding on to the bit of hope that one has to live despite the horrid odds before them.

The snowy sky held the gray clouds and the sun filtered weakly through them. Cool snowflakes landed on her cheeks, melting quickly and falling down her face like tears. Looking at the sky, she almost believed she was dying at the birth of spring and not in a winter of death and despair.

One of the clouds moved quickly, growing in her vision.

With the fire nearly kissing the tips of her muddy boots, she wondered if she had already been taken into Death's arms. Her madness surely masked her pain and fear with hallucinations of the peculiar kind.

Because the closer it got, the more silver-and-white it became. The more it looked to wear scales instead of the soft tufts she normally saw.

Come to think of it, she thought as the smoke rose and blurred her vision, *it almost appears to be a dragon.*

DAKON

CHAPTER 50

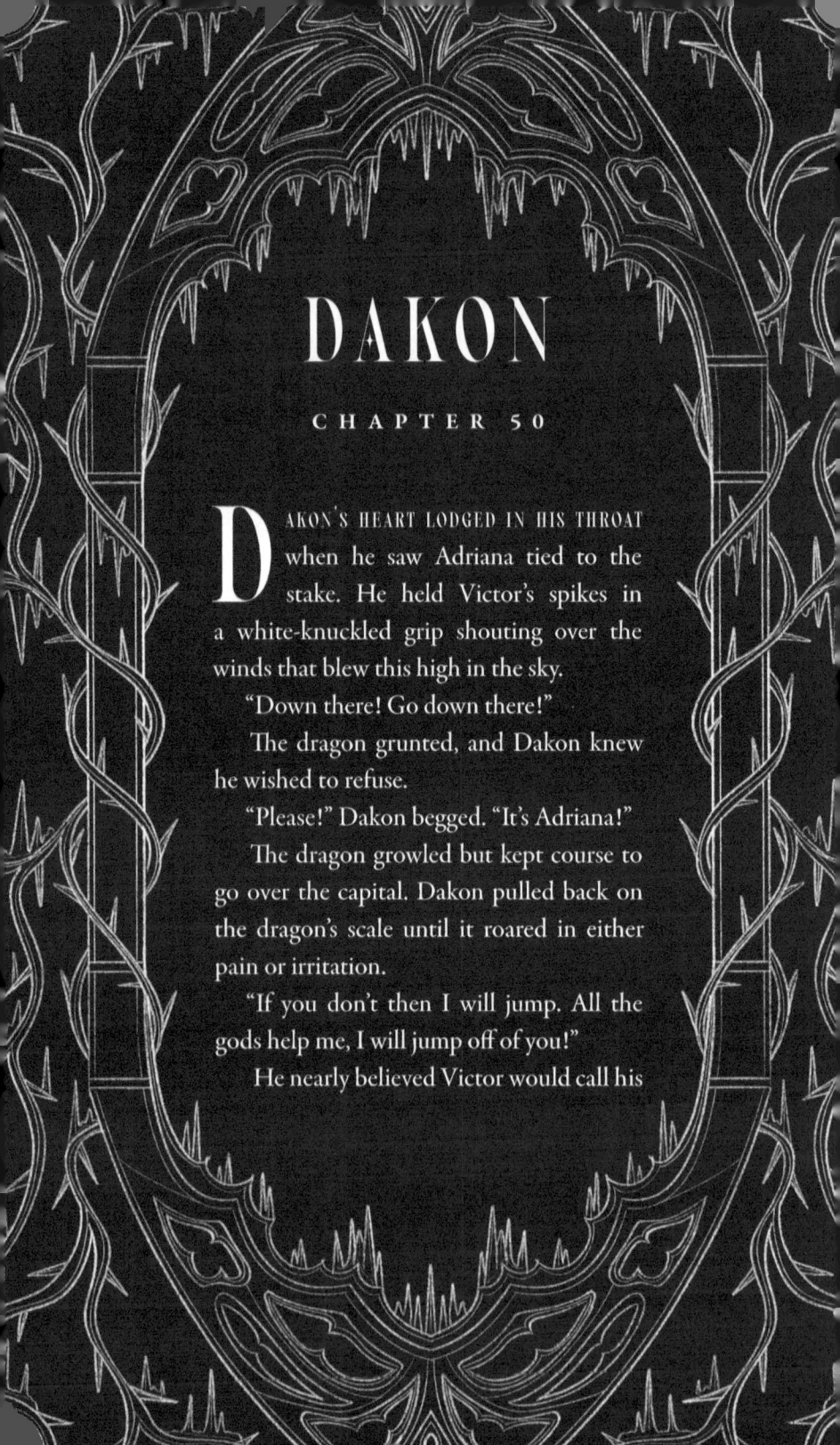

Dakon's heart lodged in his throat when he saw Adriana tied to the stake. He held Victor's spikes in a white-knuckled grip shouting over the winds that blew this high in the sky.

"Down there! Go down there!"

The dragon grunted, and Dakon knew he wished to refuse.

"Please!" Dakon begged. "It's Adriana!"

The dragon growled but kept course to go over the capital. Dakon pulled back on the dragon's scale until it roared in either pain or irritation.

"If you don't then I will jump. All the gods help me, I will jump off of you!"

He nearly believed Victor would call his

bluff, but to his surprise the dragon turned to the small fire that was building around her. It would catch quickly with the wind, and time was of the essence.

The dragon's wings flapped against the wind, forcing them down toward where the pyre was in the city square. They were only a moment away, and the ground was swiftly approaching, but the dragon showed no sign of slowing.

"On my word, use your magic! Don't kill her!" he called as the dragon raced through the air toward her, flapping its wings with reckless abandon now as they swam through the smoke and fog. Dakon could feel the heat against his face as it built higher behind her into the air. He only needed another moment, enough to not die from the fall alone. They were gaining on her, and the fire now licked the back of the stake where she was tied.

Not far off over the buildings he could see as crowds of people moved wildly toward her like mice in a maze. Many fought the guards, trying everything they could to reach her.

Were they with her or against her?

He didn't have a chance to think as they approached. "Now!" Dakon shouted, ensuring his daggers were secure in his belt, he leapt off the dragon and tumbled to the ground. Victor blew waves of cold, icy air in Adriana's direction, enough to quell the fire, but not enough to snuff it out.

Dakon looked to the dragon.

The warmth is weakening him.

He quickly tossed the satchel across his body to him. Running through the flames to Adriana, he sliced the rope from her hands.

"D-Dakon?" She coughed.

"It's me." He embraced her, pulling her off the pyre and shielding her from the fire that did little but warm his skin. "I'm here."

She coughed violently, and Dakon lay her on the ground trying to assess her wounds when hands shoved him away.

"Get off the witch!"

Dakon turned, pulling out his daggers. Timothy held his long sword out before him.

"She is no witch." Dakon held his blades before him as Timothy stepped forward.

"She is whatever I say she is." He closed the distance.

"I thought I killed you," Dakon snapped.

"A fool can never kill me." Timothy raced toward Dakon as the guards shouted around them. The crowd rushed into the city square, fighting against the guards with anything they could get their hands on.

Dakon caught his blade with the edge of his dagger, shoving him aside.

Timothy whirled around, hitting Dakon in the face with his elbow. He tasted blood, jumping back as Timothy thrust his sword at his middle. It barely scraped his midsection, and Timothy straightened, holding out his sword between both hands.

"Don't cheat." Timothy grinned. "There's no servant here to save you now."

Dakon rushed him, striking with his daggers toward Timothy's neck and chest, but each blow was deflected by his sword. One of his daggers flew across the way. Timothy shoved him to the ground, raising his sword to aim true, but Dakon kicked the inside of his calf and twisted away in time, getting to his feet. He twirled his dagger, hearing the rush of fire and chaos around him. He didn't give Timothy a moment to stand, kneeing him in the face and striking at his ribs.

Timothy let go of his sword, punching Dakon in the face. His head snapped back and Timothy wrenched his dagger hand open. He tried to blink the pain away as they wrestled on the ground for control of the dagger.

Timothy spat at Dakon, surprising him and smacking the dagger from his grip. He punched Dakon again and again, and Dakon could barely get a moment to breathe as the blows rained upon him.

He shoved his hands against Timothy's face trying to give himself space to move, to think, to do anything but be bludgeoned to death. Timothy swung for him once more but missed, and Dakon took his chance, shoving him aside. They both gasped on their backs, sweat-filled and exhausted as Dakon slowly got his broken body to his knees, reaching for his dagger. Timothy saw him, hitching a breath and forcing himself up. He swayed slightly as he shoved into Dakon, pushing him further away from their weapons. They wrestled for their lives, their cheeks red against the fierce wind that whipped at their faces, their arms screaming for relief, their breaths barely able to suck in air.

Dakon punched Timothy in the stomach and kneed him in the face when he bent over. Blood fell on the snowy, muddy ground, and they slipped as they continued blow for blow. A fight that would end only in death.

Timothy gripped Dakon's collar, shoving him up with a burst of strength and throwing him aside. Dakon groaned as his body met the ground with a sickening thud, and he tried to get to his feet, but Timothy kicked him in the chest.

Dakon hitched a breath, but no relief came. Timothy forced him to his feet, and the roaring fire caressed the back of his head. His right eye was nearly swollen shut, blood the only taste on his lips, but something moved in his vision. Just behind Timothy, Adriana slowly got to her feet.

"Rot in five hells *fool*," Timothy sneered. His face, too, was bloodied, his nose broken, his body full of scars and fresh wounds marking his once perfect veneer.

Adriana got to her feet as the guards and crowd still fought to the bitter end.

Dakon, feeling the flames lick his skin, began to laugh.

Timothy stilled, frightened and confused. His gray widened. "What?!"

"I'm no fool," Dakon said, his voice hoarse, "but you are."

He pulled Timothy into a tight embrace and let their bodies fall into the flames. Adriana screamed out for Dakon.

Timothy shrieked and fought, but Dakon held on with every morsel of strength he had left, feeling the fire give him life as it took away Timothy's.

He closed his eyes, giving himself a moment as he released his grip. Timothy's body shook and fought against the fire that feasted upon him, but he was helpless to move away from it.

Adriana cried out for Dakon.

Get up.

Get up.

Dakon slowly opened his eyes. His body ached as he lifted himself to his feet and walked out of the flames. Adriana's mouth went slack, her eyes with freshly shed tears widened, she took a step back.

"How?" she gasped.

"I wish I knew," Dakon managed, limping toward her. He nearly fell into Adriana's arms.

They turned to look at what was left of Timothy's body as it blackened and charred beneath the flames.

"You don't have to see this." Dakon said, holding her tight in his arms.

"No," Adriana said, "but I want to."

Dakon didn't argue as they watched Timothy waste away until he was barely recognizable as a man anymore.

Adriana turned to him. "Does the fire not burn you? Will you die from it?"

"No, I—I promise to tell you. But we need to go."

"By that he means that he will take a hundred years to tell it."

Victor moved barefoot through the snow, tugging on his boots one at a time as he walked.

Dakon whipped his head to him. "Where the hells were you?!"

"It seemed as if you had it handled." Victor smirked.

"I—I don't understand," Adriana said.

"He's a familiar." Victor rolled his eyes, something smashed against the ground next to them.

"More are coming!"

The three of them whipped their heads at the voices of the crowd, pointing at the approaching knights on horseback, fitted with shields and swords.

"We need to move," Victor said, pulling them away from the pyre, "and this time we have to go on foot."

They turned quickly, trying to find a way out as they took in the rest of the fight around them. The other guards were retreating if not already killed. From the edges of the city square, another large force of knights nocked their bows and arrows. The crowd turned to the knights, throwing anything they could at them.

"How do we get out of here?" Adriana asked, trembling against him.

Dakon looked around, feeling lost. Nearly every way out was filled with bodies or unruly fights.

Fuck. How do we—

He didn't finish his thought. Down a darkened, narrow alley, he saw mist and shadow. And orange-red eyes.

Beast.

His heart leapt into his throat as he grabbed Adriana's hand and led them to his gytrash. Victor followed close behind.

No sooner had they made it in the alley than arrows flew through the sky, nearly nicking Dakon's ear as he shoved Adriana and Victor in the alley. More screams rang out, and Dakon turned to see people in the crowd lying in their wounds on the bloodied, muddy snow.

"Raise the next bows!" he heard a voice call out.

He shoved himself in the alley and the next set of arrows volleyed like flocks of birds in the sky.

Adriana screamed and Dakon turned as she pointed, terrified, at Beast who ran through the alley. He grabbed her hand. "I swear I will explain everything. Just trust me and run!"

DAKON

CHAPTER 51

DAKON DIDN'T DARE TO STOP AS BEAST hurried along the narrow alley, leading them through the capital and toward Catalina's Port. He tried to forget the limp and the way his legs screamed for rest and relief, not wishing to slow their escape. Adriana and Victor held his sides as they navigated around the buildings and through the other alleys, not once looking back for fear they would see pursuers giving chase.

They managed to steal a cloak from a hanging line, giving it to Adriana to wear, hood over her head to hide herself as they made their way through the streets. Here in Givensmir, everyone knew her face, to be caught with her, and by the wrong people would mean certain death for him. And though his wounds healed slowly, he could barely flick a tiny candle-like flame in his fingers. He needed to recover, but not now.

They rushed across the bridge, hoping against hope that no one would pay them any mind. They slipped into another alley between the buildings to catch their breath. The people here, as they wandered about their business in the streets, felt different. They sauntered through the snow, moving as if they were barely clinging to life or hope. Perhaps, both.

Beast barked, getting Dakon's attention. He turned, seeing the gytrash run toward the end of the alley and to the left. Dakon and the others followed, leaving behind the port in the distance.

"Where are you and that wolf taking us?" Adriana panted.

Dakon looked between her and Victor. "It's a gytrash, and I don't know."

They made their way through the footworn paths along the coastline until they reached an unfamiliar cove. Dakon looked out; a boat waited empty at the shore, and just beyond it was a ship wading in the water.

The Wretched Sentinel.

He breathed a sigh of relief, turning to Adriana. "Do you trust me?"

"Yes"—she raised a brow—"but I may have questions."

"How do you feel about pirates?"

Hands reached out to pull them onto the deck, and as his hands splayed on the wooden deck, Dakon felt like he was home.

"Scared us half to death!" Giovani and Alonso yelled, pulling Dakon to them and giving him a fierce hug. He groaned at the pressure against his wounds, and they quickly released him.

"Sorry about that," Giovani said.

"It's nice to see you, too." Dakon mumbled looking across the deck.

"Pirates? I really pulled my luck with you, haven't I?" Victor scoffed, getting to his feet.

"Depends on who you're asking." Niani said, walking down the stairs. She gave Dakon a warm smile. "Our captain has been looking for you. But this isn't your witch, is it?"

She gestured to Adriana, who lifted herself up and quickly went into Dakon's arms.

Dakon shook his head. "I'm searching for her too. She's alive out there somewhere."

"And Pazel?"

Dakon tensed, not wavering from Niani's hopeful gaze. He shook his head slowly.

She blinked at his silence. "I see."

Niani cleared her throat. "Well, I have ... something to do. Mind the deck, crew. Let's move." She took off for the lower deck, and Dakon saw from the corner of his eyes as she wiped her own with the backs of her hands.

"She'll recover."

Dakon turned his head, seeing Amarin walk out from his captain's quarters. Dakon loosened his grip on Adriana, moving toward the captain and taking him into a brief hug.

"Amarin, you're alive."

"Unfortunately," he gruffed. His eyes flicked between Victor and Adriana. "I expect you don't have more coins for these travelers, do you?"

Dakon smiled. "I was hoping for an exception this time."

Amarin waved them to his cabin, not bothering to see if they followed.

Dakon reached back for Adriana's hand and together with Victor they went inside his cabin.

"And then he gave me this." Amarin reached in his pocket and pulled out Eve's necklace. Dakon would recognize it anywhere. Dakon reached out for it, and Amarin handed it to him.

Beneath his touch he could feel the ridges and grooves of the diamond in the center of the sun pendant. The chain held remarkably well for how many hands it passed through.

He passed it to Adriana.

"I can't believe he followed us," Dakon said.

"I can't believe you knew him," Adriana answered.

"Yes, yes. None of this is believable." Victor groaned.

"If it weren't for me and Eve, you would be stuck in that cave thinking about what other mortals to eat," Dakon snapped.

"I ate more than mortals."

"You eat mortals?!" Adriana pushed herself closer to Dakon. He nearly laughed if not for the absurdity alone.

"Quiet all of you," Amarin groaned, rubbing his temples. "I'm trying to think."

"What is there to think about?" Victor replied. "We all have what the other wants. You wish for a grimoire that Eve has, Dakon wishes for passage to find her, Adriana wishes to be wherever Dakon is and rule her land of bodies, and I wish to be anywhere but the wastes."

"But you're missing something, Dragon," Dakon said, cracking his neck. "None of us know where Eve is."

"Ah, none of *us* do, but *that* does." He pointed at Beast who lay his head on Dakon's lap.

"Thank you," Dakon said sarcastically, petting the gytrash. "But we need a plan. There are too many hostile forces around us; one wrong turn in water or land and we may not be so lucky."

"Right now, the kingdoms are about to face each other in battle," Amarin said. "Many are calling it a war of the ages."

"Seems suitable," Dakon replied. "From what me and Victor have heard on our travels, nearly every kingdom, save for Larrea, is moving their forces to fight against the capital. It was the only reason we chose to fly—too many forces walking through the forests."

"A pain in my ass having to freeze again in a lake," Victor grumbled. "Imagine, dying to live."

"Does my brother have the forces to face them?" Adriana asked trepidatiously.

Dakon looked at Adriana solemnly. "If rumor is to be believed, he has enough. But if what Amarin's sources are saying is true, then the witches can significantly impede them."

"But the witches will kill any mortal, won't they?"

Dakon nodded.

"But we need to discuss the other matter," Amarin said.

The three looked to him. He let out a drawn-out breath. "It doesn't matter if we find Eve if we aren't able to give Cassandra what she wants. She means it, the second Eve steps foot in the sea her soul is as good as gone."

"She can't take a soul if it's bound elsewhere, can she?" Dakon asked.

"I don't know, but I don't want to find out what that means for her."

"Why are you so invested in this witch's life?" Victor raised a brow. "Seems curious for a seasoned pirate, much less one who's working for a sea witch."

Amarin narrowed his eyes. "I have my reasons."

"None of my business, I suppose." Victor rolled his eyes.

"Eve doesn't want the grimoire. She would give it to you . . . with some convincing. But the problem is that it contains her soul. Unless Cassandra is willing to replace hers for it, there is no deal."

"If I bring it to her, she will. That witch cares for nothing more than power, and if she believes this grimoire will give her that then so be it."

"Fine. So, we find Eve, bring her grimoire to Cassandra, make her switch souls, and we're done."

Adriana scoffed.

"What?" Dakon asked.

"You all make it sound so simple."

"Isn't it?"

"If there's anything I've learned being around"—she gestured to them all—"different people, it's that plans are ruined frequently, and everything else is far more complicated."

"I resent that," Victor said, warming his hands against a candlelit flame. "But it's true."

"Well, we have to try." Amarin pulled a map off his desk and placed it on the floor next to Beast. He pulled out a small green booklet and opened a page.

Isn't that . . .

He cleared his throat, "I am lost and need to be found."

Beast perked his ears and turned to Amarin. Dakon watched, furrowing his brow as Amarin gestured to the map. "I am lost and need to be found."

Beast sniffed the map but did nothing.

"This worked before," Amarin grumbled.

Dakon looked to Eve's necklace in Adriana's hands. He gently pulled it from her and handed it to Amarin. "Try this."

Amarin placed the necklace on the floor and repeated his words. "I am lost and need to be found."

Beast sniffed the necklace, picking it up in his jaws and placing it on the map. Amarin looked to see, then Beast nudged the pendant lower and lower once more. Amarin raised a brow, then smiled, petting the gytrash. "Good Beast."

"Where is she?" Adriana asked.

"Your favorite type of place." Amarin smirked, turning to Victor. "Time to head north."

"Is it the Unclaimed Wastes?" Victor's eyes widened.

"No, but it seems she's on the move south from there and quickly. We may be able to reach her before dawn if we sail now."

"Can you not drown me first? I'd rather not die of cold again." Victor groaned.

"I can stab you in the chest if that makes it easier," Dakon mumbled.

"I still have some ice in me. Would you like one through your heart?"

"I can make that candlelight burn your face."

"Shut it, both of you." Amarin stood. "Worse than squabbling children. Get out of my cabin, find any spare cabins or deck space and hole up for the night. If my ship gets ruined again by any of your damn magic, I will slit both of your throats personally. And don't worry, I will live because the damn sea witch will bring me back to life."

Dakon froze, unsure of what to say.

"Out!"

The three of them clamored to their feet and rushed out the door. Even Beast who whined as he stayed next to him and Adriana.

CLARISA

CHAPTER 52

"Why did I need to see that when I lived it?" Clarisa asked her mother as they walked along the forest."

"Because I find clarity in visiting the past here." She reached out and touched the bark of a tree, admiring it.

"I only see the future . . . well, I used to." Clarisa sighed. "I suppose it doesn't matter anymore."

"Your magic matters, my dear. All magic does." She continued walking. "It's what one does with it that defines who they are."

"I killed with mine." Clarisa barely said the words aloud.

"And so did I."

She looked to her mother, wondering how someone so ethereal and graceful could ever end one's life. "But I thought you didn't kill the king."

"I didn't," she replied, "but I did kill others by letting him use my magic for his wars."

"Why didn't you ever escape?"

"Because I didn't want to risk harming those I loved. And then I had you and your sister. It became impossible to flee."

"Why couldn't you leave with us? It would have made things easier."

"I tried," her mother said. They made their way into a meadow. Here the grass danced softly in the gentle breeze, and the moon shined upon her mother's face. Clarisa felt like she was looking at Eve, for only the shortest moment. They continued walking through the grass, Clarisa feeling comfort in the night. She had nearly forgotten how it felt to walk without rain or the threat of death looming over her.

"I was locked in the tower by order of the prince. Once the king was fated to die that evening, I couldn't escape to find you and stop what Borgias had planned for you."

Clarisa stopped. "Wait. What do you mean?"

Her mother turned, facing her. "I didn't know how to get you to Amarin. The castle was heavily guarded; our every move being watched by Lord Wesley and his spies. I was desperate and went to Borgias for help."

"Why?"

"My magic was weak then. I thought I read the mind of someone willing to save us. He promised to help us escape together, without your father. But it turned out he had other plans."

Clarisa could barely think properly. Everything about that night that haunted her, everything she was told would happen if she wasn't successful in escaping with Eve . . .

Borgias lied to her.

He lied to them both.

"He was working for the crown, the prince?"

"He was working for many crowns."

"How is that possible?"

Her mother took Clarisa's hand, pulling her gently into a stroll once more. "I think better when I walk."

They moved from the meadow and into another edge of the forest, leading out to an empty city street. Nothing, not even a stray mouse, moved between the buildings or lingered in the alleys as they walked.

"Sometimes, those we think we trust are our enemies. And sometimes our enemies are the people we should trust."

"Or we could trust no one and rely on ourselves."

Her mother smiled. "That only lasts for a short while, my dear."

They made their way past the city square and toward the temple glistening under the moon, statues of the gods carved into the face of the stone. It was an impressive structure, towering nearly as high as the castle towers and filled with gold details. They stood in front of it.

"Why are we here?"

"To visit."

Her mother opened the door, letting Clarisa inside. Clarisa had nearly forgotten how remarkable the inside of the temple was. Its ceilings felt like they touched the sky, intricately painted in hues of gold and blue. Massive white pillars held up the dome. The windows were open, allowing starlight to guide her and her mother as they walked past the rows upon rows of pews lining the sides leading down the aisle to an empty altar.

Her mother placed a hand on the altar, and Clarisa did the same, feeling the smooth, cool stone beneath her touch. Before them, were five statuettes, each representing one of the five gods.

"What do you see, Clarisa?" her mother asked.

Clarisa studied them; all were carved in gray stone. "The gods."

"They see all."

Clarisa nodded.

"But especially Death." She pointed at the farthest statuette, hooded and withdrawn as if even in the stone it hid itself from the world.

"Does Death visit everyone before they die?" Clarisa asked.

Her mother turned to her. "Always."

"Then—" She swallowed, willing herself to speak the words from her lips. "Then I must be alive, if it hasn't visited me."

"My sweet girl." Her mother placed a cold hand on her cheek. "It already has."

Clarisa took a step back, nearly falling down the steps leading to the altar. She could feel her heart racing in her chest, her cool skin trembling as the goosebumps filled her flesh.

"N-no," she stammered. "How?"

The temple turned dark and her mother disappeared within it. Clarisa ran down one of the torch lit corridors, running from whatever it was that took her mother.

"By the ones who have you dreaming." It wasn't her mother's voice, but another one that was low and ominous, and Clarisa kept running to try and escape its closeness.

Dreaming?!

Clarisa ran down the next corridor. No longer feeling comforted by the temple, she rushed down to a dead end, shoving against the door that waited for her there, but this time it did not budge. She turned to see a shadow lingering at the end of the hall. It bore a long, dark robe, its face shrouded in darkness beneath a hood. Its sharp hands reached out for her. Sweat beaded on Clarisa's forehead as she looked around the temple for an escape, for any escape. But there were none.

"Mother?" Clarisa called, desperate. But there was no answer. She was gone.

"I'm here," the voice in the hood said.

Clarisa's lips quivered, her body trembling as she watched it approach her.

"I'm always here."

CLARISA GASPED INTO LIFE.

She took greedy breaths as she opened her eyes to the darkened air. Her vision was foggy for a moment, and she blinked until the shapes around her began to make sense.

Above her were wooden planks and beside her Aris slept at a small desk, snoring softly. She felt faint as the bed beneath her rocked gently. She lifted her head; the soft, dim light of night peered in through a porthole.

I'm on a ship.

Why am I on a ship?

She lifted her hand. It felt weak and feeble. She turned her palm up, willing her magic to come forth as it always did, but no water came forth, not even the familiar hint of a tingling sensation at her fingertips.

Perhaps I am too weak.

Instinctively, her hands made their way to her neck. Her necklace, the oracles, were gone. Dread pricked at the base of her spine, crawling up to the base of her neck.

I was a host for the oracles.

If they are gone, that means they took my . . .

She hitched a breath, placing a hand over her mouth as she rose slowly, trying to be as quiet as she could as Aris slept. Yet, she could only think of the worst.

My magic.

What have they done with my magic?

She nearly retched with dread as she placed her feet onto the cool, wooden floor. There were voices outside her door, so she tiptoed to it, leaning against it and listening as best she could.

". . . the king expects us to arrive by evening. He wants us to attack their fleets by nightfall."

"What about the assassin? Think she can pull forth another miracle?"

"King Navir might assassinate *her*, taking up a bed and doing nothing but burdening our ship."

She heard a faint cackle, and she removed her ear from the door.

King Navir?

Am I the assassin they speak of?

"It does you no good to listen to them, you know," Aris muttered.

Clarisa held her breath, turning to face him.

"Though, I'm glad you're awake now."

"So you can kill me?" Her voice cracked, looking down at him.

"No, not yet, anyway." He got off his chair and walked toward her. "I want to kill him."

"The king?"

"Precisely. I can admit when I'm wrong, and where he is concerned, I have made a grave mistake in trusting him."

"I could say the same of you." Clarisa lifted her chin.

"Yes, but I am not the one speaking of killing you, am I?"

"Not that I know of... yet."

Aris nodded. "Have you tried to call your magic?"

Clarisa parted her lips, thinking of a good excuse, but Aris raised a hand silencing her. "When your sister removed the oracles from you. She killed you. Now, they have gone to die or find another helpless host. And the witch part of yourself has died."

Clarisa sank to the ground, unable to stay on her trembling legs.

No, no, no, no.

She began to cry, but Aris only handed her a handkerchief. "I would be quiet if I were you. Thus far that secret is only between me and you."

Clarisa held the handkerchief over her mouth, trying to keep from retching the empty contents of her stomach on the wood. She had never known a life outside of her magic, never imagined she would live as someone who was only mortal.

Mortal.

"There are worse things than losing one's magic, Clarisa," Aris said, walking back to his desk.

Clarisa sniffled, wiping her eyes with the back of her hand as she stood. "I—I can still do spells, witchcraft?"

"Yes, I'm sure you can."

Clarisa felt angry, vulnerable, scared. Mortal.

She walked toward him. "If I am so mortal, then why have you kept me alive? Why have you not gone to tell your *dear King Marc* about me?"

Aris lifted his eyes to hers. "Because he is not *dear King Marc* to me. I am trying to temper a tyrant, and you are all I have left to try."

"I am mortal," she hissed. "I would die in a heartbeat and nothing would save me from his wrath."

Aris grinned. "But he doesn't know that. He believes you are the Clarisa that could stop a fleet of ships and set storms onto the sea."

"How would I be able to do that now?"

"You won't, but you need him to think you can."

"For how long?"

"Until you get him alone and kill him."

Clarisa scoffed. "If it was so easy, why have you not done it?"

"Because he is guarded with me."

"I wonder why."

"But he didn't used to be with you."

"I don't know how to be me without my magic."

Aris grinned. "Do what the rest of us *normal* witches do . . . pretend we have more of it."

EVE

CHAPTER 53

Eve couldn't remember the last time she sat around a fire hearing such fantastical and horrifying tales. She sat next to Theo and Callum, listening as the people lingered around the flame speaking of things they witnessed in the forests, the deserts, the sea.

It was the last night before they would make it to the capital, and they were all weary and in desperate need of distraction. She huddled against Theo, holding her cloak tight around her as the stories delved into the most absurd and macabre details. Eve thought her experiences would make her numb to such things, but she still found goosebumps raised upon her flesh, and not from the cold.

"I swear by all the gods, I barely escaped that mountain alive," one of the soldiers said.

"And not a single scar on you. I'm impressed." Emilio grinned.

The soldier narrowed his eyes. "I've got scars beneath this armor that would terrify you."

"Just imagining you taking off your armor terrifies me," Emilio replied. The group around them began to laugh as the soldier grunted and sat back down.

"Great tale," Callum said, stifling a laugh next to Emilio. "Who is next?"

A few argued about going, and Eve sighed, disinterested. She looked up. The stars twinkled in the bruised winter sky and even the crescent moon that lingered off, barely visible beyond the treetops, seemed to smile down at her. Hints of dark clouds moved around it as if they, too, had somewhere they needed to be. It pained her to look upon something so beautiful on a night before such bloodshed. Could this be an omen of sorts or the wistful welcome that Death himself gives to the damned?

She recalled looking out her balcony at skies like this, warm and safe in the maiden's keep where guards roamed the halls ensuring their safety when the kingdom was in constant battle with Larrea. The times were different then. The most she had to fret about was Theo coming home and her securing a marriage that her father would approve of. Sometimes during those nights, when she felt her loneliest, she would look out the balcony and see the moon sinking beyond the horizon and think about the ship headed for nowhere taking Clarisa with it.

But there was no such thing as *nowhere* now, was there?

Eve didn't think so anymore. After escaping to distant lands, sailing the Dallise Sea, fighting off sirens of the depths, it should have been painfully obvious how *nowhere* really meant *somewhere* she hadn't been to yet. And wherever Clarisa was out there, in the wastes or the Blackthorn, Eve hoped she was safe.

Watching the sky didn't calm her nerves, but it did settle her worries for a moment as she admired it. She looked back to the fire, ready to listen to the next tale, when Eve realized she could hear the Dallise from a distance; the waves tumbled against the shore beckoning her to touch it. She turned to the sound, though she couldn't see it through the dark, dense woods.

One of the men stood and began speaking of goblins luring wanderers deep into caves and leaving them to be lost forever. Eve stood, having had her fill of nightmares to last her for a lifetime.

"What is the matter?" Theo asked, holding her hand.

"I need some air. Stay. I will return in a moment." She gave him a weak smile as she adjusted her satchel. The book felt far heavier now than it had that morning.

Theo gave her a lingering look but nodded as Eve turned and walked toward the sound of the water.

She made her way through the woods, passing by the tents of the soldiers and the various fires they sat and talked around. She pushed through the brush, feeling as if a part of her were missing that no group present would fill. But worse, she felt guilty for feeling this way. Callum and Theo, two men she loved and had believed to be dead all this time, were alive and here with her.

Why was that not enough?

Eve wrestled with her feelings as she pushed away branches, feeling the glancing stares of the men around her. She knew they were wary of her and wondering why she had come. Eve could not lie the fault with them; she was a woman rumored to kill royals, with witchcraft, no less. Everything they had been taught to despise was something they were told now to ignore for the sake of the rebellion.

When she traveled with them, she could feel their wary gazes, the whispers around her, how they tensed and felt for their blades as if she would attack at a moment's notice. The hypocrisy of it all stabbed at her pride. Did she not feel the same way of witches so long ago too?

When witches were spoken of, did she not cast wary glances and watch as they burned at stakes saying nothing but feeling contempt at the blasphemy of their very existence?

She scoffed at who she used to be and continued making her way past them, head held high.

Eve reached the edge of where the forest and rocky shore met, pebbles crunching beneath her feet. Before her was a small inlet with large rocks jutting out of the water around, obscuring most of the sea that lay beyond it. She sat on the pebbled shore, hugging herself in her cloak. The air was chilled, but not strong. It lingered, sending the waves to and fro gently in the night. Here she could better see the sky in all its black-blue majesty riddled with pinpricks of stars. And between the jutting rocks, she saw the black of night and the end of the sea coming together as one.

A part of her missed it, being out on open water. That feeling of going everywhere, of having the limitless possibilities before you with a turn of the sail. She could be far from all the wars of mortal and magic and take off somewhere new. There had to be somewhere new.

She was not sure how long she stayed sitting there on the ground, watching the shore and sky, but when she finally lifted her head to the ends of the sea once more, she saw the most peculiar thing.

Fire. Glowing in the distance.

She stood, her eyes widening as a ship came into view.

The Wretched Sentinel.

"WHERE IN THE FIVE HELLS HAVE YOU BEEN?" DAKON SAID, PULLING Eve onboard. Eve could barely believe her eyes; she nearly believed herself dreaming if not for the feeling of Dakon's warm hand beneath hers.

Adriana, Victor, Dakon, Beast, and Amarin all waited for her on deck.

"I've died," Eve whispered, "I've died and this is Death playing tricks on me."

"No, this is my true, ugly face you're looking at." Amarin smiled, opening his arms, and Eve reached out to hug him. He held her tight and she choked on a sob.

"You found me," she said.

"I couldn't let your mother down," Amarin whispered. Eve raised her chin to face him, seeing his relieved, sincere eyes, but didn't get a chance to question him as Adriana pulled her into a fierce hug.

"I've missed you! I thought I would never see you again," Adriana squealed, tears running down her face. "Why didn't you take me with you?" She smacked the side of her arm gently.

Eve laughed, her own making their way over her cheeks, "I—I don't even know what to say. I'm so happy you're alive." She couldn't get the words from her lips fast enough. "With all the rumors of Marc. I never thought he'd let you out of his sight. Then, then, Callum told me you were taken to Zafira. Wh-what happened? How did you end up escaping?"

Adriana's face grew serious, her eyes grave as she bit her lip.

Oh no.

"What is it? You can tell me." Eve took her hand, trying to quell the rising panic within her.

Adriana turned to face Dakon and then back to Eve. She put her hand in her pocket and slowly pulled out Eve's necklace, the diamond resting within a sun pendant on a golden chain. Eve took it gently in her hands, confused.

"How did you find this?"

Adriana cleared her throat. "I didn't. Izan did."

Eve looked about the ship, the crew were staring at her, but none of them bore his face. She turned to look at Victor, Amarin, Dakon, and then Adriana again.

"Well?" Eve asked, nervously. "Where is he?"

Adriana shook her head. "He didn't make it, Eve."

Eve's stomach dropped, but she tried to calm herself.

Reyher told me as much. They said they took care of him. They did this.

"The Strix killed him. I was there when they took him away."

"No, Marc's men did."

But how?

"I—I don't understand, Adriana. How did he die by Marc? How did he find my necklace?"

Dakon took Eve's hand in his. "Come, let us speak somewhere more private."

Eve looked around once more, realizing she had been louder than she meant. She let out a shaky breath and nodded, going into the captain's quarters.

DAKON

CHAPTER 54

DAKON ROWED THE SMALL BOAT BACK to shore, the dark blue hues of night turned the soft pink of early dawn painting the sky above him. He turned to Eve and Adriana who sat next to each other on the opposite end of the boat silently. Next to him was Victor who for once didn't speak a single word as they moved through the water. It was an uncomfortable time for all, secrets and betrayals laid bare. But it was necessary. They all knew it. Though, as Dakon watched them with their heads lowered, he wondered if it was worth it.

As he felt the pebbles beneath his oar, he jumped off and pushed the boat to shore, and Victor helped the women both out. Their shoes crunched along the pebbles as Dakon walked them toward the edge of the forest.

Victor turned to him. "Well, Dakon. Wish me luck."

"Not at all. I hope you finally perish, Dragon."

Victor smiled, ruffling Dakon's hair. Dakon shoved his hand away.

"Same for you, Familiar."

He gave him a last glance and took a step back as Eve moved toward Dakon.

"Take care of my book, Dakon. Remember what we talked about."

Dakon nodded. "I will."

"I hope we see each other again at the end of this." Eve swallowed.

Dakon felt this was a goodbye he never asked for and pulled her into a tight hug. "We will," he promised. "In life or death, you are stuck with me."

Eve let out a nervous laugh. "As are you." She took a step back. "I will give you both a moment."

He watched as she moved behind a tree and Adriana reached her hand out to him. He took it, guiding her into his arms.

"Be safe," she whispered.

He kissed her temple. "I don't plan to leave when I have only just found you." He gave her a gentle smile, but knew it barely reached his eyes, because in truth he was terrified. Hundreds of ships were set to war over the seas, Adriana was a queen needing to be with her armies, and he could do nothing but finish out the plan they swore to follow.

She wrapped her hands around his neck, pulling him close. "Come back to me, Dakon," she breathed, "or I will find a way to bring you back and kill you myself."

Dakon laughed. "Anything to see you again."

She grinned, staring up at him. "You are quite a man of words, my admirer."

Dakon rested his forehead against hers. "And I will admire you past death."

She pressed her soft lips against his so suddenly, Dakon was certain his legs would fail him. He pulled her close, holding the small of her back and straightening as he held her up into his arms. He could feel the rapid beat of her heart, the sweet taste of her mouth as she wound her hands into his hair. Dakon couldn't think to breathe or move or hear the rushing of the waves against the shore; his heart was only focused on the woman he loved, kissing him as if there would be no other chance. There may not be another chance. Their warm bodies held each other in the cold morning air, fighting for every moment to stay in each other's arms, but knowing their time had come to an end.

Tears fell down Adriana's cheeks and onto his or was it Dakon's wetting her lovely face?

He lowered her slowly, holding onto that final kiss for dear life, until he felt her arms move from his neck to his chest and then away from his skin.

"Don't forget," she said, and then she turned on her heel and ran to Eve and Victor who waited for her. Dakon tightened his jaw, touching his lips where hers had been, wishing they had only a moment more. But knowing if they did, he wouldn't have been able to let her go.

He pushed the boat back into the water and jumped inside, rowing back to the ship where Amarin and the rest of the crew waited.

EVE

CHAPTER 55

They made it to the camp as the soldiers were breaking down their tents. Eve pushed through a thick cluster of brush, Adriana and Victor not so far behind when Callum rushed toward her.

"Eve, you had us scared to death. Where did you go?"

Eve hugged him. "I'm sorry, but I have good reason. I brought you something you've been looking for."

Callum furrowed his brow as Eve gestured to the brush. Adriana and Victor were making their way through it.

"Callum!" Adriana said, meeting his eyes and running toward him.

Callum nearly sank to his knees, taking

her in his arms. "Gods, you're alive! We hadn't heard from Zafira. We began to assume the worst."

"I'm here, I'm here," she repeated.

"Great, more family reunions," Victor sighed, venturing off.

Eve ignored him.

"I can't wait to show your brother. He will die," Callum said, releasing her.

Adriana frowned. "I hope so. Vile bastard."

"Is that any way to speak about your brother?"

Eve turned, seeing Theo grinning as he approached them. Adriana looked between Eve and Theo, unable to mask her surprise. "You—you—"

"I swear, no more surprises," Eve said, as Adriana ran into Theo's arms.

The soldiers around them seemed confused but didn't bother stopping their tasks as they readied their horses and weapons. It was a sobering sight, one of present happiness and one of lingering fates. Eve made her way to her horse, Callum following close behind.

"Not quite what you imagined, was it?" he asked carefully.

Eve bit her lip, nodding.

"It may not feel quite right until this is all over. And even then, I can't imagine going back to how things used to be."

He helped Eve onto her horse, though she didn't need it. She thanked him as he got on his alongside her.

"It won't," Eve said, "and it never will."

"And what of that new man you brought?"

"A dragon," Eve sighed.

"A—a what?"

"A dragon," she repeated, unable to force herself to manage any morsel of surprise on his part. "He dies of cold, he turns into a dragon."

Callum looked to where Victor stood near a dying fire.

"A fire-breathing one, like in the stories?"

"No, a talk you to death and spit ice sort of dragon."

"Well, might we get to killing him? We're at war."

Eve looked at the snowy trees and the wind that picked up. "Give it til midday with no boots and you may get lucky by the time we reach the capital." As Eve said it, something came to mind. She turned to Callum. "Order your men to remove his cloak and find a frozen lake. Quickly."

Victor was furious. The way he flew in circles and twirled in the sky she nearly lost her grip countless times.

"I'm sorry!" she yelled over the fierce wind that whipped at her hair and face, blistering it in red marks. "But I had a feeling!"

The dragon gruffed, slowing its wings and letting them fall a considerable distance before flapping them once more. Eve felt sick but tried to keep her retching under control as her vision blurred so high in the clouds.

"I swear I will never make you shift again!"

Victor straightened, gliding across the sky, and Eve could breathe again.

"Thank you," she managed.

She looked below; hundreds upon hundreds of rebellion armies marched through the Givensmir forests leading to the capital, and a short distance away glinting golden armor approached them.

It was time.

Now or never.

She gripped the dragon's spiked scale and held tight as they flew over them to the city. She wondered if the soldiers could see or even paid attention to the dragon in the sky when mortal deaths loomed before them. Eve turned her gaze to the sea and nearly lost her grip, ships as far as the eye could see littered the Dallise Sea, brown and black, sails of white and those of silver approached each other.

"The war has started," she breathed.

CALLUM

CHAPTER 56

THE WINDS WERE FIERCE THIS MORNING as the capital of Givensmir glinted against the sunlight in the distance. By the end of this day, many would die. And if Marc won, some would be tortured and imprisoned, held hostage for a high ransom to their wealthy families or executed in some remarkable display to the city folk to temper their protests. If it came to that, Callum would rather die in battle than waste another moment behind the bars of a dungeon cell. Never would he face that again in this life.

He held the reins of his horse firm as the golden armor crested the hill toward them. His eyes widened, they were far outnumbered, more perhaps than he expected. His men could sense it too; a thick tension permeated the snowy land as they grew closer.

He turned to Emilio. "Kill me if they try to take me. Promise me."

Emilio met him with solemn eyes. "Only if you promise to do the same."

Callum nodded, unable to say the words.

The large, golden army waited at the far end, and three of their riders rode to approach them.

"It's time," Callum said under his shaky breath.

Emilio placed on his helmet and together with Theo, they rode to meet them.

Ser James and Lord Wesley waited on their horses alongside one of their soldiers holding the banner of the royal sigil—a golden merlion with its talons out on a black backdrop. Callum looked up at their own that Emilio flew in the sky, it was nearly the same, save for the colors switched to represent Adriana's claim.

The grounds were muddy and snow-filled as their horses rode and Callum knew this would be a brutal fight. He wished that his aunt had not pulled her noble purse out in the war to Larrea, forcing him to stay as a castle protector while the rest had gone to war. He felt, even with all his training and experience, entirely unprepared for this venture.

"Ah, yes, our wonderful escapees. Though I am surprised to see you, Prince Theo, and among such undesirable company." Lord Wesley smirked. "Are you vying for the throne as well?"

"I am not surprised to see where you are," Theo replied. "And no, I am here to represent Queen Adriana of the people."

Lord Wesley scoffed. "Queen of the people seems quite unlikely seeing as though she is sitting in some tent I gather in the forests, whereas your brother sits on an actual throne. If anything, it makes her queen of the peasants or forest folk."

"Mind your tongue," Callum snapped, "or you won't have one."

"No need for idle threats, Lord Callum," Ser James replied. "You are only scaring the birds."

"Come now," Lord Wesley interrupted, "let us talk as civilized men." He took out a long scroll handing it to Theo. "*King* Marc's terms are simple. You all bend the knee, and we will give you light punishments, a fine for the noble houses without invitation to the royal court for ten years, and indentured labor for seven years to the poorest among you. I consider it very fair. Oh, and of course the head of your sister for treason."

"Denied," Theo replied.

"Are you sure you don't want to think about it? I have heard the horrible plans our king has for any who survive this, and he has made it clear he wants as many survivors as he could get." Lord Wesley looked to Callum. "I'm sure you could vouch for sanity here, having experienced *a little* bit yourself?"

Callum swallowed, remembering those scars, the stabbings, the beatings, the dungeon where rats climbed over his sleeping body. He shivered, turning his head away.

"I thought so," Lord Wesley replied.

"We will fight." Theo tore the scroll in two, tossing it to the wind. "I hope you make it out alive, Lord Wesley. I have plans for you too."

Lord Wesley smirked. "Looking forward to seeing you in chains, *Prince*."

The three of them rode back in silence and all the while as the air howled and the snow fell, he could see in the sky the storm that promised to arrive soon. He looked to Emilio, hoping that he would stay true to his word, because Marc would keep him alive for as long as his body could take it.

CLARISA

CHAPTER 57

SCREAMING AND FIRE FILTERED THROUGH Clarisa's cabin. Aris stood on the desk, peeking through the porthole as water splashed against the glass.

"It seems our time is now." He turned his eyes to her.

"It sounds like death out there." Clarisa trembled, feeling too vulnerable as she huddled in the corner of the bed.

"It is death," he replied, grave.

"But how? Navir's ship is the last in the fleet to fight. How are they already here?"

"This is a mortal war we're fighting." Aris climbed down the desk. "We are in uncharted territory here."

There was a scream and a bang on their

door, and Clarisa turned in time to see a witch run inside. "The king requests Clarisa's presence immediately!"

Aris turned to Clarisa with serious eyes. They stared into one another, and she wanted to ask, no beg, him to let her run for it. To try and escape into the water if it meant not having to face Navir as a mortal woman. But he shook his head, barely discernible as he replied, "she is ready."

She tried to still her shaky breathing. As they made their way to the main deck, the ship was in chaos, mortal and magical ships converging on one another in broken pieces of wood and rope not far in the distance. Some of them not even war ships, but vessels it seemed—people finding themselves in the midst of war. The witches on board her ship moved the sails, readying their weapons and magic as best they could for the bloodbath that awaited them. They pulled aboard survivors from the water, killing those that were mortal and leaving the witches aside with weapons.

Aris ushered Clarisa to the door of the captain's quarters, and she realized then how shallow and quick her breathing was. She couldn't part her eyes from it all. The mortals were fast. Even without magic, they cut through ties and fought with swords, daggers, and even their bare hands. It was gruesome and terrible.

"Look at me," Aris said. "Look at me, not that." He pulled her head to face him. "We can end this. You and I, all you have to do is go in there and end this madness."

Clarisa could barely hear him through the screams. They pierced through her heart, her soul, finding fear that she had never known before.

Aris snapped in front of her face, getting her attention. "Kill him, and I will turn all our ships around. I will take us back home. Do you hear me? We still have time to retreat."

She stared into his wild, desperate eyes. This was their only hope. Killing Navir was the only way she could stop this.

Aris opened the door. "Your Majesty, I have Clarisa for you."

Navir paced before them, stopping as they entered. A guard inside stood by the doors.

"Well?" Navir walked to Clarisa but spoke to Aris. "Is she fixed? Can she kill them now?"

"She needs to channel her magic, but yes," Aris replied.

Clarisa tried to mask the fear that lingered within her as Navir stared into her eyes.

"Why are her eyes brown? They are supposed to be blue."

Oh no. My eyes.

Aris tensed next to Clarisa, but quickly responded, "Because she is in her mortal form at this moment, Your Majesty. Give her space and she will show you what she is capable of."

Navir took a step back, gesturing for Clarisa to begin.

Clarisa swallowed, stepping forward toward him. "I—I can only channel my hidden magic when I am alone. It is too crowded in here."

"That never seemed to bother you before," Navir snapped.

"Because I had the oracles. Now I don't," she snapped back.

Navir swallowed.

Keep going.

"All of you need to leave, I can't concentrate."

Navir narrowed his eyes. "No, do this here, now."

Clarisa stood her ground. "No."

"So, you will let poor witches die because you aren't getting what you want."

"I could say the same of you."

Navir closed the distance. Clarisa couldn't help it, she flinched. He smiled. "I think you've lost it."

"No, I haven't," she said quickly.

"Prove it." He grabbed a cup from his desk and handed it to her. "I'm quite parched. Fill it."

"I won't lower myself—"

"I said fill it!"

Clarisa bit her lip, knowing full well the magical feeling she had all her life was missing. Even as she thought to summon it to her fingertips, to feel that familiar tingling as her magic ran through her veins, nothing was there anymore.

In that single moment between his request and knowing the dire truth of their fates, Clarisa could do nothing but feel rage.

No. She felt wrath.

She kept Navir's smug gaze as she tossed the cup to the side. "I will not be ordered by you any longer."

"You are mortal," he shouted, pointing a finger at her. "Kill her!"

It happened too quickly, the guard rushed toward her as Aris shoved himself between them, catching the knife meant for her in his chest.

"No!" Clarisa screamed. The guard ran to her, but she twisted from their grip, running out of the cabin door as Navir cackled madly behind them. She ran across the busy deck, no one stopping to help her as the mortal ships made their way to them. Clarisa climbed the steps to the steer and the guard followed. She slipped on the wet deck, water sloshing against the skies, a storm rising in the distance. Snow fell harder, nearly obscuring her vision as the guard leapt for her, missing, but losing their knife in the process. Clarisa rushed toward it, needing anything to save herself. The guard saw her and gave chase as Clarisa bent to grab it. She turned just in time. The guard pummeled themselves into her blade, piercing through their stomach. The blood spurted onto Clarisa, and she let go, horrified as the guard fought for life and then quickly gave in to death.

She could barely stop her ragged breathing as she raised her hands before her. They were filled with dark, sticky blood that dripped onto the wet deck. She lifted her head, looking at the carnage that raged around them. People, magic and mortal, fought for their bitter lives, the steel on steel of swords, the brutal fists that met flesh, and screams. The screams were the worst. She closed her eyes, feeling so vulnerable as she looked upon it all.

I will not make it out alive.

"It's beautiful isn't it, so poetic?" Navir's voice carried through, and Clarisa turned to see him walking up the steps toward her with his dagger in hand. "The mortals name their battles, you know? Something to make them feel good when they sleep at night." He reached the landing and took a step toward her. "I wonder what they will call this? The Battle of the Dallise? No, that is too simple, it lacks a certain charm, a certain gusto for the singers to belt out in taverns for weary travelers." He continued closing the distance, and Clarisa could do nothing but face what was coming for her. She couldn't bend to remove the blade without risking him rushing toward her. She took a step back to the wall of the ship.

"The Battle of Witches? The Battle of Mortals and Magic? What do you think?" He grinned, wickedly.

Clarisa said nothing, her lips trembling as her eyes made their way from his to his blade. She hoped it wouldn't hurt for long.

"You're right, it's not nearly as impressive." He tapped the pointed end of the blade to his chin, pretending to think. "Ah, I got it. Listen to this, my dear Clarisa."

He was only a few steps away now, and Clarisa was certain her heart would give out.

"The Battle of Mortals and Magic." His wide smile petrified her. "That's what they should call it, because no matter who wins, both of us die. Mortal." He pointed the tip of the blade to her chest, then back at himself. "Magic."

"You first!" someone from behind him shouted.

Navir turned, and Clarisa only saw the sword slash deep into Navir's neck. He fell to the ground, groaning as he clutched his fatal wound. Clarisa raised her eyes, shielding her face with her hands ready to be next, but instead her breath caught in her throat.

Ana stood before her, hands on her weapon as she struck Navir again and again, until he stopped moving. She could barely speak, her limbs shaking against the wall as Ana held her weight against her knees. "I was tired of hearing him talk," she said between breaths.

"H-how did you?"

"I took the wrong ship, it seems." Ana gave her a grim smile.

Clarisa lowered herself to her knees, barely able to keep herself upright.

Ana bent down to her. "You didn't think you had gotten rid of me, did you?" She pulled her sleeve down and wiped Clarisa's face gently. Clarisa looked into her brown eyes, those of amber kisses in bloom, and wiped her hands on her dress before raising them to Ana's cheek.

"I never should have told you to go."

"Then stay with me." Shouts carried over the ship, and Clarisa turned to look at it, but Ana gently brought her back to face her. "Until the end."

"And even after," Clarisa promised.

Ana kissed her, deeply, urgently and Clarisa wrapped her arms around her neck. Time was moving quickly, and if she died here, now, on this ship, it would be in Ana's arms.

Forever in Ana's arms.

AMARIN

CHAPTER 58

Amarin's ship was the fastest in the Dallise Sea, but never did he think there would be a time when he was pursued. New brown ships with golden sails raced toward him as he tried to move swiftly through the water. He cursed himself for not seeing them sooner, but it was too late, and they were closing the distance quickly.

"Cassandra!" he called out again from the main deck.

Niani shouted orders to the crew, ordering them about as she took hold of the steer. They tumbled over one another running to lighten their load, to ready their weapons for the approaching ship. The snowfall hastened as most slipped on the slick deck.

"You monster!" he shouted to the air. "We have it! Now make good on your promise!"

Dakon rushed toward Amarin, handing him the satchel. "It's there. This is it."

Amarin pulled the grimoire out, feeling its horrid, heavy weight beneath his trembling hands. The owl stared at him like a deadly omen and the stars seemed to twinkle at him from the leather binding.

Beast barked nearby, and Amarin raised his head, seeing the creature rush inside his cabin.

Dakon followed the gytrash and as soon as he crossed the threshold, it became silent.

Still.

She's here.

It returned. That familiar, dreadful sense in his body, the one that sent goosebumps crawling along his skin and pricks of fear down his neck.

She's here.

Amarin looked about. His ship was empty, not a single soul on board.

"I hear you've come bearing gifts, my handsome captain."

Amarin turned. Cassandra rested her hands on the railing of the ship, facing him. He took a precarious step toward her, glancing overboard. She was floating on a wave that lifted her to the edge.

Amarin met her eyes. "Yes, I have it."

"Well, give it here."

"Not yet, I need to know you've kept good on your word."

Cassandra rolled her eyes but reached into the water and tossed a black pouch to him. "Your freedom, Amarin."

Amarin swallowed, bending down to pick it up quickly. He untied it as he watched her watching him and peeked inside. Within was a single, black coin. Only the letter A inscribed in silver on its face.

"All right. Here."

He stuffed the pouch in his pocket and with both hands lifted the book to her. She took it greedily, running her fingers along the binding.

"I must admit, Amarin"—she grinned, opening the book—"I never thought you could do it. It seems I've underestimated y—"

She turned the page, it was blank. She turned the next page, and it too was blank, as was the next and the next.

"Why is it like this?" Her furious eyes rose to Amarin. "Where are all the spells, the magic, the—the curses?!"

Amarin shook his head. "I'm not certain. Eve might have mentioned something."

"What?" Cassandra narrowed her eyes, the water pulling her higher into the air and over the railing. She walked toward him angrily, the book clenched in her hand. Her curls fell wet over her dark, silver dress and she walked barefoot along the wood until she closed the distance. "Tell me or I will rip out your heart with my bare hands."

"I did what you asked, Cassandra. Is that not enough? I am a mortal man, a pirate. I know nothing of magic and grimoires."

"But you know the witch who had this. What did she tell you?"

Her silver eyes swore fury and swift consequences, and Amarin stepped back. He was unarmed, with nothing in his pocket to protect him now, not that it would do him any good.

"Sh-she said one had to give themselves to it, then it would show you everything."

Cassandra lifted a brow. Amarin continued. "The lengths I had to go to to steal it from her. I lied to her, Cassandra. I *lied* to her! I have given my life doing everything you asked, and it is never enough."

"How am I supposed to use this?" She shoved the book at Amarin. "You have given me wasted pages!"

Amarin clutched the book to his chest and then let it go. It hit the deck with a solid thud echoing around the silent ship. He lowered his head as he could feel Cassandra's rage emanating from within her. "I lied."

"You've said that," Cassandra made to turn, but Amarin grabbed her wrist.

Cassandra lifted her furious eyes to his.

"I don't want you to be consumed by it," Amarin breathed, placing his free hand on his chest. "I want you to be as you are, with me now."

Cassandra stilled, and Amarin pulled her gently toward him.

"Tell me," she whispered as Amarin brushed his fingers through her hair. This enthralling woman, this witch who had been in his life for as long as he could remember. She never broke her promises, never doubted him. Everything he had, he owed it to her.

"Tell me," Cassandra whispered. "Together we can rule over all."

Amarin looked into her soft, silver eyes. He nearly forgot how much mischief they held, because where he stood with her now in peace and solitude, they were enchanting.

"Don't make me," he pleaded. "I don't want to lose you."

She caressed his cheek, running her hands along his beard and down his neck. "I will never leave you."

He kissed her then, soft at first, then as she pressed against him, he pulled her close. He ran his fingers through her smooth, dark curls, deepening their kiss. His heart thudded against his chest, every bit of him feeling the fire beneath his skin as he lost himself in Cassandra.

She pulled away slowly, looking at him with eager eyes. "Together," she said, bending down to pick up the book and opened it to one of the blank pages.

Amarin let out a shaky breath, meeting her eyes with pain and sorrow. "Your blood and soul, Cassandra."

She hitched a breath, then looked down at the pages. He nearly believed she would abandon it, let go of this folly idea to have more power than simply wish to be with him. But a slow smile rose on her face. "Done."

She placed a hand on the book, and he gently pulled it away.

"Don't leave me."

She moved her hand from his, placing it back on the book. "Together, remember?"

She twirled her wrist and procured a small blade from thin air. Amarin clenched his jaw, holding the book as she pricked her finger, placed it on the book, saying aloud, "My soul is yours."

The book grew hot in Amarin's hands; he dropped it as it began to glow blue and branches, sharp and thorny, crawled out from it. Cassandra stood before it, cackling and embracing it as it wrapped around her arms and legs. The pages began to flip and now they were filled with words and sketches, drawings all written in an orange-brown ink. She rose into the air as the branches continued wrapping around her. Shadows emerged from the book, and Amarin jumped back.

Storms raged in the sky, and the cold wind whipped at his face once more. The shouts of his crew and Dakon and Beast as they emerged from his cabin, calling his name, filled his ears. Snow fell from the pregnant clouds as lightning struck the water.

The Givensmir ship raced toward them, closer than it was before.

"Cassandra!" Amarin shouted.

The branches turned to smoke around Cassandra as the waves tumbled against the ship, knocking it nearly to its side. Amarin gripped a rope on the main mast, and Dakon leapt toward him, grabbing the grimoire before it fell into the sea.

Cassandra looked down, cackling, "Fool. You worthless, mortal fool."

The ship righted itself, and Amarin stood, gasping for air as he walked toward her. "No, you promised!"

"Pathetic pirate, you have no power over me!"

Amarin took a deep breath, as Dakon opened the grimoire. He smiled up at Cassandra. "I know . . . but he does."

Cassandra turned to Dakon. He raised a dagger before the book, turning his fist and the weapon to flame.

"No!" she screeched, sending waves ashore.

Dakon stabbed the Blood of the Blackthorn. Cassandra cried

out as she raced toward him, the waves doing nothing against the magic of his fire.

"Stop!" she screamed, reaching out to touch him, but Amarin shoved himself against her, holding down her arms as Dakon stabbed the grimoire again and again.

It turned to fire, all of it, as the branches clawed out once more.

Cassandra pushed Amarin away as the branches and smoke wrapped themselves around Cassandra once more. This time, they drew blood. She screamed, fighting the bindings, but they tightened around her body, pulling her toward the book. Dakon leapt back as the branches clawed for anything around it. The crew ran to the upper deck.

"It's mine!" Cassandra shrieked. "It's mine!"

Amarin pulled Dakon to his feet, forcing him up the stairs. Amarin himself nearly took the first step, but a branch clawed at his ankle, pulling him back.

"Damn you!" Amarin shouted.

"Amarin!" Dakon reached out, but Amarin shoved him away. "Go!"

Dakon held Amarin's desperate gaze. "I said go!"

He fought against the bindings, but they were too strong, piercing his skin, and he watched in horror as Cassandra's hand, desperately clinging to nothing but air, was the only thing left of her through the blackened pages. Lightning struck the edge of the ship and waves, forcing the Wretched Sentinel nearly on its side once more. The book swerved down the main deck and over the edge of the railing, falling into the sea.

Taking Amarin with it.

EVE

CHAPTER 59

THE CORRIDORS LEADING TO THE DUNGEONS, what was left of them, were surprisingly empty. Not a single guard, it seemed, was spared for the war effort. And Eve knew why as Victor walked alongside her. Their footsteps, no matter how gently they tried to walk, sounded throughout the halls.

It felt wrong to be here now. Her last memories of the castle bathed in blood and terror. She could see Marc's smug grin as he watched her suffer on the floor of the throne room, she could see the Blood of the Blackthorn opening and tricking her into giving her its soul, she could see herself, so long ago, arrested for the murder of a princess her sister had killed.

No. This place was not home anymore.

She could hear the cries of women through the walls, there had to be nearly a hundred if not more, locked in pitch-black cells. They needed to do this fast, release them all before Marc had a chance to send more of his guard down here.

They turned the corner and there was a single guard standing at the closed entrance of the dungeon. Eve looked to Victor. "You or me?"

Victor didn't answer her, waving a hand in the direction of the guard. A sharp icicle went straight through the air and landed in his throat. He fell with a clanking thud on the marble floor. She nearly stepped into the hall, but Victor held her back in time to see dozens of guards approach the dead man.

Shit.

"You go on my signal," Victor said. "I think I have just enough in me to handle them."

"But—"

Victor didn't hear her out, running toward the guards, and Eve watched, terrified, as he pummeled one to the ground. The others, shocked, barely had a chance to move before Victor shoved another icicle in his chest and removed the guard's sword. The others pulled out their own, fighting him on all sides as Victor juggled between magic and sword trying to fend them off. He shoved one of the guards aside and ran down the hall further into the dungeon where the prisoners were held; the guards gave chase.

"Run!"

Eve didn't wait, rushing toward the dead guard, and removing his set of keys. She ran with them down another hall, but the first few cells were empty and led to a dead end. She gave up, not bothering to check the ones at the end, when she heard a voice.

"Are you looking for me?"

Eve turned quickly. In the darkened corner of the farthest cell, Marc emerged from the shadows. And in his grasp was Borgias' head.

Eve hitched a breath.

If not for the crown on Marc's head, she would never have thought it to be him. His skin, spotted and gray, peeled from the flesh, he was missing an eye, he only had clumps of his hair, white now, left on his head. He hunched over, barely able to stand straight.

But as her eyes went to his mouth, she realized there was fresh blood. She looked between him and Borgias... what was left of him.

Her heart sank, she could barely breathe, and she took a step back as Marc released Borgias's head to the floor. It landed with a thud and rolled once. Its eyes staring straight at her.

She could barely think, holding the key before her as if it were a weapon.

"Who knew he was one of you, right under my very nose?" Marc grinned, his teeth stained with blood. He turned to her. "I grow quite hungry, you see. But mortals won't do for the thing inside of me, no. It only wants witches. Fresh and alive witches."

"M-Marc, this isn't you," Eve said, taking a step back. "It's Isila. She's taken over you."

"Yes, that's her name, isn't it? Your goddess." Marc cackled, and it turned to a cough. "She has taken nearly everything from me. Every strand of hair, every touch, taste, even my sight." He pointed at his missing eye, moving out of the cell.

"I have to kill her, Marc. It's the only way she will stop—"

"Stop?" He coughed. "She will never stop. None of you witches ever stop." He lifted his bloody hands. "Do you think I want to taste you, to hear your screams in my darkest nightmares? I only wanted to save us all from your kind, your despicable, monstrous kind. And look what you have done to me!"

He roared the last word, and Eve could nearly feel the dungeon shake.

"You asked for this power."

"I asked for *power*, not this curse." Marc stepped closer, but Eve held her ground, feeling the flames at her fingertips. She dropped the key.

"Aren't we all cursed?" she breathed, and as he neared, she could see her red eyes reflected in his eyes.

"Remove this thing, Witch. I command you as your king!"

Eve wanted to set him to flames, to feel his burning corpse beneath her touch.

That's what he wants too. Isn't it?

She heard voices behind her, rushing toward her, but dared not turn. If Dakon was successful, her soul would be free, and Isila could die along with Marc, but she didn't know what else they could be capable of.

"You are not my king," Eve said.

"Oh, gods!" Victor's voice carried through the hall behind her, and she knew he was successful. She could hear him approach them among the dozens of other footsteps. He freed the women.

Marc's eyes widened. "Get back in your cages!" he shouted to them. "Back or I will kill you all!"

Eve lessened her flame. Looking upon this pitiful horrid excuse of a man. She took a step and closed the distance. "Goodbye, Marc."

She turned away from him, but his claw-like hand gripped her shoulder. "I order you—"

Eve whirled around sending him back with a fiery blow. He hit his head against the wall and fell to the floor.

"You are not my king."

She picked up the key, placing it in her pocket and walked away to Victor. The women around him, those now freed from the shackles of their prison for crimes of simply existing, glared at Marc. She met their faces, fierce and wrathful, as they moved past her and stalked toward their fallen king.

Eve didn't care to look back as she heard his piercing cries and those of a voice she had once heard long ago fade in the distance. This would be the last time she heard them both.

The last time she gave either of them any more of herself.

THEO

CHAPTER 60

The sounds of battle surrounded him. Men in gold and silver and black slipped and fought in the brutal grounds of mud and snow. His horse had been slain, and he only made it off in time to save himself from another pursuer. The cries of dying men and the shouts of those who fought to live echoed around him, sending chills, as he turned around and around thrusting his sword in the crowd and taking down all those who wished to kill him first.

He had been a prince, their prince once. Fighting for the rebellion, knowing they could win a large sum from his brother for bringing back his head, garnered the interest of men who would risk their lives fighting him.

He didn't know how much time had passed as the sky darkened into a snowstorm threatening to take them all should they stay, but leaving was not a choice.

Death was the only way out.

"Release the flank!" Theo shouted. "The flank!"

His men echoed across the battle, and the Rubianes forces rode on their stallions from east toward them. He could barely catch his breath as a knight charged him. Theo ducked and slipped in the mud, the edge of the knight's sword cutting into his ribs. He howled, stumbling to his feet as he lifted his sword to deflect another blow. But the knight trampled on top of him, gripping the hilt of Theo's sword as they fought for control of it. Theo kneed him in the groin and the knight fell to his side as Theo gasped for air, gripping his sword tight.

The knight removed his helmet, tossing it into the mud as he picked up his fallen sword. Ser James ran toward him, bellowing into the air as he tried to slice Theo's face. He ducked again, shoving his body into Ser James's stomach and thrusting him into the mud. He raised his sword, but Ser James smacked him with the back of his hand, sending Theo into the ground on his back. He wrestled on top of him, forcing the sword from his hands and placing his own around Theo's neck.

Ser James' face was bloodied and tortured, nearly purple as he forced all his might into strangling Theo. Mud circled Theo's vision as he tried in vain to pull Ser James's hands away.

"Die like the filth you are," Ser James spat.

Theo couldn't reach his sword as he sank into the mud.

"Die."

The edges of his vision turned to black as he did the only thing he could think of. He let go of Ser James's hands and grabbed as much mud as he could, throwing it in his face. Ser James loosened his grip enough for Theo to shove him off and grab his sword. Ser James barely had a moment to turn before Theo sent his head flying into the dirt.

"Die," Theo panted, "like the filth you are."

Horns blared across the battlefield, and Theo raised his head in time to see the last of the golden armor, no more than a few dozen, fleeing back to the capital. He turned to Callum, not far from him. Their eyes met, as they took ragged breaths.

And smiled.

"We've won!" Emilio shouted, racing toward Callum and taking him in his arms. "We've won!"

The men shouted around them, taking Theo and Callum into their arms and lifting them into the air. "We've won!"

Theo raised his fist in the air. "Long, live the queen!"

PART 4

TIME OF PEACE

May The Creator give you faith in times of darkness,
May The Sage guide you to reign justly,
May The Lover guide you to reign true,
May The Warrior give you strength against the wicked,
And above all, may Death protect your soul.
This crown, forged through centuries of
your blood, is now entrusted to you.
May you reign as one chosen by the gods.

ADRIANA

CHAPTER 61

THE ELDER PLACED THE CROWN ON Adriana's head. "Adriana Ebron of the Mistral Islands, Queen of Givensmir and the Four Seas, Defender of Mortality and the Faith of the Five! Long may she reign!"

It didn't feel as heavy as she expected as she rose from her knees and turned to face the people at the bottom of the temple steps. It was spring morning, the skies were a soft, blue hue as the sun shone down upon the capital bathing it in light. The city was alive with celebration as the elder spoke his final words. "Long reign Queen Adriana!"

"Long reign Queen Adriana!"

Long reign Queen Adriana!

She felt her heart in her throat; the

crown she never imagined having rested on her head. She could only hope that she would be deserving of it, of the love of the people, of the peace she wished to bring them all.

She gave a gentle wave, looking out into the faces of the crowd, so many women that had lived through the worst of times met her eyes with pride and hope. She turned to the guards, her new knights, the people around her that made her feel safe.

Callum stood off to her left with Emilio and the rest of the nobles. He grinned impossibly wide as he nodded to her. She smiled back, her eyes moving to Theo and Eve, holding hands as they cheered for her. Eve held a handkerchief to her eyes, beaming with pride.

She turned to her right. Dakon stood with the rest of her guard, watching with pride and admiration. Her lips parted as she mouthed to him.

Come with me.

She raised her hand to him, and he stilled, raising a brow. She repeated over the cheers that nearly deafened her.

Be with me.

Dakon took a careful step, as if asking permission, and she smiled, lifting her hand higher. The crowd seemed to notice watching the man who was once a servant, a fool, a familiar, and then something more walk toward their queen.

He took Adriana's hand in his and smiled.

"Is this everything you wanted?" he asked.

"Almost," she said.

SHE LED THE CROWD OF PEOPLE TO THE CITY SQUARE, HER HAND IN Dakon's as they raised their torches. Behind them, the people celebrated, singing and laughing and even drinking as they moved along the path.

In the center was the pyre, tall and wide, looming like a shadow on their bright day. Adriana turned to the crowd, lifting her torch as she spoke as loud as she could.

"This will be the last day the fire burns in this square. It will be the last day mothers will be separated from their children, wives from their partners, and women from their lives. Henceforth, there will be no pyres in my kingdom, there will be witches welcome where they come in kindness. For this is the dawn of a new age. One of Mortals and Magic!"

Together, she and Dakon thrust their torches in the pyre, and it took to flame. Surprisingly the crowd surrounded them, throwing their own torches, letters, trinkets, rope, anything they wanted to free themselves from. The fire burned, the smoke rising as Adriana and Dakon moved back toward Eve and Theo. But the fire was growing weak with all the objects smothering it. She held Dakon's hand tight and grabbed Eve's with her free one.

"A little help, please?" she asked them.

Dakon and Eve looked to one another smiling, and Adriana saw the smallest hint of red in Eve's.

She turned in time to see the fire roar to life, nearly reaching the skies, as it consumed everything within it. The crowd stepped back in surprise and then once again burst into celebration.

Long reign Queen Adriana!
Queen of Peace!
Queen of the People!

EVE

CHAPTER 62

"I'M NOT GOOD AT GOODBYES, SO I WILL give you a brief hug, wait for your thanks for saving your life, and send you on your way." Victor pulled her into the shortest of hugs and released her.

Eve lifted a brow. "I distinctly remember turning you into a man for the first time in centuries."

"It would have happened sooner or later."

"I'm certain it would have." Eve smirked. "But thank you, Victor. Take good care of Dakon for me, please."

"That's too easy. He loves having me around." Victor turned to wave at Dakon who approached them. And Dakon rolled his eyes, pretending not to see them. "See, best mates."

Victor walked toward Dakon, and Eve watched, trying to stifle a laugh as Victor ruffled Dakon's hair. Dakon shoved him away.

Adriana scoffed, standing next to her. "They're quite ridiculous."

"Imagine being in a cave with them both."

Adriana shook her head. Then she turned Eve to face her, taking her hands. "Can I not say anything to make you stay?"

Eve looked between the ship and Adriana, giving her a slight smile. "This isn't my home anymore."

"But am I not your home?"

Tears pricked at the corners of Eve's eyes as she took her dear friend into an embrace. "You are always my home."

"I don't know what I will do without you," Adriana managed.

"Rule, perhaps."

"Oh, quit speaking sense." Adriana swatted her arm gently. She took a deep breath, closing her eyes for a long moment. When she opened them, she gave Eve an endearing look. "I want your happiness. No matter what that means to me. Please, at least send a dove or two and let me know you're safe."

Eve kissed Adriana's forehead. "Of course, My Queen."

"It's Adriana between the two of us."

"I know," Eve replied, grinning. "I like to tease you."

"That makes two of us," Dakon said, walking toward them.

"I will say goodbye to my brother now," Adriana said, looking between them and sauntering off.

"Oh, no." Eve wiped her eyes. "I knew this was going to be difficult."

"I thought saying bye to Callum was?" Dakon smirked.

"Oh, for different reasons." Eve shoved him playfully.

Dakon grinned. "I couldn't let you go without seeing you."

Eve didn't bother to conceal the tears that ran down her face; her skin heated as her heart ached. "I wish you had. Now look at me. A mess."

"I thought the spoiled, rich lady was gone. Is that a hint of her I see there?"

"I never left." Eve scoffed. "I simply... grew up."

"That's one way to see things."

"And what about you?" Eve said. "You're betrothed to a queen. Mighty high ladder you made for yourself from a stable boy."

"I can scarcely believe it myself."

"I suppose you'll be acting high and mighty soon."

"No, I still find myself cleaning the horse stables and sparring with wooden swords."

Eve laughed. "Old habits die hard."

"Some are good for my health."

They stared into each other for a long while, until Theo's voice rang out from the ship. "Eve, it's time!"

Eve looked between him and Dakon, nodding.

"I want you to know, everything I have now is because of you," Dakon said, taking her hand in his. "I owe you my life."

Eve sniffled. "It's too cheap for me."

Dakon laughed aloud. "Well, it's still yours."

"No. Keep it. It's yours to live." Eve laughed through her tears. "Though I want to warn you, I'll forget to write to you sometimes, but I'll be thinking of you."

"I'll cherish them even more."

Eve took Dakon in a fierce hug, feeling the warmth of his skin on her. It was always their kind of warm.

"I love you, Eve."

"I love you, Dakon."

She released him, looking into those summer-green eyes and wiping the tears from her face as she boarded the ship and into Theo's arms. They sailed away from the port, the capital slowly fading in the distance. Eve couldn't help but cry bittersweet tears, never once moving until it was gone.

She didn't wish to go back to Givensmir, but her leaving still pained her. Every friend she made along this treacherous, rewarding journey stayed behind to forge new lives for themselves. And she felt lost there. Eve wanted something new and so did Theo. She looked up at him as he stood beside her. He gave the top of her head a kiss and wrapped his arms around her.

"Are you ready for paradise?" Theo asked against her ear.

A smile tugged at Eve's lips. "Paradise?"

"I heard someone tell me about it once. Maybe one day we'll even see them there."

"In paradise? Who was this?" Eve raised a brow.

Theo placed a gentle kiss on her lips.

"It's a long story."

"Well, we have time now."

LUCIA

CHAPTER 63

Lucia watched the darkening sea from her window. She could feel his presence somewhere not so far out there and wondered if he missed her after all these years, if he was afflicted with the same heartbreak as she since they were separated as young lovers. She closed her eyes, still imagining the feel of Amarin's lips on hers, his warm touch on her skin, the way he would say her name as he held her in his arms at the old inn in Catalina's Port.

She would give nearly anything to be there with him once more, the three days that never left her soul no matter how much time willed it. Her hands trembled as she made out the faintest dark ship where the early night sky met the glistening water, reflecting the faint stars like tiny jewels on its surface leading him to her.

"You came for me," she whispered, a lone tear making its way down her cheek. Her heart ached, knowing that she would not be able to fulfill the promise she made him. The letter she had sent begging him to take her and her daughters away, to save them from certain death. She hoped he would take good care of them in her absence as he sailed them to the Blackthorn where Malin would be waiting for them.

Lucia breathed deeply, the scent of the sea filling her, and even the scent of chamomile, like those of Amarin's home that he often dreamt of in her presence, caressed her. She had been so consumed with the loss of her magic over the years that she nearly forgot that life itself could be magical too.

Footsteps came up the tower steps and she knew. Lucia made her way to her bookshelf, taking out the poisoned knife and hiding it in her dress skirts.

She needed to buy her daughters a little more time, needed to distract the new king before he thought to look for them. Because somewhere in the tunnels and through a broken part of the castle wall, her daughters were running for their lives, and she would be damned if she let them meet the same fate as hers.

The footsteps were louder now and echoed her beating, thunderous heart. Any moment now, they would knock on her door, summoning her to the new king.

She begged herself for strength as her hands shook and lips trembled. She moved once more to the open window, willing herself to be brave.

The ship was closing in, headed toward the cove as she had instructed and disappeared behind the Temple of the Five.

"Be brave," she whispered, to herself, to Amarin, to her daughters.

There was a knock on her door.

She turned, ready for them to take her away as they always did in this cursed, wretched place after death.

But the door opened to only one person.

Lucia's heart rose as she met his eyes.

"Amarin."

DAKON

EPILOGUE

Twenty Years Later

Dakon lifted the large, brown book from his satchel, the children squealing in delight around him. He looked upon all the little faces and bright eyes of the orphanage as they eagerly awaited the next tale he had for them. He adored these weekly visits and found himself writing all sorts of tales in the many books he had in his personal library.

This time, however, when he went to pluck one about a swordsman facing a monster in the woods and saving the villagers, Beast nudged him gently toward the far corner of his bookshelf. Dakon followed his gytrash's wish, placing a finger on each spine until it seemed the gytrash was happy enough. Dakon pulled the book from the shelf, much larger than he remembered and felt it in his hands. He had not written in these pages nor read from them in over a decade. In truth, as life and time passed, he even forgot it existed. He opened it and read the inscription.

The Eternal Curse
Heart of Dakon
A Book of Tales For Mortals & Magic

As the carriage took him to the orphanage, he felt the leather-bound cover beneath his fingertips, the weathered, yellow pages torn at the corners. He looked outside. The slums he remembered riding through were nothing like they were today. Children, recognizing his carriage, ran alongside his open carriage window with dolls and toys. They even tapped against his door to bid him good morning. The alleys were not dark and foreboding, but light and decorated with trinkets in the summer day. The sky was cool and while the sun settled in the midday sky, the clouds offered the people below a reprieve from the heat. The carriage turned to go over the bridge to Catalina's Port, and Dakon watched as the ships moved to and fro on the water going about their business for the kingdom. He wondered if the Wretched Sentinel was among them somewhere in the Dallise Sea. He even wondered if Niani still captained it.

He smiled to himself.

Of course she did.

He settled on the chair in the orphanage. It would be the first time he ever read this tale aloud to anyone. He loosened the collar of his tunic, seeing their barely contained excitement, children of all ages and even a few grown that still visited when he did long after they left. He smiled to a few, recognizing them.

He wondered if Cerene felt this way when she would read for the servant children in the castle, distracting them for a moment from the brutality of their work and the hopelessness of their poverty-stricken lives. She was the beacon of hope for him, the only mother he ever knew, and the woman who saved his life through her tales, even when hers had long ended.

He opened the book before them, blowing a bit of dust that lingered.

"What do any of you all know about magical curses?"

A few children raised their hands and others shouted their answers aloud. Soon the orphanage was filled with the sound of laughter and shared ideas and imagination.

Dakon smiled, listening as each of them spoke and when they were all done, he raised a finger to his lips as he always did, beckoning them to silence. "Shh, hush now. This time, my good children, we will hear the story of The Eternal Curse."

He watched as their eyes grew wide and their mouths slack as they listened. Dakon began to read aloud.

"*The Enchantress is Dead...*"

For a long while, he read of a witch who opened a magical book that promised her the world. He spoke of a servant boy who became a familiar and then a man of free will who fought alongside mortals and magic folk alike. He excited them with the story of the servant boy's friend fighting the sirens with swords and fists, sending them back to the sea. He raised his hands and voice theatrically as he read of the gytrash that led him through the darkened streets and into battles not of sword and daggers.

Many of them cheered as the mad king fell and cried when the servant boy's friend perished in the snow. But Dakon carried on, wishing to give their lives and deaths the dignity of a rewarding tale.

And when he was done, he looked outside the window next to him. The morning had become shrouded in the blanket of night and even the man who managed his carriage, the very one who was supposed to retrieve him when it was time to go after his hour, was standing by the window listening to his tales.

For the first time since he began reading stories to the orphanage, not a single child stirred, as if they were captivated beyond reason. He closed the heavy book with a light thud on his lap and watched as the people stared in silence for a long moment.

A young girl raised her hand. "So, the curse is not eternal?"

Dakon shook his head, smiling. "No, it was broken."

"How do curses break?" another child asked.

"I suppose it depends." He smiled.

"And what abou—" A third child made to speak but was silenced. Dakon raised his head, the entire room was silenced and still. Everyone save for him.

"You tell it so well," a voice said from the doorway.

He flicked his eyes up. Eve stood there. She seemed to stand the test of time itself, her long brown hair spindled down to her waist, her brown eyes with hints of gold met his, her burgundy dress flowed to the ground beneath her black cloak. She was older, but more enchanting than he ever remembered before. His heart leapt in his chest, that familiar warming sensation moved across his skin. It was warm. Their kind of warm.

"Eve," he breathed.

APPENDIX

HOUSE RUBIANES

The Rubianes have stood the test of time in Serit. Their house was forged from centuries far beyond that of written record. In the fertile lands of their namesake, the lineage has amassed a large fortune from their wines and other crops sent throughout the kingdom. Generations ago, Andren I of House Rubianes swore fealty to King Nikolas Ebron I after losing the Battle of the Vines. King Nikolas granted Lord Andren continued ownership of Rubianes and the surrounding lands after he successfully aided in a negotiated surrender of Larrea to the crown.

Centuries later, Lord Marcelo I was ordered to marry the first Royal Enchantress, Lady Lucia of the Blackthorn. Deemed a scandal for the known nature of witches and mortal couplings to bear no children, House Rubianes was in uproar. However, the wedding proceeded and yielded two daughters, Clarisa and Eve, the former perished in the Battle of Mortals and Magic. Following a remarriage to Lady Natalia of Granata, Lord Marcelo had a son Isidro.

Lord Isidro is the current head of House Rubianes and the youngest lord of the major houses.

SIGIL
Cross swords between olive branches

BANNER COLORS
Burgundy and Gold

HOUSE EBRON

House Ebron originated from the Mistral Islands where they saw much success in naval trade as they were positioned between the Blackthorn and mortal kingdoms. After the fall of the Blackthorn witches, Gale Ebron I took advantage of the vulnerability of the mortal lands, securing an alliance with Teros and creating the kingdom of Givensmir. Following the creation of its capital north of what is now known as Catalina's Port, Gale secured his title as Givensmir's king, a lineage that has lasted for centuries.

Following a tumultuous rule by King Eryck and the death of his first two heirs, Prince Eryce and Prince Theo, Prince Marc took the helm of the throne. His reign marked a remarkable rise in witch burnings, resulting in the deaths of thousands of women whose affinity for witchcraft is still debated to this day. The chaos of his rule resulted in his death at the Battle of Mortals and Magic.

Queen Adriana I is the head of House Ebron and ruler of the Givensmir kingdom.

SIGIL
A Merlion

BANNER COLORS
Gold and Black

HOUSE TEROS

Following the alliance with House Ebron, the Teros have remained a stronghold of the north. Occupying the dense forests, silver mines, and warhorses that make up a sizable force of Givensmir's battle trade, the Teros have long been suited for battle. Their lands are separated from the Unclaimed Wastes by the icy river of Gods' Protection with no suitable plans to occupy further. They have the highest regard for loyalty to family, duty, and honor.

During the reign of King Marc I, they were among the many major houses who declared for Queen Adriana and the rebellion and fought against the Givensmir royal forces at the Battle of Mortals and Magic.

Lord Callum is the head of House Teros.

SIGIL
A War Horse

BANNER COLORS
Forest-Green and Silver

HOUSE ZAFIRA

House Zafira, named for the family that has ruled the desert lands for nearly four centuries, is rich with minerals, jewels, and sea trade. It has remained a vital key to the Givensmir southern defense. In the years 613 and beyond, there grew a considerable witch presence when the Blackthorn exiled a coven from their kingdom. Over the years, the witches and mortals there have lived in turmoil fighting against one another for land, power, and control.

Under Lord Ybara, House Zafira struggled to temper the witches and under the oppressive rule of King Marc I, they were forced to execute many innocent mortals believed to be witches. Lord Ybara was executed by the crown before the Battle of Mortals and Magic, leaving his reign to his husband who fought in the Battle of Mortals and Magic.

Lord Varik is the head of House Zafira.

SIGIL
Scorpion

BANNER COLORS
Blue and Gold

HOUSE FARRIN

House Farrin has manned Pleasant Peak for nearly a century and is under Lord Dario's charge. It was sworn to House Ivari of Larrea and fought in its uprising against the crown under Fidel IV. After eight years of war and hardship on his people, Lord Dario brokered a deal with the crown for clemency in exchange for allowing Givensmir forces to pass through the Canys River, a stronghold of the Pleasant Peak army. Many accounts differ on the reasons for Lord Dario's decision to fold for the crown between threats of violence against his wife and children or coins being passed to assuage his guilt. The circumstances remain unknown and are spoken only in secret confidences.

Following the fall of Fidel IV, House Farrin claimed fealty to Larrea's newest ruler, Lord Moryn of House Ivari. Yet, their loyalties swayed during the rebellion against King Marc I's rule when they declared for Queen Adriana and fought against the Givensmir royal forces.

Lord Dario is the head of House Farrin.

SIGIL
River Elk

BANNER COLORS
Red and Silver

HOUSE IVARI

Rife with internal conflict and continuous wars throughout the centuries, House Ivari has felt its share of struggle and hardships. While Larrea has miraculously remained in the hands of the Ivari lineage, it has transferred between cousins, daughters, uncles, and legitimized bastards alike. Forced into the expansion of Givensmir's kingdom, House Ivari and its lands remained faithful for a few years. Following the rise in taxes and underwhelming support of King Eryck following his ascension to the throne, Fidel III of House Ivari began an uprising against the crown, declaring themselves a separate kingdom once more. Civil war waged for eight years and three different false kings before Prince Eryce was ordered to execute Lord Fidel IV, ending the war. The immediate family was exiled to Bastard's Haven, after their acts of submission. A new noble, after swearing fealty to King Eryck and accepting terms of surrender, was appointed as the Lord of Larrea.

Lord Moryn, distant cousin of Fidel IV, is the head of House Ivari.

SIGIL	BANNER COLORS
Sea Serpent	Blue and Black

HOUSE MYTAR

The Mytars have developed a complex mining system in the mountains where they have forged precious resources and established effective trade with Givensmir. However, they remained resistant to joining the kingdom over the centuries until the year 798 when Lord Joseph I of House Mytar met with the Royal Enchantress. After a single meeting, he is rumored to have declared that he would have "sold his left arm if only to spend another moment listening to her speak." Lord Joseph and King Byron III of Givensmir remained steadfast companions until the king's untimely death years later.

Following the execution of Lord Joseph I and Lord Joseph II during King Marc I's reign, House Mytar changed allegiances for the rebellion, declaring for Queen Adriana and fighting for her cause in the Battle of Mortals and Magic.

Lord Allyn, cousin of Lord Joseph I is the head of House Mytar.

SIGIL
Cloud pierced by a Pickax

BANNER COLORS
Bronze and White

BLACKTHORN COVENS

The Blackthorn covens were created following the fall of Isila and the Original Witches. Bound to remain in the Blackthorn isles where their magic was strongest, the remaining witches formed covens which remained in relative harmony across the Dallise Sea from the mortals who sought revenge. Despite all attempts at invasion, the Blackthorn and its covens have yet to be conquered. Under the same lineage of rulers, the isles are led by its capital coven.

One of the covens, Strix, known for their disastrous methods of witchcraft were exiled in the year 613.

Queen Rinya is the head of the capital and Alyna covens and ruler of the Blackthorn kingdom.

SIGIL
Owl beneath Three Stars

BANNER COLORS
Silver and Black

ACTIVE COVENS
Capital
Alvyna
Luna
Veneno
Petris
Arric

EXILED COVEN
Strix

PRIALIS

The island of Prialis is a territory of Givensmir's kingdom. The people of Prialis are known for their peacemaking and tend to stray from violence. Despite much opposition, the land was claimed by King Byron III to be used as a port for supply lines running to the east during his conquering of the Larrea kingdom. At the urging of the Enchantress and the successful invasion of Larrea, King Byron largely ignored the island, deeming it a waste of resources. Prialis and its people live in villages and worship the land and sea nearly as much as the five gods. It has been widely regarded as the land of paradise.

A council of four, the eldest of the island's leaders, rules the people as is their sacred tradition.

SIGIL
A Jasmine Flower above Four Sea Waves

BANNER COLORS
White and Blue

AUTHOR'S NOTE

It is bittersweet, closing out the first completed series of my career.

When I was a little girl, I would find myself buried in stories of witchcraft and folklore, magic and mayhem—flipping pages out of control as my brain tried to consume the tales as quickly as possible. I would write in my diary, the popular one from the early 2000s that was purple and fluffy and had its own flimsy lock and key. (Though, to be honest, I lost the key after a week and never bothered to lock it anyway)

I scribbled on most every papered surface I could find, making up incredulous worlds that helped me escape my own for just a little while.

You see, since then, I never stopped being that little girl. I never stopped dreaming, even when I would look out the window in my corporate office building years ago wishing for the day I could start to live.

And as I wrote in the first Author's Note of my career, it all changed in the winter of 2024, when I went on a road trip through the incredible forests of Washington State.

And well . . . you know the rest.

If I could impart any advice to you, dear reader, it would be that dreams happen when you take the first step. So go on, what are you waiting for?

With Love,

Rocio

ACKNOWLEDGMENTS

Thank you to my incredible editor, Heather, who has supported my work since the first day we followed each other on social media. Before she ever knew a single word I wrote, she was in my corner, cheering me on and giving me the courage to reach out and ask if she would be interested in editing my witchy fantasy book. Wow, am I glad I did!

Thank you to Mariska, my interior formatter, who gave my series (and most of the other books in my catalogue) such life. Every time I flip one of my pages, I am in awe of such artistry and design. You are truly a talent in your craft.

Thank you to Irina, my cover artist, for taking the leap of faith on an unknown indie author and agreeing to create such incredible, jaw-dropping art for my series covers. I am honored to be your first book covers, and I can't wait to see what other works you have in store.

Thank you to my family for supporting me on this journey. Every success I have is due to you. The love I have for each of you is more than I could put into words. (And I know, I've tried)

And finally, as always, thank you, dear reader, for picking up my books and finding yourself lost in my worlds and words.

Here's to many more stories coming soon.

AUTHOR BIO

ROCIO CARRANZA is the international bestselling author of *Blood of the Blackthorn* from *The Eternal Curse* series which includes *Flame in the Silver Storm* and *Wrath of the Cursed Witch*. Other works include *My Dreams Come True*, and short stories *Lana Lang*, and *Miss Reliable*. She is the co-host of the *Chat You Up Podcast* where she and her co-host discuss sisterhood, fashion, pop culture, dating, and lifestyle. Rocio is forever a dreamer and creative who spends her free time building worlds on paper and film that may never see the light of day but spark joy in her soul. She lives with the ever-jovial Allen and their two sons in Austin, TX.

VISIT THE AUTHOR ONLINE:
www.rociocarranza.com

INSTAGRAM & THREADS:
@rociocarranzawrites

www.ingramcontent.com/pod-product-compliance
Lightning Source LLC
LaVergne TN
LVHW091658070526
838199LV00050B/2199